The Peace Killers

Zeb Carter Series, Book 2

By

Ty Patterson

Books by Ty Patterson

Warriors Series Shorts

This is a series of novellas that link to the Warriors Series thrillers

Zulu Hour, Book 1
The Shadow, Book 2
The Man From Congo, Book 3
The Texan, Book 4
The Heavies, Book 5
The Cab Driver, Book 6
Warriors Series Shorts, Boxset I, Books 1-3
Warriors Series Shorts, Boxset II, Books 4-6

Gemini Series

Dividing Zero, Book 1
Defending Cain, Book 2
I Am Missing, Book 3
Wrecking Team, Book 4

Zeb Carter Series

Zeb Carter, Book 1
The Peace Killers, Book 2

Warriors Series

The Warrior, Book 1
The Reluctant Warrior, Book 2
The Warrior Code, Book 3
The Warrior's Debt, Book 4
Flay, Book 5
Behind You, Book 6
Hunting You, Book 7
Zero, Book 8
Death Club, Book 9
Trigger Break, Book 10
Scorched Earth, Book 11
RUN!, Book 12
Warriors series Boxset, Books 1-4
Warriors series Boxset II, Books 5-8
Warriors series Boxset III, Books 1-8

Cade Stryker Series

The Last Gunfighter of Space, Book 1
The Thief Who Stole A Planet, Book 2

Sign up to Ty Patterson's mailing list and get *The Watcher*, a Zeb Carter novella, exclusive to newsletter subscribers. Join Ty Patterson's Facebook group of readers, at www.facebook.com/groups/324440917903074.

Check out Ty on Amazon, iTunes, Kobo, Nook and on his website www.typatterson.com.

Acknowledgments

No book is a single person's product. I am privileged that *The Peace Killers* has benefited from the input of several great people.

Paula Artlip, Sheldon Levy, Molly Birch, David T. Blake, Tracy Boulet, Patricia Burke, Mark Campbell, Tricia Cullerton, Claire Forgacs, Dave Davis, Sylvia Foster, Cary Lory Becker, Charlie Carrick, Pat Ellis, Dori Barrett, Simon Alphonso, Dave Davis, V. Elizabeth Perry, Ann Finn, Pete Bennett, Eric Blackburn, Margaret Harvey, David Hay, Jim Lambert, Suzanne Jackson Mickelson, Tricia Terry Pellman, Jimmy Smith, Maria Stine, Theresa and Brad Werths, who are my beta readers and who helped shape my book, my launch team for supporting me, Donna Rich for her proof reading and Doreen Martens for her editing.

Dedications

To Michelle Rose Dunn, Debbie Bruns Gallant, Tom Gallant
and Cheri Gerhardt, for supporting me.

If you want to make peace, you don't talk to your friends. You talk to your enemies.

— Moshe Dayan

Chapter 1

—⊗⊗⊗—

Jerusalem, Israel

Eliel Magal woke up when the city was still dark.

No, he corrected himself, when he cracked open the window and peered out at the quiet neighborhood. It was grey. Dawn was approaching fast.

Five-thirty am. He didn't have to look at the bedside clock to know what time it was. He always woke up at that hour, a deeply ingrained habit.

He padded to the small bathroom and, when he emerged, knocked on the door down the hallway. Navon Shiri opened it instantly, eyes alert, hair brushed neatly, dressed in plain white.

The two men went to the kitchen and prepared breakfast. Warm milk for Magal, cereal and a banana for Shiri, who took his bowl to the living room and turned on the TV, to the Palestinian Broadcasting Corporation, PBC, channel. The programming wasn't available in Israel, but the two men had piggybacked on an illegal feed and were able to watch the content.

Magal joined him on the couch, and the two watched the news in silence.

The two men could have been brothers. They weren't. They were lightly tanned, with dark eyes, short cropped hair, clean-shaven. Five feet, six inches tall. No distinguishing features. Nothing about them stood out.

Magal's glass clinked when he placed it on the table as he watched the screen.

Gaza was burning, as was the West Bank.

The United States had opened its embassy in Jerusalem, and that had triggered intense outrage and violent protests in Palestine.

Thousands of Palestinian protesters had gathered at the border fence and had thrown Molotov cocktails, burning tires, stones, whatever missiles they could find, at the Israeli Defense Forces, IDF, on the other side of the fence. The IDF had fired in return, and dozens of people had been killed.

Shiri peeled his banana and flicked to another news channel. Different reporter, same coverage. He went back to the previous one and bit into his fruit.

The two of them didn't need to discuss the riots. They knew what had happened. Every person in Israel and Palestine knew of the region's history and that of Jerusalem in particular.

Palestinians believed they were an oppressed people, Israel the oppressor. The majority of Israelis believed they were defending their country and their land.

Nabil and Shiri didn't look at the screen when the reporter brought up a map and went through a history recap.

In 1948, Israel declared itself an independent state. The next day, war broke out between a coalition of Arab nations and the newly formed country. Jordan occupied West Bank and East Jerusalem. Egypt took over Gaza at the end of the war.

In 1967, there was another war, at the end of which Israel occupied East Jerusalem, Gaza, Golan Heights and Sinai. In 1979, Israel and Egypt signed a historic peace treaty and Sinai was returned to Egypt.

That eventually led to what the Palestine state currently was, a country in two geographical parts. West Bank, bordered by Jordan to the east and Israel in all other directions, and the Gaza Strip, which had the Mediterranean Sea behind it, Egypt to the south and Israel at the north and west. Palestine's two regions did not share a border between them.

The politics and governance of the state were divided, too. The West Bank was administered by the Palestinian National Authority, while Gaza was ruled by Hamas, which, Israel, the United States and the European Union regarded as a terrorist organization.

The reporter droned on about the status of Jerusalem, that East Jerusalem was claimed by Palestine but was controlled by Israel. Shiri tuned to Kan TV, the Israeli channel. Similar news, with an Israeli slant. He grunted in disgust and was about to turn off the TV when Magal raised his hand.

The reporter went into breathless excitement mode.

'There are several rumors,' she said, leaning forward, her eyes sparkling, 'that Israeli and Palestinian negotiators are meeting in secret to work out a historic peace accord. Government officials on both sides have declined to comment on this.'

She went on about the significance of the development, if true, and at that point Shiri turned off the TV. He finished his cereal and went to the kitchen, where he washed and rinsed his bowl.

Magal yawned and stretched. 'I'll get ready,' he said.

Shiri grunted and peered out of the kitchen window. It was seven am. Light traffic outside in German Colony, the Jerusalem neighborhood they were in. He went to his room and changed into a white shirt and khaki trousers. Walking shoes over his feet. A Glock 17 went into a holster attached to his belt. He adjusted his loose shirt to ensure the gun wasn't visible to the casual eye. In his trouser pockets went several spare magazines.

He emerged from his room to see an old woman in the hallway. She was in a patterned dress that fell below her knees. Hunched over, her white hair tied in a neat bun. Glasses on her wrinkled face. Left hand trembling as she held a walking stick. Right hand clutching a large bag, which seemed heavy.

Magal, the woman in disguise, placed the bag on the floor and flexed his fingers. Shiri toed it and felt something hard inside it. He peered down and nodded in satisfaction when he saw the shape of a Galil MAR, an Israeli automatic rifle.

'Ready?' he asked in Hebrew.

'Let's go,' Magal replied.

Chapter 2

———— ❧ ————

Kadikoy, Istanbul
Three Days Before

Zeb Carter was breaking into a hotel room rented by two Mossad kidon. Mossad was his closest ally, but on this particular mission, he wasn't sure.

It had started a month ago, in New York.

He had been on the trail of one Uzair Hussain, a Pakistani nuclear scientist. Hussain's international travel had been flagged by his team's supercomputer. Werner.

The scientist traveled often to Europe, which in itself wasn't a big deal. What was interesting was that, once on the continent, he seemed to drop off the radar and surfaced only when returning.

Beth and Meghan looked into it. The twins oversaw the Agency's intel gathering and analysis, along with Broker. Cracking into airline databases and Pakistani networks wasn't hard for them.

'Six visits to the Middle East in two years,' Beth had told

Zeb, a month earlier.

'Middle East? I thought he went to Europe.'

'That was the entry point,' she explained patiently. A lot of it was needed when dealing with Zeb. 'He flew into Paris or Amsterdam or any one of the large hubs. From there he took trains. Used fake IDs. Good trade craft. But not good enough to escape all the security cameras in Europe.'

'Where did he go?'

'Turkey. Istanbul.'

'All six times?'

'Yeah. Fewer cameras in that country, but we ran facial recognition on the CCTV feeds in their train and bus terminals and got these.'

She dumped a bunch of photographs on his desk. Zeb flicked through them rapidly. Blurred images in several of them, but clear enough to make out Hussain's profile.

He looked up when Meghan joined her sister. Something in their faces...

'What's up?'

'There's a café in Kadikoy, which is in—'

'Istanbul. What about it?'

'There's a security camera across the street. A bank. We hacked into it and got this.'

Meghan's right hand came from behind her back, holding another photograph.

Hussain seated at a table outside the café. Another man facing him. Both of them drinking what seemed to be tea.

It was the second man that got Zeb's attention.

'That's—'

'Kamran Shahi.' Meghan brushed a stray curl of hair back. 'Iran's nuclear guy. He's responsible for their weapons program.'

Zeb studied the photograph again. Both men were in suits. Neatly trimmed beards. The Iranian seemed older, with grey flecks in his hair.

Iran had stopped its uranium enrichment program after it had struck a deal with the United States and Europe.

'It could be innocuous,' he said half-heartedly.

'Could be,' Beth agreed. 'But you know what happened with another Pakistani nuclear scientist.'

Zeb nodded. The whole world knew.

A.Q. Khan, the 'father' of Pakistan's atomic bomb, had sold nuclear secrets to Iran, North Korea and Libya. He had played a major role in nuclear proliferation in some of the worst regimes in the world.

He tossed the image on the desk and stretched his arms. Caught himself when he sensed something. The sisters seemed to be buzzing with excitement.

'There's more?'

'Heck, yeah!' Beth's eyes flashed. 'He's planning another trip. To Europe. In a month's time.'

And that led to Zeb flying to Istanbul a week before the Pakistani's arrival, checking in to a decrepit hotel in Kadikoy as a local businessman.

His plan was to shadow the scientist and place a bug on him.

That plan changed when he spotted the couple who frequented the café each day. Mediterranean looks. Seemingly in love.

Zeb wore a different disguise each day: an elderly man one day, a woman returning from shopping the next.

He was in his third older-man disguise when he got close

to the couple and overheard their conversation. They had their heads close together and were almost whispering.

Zeb caught snatches of their conversation. How long they would be staying. When *it* would happen. How *it* would go down.

The *it* aroused his suspicions. Just that word, nothing else describing whatever the event was.

Then it was their language. They spoke Turkish with the servers, occasionally Arabic with other patrons. But when together, when whispering, they spoke Hebrew.

He followed them and found they practiced exceptional tradecraft. They paused several times, appearing to be window-shopping, but Zeb knew they were checking out their six. They used the mirrors of parked vehicles, detoured elaborately.

He could think of only one agency whose operators were this good and who spoke Hebrew.

Mossad.

Of course, they would be interested in a Pakistani nuclear scientist's movements.

Zeb tailed them to their hotel. A shabby, rundown one like his. Their room was on the ground floor, just as his was. Good operatives chose the lower floors. They enabled quicker exits.

He broke into their room on the fourth day, when they were away, and wasn't surprised when he didn't find much, initially.

His bag. Her bag. No brightly lettered identification cards that said they were Mossad agents.

No surveillance equipment. No weapons.

He stood in the center of the room and surveyed it. Walked toward the bathroom. A loose floorboard moved under his weight.

He looked down.

Carpeted floor.

But an almost invisible crack in the fabric.

He bent down, pried it open, tested the board beneath it and discovered the treasure trove.

Two Glock 17s, several magazines, knives, surveillance gear.

He laid back the board, adjusted the carpet and waited behind the door.

It was confrontation time.

Chapter 3

———⊗⊗⊗———

Jerusalem
Present Day

Shiri held the elevator door open for Magal and pressed the button for the ground floor. He wasn't worried about prints. Both men were wearing adhesive pads on their fingers and, before leaving their apartment, had wiped it clean. They wouldn't be returning to it again.

He held the door open for Magal, and to any onlooker it would have looked like an act of politeness. A young man helping an old woman.

The old woman turned right when she reached the street, trudging slowly. Shiri donned shades and looked in her direction casually, until she turned a corner and disappeared from sight.

He walked a hundred yards and came to a parked vehicle, a white Skoda, bearing the logo of a taxi company. He turned off the yellow sign on the roof and drove out.

He headed down Hazefira Street, turned left on Yehoshafat Street, went toward the Museum of Natural History, where he circled round to join Emek Refaim, the main drag of German Colony.

He parked on the street opposite the entrance to a luxury hotel. Lowered the sun visor, leaned back in his seat and half-closed his eyes. A cab driver resting between jobs.

An hour passed. Traffic picked up. Tourists walked past. A uniformed cop strolled past, glancing at Shiri. The cab driver didn't react. The taxi was the real deal; his driver credentials would stand up to any scrutiny.

At ten am he stirred and made a show of rubbing his eyes and yawning lustily.

Half an hour later, there was movement at the hotel's entrance.

A couple came out of the revolving doors and stood outside. The man was bearded and dressed in an ill-fitting suit. The woman was slim, in a dress, and was laughing. Two men came behind them and waited.

A Range Rover drove up. The couple climbed down the steps, greeted the driver and settled into the back.

Another Range Rover arrived. The two men, who looked like heavies, got inside.

The two vehicles left, the couple's vehicle in the lead.

'They are coming your way,' Shiri murmured.

Maryam Razak snorted a laugh at Farhan Ba's joke and wriggled back in her seat in the first Range Rover. The two of them had this routine.

They went out for a drive after breakfast, a brief spin through German Colony, the city center, further if there was time, or else they returned to the hotel. The outing cleared her mind and prepared her for the day ahead. Farhan? She had a sneaking suspicion he came along with her just for her company. That flattered her, but she wasn't looking for a relationship.

She whipped out her make-up kit and reapplied her lipstick, listening as Farhan talked about the previous day.

Their vehicle slowed. It came to a stop.

She flicked her eyes up.

A pedestrian crossing. An old woman walking slowly, hunched, a bag in her hand.

Maryam and Farhan and the rest of them had been briefed about security. The vehicle behind them had their protectors.

She saw no reason to be alarmed by an elderly woman getting to the other side of the street. Maryam went back to her lipstick while Farhan fidgeted beside her.

He gasped. She didn't look up, dabbed the corner of her mouth with her forefinger.

He yelled. Fright in his voice. She jerked her head up. Her eyes widened when she took in the scene.

The old woman had stopped in the middle of the street. She had whipped out something long and metallic from her bag.

Their driver was cursing and reversing when a starburst pattern appeared on the windshield. A hole appeared. More of them. Maryam screamed when she realized what was happening. The driver slumped forward. Their vehicle yawed to the left.

The old woman came to their right. Windows shattered. Farhan shuddered and jerked. Something hit Maryam. She looked down, amazed at the red blossoming on her blouse. She felt like she was underwater, everything was moving so slowly. Her mouth opened to scream when she looked up and saw a cannon, the weapon's barrel, trained on her.

Maryam Razak didn't see anything else.

Magal moved swiftly and cut down the occupants from the second vehicle as they lunged out of their Range Rover. They were police officers, trained, but not as well-trained as he. They fell before any of them could reach for a weapon.

He threw the MAR, moving fast down the pavement. There was screaming on the streets. Pedestrians fled. Cars swerved and their occupants cowered. He saw movement from the corner of his eye. A driver raising his hand, holding a cell phone. The man ducked when he felt Magal's eyes on him.

Ahead, he saw the white Skoda, a barely perceptible trail of exhaust coming out of its pipe. He broke into a jog when he heard the wail of sirens in the distance.

He glanced back briefly. A few people had gathered around the wreckage of the two vehicles. At least two hands were pointing at him, but no one made any move toward him.

The Skoda was moving as he reached it. He opened the rear door, jumped in, and Shiri took off with a squeal of tires.

Magal removed his wig and the mask over his face and ripped the dress away as Shiri took the first left, then right, straight ahead and another left. A residential street.

The Skoda stopped behind a van parked on the street. The two men got out, moving in controlled haste, and went down the line of parked vehicles.

Shiri opened the driver's door to a dusty Volkswagen and slid inside. He reached beneath his seat and extracted a mustache from a plastic bag. He attached it to his upper lip and looked at Magal, who nodded.

Shiri nosed out of the parking space, circled back and joined the growing line of traffic on Emek Refaim. People were bunched on the pavement. Huddled together. Heads bent, talking softly as if they could be overheard.

Magal lowered the window and snatches of conversation floated in.

'Six people shot ...'

'Old woman ...'

'No, that must be a disguise ...'

'Escaped ...'

Their VW came to a stop at a police cordon. A bunch of cops, alert-eyed, hands on weapons, approached them.

Shiri lowered his window and answered their questions respectfully.

They were office workers. He pointed to the briefcases in the rear seat. They were already late to the office.

Did the cops want to see their identity cards?

No, they didn't.

Did Shiri or Magal see anything suspicious?

The police officers directed them to a detour and waved them away.

Magal drew out his phone when they were heading away.

He went to a social media app.

'Now?' he asked his partner.

'Yes.'

Magal typed out a single sentence.

Mossad Killers Assassinate Palestinian Peace Negotiators.

And with that, the Middle East exploded.

Chapter 4

Kadikoy, Istanbul
Three Days Before

Zeb heard their voices at the door two hours later.

The woman was arguing with the man, words indistinct, but the tone was unmistakable.

The door swung open into the room. She entered, followed by the man.

Zeb had lowered his chi, slowed his breathing, had made his consciousness almost undetectable.

He was the wall. He was the room.

The woman tossed her bag onto the bed and loosened her hair. The man headed to the bathroom. She loosened her shirt and turned.

And saw the old man at the door.

She didn't shout or scream. She dived toward the bed, her hands outstretched, reaching for her bag.

The man whirled. His hand dipped toward his waist.

The woman shoved her hand inside the bag.

Started drawing out her Glock.

The man's weapon started rising.

Zeb shot into the mattress.

The report was loud in the room, despite his silenced Glock 41.

'I am a friend,' he said in Hebrew, his eyes taking them both in. He was alert, ready for any move. Body armor beneath the shirt he wore.

I hope I've guessed right about them.

The couple didn't respond. Their eyes were wary. Their hands still gripping their weapons. The woman lay at an acute angle, heels digging into the floor, left hand braced against the bed, right gripping her gun, her body in the air.

She was breathing evenly despite the unnatural pose.

She would, if she's a kidon.

'I could have killed you,' Zeb tried again, mildly. 'I didn't. That should give you a clue. My language as well.'

'Who are you?' the man demanded.

'He was at the café,' the woman replied.

Zeb watched them watching him.

Time to take a leap of faith.

He bent down slowly and placed his gun on the floor.

'I'm friendly,' he repeated in Arabic, just in case he had misheard them.

Their Glocks came up and trained on him. Neither fired.

He moved his hands slowly and removed his wig and the prosthetic mask. 'You saw me yesterday, as well.'

'No,' the woman replied, in Hebrew. 'We would have noticed. The regulars were pensioners who look nothing like you. They play chess. They're harmless.'

Zeb saw a flicker of emotion cross her face.

Harmless. She knows she shouldn't have said that word. A

stranger would wonder at its choice.

'Did you see the old woman who was carrying a Food Bazaar bag? She sat close to you and sipped her tea noisily?'

The stillness in them gave them away. They had noticed the woman.

'You're from Mossad? To assassinate Hussain?'

A muscle twitched on the man's face but no word escaped them.

Zeb sighed. 'Look, I told you. I am not a threat. We both are after the same person. We can work together ... but if you're here to kill Hussain, then we're not friends.'

'We don't know any Hussain. We are not from Mossad,' the woman replied.

Looks like she's the khuliyot leader.

'I'm sure you can explain those Glocks you're carrying. And those beneath the floorboards, as well as the other gear.'

They didn't explain.

His hand slid inside his pocket and he withdrew his phone carefully.

He dialed a number, and when a voice came online, he put the phone on speaker.

'Avichai,' he said loudly, eyeing the two agents, 'I am with two of your kidon. I think.'

'My kidon? Where are you, Zeb?'

'Kadikoy. In a hotel room. With a male and a female who're pointing their guns at me. If they're not your people, then I am a dead man.'

Levin didn't respond.

'Why are you there, Zeb?'

He's not denying their existence.

'I'm tracking Uzair Hussain. I noticed your operatives. I

think we both have the same objectives. It's better if we work together … unless your people are working on a *wet* assignment. In which case, we're on opposite teams.'

'Hang up. Stay there.'

Zeb hung up.

A phone buzzed. The female patted her pocket and withdrew her cell.

She brought it to her ear, her gaze still on Zeb. 'Ken?' Yes.

She listened intently for a while, nodded, turned away and spoke softly. She handed the phone to her partner when she had finished. The man listened as well, grunted an acknowledgement and hung up.

Zeb couldn't help grinning when the two stood motionless for a moment, expressionless.

'I bet you two haven't done this before. Worked with someone else on a mission.'

'You're American?' the female asked, flatly.

'Zeb Carter. *Avichai* might have told you about me.' He deliberately used Levin's first name to convey the relationship he had with the ramsad.

It didn't have the desired effect. Neither of the two introduced themselves.

'You speak our language well,' the female kidon stated.

'I'm sure you speak English fluently.'

'What is your mission?' the man tucked his weapon in his waist and stood beside his partner.

'You aren't going to make this easy for me, are you?' Zeb picked up his Glock and holstered it. 'I want to know what Uzair Hussain is up to.'

'You'll grab him?' The female operative still held her gun.

Looks like she's less trusting than her partner.

'No. I plan to bug him. What about you?'

She didn't say anything until the man nudged her.

'You know who he's meeting?'

'I can make a guess. Kamran Shahi, the Iranian nuclear—'

'We know who he is.' The female kidon finally put her gun away in her bag and turned toward him.

'I am Riva. He is Adir.'

No handshakes. No second names.

'You're kidon?'

No reply. Standard operating procedure for Mossad's deadly operatives.

'What is your mission?' Zeb asked.

'Grab Hussain. And Shahi.'

Chapter 5

———⊶⊷———

Jerusalem
Present Day

Prime Minister Yago Cantor was still in his residence in Beit Aghion, in Jerusalem, when news of the shooting filtered out.

He normally headed to his office at seven am, but that day had stayed back for several meetings.

He had just finished a briefing with his public security minister, Jessy Levitsky, when an aide knocked on the door and rushed in without an apology or a greeting.

'You've got to see this.' He picked up a remote and turned on the TV.

Cantor's face paled when he read the scrolling banner beneath the images of the shooting.

'That hotel … that couple,' he whispered.

'Those are the Palestinian negotiators,' Levitsky replied grimly.

'No one knew about them. How did it happen?'

'I'll find out.'

The prime minister leaned against his desk, following the

news, while Levitsky, whose department oversaw the police, left the room, speaking softly in his cell phone.

Already, the Islamic countries were saber-rattling. Jordan and Egypt, Israel's immediate neighbors, had threatened military action if Israel didn't identify the killers quickly.

Saudi Arabia's defense minister had upped the country's alert level.

A phone trilled. The aide picked it up, listened, cupped the receiver and looked at Cantor.

'It's the American ambassador.'

'I thought she was on vacation.'

'She is, sir. She's calling from the U.S.'

'I'll call her back.'

The aide murmured in the phone and left the room. Yago Cantor muted the TV, rubbed his eyes and passed a hand over his thinning hair.

He was powerfully built and had a personality to match. He looked around in his home office, at the pictures of various prime ministers hanging on the wall. Some with families, others with American presidents or alone in the photograph.

A quotation by David Ben-Gurion, the first prime minister of the country, caught his eye.

In Israel, in order to be a realist, you must believe in miracles.

Cantor was a pragmatist. He was the leader of his right-wing party, had held together his coalition government through no-confidence motions, and was in his second term.

He had welcomed the U.S. administration's Jerusalem embassy move. He also knew how that would affect the Palestinians and had set his plan in motion: bringing the Palestinians to the peace table, because he didn't want to see subsequent generations of Israelis warring with their neighbors.

It hadn't been easy.

Many in his party had criticized him. They said he was going soft. That the Palestinians had shown their true nature during the failed peace talks of 2014.

Cantor used his charm. He cajoled and persuaded, threatened and swore. He outlined the bigger picture. Surely everyone wanted lasting peace. Did anyone want to see terrorist attacks in Israel?

'Do you want to see that for the rest of your lives?' he challenged his party members, pointing to the TVs on the wall, which showed the scenes in Gaza. *That was the Palestinians' fault*, his party roared back.

'And they say Israel is the culprit. This will never end. Our two people, ours and theirs, have been at war ever since our country was born. Do you want this to continue forever? Your grandchildren and their children … you want them to live like this?'

There were a few feeble protests at that, but not as widespread as he had thought. That had given him confidence. He had pressed on, convincing his party, those in his coalition, as well as his cabinet.

Some in his party had wanted the Americans to mediate the peace process.

Cantor had exploded. 'This is our country,' he had stormed. 'We don't need the United States or any other country to broker peace for us.'

He had won his party over slowly, and then started working on the coalition partners. At no time did he reveal the full extent of his peace plan or when the negotiations would start. Only select members of his cabinet knew, and they were sworn to secrecy.

He had reached out to Ziyan Baruti, president of the State of Palestine, who had been initially distrustful.

'Why should we believe you?' that leader had asked Cantor.

'Would I call you if I didn't mean it?' the prime minister had countered. 'Can you imagine how hard it was to sell this to my party and my coalition?'

There had been silence on the other line. Baruti was familiar with Cantor's party and with its sometimes hard-line stance toward Palestine.

The two men had spoken at length; then the Israeli stunned the Palestinian with his dream.

'Do you mean it?' Baruti had whispered after several moments of silence.

'Yes.'

'This could mean the end of your career. Your party will never accept it. Your country will not, either. You might even be assassinated by your own people.'

'I am aware of that,' Cantor had replied irritably. He hadn't arrived at his vision in one morning. He had spent sleepless nights agonizing over it before deciding it was the right thing to do for his country.

'That is why we do this my way. We negotiate and agree first, and then announce it to my country. The Americans, the British, the French, everyone will support this treaty. That will put pressure on my party. My country, my people will then accept the deal.'

'Not immediately.'

'No,' Cantor had admitted. 'There will be rioting in West

Jerusalem. All over the country. It will take time. Maybe years. But in the end, it will be worth it.'

'Inshallah. Enta ragel hakim,' Baruti said in Arabic.

Cantor understood the words. He was fluent in it, even though Hebrew was his country's language.

'Thank you,' he replied, touched at being called a *wise man* by the Palestinian.

He and Baruti weren't friends. They had met a few times at carefully orchestrated diplomatic functions. Their private discussions had escalated to hostility very quickly.

That was just the way it was. No Israeli leader could be a friend with his or her Palestinian counterpart.

Cantor had researched Baruti for a long time before discussing the peace plan.

The State of Palestine had a complex government, partly because the region was split into two distinct territories, Gaza Strip and the West Bank, run respectively by the two major parties, Hamas and Fatah.

Both sides were in a continual state of conflict that often erupted in violence. Hundreds of Palestinians had died over the years because of the parties' antagonism.

The West Bank was the seat of the Palestinian National Authority, PNA, the internationally recognized government of the state. This was a Fatah majority government, with Ziyan Baruti as its president.

The two governments in the Palestinian territories did not work together. They had their own budgets—both of which relied extensively on foreign aid and donations and had different administrative machinery.

Baruti, whom the world recognized as the leader of the State of Palestine, was widely perceived as a moderate, and the Mossad's psychological profiling on him confirmed that.

By all accounts, Cantor's counterpart was a mature man, one with a long-term vision. That personality had led the prime minister to take a leap of faith in Baruti.

To be called that by him ... I reached out to the right man.

Encouraged, he had gone into the details of the logistics of the peace plan with the Palestinian, and the two men had discussed it at length.

'You should not tell this to anyone,' he had warned his counterpart.

'Why?' Baruti had demanded. 'Surely, it is better to have this in the open.'

'No. No one should ever know what exactly is being negotiated.'

Baruti had grumbled but had finally relented.

The two men had spoken a few more times after that, and a negotiation plan was struck.

Each country would have six delegates. The two teams would meet in Jerusalem, in an upscale hotel that was frequented by business people. Each negotiator would pose as a business person. Both teams would have security provided by Israel. The bodyguards would think they were protecting high net-worth individuals.

For added security, only Cantor and a few in his cabinet would know the hotel's details. On top of that, the Palestinians would have to surrender their cell phones, and any calls they made or received would be monitored by the Israelis.

Baruti had balked at that but caved in when the prime minister insisted. The big picture was important.

Cantor was firm on an additional point: Neither team would know of his dream.

'Why are they even meeting, then?' Baruti had burst out.

'They will start off as if they are discussing a conventional peace treaty. Later, we will tell them what the real goal is.'

The Palestinian understood. Cantor's vision would be hard to negotiate. It was better that a conventional peace treaty be hammered out first and then the thornier issues be dealt with.

Nevertheless, he had protested. 'This cannot be done in a few weeks. It requires months.'

'Yes, I know. But in a few weeks, we can set the parameters of what we want to achieve. With the objective very firmly in sight.'

The negotiators were identified. Well-respected, experienced hands on both sides. They were all sworn to secrecy. The hotel was identified as well. One in German Colony, popular both with tourists and business travelers. The security personnel were handpicked by Levitsky.

Cantor's plan worked perfectly. Both teams of negotiators arrived at the hotel. No lay person in Israel or Palestine knew who they were, or their purpose. Each night the prime minister called Baruti and briefed him on the day's progress.

The first week was nearing an end. Cantor was feeling optimistic. He felt it was time to tell the negotiators of the big plan. His vision.

And then the killing happened.

Yago Cantor held his face in his hands, his shoulders drooping. *I am lucky I am a widower and have no children,* he thought. *My marriage, my family, wouldn't have survived this pressure.*

He raised his head when his aide burst in again.

'Did you see?' his assistant asked.

'What else is there to see?'

The young man pointed at the TV in silence.

The prime minister's heart clenched when he read the latest rolling banner.

MOSSAD SUSPECTED OF KILLING PALESTINE NEGOTIATORS.

Chapter 6

——❦——

Kadikoy, Istanbul
Three Days Before

It took a couple of hours for Riva and Adir to open up, and it happened gradually.

Zeb went to the small refrigerator in their hotel apartment and brought out two bottles of beer. He handed one to each of them and picked a water bottle for himself.

'What about you?' the female operative asked, as she sat on the bed. She was dark-eyed, with a narrow face, hair tied back in a ponytail.

'I don't drink.' He held up his water. 'This is good for me. How will you grab them?'

The kidon looked at each other. Sharing operational details with a third party didn't come easily to them. Even if said party was a close friend of their boss, who had instructed them to cooperate fully.

'We'll drug them. Make them passive.'

'Just the two of you? What about a getaway vehicle?'

Adir took a swallow, placed his bottle on the table and bent to the floor. He ripped up the loose carpet piece and removed the floorboard. He ran his eyes over their cache of weapons and equipment. Nodded to himself, and removed the neighboring floorboard.

'Huh?' Zeb exclaimed in surprise. He hadn't checked out the surrounding boards.

The kidon reached into the opening and brought out two white shirts and two pairs of dark trousers that had high-visibility strips at their bottom.

'Emergency services?' Zeb guessed.

'Ken,' Adir confirmed. 'We'll go as ambulance staff. That café is near a hospital. We have observed emergency vehicles park near it, and the staff go inside for tea and snacks.'

'What about the vehicle?'

'We've arranged it.' Riva finished her drink and placed the empty bottle beneath her bed. 'It's not far from here. What role will you play?'

'Walk me through it again?'

The two kidon broke down their plan for him, answering his questions patiently.

'What if police come?'

'The ambulance is genuine. Our paperwork is good. We'll take the two to the hospital.'

'Then?'

'It's a busy hospital,' she shrugged. 'We'll lead them out through the rear. We've been through dry runs.'

'What if passersby interfere?'

'We are ambulance staff. We can keep them away.'

'What if other vehicles crowd?'

'They won't crowd an ambulance.'

'Does Shahi have any security with him?'

'He's come alone, always. We don't see any reason for this next meeting to be different.'

'Why do you think they're meeting?'

'That's why we're taking them,' Riva replied, drolly, 'to find out.'

'What role will you play?' she asked again.

'I'll watch. Provided you share intel with us.'

'That's what the ramsad told us. We have our orders. You'll get your information, without your doing anything,' Riva told him with an undertone of anger.

Zeb pocketed his disguise and left without a word. He took counter-measures when he reached the street, to shake any tails. Just in case the Mossad operatives tailed him.

Once he reached his hotel room, he drew out his screen from his backpack and turned on an app.

Two green dots glowed on it. Riva and Adir, the soluble GPS trackers in their bodies signaling their location. It had been a simple matter to slip the trackers into their drinks as he opened their bottles.

It was clear the female kidon didn't trust him. Now, it didn't matter.

He had eyes on them.

Chapter 7

—✦—

Jerusalem
Present Day

'Get me Levitsky,' he roared. 'And Avichai Levin and Nadav Shoshan as well.'

The aide fled the room.

Cantor grabbed the remote with trembling fingers and turned up the volume.

Unconfirmed reports ... Mossad accused ... Social media trending ... Questions being asked ... Why were these negotiations conducted in secret? ... Did Israel authorize Mossad to kill those negotiators?

The prime minister swung around when the door burst open and Levitsky hurried in. He jabbed the remote at the TV and turned down the volume.

The minister held his hand up before Cantor could let loose. 'I've heard. The police are investigating.'

'I didn't authorize any assassination,' the prime minister yelled.

Shabak, also known as Shin Bet, was Israel's internal

security service, similar to the United States' FBI. Mossad, which in Hebrew meant the Institute, was the country's foreign intelligence agency, much like the CIA.

Mossad's ramsad, its director, reported only to the prime minister, and only he could sanction an assassination.

'I know,' Levitsky replied soothingly and brought a glass of water to the prime minister.

Cantor emptied it in one large swallow and took several calming breaths.

'Shoshon and Levin are on their way,' the aide said, popping his head again.

'No calls,' Cantor warned him.

The aide bobbed his head and disappeared.

'These rumors ...' the prime minister gestured toward the TV.

'My people,' Levitsky, referring to the police forces, 'are still investigating. It looks like they first surfaced on Twitter and then they spread.'

'Who posted it first?'

'We do not know.'

A sharp knock sounded on the door before it opened. Nadav Shoshon, the director of Shabak, entered first. He was middle-aged, bald, with brown eyes that were usually mirthful. They were somber now.

A second man followed him. He was in a suit, no tie, and looked like any businessman. Clean-shaven, piercing eyes, tightly cropped hair that was turning steel grey. Avichai Levin, Mossad's ramsad, was feared by terrorists and revered by the directors of foreign intelligence agencies. Both men knew of the negotiations. They had to, since they headed two of the three intelligence agencies in the country. The third, Aman, was the intelligence branch of the Israeli Defense Forces.

'Avichai,' Cantor rumbled, having gained control over himself. 'Explain this.'

'I can't,' Levin replied honestly. 'As you know, we don't have any such sanctioned operation.'

'How did these rumors start, then?'

'It looks like the first post was made on Twitter just after the killing. I just found out,' he clarified when the three men looked at him in surprise. 'A user who had never been on the site before. Looks like an account that was created for sending that message only. The tweet was then picked up by other users. I am sure there were some bots, too, that kept retweeting. The rumor spread from there.'

'How did the killers know about the negotiations?' the prime minister asked.

No one knew.

'This isn't something that was planned overnight,' Shoshon said, breaking the silence. 'The killers would have to know who the Palestinian negotiators were. Where they were staying. Maryam Razak and Farhan Ba used to go for a drive every day—'

He stopped when a sharp sound echoed in the room. The prime minister slapping his forehead dramatically.

'The others!' Cantor exclaimed. 'We've got to—'

'They have all been moved, sir,' Levitsky broke in. 'Our negotiators as well as the Palestinians. We've put them up in another hotel on Emek Refaim Street. Yamam and Yasam units are protecting the hotel. The street is shut down.'

Yamam was an elite police unit, whereas Yasam was the counter-terrorist unit present in each Israeli district.

'No one can enter that hotel,' the public security minister concluded.

'I am putting together an investigative unit.' Cantor straightened from the desk he was leaning against. 'Representatives from Mossad, Shabak, and IDF. Reporting only to me. We need answers fast. We have to find those killers.'

'Sir,' Levin held up a hand.

'What?'

'Can I have a moment with you?'

The prime minister paused. Mossad was one of the most secretive agencies in the world. Even Shoshon or Levitsky weren't privy to its working. *I, too, don't know all of it.*

'Do you have any objections to this investigative unit?'

'No, sir,' Levin replied.

'Shoshon, you'll put this team together. Right away. I want hourly updates. Thank you for coming.'

The minister and the Shabak director left the room.

'What is it, Avichai?' Cantor asked wearily when the two men were alone.

'I don't want anyone external investigating Mossad, sir.'

The prime minister nodded. He had suspected something like this was behind the ramsad's request.

'You're aware of the implications of these killings?'

'Political, sir?'

'Not political. What it means to your agency.'

'Yes, sir. If these rumors are true, it means some of my operatives have gone rogue.'

Chapter 8

Kadikoy, Istanbul
Present Day, Before the Jerusalem Assassinations

Zeb wore a balding man's disguise on the day of the grab. Dark shirt, stained, dark trousers, comfortable shoes on his feet. A linen bag in one hand, he was the picture of a man heading home after grocery shopping. No one paid any attention to him. There were millions of men like him in the city. He was invisible.

He reached the café several hours before and checked it out by ordering a tea. Hussain wasn't present. Neither was Shahi. *Meghan said the two met around noon, the previous times.* It was ten am. There was no sign of the Mossad kidon, either. That didn't worry him. The operatives would be planning, and it wouldn't surprise him if one of them was watching the café.

The regulars came in an hour later, the chess players. They occupied their usual table, greeted the owner and placed their order. One of them laid out a chess board and they began. Zeb had followed two of them previously and knew they were harmless. No lethal operative among any of them.

He put his drink down and rose hastily, mumbling to his server that he had forgotten an item on his list. His wife would kill him.

He departed, turned a corner and circled back. Entered the street at the far end and walked behind a family. Checked out the cars parked on the streets, testing their doors discreetly. One opened. He slid inside. No keys anywhere. That was okay. He wasn't planning on driving it.

If the owner turned up, he would look apologetic. Say that the door was open and he had taken the opportunity to rest his legs. Who would begrudge an old man his respite?

He peered through the windscreen. Good view of the café and its approach.

Forty-five minutes later, he lumbered to the establishment. Settled heavily into a vacant seat and placed his bag down. He mopped his brow and checked his shopping against a list he produced from his pocket.

The chess players looked at him and clicked their tongues in sympathy when he grumbled about his wife. The universal brotherhood of harried husbands at play.

The server came, placed his tea on the table and headed back inside. Zeb took a sip and smacked his lips loudly in appreciation. Did the mopping thing again. Looked around. Spotted a newspaper on another table that someone had left.

Grabbed it and sat back in his seat with a sigh.

A few customers drifted in and out. Noon arrived. Half an hour later, Uzair Hussain came.

He was alone, in his black suit. Scuffed shoes. A worn leather satchel in hand. He occupied an empty table and looked around. His gaze passed over the pensioners and the man with the newspaper. He didn't seem to sense any threat. He waved his hand to the server and placed his order.

Zeb had his head bowed, a finger tracing the column he was reading, his lips moving silently. He was watching from the corners of his eyes, the Glock snug in his shoulder holster.

Hussain checked his phone. Looked around impatiently and shifted in his seat.

Twenty minutes later, Kamran Shahi walked up briskly.

Hussain rose, hugged the man and exchanged greetings with him. The two men sat opposite each other, and when the new arrival's drink appeared, they conversed softly.

Zeb didn't attempt to overhear them.

His eyes were on two men who had accompanied the Iranian.

They wore short-sleeve shirts left untucked. Jeans. Combat boots, and when a breeze drifted through the street, their shirts flattened against their chests and revealed the angular outlines of the weapons at their waists.

Shahi hadn't come alone, this time.

He had heavies with him.

Chapter 9

Jerusalem
Present Day

'Won't it be better if we get Shabak or the police to investigate? You won't know whom to trust in Mossad.' The prime minister turned off the TV and settled in his chair.

Levin remained standing, though Cantor had nodded at an empty chair. 'One of the reasons Mossad is successful is its secrecy. Once I allow other agencies inside, that is lost. Let me clean my house, sir. My way.'

The prime minister swore softly and was waving a hand to dismiss the ramsad when his desk phone trilled and the aide popped his head through the door.

'Sir, you should take this.'

'I said, no calls,' Cantor grumped. 'Who is it?'

'President Morgan, sir.'

The Israeli leader motioned for Levin to sit, cleared his throat, took the call and turned on the speaker.

'Mr. President, it is good to hear from you, sir,' he greeted the leader of the free world.

William (Bill) Morgan had been elected based on his manifesto to deliver change. Reposition America's standing in the world, have closer ties with allies, regenerate employment, and, perhaps the most ambitious of all, bring peace to the Middle East.

He and the British prime minister were the only two world leaders to know of the peace negotiations and of the Israeli's vision. Morgan and Cantor had become closer when the prime minister had revealed what he wanted to achieve.

'Yago, I can imagine how things are at your end.' The president's Texas drawl sounded loud and clear in the room. 'I wanted to check if you needed any help.'

Cantor knew what that meant. *The offer's genuine. But Morgan also wants to know what's happening.*

'Sir, at this moment, what we have is not much more than what you're watching on screen.' He went on to brief the president with the available facts.

'Could this be a false flag operation?' Morgan asked. 'Someone wanting to discredit Israel as well as Mossad?'

'That's a possibility, sir. Avichai Levin is with me and he'll be investigating.'

'Hello, Mr. President,' the ramsad said, leaning toward the speaker phone.

'Avichai, I have instructed our agencies to cooperate with you. Any help you need, any intel … nothing will be held back.'

'I appreciate that, sir.'

'Yago, has anything changed?' The president asked, referring to the negotiations.

'I haven't had the opportunity to brief President Baruti, sir. I'll be doing that shortly. We want the peace talks to progress. These killings haven't altered that.'

'That's great to hear, Yago. I have instructed Alice to cut short her vacation and to return to Jerusalem. She will be more than happy to help you with anything.'

Alice Monash was the American ambassador to Israel. An experienced diplomat, she was widely respected by both Israel and Palestine.

'We appreciate that, sir.' Cantor hung up after speaking for a few more minutes with the president. He sat for several moments staring at the photographs framed on the walls. Muted sounds drifted in through the closed door. A phone ringing somewhere in the residence. Indistinct voices. Since he lived alone, Beit Aghion had become more of a second office and less of a home.

'A bird cannot fly with one wing,' he mused. 'Shimon Peres used to say that. For peace, we need two parties. We cannot deviate. We will not waver.'

He reached for the phone and dialed a number from memory.

'President Baruti?' he asked when a voice came on the line.

He winced when a tirade erupted from the other end and held the phone away from his ear.

He gestured at Levin, who was rising, to remain seated and put the phone on speaker.

'Mr. President,' he interrupted the Palestinian's angry words. 'Mr. President ... allow me to speak, sir.' The two men spoke in Hebrew, as they usually did.

'What is there to speak, Prime Minister?' Baruti demanded, angrily. 'You betrayed my country. You made false promises. You spoke nice words and I was drawn in. I thought, here's an Israeli leader who is different. He wants peace and means it. I can do business with him. Business? Your only business was to kill my negotiators. You are a liar, Prime Minister. A liar who—'

'Mr. President, I meant every word I said.' Cantor's face was flushed, but his voice was controlled. 'I was committed to the peace process then. I am committed to it now. I was the one who told you my vision. Palestinians and Israelis living side by side, in harmony. That vision remains undimmed.'

'Your Mossad killers have ended that vision,' Baruti shouted.

'Sir, we do not know if they are Mossad—'

'Don't know? Do you read the news, Prime Minister?'

'I am aware of what's being reported,' Cantor replied stiffly. 'However, there's no proof. I have not authorized this operation. Director Avichai Levin is with me. He can confirm what I am saying.'

The ramsad switched to Arabic when he spoke, a mark of respect for the Palestinian president. 'Sir, the prime minister is right. Mossad is *not involved* in these killings.'

'But—'

'I will be investigating those claims, sir. If any of my operatives were behind it, they acted on their own and will be dealt with. You have my word, sir. I know it is difficult for you to trust an Israeli's word at this time. Nevertheless, this is a promise I make, in the holiest city of the world, Jerusalem.'

Baruti remained silent for a moment. 'Yago?'

Cantor closed his eyes in relief at the mention of his first name.

'I am here, Ziyan.'

'You and Levin mean what you said?'

'Yes, Ziyan. We are deeply sorrowed by the killings of

Maryam Razak and Farhan Ba. We will investigate those killings and find whoever is responsible. But the peace talks should go on.'

'Very well. I am taking a leap of faith in you.'

'I will not let you down, Mr. President.'

'I will send two more negotiators.'

'That would be welcome, sir. Perhaps we could also release a joint statement.'

'I thought you wanted to keep your vision a secret.'

'We will not mention it in the statement. Both sides are committed to peace talks. That's what the declaration will say.'

'Let's do it today, Yago. Let's not waste time.'

'I'll instruct my office to work on this, Ziyan. They will contact your people.'

'Shalom.'

'Shalom.'

Cantor's face was lined with fatigue. His eyes were narrowed with stress. Despite that, he managed a smile.

'Avichai, I didn't know you could speak so well.'

Levin rose and adjusted his suit. 'It must be your proximity, sir.'

'You fox,' the prime minister laughed. 'You'll do very well in politics if you want to enter it.'

'That's not for me, sir.'

'Avichai,' the prime minister stopped him as he was opening the door. 'This will bring pressure on me. My party, the coalition, the Knesset ... there will be many calls to abort the negotiations. Many of our people will call me a traitor. You need to act fast.'

'Yes, sir.'

'Find them.' Prime Minister Yago Cantor's eyes turned

steely. 'Find these killers. If they are Mossad ... deal with them.'

Levin nodded. He knew what the prime minister meant.

If the assassins were his operatives, justice would not be administered through any court of law.

It would be delivered the Mossad way.

Chapter 10

⸺⸺∞⸺⸺

Kadikoy, Istanbul
Present Day, Before the Jerusalem Assassinations

Zeb had no means of warning the kidon. He hoped they were observing the café, were aware of the two men and had adapted their plan accordingly.

Then he remembered: Riva and Adir were acting alone. *Two operatives aren't enough.*

The heavies had swept the café with practiced eyes as soon as they had arrived. They had lingered on the pensioners and dismissed them. Zeb had similarly been disregarded. There was nothing about a balding, perspiring elderly man that aroused suspicion. Not many operatives took such a person for a threat.

Hussain and Shahi continued their discussions, glancing occasionally at a sheet of paper that the Pakistani scientist had produced.

Zeb turned a page clumsily and got to his feet when his newspaper fell down. He shuffled over to retrieve it and, when he bent down, snatched a glance at the scientists' table. It was some kind of a drawing. A layout of a building.

He went back to his seat, and when he had finished folding his newspaper to the right column, an ambulance was turning up.

It idled for a few moments, and then its engine shut off. A man jumped out from the driver's seat. He waited for his companion to join him. Adir and Riva, both in the Turkish Emergency Services uniforms.

The two laughed at something and high-fived each other. Shahi's heavies watched them but made no move.

Riva went to the café, turned around to say something to Adir, lost her balance and stumbled against the seated Hussain.

The scientist's tea spilled on the table. Shahi grabbed the sheet of paper and folded it quickly. He admonished Riva, who apologized profusely to Hussain. The Pakistani brushed her off in irritation and, when Riva spoke to him again, snapped at her.

She raised her hands in apology and went inside the café.

Zeb watched, as did the chess players. The difference was, he was observing the heavies. They had started forward but then had stayed back at a barely perceptible shake of the head from Shahi.

It was when the kidon were returning, drinks in hand, that it happened.

Hussain slumped forward, clutching his chest. He groaned. Shahi spoke urgently to him. The Pakistani moaned louder.

The Mossad operatives were heading toward their ambulance when the Iranian shouted in alarm.

Zeb got up from his seat and hurried over to the Pakistani. He put a hand on the man's shoulder and brought his face close. He cupped his palm in front of the man's nose and, with sleight of hand, slipped a soluble through his parted lips. The Pakistani allowed it involuntarily.

'He's alive,' Zeb cried out. He took the opportunity to check out Shahi swiftly. Close-up, the Iranian was swarthier than he appeared in photographs. His beard didn't seem to have been trimmed for a couple of days. Bushy eyebrows. Dark eyes that looked concerned. A small tattoo on the left side of his neck that was normally concealed by his shirt collar and exposed only because he was looking around helplessly. The body-art was incredibly rich in detail and no bigger than a quarter-dollar.

Zeb took it in for as long as possible without arousing suspicion and then looked toward the kidon.

Riva turned at his shout. Dropped her drink when she took in the scene and hurried forward. Adir joined her, and the two kidon bent over the fallen scientist.

'It looks like a heart attack,' Riva spoke crisply. 'We'll have to take him to the hospital.'

Shahi protested.

'Sir,' she snapped at him. 'We are from Kadikoy Sifa Hospital, which is just around the corner. Unless you are a doctor, let us do our jobs.'

The Iranian wasn't a doctor. He looked back at his heavies, who had come closer. He shrugged his shoulders in defeat and whispered something to the Pakistani, who groaned louder.

Adir ran to the ambulance and wheeled out a gurney. Shahi looked on helplessly as the two operatives maneuvered Hussain onto it. The chess players offered to help, Riva shook her head.

'Sir,' she addressed Shahi. 'You know this man?'

'He's … a friend.'

'It's best you come with us, in that case. You can contact his family.'

She placed a hand on his shoulder, her other hand pushing the gurney.

Shahi was clearly of two minds. Events were happening faster than he could comprehend. His heavies made their minds up.

They surged forward, their hands reaching toward their waists. They were focused on the bunch of people heading to the vehicle. They didn't see the old man move toward them.

Zeb acted fast to cut them off. Skirted the tables and chairs. Ignored the chess players, who were watching the gurney getting loaded into the ambulance.

His left elbow rose in a point and smashed into the nearest heavy's temple. The man went down like a collapsing sack.

His partner turned swiftly, his hand coming out, a snub-nosed gun in hand. Zeb jabbed him in the throat with the outstretched fingers of his right hand.

The man choked. His weapon clattered to the ground. Zeb punched him in the gut and followed up with a chop to his neck.

The heavy joined his companion on the ground.

Zeb felt eyes on him.

The pensioners were staring at him, mouths agape.

'Enjoy your game,' he told them, grabbed his bag and walked away quickly as the ambulance disappeared in traffic.

Once out of sight, he reached into his bag and withdrew his screen.

Three green dots on it.

Two representing Riva and Adir. The third indicated Uzair Hussain.

His mission was done.

Chapter 11

———— ⊙∞⊙ ————

Tel Aviv
Evening of the Assassinations

There were varying estimates of Mossad's size. The lay person thought it was a vast organization with a global reach. Those in the intelligence community thought Mossad had about a thousand staff. The CIA, MI6, other Western agencies had their own estimates about its size.

Levin and his predecessors never commented on those estimates. It added to the mystique and the legend of Mossad.

In reality, the organization was smaller than the CIA and MI6. It was also smaller than Hollywood's portrayal of the agency. What gave the organization incredible reach was the network of sayanim, helpers, Jews who in many cases were dual nationals, scattered all over the world.

Sayanim helped Mossad's operations the world over. A travel agency in Dubai could arrange the right documents for the operatives. A landlord in London could provide accommodation. Sayanim sometimes worked closely with katsas, Mossad's field intelligence officers. Often, they worked alone, driven by their commitment to the state of Israel and to the welfare of Jews the world over.

Sayanim were the furthest thing from Levin's mind as he reached his office in Tel Aviv. The CIA had its headquarters in Langley, MI6 had its at Vauxhall Cross in London. Neither agency made any attempt to hide those locations.

Mossad never advertised where its headquarters was. Other than current and former employees and a few politicians, no one knew where the ramsad ran his agency from.

To the naked eye, the building looked like any office block. Staffers clocked in with key cards, some wearing business suits, some casually dressed. Unsurprisingly, given that many Mossad operatives were stationed overseas, hot-desking was the norm. There were conference rooms scattered around the building, with Levin being one of the very few who had a separate office.

The building's interior had the feel of a university campus, though its security wouldn't be found in any college.

Levin greeted people around the office, went into his own and shut the door.

He logged in to his computer and brought up the files of all his kidon.

Kidon, Hebrew for "tip of the spear," was a special-ops unit in Mossad so secret that most staffers didn't know who was in it.

It carried out high-profile assassinations, gathered highly sensitive intelligence, and engaged in sabotage operations. Kidon members, male and female, were usually drawn from elite units such as Sayeret Matkal within the Israeli Defense Forces.

They underwent intense psychological profiling before

being admitted and trained in the Negev desert. They worked in small teams, *khuliyot*, of two to four. Each team member was responsible for specific tasks such as recon, logistics and assassination.

If Mossad operatives had been responsible for the killing, they had to be kidon.

It wasn't hard to reach that conclusion. Like any other intelligence agency, Mossad had several departments. Collections was responsible for espionage; Political Action dealt with relations with other countries, both friendly and hostile; there was a research department and a technology one; and then there were Metsada and Kidon.

Metsada was a special operations unit, and its operatives were trained assassins. However, Levin knew the location of every one of them and received daily video reports. Those calls triangulated their position. It was logistically impossible for any of them to have arrived in the country and carried out the killing.

No, if the killers were from his organization, they had to be kidon. Levin brought up their profiles. Just two of them were in Israel, the rest overseas on various missions.

That didn't mean much. Unlike the Metsada teams, kidon didn't call in or send daily reports. Any one of them could have come into the country using fake credentials. After all, they lived large parts of their lives under assumed names and false identities.

Levin looked out at the open-plan office. Men and women going about their work. A lot of it was simple administrative work that held together intelligence-gathering operations and the more lethal missions.

How could he identify the killers? Who could he trust?

President Morgan's words came to him. *Any help you need...*

Of course. How could he have forgotten? He deliberated for a moment, going through his decision. Bringing in an outsider to investigate the Mossad? It had never been done before.

But these were exceptional times, and Avichai Levin was an exceptional leader, which was why he was also considered a legend.

And the man he had in mind?

Exceptional was an understatement.

Washington DC, That Evening

The woman who took Avichai Levin's call could have passed for a banker on Wall Street.

She was dressed in a cream suit over a white blouse and wore a string of pearls around her neck. No rings on her fingers. She wasn't married or engaged and, other than the necklace, didn't wear jewelry.

She went by Clare. No second name. Those who knew it, never used it.

She had just returned from briefing President Morgan and had been in the Oval Office when he had spoken to Prime Minister Cantor.

Clare headed the Agency, a virtually unknown black-ops outfit that was answerable only to the president. While the country had many covert units to fight terrorism and deal with national security threats, the Agency was structured differently.

Clare was its only employee and had the opaque title of

Director of Strategic Affairs. She had eight agents, all of who worked for a security consulting firm in New York. The firm was genuine; it had real clients and delivered exceptional advice ... when the operatives were not on Agency missions. The security business housed all the assets that the covert unit needed, and this resulted in a near-zero administrative footprint for the Agency.

Zeb Carter was the outfit's lead operative. Prior to joining Clare's outfit, he had been a private military contractor.

Her phone buzzed. She looked at the number and smiled briefly. She had won a bet with President Morgan.

'Avichai,' she said as she took the call, 'I heard what happened. How can I help you?'

She listened as the Mossad director outlined his request.

'You know Zeb's on a mission.'

The ramsad said he was aware of that.

'You can take my other operatives. They are as good.'

'I know,' Levin replied. 'But I want him. He can pass for an Israeli. Or a Palestinian. I know he's in Turkey. I spoke to him a few days back.'

Another smile escaped Clare. She knew about that call. Zeb had briefed her, and the incident in the kidon's hotel room had made her chuckle.

She knew the reasons Levin gave weren't the real ones. There was history between the Mossad head and Zeb. Good history. They were almost like brothers. It wasn't surprising that the ramsad wanted that particular operative.

'I'll tell him.'

'Thank you.'

'Anything you need, you just have to ask.'

'I know,' Levin acknowledged. In the world of counter-intelligence agencies, Mossad and the Agency had a history of unstinting cooperation.

Clare broke mission protocol when the call ended. She sent a text message to Zeb Carter.

A friend will call.

Chapter 12

———— ∞∞∞ ————

Kadikoy, Istanbul
Evening of the Assassinations

Zeb was in his hotel room. All traces of the old man had gone. In his place was a younger person, dark hair, neatly trimmed mustache, a black T with a peace sign on it. Jeans and trainers completing his look.

He looked around the room one last time. It was clean. No prints anywhere.

He opened the door and peered out into the hallway. Waited for a bunch of tourists to head toward the reception area and, using them as cover, baseball cap low over his head, walked out of the hotel.

He would never return to it.

In his original plan, he was to stay back in the country for as long as Hussain was around. That would give him the opportunity to listen in on the scientist, follow his movements and find out what he was up to.

That plan wasn't needed anymore. Riva and Adir would move Hussain and Shahi and wring every bit of information needed out of the two men.

Zeb shook his head imperceptibly, smiling grimly.

Did those two think they could meet and no one would know?

He was heading in the direction of the Kadikoy metro station, which was served by the M4 line. He would have to change twice to catch the M1B line to get to Ataturk airport.

He spotted a relatively empty coffee shop and entered it. Ordered a drink and powered up his screen while he waited for it to arrive.

Booked several flights to London, all in different names. He would randomly choose one once he reached the airport, produce the relevant passport and check in.

He thanked the server when he arrived and searched for the Iranian tattoo images. He browsed through several until he found one that came closest to the one on Shahi's neck.

It was that of an Achaemenid warrior, from the first Persian Empire, which had once stretched from Eastern Europe to the Indus Valley. It spanned five and a half million square kilometers, larger than any previous empire.

Tattoos were taboo in Iran. They were officially banned by the government as signs of devil worship or Westernization. However, there was a strong demand for them … *and there's only so many people the cops can arrest.*

He turned off his screen when he became aware of a change in his surroundings. A bunch of people were crowded at the counter.

Listening to the radio.

He frowned. Looked across the street at an electronics store. More people gathered around the TVs on display in the shop window.

He reached into his rucksack and brought out his cell phone. He rarely turned it on during missions. If the twins or Clare needed to get in touch with him, they would find a way.

There was just one text for him, from his boss, sent that very day, a few hours earlier.

A friend will call.

He didn't understand it.

He was tempted to call her when a shout distracted him.

People were gesticulating furiously and arguing with one another at the counter.

He left a few bills on the table and crossed the street. Joined the throng at the TVs.

Watched in disbelief at the scenes in Jerusalem. He and the rest of the Agency operatives had known of the peace talks. Clare had broken security protocols and briefed them.

He read the scrolling banner in shock.

Mossad Killers Assassinate Palestinian Peace Negotiators.

And knew which friend would call.

Chapter 13

————⊙⊗⊙————

Gaza Strip, West Bank
Evening of the Assassinations

President Baruti had had better days. He had caught a brief nap after the call with Prime Minister Cantor and then been awakened for a series of calls.

Two of those interactions worried him deeply. The first was with Masar Abadi, the Gazan prime minister.

'These peace talks must stop,' he declared as soon as Baruti took his call.

'Don't you want peace?' the president countered.

'Peace? Bah!' Abadi snorted. 'These Israelis are playing with you. They have fooled you into believing a dream. If they wanted peace, why did Mossad kill our negotiators?'

'Prime Minister Cantor—'

'DON'T SAY THAT SNAKE'S NAME,' Abadi yelled shrilly. 'That man wants to kill every Palestinian. He is an American pawn. He and the United States want to finish us.'

Baruti allowed him to rant and spoke when the man paused for a breath. 'The negotiations will proceed,' he told the prime minister firmly. 'There is no going back. The world's eyes are on us. We will not be the ones to back off.'

'Israel is our enemy,' Abadi roared. 'We will have peace only when that country is destroyed—'

'Enough,' Baruti cut him off. 'We'll speak no more of enemies. Just so you know, it is Cantor who reached out to me. He took the initiative.'

'And he stabbed you in the back,' the prime minister hissed. 'Be warned. You aren't as popular as you think. You will not survive these talks. I have heard about Abdul Masih. He does not like what you are doing.' And with that, he disconnected the call.

Baruti felt cold even though it was a warm evening. Masih was the commander of the Al Qassam Brigades, EQB, the military arm of Hamas. It carried out attacks on Israel, and while it took its political direction from its parent party, it often operated independently.

Masih, one of the most-wanted men in Israel, had survived numerous assassination attempts and remained at large. And very active.

EQB can kill me. Baruti spread his fingers and inspected them. He was pleased to see that they didn't tremble. He snorted at this thought. *Why EQB? Someone from my party or anyone from the street could assassinate me.*

Abadi was right. His popularity ranking had tanked after the killings. Many Palestinians echoed the thought that the prime minister had partly articulated. That Cantor had initiated the talks to shore up worldwide support, to be seen as the good guy. And had then acted traitorously.

I trust him, Baruti thought, looking at the view of Ramallah, the capital of his government. *And if I die, so be it.*

He had three children, all of adult age, all of who were gainfully employed. His wife had passed away the year before.

If my children and grandchildren grow up without the threat of war ... that was a dream worth dying for.

The second call wasn't a threat to his life, but to his political well-being. It was from his deputy prime minister, Muhammed Bishara, who was from the same party, Fatah.

'You're in trouble,' the caller began without preamble. It was turning into that kind of day—no one wasting time on greetings or pleasantries.

'I just got off the phone with Abadi. He threatened me. How much worse can it get?'

'This is about your political life. Many members of the executive committee are unhappy. They are talking about a no-confidence motion.'

Baruti sighed in frustration. He had met each of the committee's members and had convinced them of the importance of the discussions in Jerusalem. They had agreed to back him.

Just two killings later, they have lost faith in me.

He knew he couldn't underestimate Bishara's warning. The committee wielded tremendous power and could remove him from office if all its members got together.

'This must be the only country in the world which doesn't want a peaceful existence,' Baruti protested.

'Have you seen the news? Have you stepped outside your office? There are riots in the West Bank and in Gaza. Our people are protesting, strongly and violently, against the Israelis.'

'I know. But don't they get it that continuing these discussions is our only hope?'

'Emotions are high. Tempers are frayed. Right now, not many Palestinians trust the Israelis.'

'I do. I trust Prime Minister Cantor.'

'Yes, I know,' Bishara replied sharply, 'and it is your trust and nothing else that has brought us to where we are.'

'You are doubting me?'

'No,' his deputy adopted a more conciliatory tone. 'We, the cabinet, believe in you and this course of action. But we should not ignore what the people think. We have lived with war for so long, it has become almost a normal state,' Bishara explained. 'You have got to deliver something to our people to quiet them.'

'The talks—'

'Will take time. You have yet to appoint replacements for those killed. And who knows what the outcome will be?'

I can bring our people together if I tell them what Cantor has in mind.

But for that, he would need the Israeli's permission. 'I'll see what I can do,' he replied.

He flicked open the files on his desk and put aside two of them. The new negotiators who would replace Maryam Razak and Farhan Ba.

He then made a call of his own, to Prime Minister Yago Cantor. He kept it brief, just one line.

'We need to meet.'

Chapter 14

Tel Aviv
Night of the Assassinations

'We have to meet.'

Those had been Avichai Levin's only words to Zeb, an hour after he had watched the news in Kadikoy.

That cryptic call, five hours back, had led to his catching the first Turkish Airlines flight out of Istanbul. Direct to Jerusalem. Flight time of just two hours. He was traveling as Jarrett Epstein, exporter of Israeli olives.

He had spent part of the flight trying to make sense of the killings. The entire world wanted a stable Middle East. The assassination of the two Palestinians benefited no country.

He had spoken briefly to Meghan before boarding, but she had no insights for him, either.

'Need any help?' she had asked. 'We're all free. We can come. There will be enough of us to start a war.'

'I think the idea, the world over, is to stop one,' he had replied drily.

He had given up finally and slept. Food and rest. An

operative never passed up opportunities for both.

Jerusalem was pleasant, dry, when he landed. He hailed a cab. 'Tel Aviv,' he instructed the driver, who set off as if it was NASCAR.

Zeb stopped the driver several blocks from Levin's office and set off on foot. He backtracked for tails but didn't spot any. He texted Levin when he was ten minutes away.

The ramsad was waiting for him when he arrived, and hugged him.

'Shalom,' Zeb greeted him.

'Shalom,' Levin replied automatically and glanced at the passport held in front of him. 'Jarrett Epstein?'

'Ken,' Zeb replied in Hebrew.

'Wait,' the Israeli said and disappeared into the building. He returned fifteen minutes later, carrying a lanyard with a keycard dangling off it.

Zeb's photograph was on it, as was his cover name. They proceeded through the security barriers and went up the elevator in silence.

Levin pointed to a chair when they entered his office and shut the door.

'What was so important?' Zeb crossed his legs and surveyed his friend.

The Mossad director had fine lines around his mouth and eyes. His lips were pinched and his cheeks were hollowed.

I've seen that look before. When his daughter was killed in New York.

Zeb had hunted the killers down, for which Levin had said only two words, *thank you*, but had meant much more.

Levin poured water into two glasses and offered one to Zeb.

'I want you to investigate me.'

Chapter 15

———∞∞∞———

Zeb looked at him in astonishment. 'Investigate you?' he repeated.

'Not me, personally,' Levin growled. 'Look into every Mossad kidon member. Find out if any of them were the killers.'

'Why me? Surely you have investigators yourself.'

'You know why,' the ramsad glared at him.

He doesn't know whom to trust. If a kidon had gone rogue, who else might have?

Zeb fingered the keycard around his neck and now knew why the ramsad had arranged for it. In normal circumstances he would have been given a temporary pass.

'I don't know what to say,' he said helplessly.

'Say yes,' the Israeli snapped, 'and get to work. We don't have time. We don't know what those killers are planning.'

'The negotiations are going ahead?'

'Don't you follow the news? Our prime minister and

Baruti put out a statement. That they will not be deterred by these assassinations.'

'Which means there are—'

'More negotiators out there, yes. And the killers might know that, too.' He passed over a thumb drive to Zeb. 'Every one of my kidon is in there.'

'They must be all over the world.'

'Not any more. I have recalled them. They are dropping their missions and returning.' He glanced at his watch. 'In a few hours, all kidon will be in Jerusalem.'

'Which means they weren't far … maybe in neighboring countries?' Zeb probed.

'I will be asking them to come to the office immediately. I'll conduct a lie-detector test on each one of them. Those can be beaten, but I have to do it. You'll find their mission details in that drive,' Levin continued, stony-faced. Just because he and the American were friends didn't mean he was liking the prospect of an outside investigation.

'You have other departments, other teams.'

'I might get Shabak to investigate them.'

Zeb's jaw dropped. 'You'll allow another agency access?'

'I am giving you access, aren't I?' Levin exploded and then put up a palm in a peace gesture. He rubbed his eyes and sighed. 'The prime minister is putting together a special investigative unit from Shabak, the police, other departments. He suggested I should let Shoshon's people look into my people. I rejected it outright … however, now that I think of it, there might be merit in it. So long as you focus on the kidon.'

'The killers could be anyone. They could be Shabak operatives. They could be foreign agents.'

'I know. You'll carry out your investigation, they'll conduct theirs ... the goal is the same. We have to find them. Failure isn't an option.'

Zeb hadn't heard fear in Levin's voice before. He could feel it emanating from his friend and understood its reason.

The Middle East can burst into war if the killers are not found.

It was almost inconceivable that the killing of a couple could trigger military conflict. However, this was the Middle East, a perennial powder keg. Something about the assassinations had grabbed headlines and had stoked rage and fear in the region. Accusations and counter-accusations had slipped out of every political leader in the geography.

And if conflict erupts here, there's no way in hell it will stay contained.

Zeb inspected the grey, inconspicuous storage device. 'Have you have got any security camera footage of where it happened—'

'Everything's in that,' Levin pointed to the thumb drive. 'Not many cameras in the area, but a few passersby used their phones. Not much help there. The shooter was an old woman, a male in disguise. We gait-analyzed the footage to confirm. The killer went down the street and disappeared from view. No trace of him. No sign of a getaway car.'

Zeb knew German Colony well. He was aware of the hotel's location and the busy street that was Emek Refaim. 'A getaway wouldn't be that difficult that time of the day,' he mused. 'The killer knew what he was doing. He capitalized on shock and traffic conditions.'

'How would you do it?'

'Two-person team,' Zeb answered immediately. 'Three at the most, but I would prefer two. Easier to coordinate and less conspicuous. A getaway vehicle out of sight but within walking distance. Another vehicle a block away. Remove the disguise in the first vehicle. Put on another. Dump vehicle. Take the second one and drive away. Any reports of stolen cars?'

'Several. The police are checking.' Levin rose and pointed to a glass-walled cabin down the hallway. 'You can use that office. No one will disturb you. Jarrett Epstein is a field agent who has come in for some administrative work. That's your cover.'

'I don't need it. The less anyone sees of me, the better.'

'There's one more thing.'

'What?'

'I'll be letting every kidon know about you. Inform them that you are the investigator.'

Zeb shook his head and grinned ruefully. 'You aren't making it easy for me.'

'At Mossad, we don't know what that word means.'

Zeb rose, stretched and pocketed the thumb drive.

'You know I can't offer you any protection.' Levin came around his desk and gripped Zeb's arm.

'I know.'

He returned his friend's clasp and left the Mossad HQ. He wouldn't return to it again.

He knew why the ramsad had mentioned his name to every kidon and what he had meant about protection.

The kill team, if they were kidon, could come after Jarrett Epstein.

Chapter 16

Ein Kerem, Jerusalem,
One day after Assassinations

Magal and Shiri were up at their usual time the day after the killing.

They had dumped the VW and had taken a Toyota, which had been parked in a public lot in the city center. From there, they had driven to Ein Kerem, a neighborhood in the southwest of Jerusalem. It was away from the main city but received tourist traffic on account of its Christian heritage.

Shiri had rented a stone house a month ago, at the end of a cobbled street. They were university researchers, writing a book on Jerusalem. That was their cover.

The house was utilitarian but had everything they needed. They watched the news on TV as they ate their spartan breakfast. The Skoda had been found by the police. No prints on it, no leads.

The host read out Cantor and Baruti's statements and then cut to scenes in Gaza and the West Bank, where angry mobs were rioting and burning effigies of Avichai Levin.

Mossad was trending on social media, as were the names of the dead negotiators.

'You checked your email?' Magal asked Shiri.

'Yes. The ramsad acted fast.'

'He had to. There's tremendous pressure on him.'

'Jarrett Epstein. I've never heard of him. No description. We don't know what he looks like.'

'We could ask the ramsad.'

'And put ourselves on the radar? No. He may not be kidon. The ramsad said he was an experienced investigator with field experience. That could mean anything. He could be from Shabak or the police.'

'We are prepared for this,' Magal replied, unconcerned.

'Yes, but we were expecting a police investigation … Shabak. We didn't expect Levin to appoint someone. An inside man will know how we work. We need to find where he is and take him out.'

'Is that necessary?'

'We need time for the second phase. He cannot interfere with our plans.'

Magal went to the kitchen sink, rinsed his glass and placed it on a plastic tray. He wiped his hands on a kitchen towel and went to his room. He returned with the MAR and disassembled it with practiced ease. He set about cleaning it. 'Why don't we meet him? He will want to interview all of us, won't he?'

'Let him contact us.'

'No, let us take the initiative. Offer to meet him. Then we'll decide how and when to take him out.'

'It could be a trap—their telling us he's the investigator.'

'Yes, which is why I'm suggesting we meet him first.'

Downtown Jerusalem, That Day

Zeb woke up to the noise of Mahane Yehuda Market as vendors put up their stalls, vans drove up, and produce and products were unloaded.

He had rented a room in a small hotel almost next to the market—which sold everything from vegetables to textiles—the previous night. He had collapsed on the bed as soon as he arrived and woke up when the market came to life.

He yawned and padded to the window, which looked out into the city. Smoke rose lazily in the air from rooftops. Sounds of traffic, honking and the squeal of tires. Having been unable to get a round on the ground floor, he was on the fourth and could see masses of people in the winding streets below. Office-goers and tourists ambling by.

To the southeast was the Old City, home to the Dome of the Rock, whose gold cupola featured in many travelers' photographs. The Western Wall and the Church of the Holy Sepulcher were also located in that vicinity.

Three of the oldest religions came together in Jerusalem. It was a holy land for billions of people the world over.

Now, two killers are threatening its very existence.

Zeb worked out for forty-five minutes in his room, showered, and then hit his screen. He hit a block when he plugged in the thumb drive. It needed a password. He checked his email. No password sent to him by Levin. No text message either. He got the hint.

He called the ramsad, who sounded as though he had been awake all night. Levin recited the password to him, and the drive responded by revealing a set of files. He clicked on one. It was encrypted. He checked the others; they were the same.

'Check your phone,' the director told him. 'You should know, all kidon are here. All passed their polygraph tests.'

Zeb nodded unconsciously as he checked for the link. Passing such a test wasn't that difficult for a highly trained operative. He and everyone else at the Agency could sail through them.

He hung up, copied the link that held the keys to the encryption, and got access to the files.

There were twenty-eight kidon listed, detailed profiles for each one of them. Addresses—all of them in Jerusalem, a condition Levin insisted on—relationship data, physical and psych evals. Everything that he would expect from one of the best intelligence agencies in the world.

One particular detail surprised him.

All of them go by their first names, even though the files have their full nomenclature. He thought about it for a moment, then nodded.

Makes sense. Makes them more anonymous when they are on missions.

Many of the kidon had expressed preferences for working with other members. Zeb glanced through the teams in operation. It looked like Levin had accommodated such requests. *Most of those khuliyot have been unchanged for a long time.*

Not every team was of the same size, and not every kidon was currently in one.

Some khuliyot were four-person operations, some two, and there were several lone-ranger missions in play.

Zeb raised his eyebrows when he found where they had been deployed. Two teams were in the U.S. and would have landed late the previous night. Both on separate missions, one tagging a Russian arms dealer, another gathering intel on a

Qatari businessman. No wetwork involved.

As he scrolled down the list he found that no khuliyot was tasked with assassination in their current missions. That wasn't surprising. Popular culture overstated the number of kills any counter-intelligence agency carried out.

He looked up Riva and Adir's profiles, both of them from Sayeret Matkal. Both unmarried, though Adir had a girlfriend. The percentage of married kidon was low. The job took a heavy toll on relationships and family life.

He ruled the two out. They hadn't left Istanbul … which reminded him. He opened another app and looked up their location. The three green dots were still in Turkey's capital.

Probably in a safe house, sweating Hussain and Shahi. Looks like Levin didn't recall them. He knew I was with them.

He had pushed the nuclear scientists to the back of his mind. Clare would pursue the intel-sharing with Levin. She knew he was currently helping the Israeli and would let him get on with it.

The kidon were evenly split gender-wise, an equal number of men and women, with the majority of them coming from the IDF. All the operatives were staying in Jerusalem, and the drive had their addresses.

A ping on his screen. Incoming email from Levin. He opened it. Some kidon had responded to the ramsad's terse announcement of Jarret Epstein's appointment. The ramsad had forwarded all those replies to Zeb.

Okay, some operatives had answered, with just that one word. *Who is he*, a few had asked, to which Levin hadn't replied. A couple had offered to meet at the earliest. *Best to get this out of the way quickly*, the team lead of that khuliyot had said.

Standard responses. Nothing surprising there.

Zeb looked up the locations of the kidon on a map of the city, their relative proximity to his hotel. Two female operatives were the closest, sharing an apartment in a nearby neighborhood.

Zeb decided to check them out first. The ramsad had said the killer was male, but gait analysis wasn't definitive. In any case, the gender of the accomplice was unknown.

He made a secure copy of the thumb drive, made a hole in the wooden window jamb and stuffed it inside. He covered the opening with putty that looked like wood.

He filled his backpack with what he thought he would need. Spare mags for his Glock, listening devices, rappelling gear, balaclava masks, wigs, prosthetic noses, and, almost as an afterthought, a building maintenance worker's uniform.

The rucksack bulged when he had finished, but the weight wasn't significant.

He donned a pair of clear glasses, ruffled his hair, pulled on his baseball cap and set out.

He had armor beneath his tee, trainers on his feet and comfortable jeans. He wasn't looking for confrontation with the kidon.

But if there was one, he was ready.

Chapter 17

———⌘———

Jerusalem
One day after Assassinations

Carmel and Dalia. Early thirties. Returned from Tunisia,
where they were stalking a military commander suspected of
ties with Hezbollah. Zeb recalled the contents of their files as
he walked down the stairs and stepped out into bright sunlight.

He squinted his eyes in the light, brought out a map and
studied it in the shade of an awning. Checked out the surroundings of the market covertly.

No one looked away quickly or stopped abruptly. His inner
radar stayed quiet. He stuffed the map into his pocket and
walked purposefully away from the market toward Rehavia,
where the two kidon were.

Not in a romantic relationship with each other. No
boyfriends. Renting the apartment jointly to share costs.
Good friends. Both from the IDF, both had several kills to
their names.

'Which way to Rehavia?' he asked two suited men who
were chatting at the end of the market.

One of them pointed toward the south and gave him directions.

'Follow Mahane Yehuda Street, turn right into Agripas Street …' Zeb tuned him out after a while and thanked him when he had finished.

He hurried toward the apartment building, dodging and weaving through travelers and locals. He knew where he was. To his right was the Knesset, the Israeli Parliament. To his left, a mix of government offices, residential and religious buildings, and offices.

His earpiece buzzed. An incoming call. He glanced at his phone.

Meghan. He took the call.

'You're up late.'

'Yeah, couldn't sleep.' Her voice was warm, cheerful. That was characteristic of the sisters. The world could be coming to an end, but they always managed to see the bright side of it. 'Beth was grumbling that things were too quiet. She was wondering if you'd started a war, yet.'

'Nope. Where's she?'

'I sent her away. She was distracting me.' She turned serious. 'Werner's looking into the profiles you sent.'

Zeb had emailed details of the kidon to the twins before he left the hotel room. Had asked them to see if there was anything off that they could find.

'And?'

'Nothing,' she said in disgust. 'We checked their phones. Nothing unusual there. They were in the countries they were supposed to be. But then, you expected that, didn't you?'

'Yeah. They are kidon. Those phones are their official ones, issued by Mossad. If any of the operatives are the killers, they'll be smart. They would know their devices would be tracked. They would work around that. I'll have to find another way.'

'You're going up against them?' she sucked her breath sharply. 'We thought you were just analyzing data for Levin.'

He blinked and realized he hadn't briefed any of them on the details of his assignment. Broke it down for her swiftly, cut her off when she protested.

'I don't intend to take them on at all. Heck, the killers might not even be kidon. My job is to check them out, go back to Levin with my findings. That's all.'

He stifled a grin when she snapped, 'You should write fiction. You make it sound easy. You know it never is. You have a plan?'

'Yeah. Get hold of their phones, their personal ones, that Levin doesn't know of. See where those devices have traveled. Get their laptops and any screens they have. Analyze the data. I might meet them as well. See what they say. I'll play it by ear.'

'You're sure they'll have such cell phones?'

'Yeah. Every operative has one.'

'We don't.'

'That's because we're a very different agency. I don't think there is any other that's structured like us—each of us with only one number that Werner tracks.'

'They'll give you their phones just like that? How would you know it isn't a burner or a fake? These are Mossad kidon, for Chrissakes.'

'I might have to break into their apartments. If necessary, plant a bug.'

'And their screens?'

'Same MO.'

She fell silent. He heard a door opening, a voice calling, 'Who is it?'

Beth.

Meghan quickly briefed her twin, who latched on to two words that Zeb had let slip.

'You might have to *meet* them?' Beth shrieked.

'Yes,' he bit his tongue, cursing himself for revealing too much. 'I'll have to try all means. Meeting them, breaking into their apartments ... Levin has let them know there's an investigator.'

'That'll bring the killers after you,' she yelled.

'No, he hasn't given out my description. And the killers wouldn't be that stupid.'

'You don't know that. Besides, phone and laptop data can be tampered with.'

'I thought you two had upgraded Werner. That it can detect if a phone's data has been altered. If you haven't—'

'Of course, we have,' she said indignantly.

'He's deflecting,' Meghan told her sister.

'Yeah, I know,' Beth grumped. 'We're coming—'

'No,' he said firmly. 'You and Meghan will blend in here, but the rest ... can you imagine Bear or Bwana trying to look like a local?'

She chuckled reluctantly at the images of the huge men trying to look like Israelis.

'We'll keep digging,' she sighed. 'We checked cameras at various airports. The countries they were in, Israeli ones ... nada. Zilch.'

'Doesn't surprise me,' Zeb said, swerving around a couple. 'They wouldn't be that careless. I gotta go,' he told her when he saw Carmel and Dalia's building came in sight.

He hung up and stopped at a street-side vendor. Bought an ice-cream and licked it slowly as he removed his map and made a show of looking at it.

The apartment building was made of pale stone and concrete, like many in the city. It had six floors, with the kidon's apartment on the fifth. Each apartment had a balcony, and the one the operatives occupied overlooked a street crossing.

Good location. They have a good view of anything happening on the street. I'm sure they'll have escape routes mapped out.

The building's lobby had a revolving glass door, mirrored, and while he was watching, it rotated.

Carmel and Dalia came through.

Chapter 18

———— ⊖⊗⊗⊖ ————

Jerusalem
One day after Assassinations

Zeb acted instantly, without haste. He turned to the vendor and presented the map to him.

'How can I get to the Temple Mount?' he asked in broken Hebrew.

From the corners of his eyes he saw the two operatives check out the street. He felt their gazes linger on him. Apparently, he wasn't a threat, because they headed toward Mahane Yehuda Market.

The two women had replied to Levin's email, said they were open to meeting Epstein. The quicker it happened, the faster they could get back to their missions.

Twelve of the kidon replied to Levin similarly. Nothing can be read into those replies.

He thanked the vendor, stuffed the map in his backpack and decided to follow the women. He had to detour first, however, to keep the vendor from becoming suspicious, since his directions had pointed in a different direction.

He followed the length of the operatives' building and, once he was out of sight of the kidon and the vendor, sprinted around it.

He used the cover of a car to bend down swiftly, don tinted shades, turn his jacket inside out to reveal a different color, and remove his baseball hat.

A slight change to the way he walked, with his left shoulder drooping, and his new disguise was complete.

He hurried until he caught sight of the women, who were walking leisurely.

They aren't on a mission. These times must be rare for them. They're making the most of it.

He got as close to them as he could risk. Heard snatches of their conversation.

Neither Carmel nor Dalia talked about killing the Palestinians. They were conversing about the weather, their families, a movie they had seen.

Zeb hung back when they went inside the market and checked out vegetables.

An hour to complete their shopping?

Zeb figured it would take that long, from his limited experience of women.

He returned to the apartment building in ten minutes and entered its deserted lobby. No security. A camera in the ceiling. He lowered his head and went up the stairs at a jog. Entered the fourth-floor hallway through a service door.

Two apartments on each floor. Two elevators in the middle of the hallway. Carmel and Dalia's apartment was to Zeb's right. Dark windows, thick glass, overlooking the street, on the sides of the corridor.

He inspected the door from a distance. Didn't see any

cameras. *The apartment could be alarmed. Don't want to risk an entry that way.*

He went back to the staircase and looked around for a maintenance door.

There it was, painted white, the same shade as the wall. He opened it and went inside a narrow corridor filled with cables and air-conditioning ducts ... and reached a dead-end.

He went down the stairs as another idea emerged. Twenty minutes since he had left the kidon at the market. Forty to go.

He left the building and checked out the balconies. He could leap to the bottom of the first one. Get onto it. The vertical wall was uneven, with stones jutting out, an architectural motif.

Zeb looked around casually. Not much traffic. The vendor was out of sight. The balconies on all the floors were unoccupied, their doors shut.

He put on gloves and leapt without further thought. Caught the bottom railing of the lowermost balcony and pulled himself up.

Leaped sideways and grabbed a jutting stone. He had done a fair share of bare-hand mountain climbing, and those skills were useful. He used his shoulders to take his weight and climbed fast, his feet instinctively and easily finding footholds.

In fifteen minutes, he was on the fourth-floor balcony, breathing easily.

No one had shouted at him. No one had taken shots. He looked down. No upturned faces, either. No sign of Carmel or Dalia.

He tested the doors and sent up a silent prayer of thanks when they slid easily.

That's the second mistake those operatives made. The first one was to rent in this building, with that kind of outside wall.

He entered the living room silently, the carpet beneath his feet killing all sound. The apartment was air-conditioned and cool. A dining table in one corner, around which were four chairs. A TV against a wall. A couch set against another wall. An ornate showcase in another corner. Two doors that led to bedrooms, each of which had a bathroom, and a hallway that went to the kitchen.

He couldn't see any security cameras; nevertheless, he removed a rectangular device from his backpack and turned it on: an RF detector that could sniff out electronic devices across a broad spectrum of radio frequencies.

Broker and the twins had customized the device further to detect a wide array of surveillance and counter-surveillance equipment.

No cameras. There weren't any in the apartment. No bugs, either. A standard security alarm that he could easily turn off and on, next to the entrance door.

Zeb wondered for a moment at the lack of surveillance equipment. *Maybe these two aren't the killers.*

The device in his hands had a screen that indicated two pieces of equipment that interested him.

Laptops.

One was beneath a pillow in one bedroom. A quick look around indicated it was Carmel's. A set of passports, a Beretta and a wicked-looking knife in a drawer.

He picked up the device and turned it on. Grimaced when the screen asked for a password.

He removed more gear from his rucksack and inserted a thumb drive into the machine. A light on it blinked as it got to work, copying the hard drive. He removed the flash drive when the light disappeared and returned the laptop to beneath the pillow.

His eyes lingered on the bed. Sturdy bedposts. Wooden. He fingered one. Yeah, it would do. He used his knife to make a hole in it, inserted a listening device and filled the hole with putty. Same color as the wood. The material wouldn't keep the bug from working.

He went to Dalia's room and found her laptop in a bag in a closet, along with a bunch of passports and fake IDs. He didn't search the room anymore. He copied her laptop, too, and left another bug in her room.

He planted the last listening device in the living room, by gouging out the bottom of the dining table.

He went to the balcony and peered out cautiously. No traffic, still.

He extracted the last piece of equipment from his backpack. A cellphone tower shaped like a miniature TV antenna. He coated it with adhesive and went outside. Climbed to the fifth-floor balcony, next to which was a dish TV antenna. He attached his tower to the wall behind it, smoothed down the excess adhesive and dropped to the kidon's balcony.

Ten minutes more.

He didn't want to risk an exit through the exterior and decided to leave through the front door.

That was his mistake.

Chapter 19

Jerusalem
One day after Assassinations

Zeb slapped a mustache on his face, put on a prosthetic nose and added cheek pads to make his face look fleshier.

He turned his jacket inside-out again and stepped out of the door. He used a master key to lock the apartment and went down the stairs.

The steps went down in a square, and from the banister, one could peer all the way down to the ground floor.

He took a peek. No residents climbing up or going down. The building was quiet on the inside.

He bounded to the third-floor landing and went down, taking two steps at a time.

Turned a corner of the square and was proceeding at a rapid pace when he came face to face with Carmel and Dalia.

The two kidon were running up, holding the bag together, sharing the handles. No squeaks from their shoes. They were breathing easily.

Zeb kept his face composed even as he tightened on the

inside. He nodded to them politely and moved to the railing to let them pass. Felt their eyes run over him swiftly, as they nodded in return.

Dalia closer to him. Her hair bouncing on her neck, the faintest sheen of sweat on her forehead.

Carmel looking away from him and upwards. It didn't feel as if either viewed him as a threat.

And then his foot slipped. He stumbled, and Dalia's shoulder slammed into his chest.

His breath escaped him.

His backpack clinked.

His jacket pressed hard against his chest, showing the outline of his Glock.

And his mustache fell off.

The women's reflexes and speed of reaction amazed him. Both of them let go of the bag. It fell, its mouth gaping open, groceries rolling down the steps.

Carmel said something that didn't register on him. Not then.

Dalia's elbow came up swiftly, going for his throat, her eyes narrowed. Carmel was leaping back, making room for herself, her hand darting behind her back.

Zeb slapped away the incoming blow.

Don't shoot, he wanted to yell at them. But he understood their reactions. They didn't know who he was. They had come to a conclusion based on his disguise and his weapon.

They were kidon. A stranger was either an enemy or a noncombatant. A stranger in their building, carrying a gun, was hostile and had to be treated as such.

Zeb was still off-balance from slipping, one foot on a higher step, one on a lower. He twisted his body to take Dalia's second blow high on his chest. The knuckles of her hand bit hard, sending lancing pain through him.

Carmel's hand was rising. A Beretta, black and lethal, snug in her palm. He didn't know if she would shoot to kill.

He risked a quick glance to the stairs. Still empty. Made a quick calculation even as he countered Dalia's punches automatically, which were coming thick and fast.

Mossad was his friend. Yes, he was investigating the kidon, but he didn't know if these two were the killers. He wasn't going to shoot them or hurt them.

He deliberately leaned in, giving her less room, reducing the weight of her punches. He used her body as a shield from her gun-toting partner.

Rocked back on his heels when an open palm slapped him, stinging his eyes with involuntary tears.

He grabbed Dalia's retreating hand. Got a hold on it, twisted it, wrenched it behind her back and, using momentum, shoved her against Carmel.

He got a few seconds of respite as the two kidon slammed into each other, their harsh breathing punctuated by swearing. He grabbed the fallen mustache and pocketed it. His left hand caught the railing. He checked the two operatives one last time. Carmel was pushing Dalia away, her face angry, her gun hand rising again.

And then he was vaulting over the stairs.

He fell.

His arms outstretched, his body loose.

Counting rapidly in his mind. Looking down.

One second.

Two.

NOW!

He caught hold of the railing on the first floor, gritting his teeth as his fall came to an abrupt stop, his arms feeling as though they were being yanked out of their roots.

He let go and dropped lightly to the ground floor.

Looked up and saw both women peering down at him.

He strode out of the lobby and, once outside, ran around the building, away from the cross road.

Away from the balcony's view.

Started checking out cars on the street.

There was a van that had seen better days. Parked close to a Toyota. He looked up and down the street. No alarms had been raised. No one pointed at him.

He slipped between the two vehicles. Dropped his backpack to the ground and opened it.

Removed a long dress. Slid it over his head. Kicked away his trainers and slipped into sandals.

Removed his cheek pads and nose. Donned a greying wig and put on dark shades. Applied lipstick and checked himself out in the reflection from the van's metallic surface.

He stepped out and held his phone to his ear, speaking softly, laughing occasionally. He now looked like an office-going woman, speaking to a co-worker.

He crossed the street and walked on the pavement on the other side. Swaying his hips a little more.

Carmel came out of the building. She stood casually, looking up and down.

Dalia emerged, flanked her, and the two women stood, bodies relaxed, eyes checking out every movement on the street.

They saw the old woman. Considered her carefully. Zeb didn't look at them. He spoke of meetings and deals. Willed his chi to go lower.

He passed them. His back prickled as he sensed their eyes on him.

The shades on his face were custom. They projected the rear-view on the lenses. He saw the two kidon talking to each other.

They came forward to the cross street and looked to the left and right.

'Hold on,' he told his nonexistent caller.

He went to the ice-cream vendor and ordered a lolly. Sucked on it as he returned to his call and headed toward Mahane Yehuda Market.

The kidon disappeared from sight, and when they did, he heaved a sigh of relief.

However, he wasn't done.

He searched for a bar, found one, entered it and headed toward the restrooms.

Went to the door labeled Ladies and occupied a stall. Removed his disguise and put on his previous one, the fleshy-faced man that the female kidon had seen.

Zeb cracked the door open and checked for traffic.

The restroom was empty.

He went out of the bar quickly and, once on the street, turned in the direction of Rehavia.

He was going back to Carmel and Dalia's building.

Chapter 20

---⚬⚬⚬---

Jerusalem
One day after Assassinations

'*Tunisian hitter!*'

That had been Carmel's warning to her partner on the staircase. The words had come to Zeb as he was falling to the ground floor.

Why would they think I am Tunisian? he wondered as he headed back to their apartment.

He was sure of one thing. They weren't involved in the Palestinians' killing. Otherwise, Carmel would have warned her partner differently.

Well, I'm almost sure. Only one way to find out. I'll ask them.

He donned a pair of headphones and plugged them to his cell as he hurried. His phone would pick up the conversation from the bugs he had planted.

If I was them, I would sweep the apartment ... so those devices will be spotted soon.

Sounds from the apartment came to him. Bodies moving. Objects being shifted.

They're checking out their place.

'You're sure about him?' Dalia's voice.

'I think so. Who else would it be?' her partner replied. 'His reactions. The way he counter-punched. He wasn't someone from the street.'

'Yeah, but I'm not sure if he was the commander's man. It's not as if we got an opportunity to question him.'

Commander? That must be the Tunisian they were gathering intel on.

The operatives fell silent. Something heavy moved. One of them grunted and silence fell. Zeb looked at his screen. The bug in Carmel's room had turned off.

Looks like they've discovered it. They'll find the other one too. Will they think of checking the dish on the upper floor?

He thought not. The device he had planted there wasn't just a tower. It also had a powerful bug in it, and that kicked in as the one in Dalia's room turned off, too.

Looks like the fifth-floor apartment is empty. Lucky, otherwise it would have been a pain to separate conversations from the two places.

Zeb was within sighting distance of their building, now. The sliding doors to their balcony were open.

To let in air? Or to keep a watch on the outside.

'That's the last of it,' Dalia spoke.

'Let's check once again.'

He thought he saw shadows move inside the apartment, but he couldn't be sure. He reached the cross street and waited for the light to change. Heard bodies move in their flat.

'We're clean,' Dalia announced.

'Yes, but we need to move,' Carmel announced. 'Our place is compromised.'

'We'll go in fifteen minutes.'

No acknowledgement.

Zeb joined a bunch of tourists as they crossed the street. Kept his head down and reached the building. He was directly underneath the first-floor balcony.

They can't see me.

He waited for the group of people to make their way through the neighborhood. Looked in all directions. A car passed. A couple, holding hands, approached, their attention on each other.

He waited until their backs were to him and then jumped up and caught hold of a railing on the balcony.

He climbed swiftly, knowing he was under time pressure. *Also, either of them could come out. And they wouldn't greet me warmly if they saw me.*

He reached the bottom of the kidons' balcony. Raised himself cautiously until he could see inside.

Curtains swishing at the side. Living room seemed to be empty. He listened hard. Muffled sounds in his headphones.

Packing. In their rooms.

He hauled himself over the railings and climbed inside. Padded silently across the marble floor, Glock in hand. There was a couch that faced the sliding doors. An ornate mirror mounted on a showcase in a corner.

Zeb seated himself on the couch, his backpack to one side of him, his weapon to the other. Narrowed his eyes when he noticed that, by shifting his position, he could see the insides of both the rooms reflected in the mirror.

Another security measure.

Shadows moved in one of the rooms. Carmel came into view ... hugging Dalia, brushing back the hair from her face.

99

She pressed her lips to her partner's.

Levin's files on them are wrong. The two are in a relationship.

They drifted out of view. He heard soft murmurings and footfalls. Carmel came into the living room holding her girlfriend's hand, their bags strapped over their shoulders.

They didn't see him initially, and when they did, both kidon froze for a moment.

'Don't,' Zeb warned them in their native language, raising his Glock. 'If I wanted you dead …' He didn't complete it.

'Kalb must have sent you,' Dalia spat, her eyes flashing. No fear in either of them.

Rashid Kalb. Zeb recalled the name from the ramsad's dossier. *The Tunisian they were targeting.*

'You're an Israeli killer?' Carmel asked contemptuously, as she inched toward Dalia's room. 'He must have paid you a lot for you to go after your own people.'

Zeb shot into the floor near her feet, the report echoing loudly in the room.

'Don't move,' he told them. 'I want your phones.'

They think I am a shooter, here to finish them. No fear in them, however. They didn't even flinch when I fired. He couldn't help admiring them, even though they could be the killers.

'Your phones,' he repeated. 'Reach into your bags and bring them out. Carefully. One at a time.'

The women looked at each other. Phones? Carmel shrugged her shoulder and her purse dropped into her palm. She opened it and fished out her cell.

'That's your Mossad one?'

'Mossad? We aren't—'

'Please. We are beyond that.'

She glared at him, and then nodded once.

'I want your personal one.'

'Since when did a killer go after phones?' she snarled. Nevertheless, she brought out her personal device.

'Drop it to the floor.'

It fell to the carpet.

'Kick it toward me.'

The phone slid across the surface and came to rest near him.

'Now you,' his Glock pointed at Dalia, who went through the same maneuver.

'Drop your bags to the floor.'

The women followed his orders.

'Go, sit on those chairs.' He gestured at the dining table.

They seated themselves and glared at him.

'You know who we are.' Dalia cocked an eyebrow at him. 'You'd better kill us fast. The more time you take, the more we have to figure out how to overpower you.'

Zeb didn't reply. He swiftly grabbed the phones from the floor and powered one on.

'Password?'

Dalia uttered one.

He entered it, his eyes flicking between the screen and the women. He navigated to the various apps but didn't find the one he was looking for.

He reached into his backpack and brought out a cable and another device. Hooked his equipment to Dalia's phone and copied its contents. Did the same with her partner's cell. All the while, the kidon looked at him, a thoughtful look now in Carmel's eyes.

He fingered his cell, put it on speaker and called Meghan. He knew she would be awake and at her screen.

The women's eyes widened when the international dialing tone sounded in the apartment.

'You've got two data dumps coming,' he told his friend when she accepted the call.

Carmel looked at Dalia swiftly. Seemed to tense, ready to spring at him. Froze when he raised his Glock.

There was a reason he had asked them to sit. It put them at a disadvantage, since it would take them more time to act from that position.

'Got it,' Meghan replied crisply.

'Check out where those cells have been for the last week.'

A keypad clicked as she worked.

'You're American,' Dalia stated flatly, switching to English.

He didn't respond.

'Who's with you?' Meghan asked.

'Later,' he told her, feeling a surge of pride within him. A lesser operative would have called him by his name. None of his friends would do that.

'Tunisia,' she came back a few moments later. 'I'm narrowing it down.'

'I'll call later.' He hung up.

And then Dalia acted.

Her hand flew to the fruit bowl on the table. She grabbed an apple and flung it at him. Carmel slid out of her chair, pivoted on her heel with balletic grace, grabbed the back of the chair and threw it at him.

The two kidon spread out and charged toward him.

Zeb was anticipating a move like that. He was moving

even before the fruit reached him. He dived out of the couch and landed on the floor on his left shoulder.

The women lost a fraction of a second as they changed direction toward him. Which worked to Zeb's advantage.

He fired over their heads, the round thudding in the wall behind them.

They stopped, their eyes glittering.

'You were in Tunisia all along?' he asked them in Hebrew.

'Kill us, or fight us.' Dalia pounced at him, Carmel close behind.

Zeb twisted his body quickly, but he wasn't fast enough. She landed on top of him, her palms clamping around his gun hand.

'Keep him down,' Carmel yelled and sprang toward her bag.

Zeb kept down, offering no resistance, and when she returned with ties, he couldn't help grinning.

'That's not needed,' he told both of them.

Dalia didn't relax, but that questioning look returned to Carmel's face.

'Just who are you?' she asked.

'I'm Jarrett Epstein.'

Chapter 21

Jerusalem
One day after Assassinations

'Prove it,' Dalia demanded, not relaxing on top of him.

'Call the ramsad. Ask him.' He could have given them the card Levin had provided him. *They won't trust me, however. They'll think it's a forgery.*

Carmel fished out her work phone and dialed a number.

'Sir,' she told him, 'there's a man in our apartment. Says he's Epstein, the investigator.'

She turned away and described him softly. 'We passed the lie tests,' she added. Fell silent, listened, then nodded several times. 'Rega.' One moment. She came to Zeb, who was still being held down by Dalia, and held the phone to his ear.

'Carmel says they've captured you.' There was a hint of a smile in Levin's voice.

'That's one way of putting it,' Zeb acknowledged.

'You think they're—'

'No.'

'I'm glad to hear that. They're two of my best. You can trust them fully, now. Give the phone back to her.'

Carmel rose, listened and nodded some more. 'Toda,' she said, *thank you,* and hung up.

'He's Epstein,' she told her partner, and only then did Dalia release her hold on Zeb and climb off.

'Levin explained?' he asked Carmel.

'Yes. We're clear?'

'Yes, unless you've tampered with your phones.'

He knew they hadn't. Meghan would have run through a few checks before confirming her Tunisia announcement.

'We haven't.'

Dalia kept quiet as she went to the couch and straightened it. She pocketed their phones and returned the chair and the fruit to their positions. No questions from her, and that impressed Zeb again.

They aren't asking why I tapped their apartment. They know I had to use any means to investigate.

'What now?' Carmel asked him.

'What do you know of the rest of the kidon?' He went to his backpack and stuffed its contents back inside.

'Not much,' she shrugged. 'We, Dalia and me, have been working together for a few years now. Before that, we were in different teams. It's not as if we socialize a lot. Some kidon are good friends with others. We aren't like that.'

'You've met all of them?'

'I don't know. It's not as if the ramsad tells us who else is a kidon. For instance, we didn't know about you.'

'He isn't one of us,' Dalia asserted.

'Is she right?' Carmel asked him.

Zeb debated with himself for a moment. *Levin said I can*

trust them. His gut agreed with the director. He decided to go with his gut.

'Yes. Dalia was right. I'm from the U.S. A long-time friend of the ramsad.'

'You're with the CIA?' Dalia probed. 'You speak Hebrew fluently. With the right accent. I have never come across any American who can speak so well. Your name … Epstein. Why do I think that's a cover?'

'None of that's important,' he deflected. He headed to the table and occupied a chair. His lips quirked when Carmel sat to his right, Dalia to his left, pinning him between the two of them.

He brought out the list of operatives and laid it on the table.

'You know them?' he asked the kidon.

Dalia ran a finger down the list and nodded. 'Yes, we both have either trained with them, met them or have worked with them.'

She lingered over two crossed names, Riva and Adir. 'What about them?' she asked.

'How well do you know those two?' he countered.

'Carmel said we didn't have friends. She was wrong. We have one. Riva. We know Adir well, but not like a friend.'

'You know what this is all about?'

'Let me guess,' Carmel replied sarcastically. She held a finger up. 'First, there were those killings.' Another finger shot out. 'Then those accusations on social media.' A third digit extended. 'Of course, there was that email from the ramsad, about Epstein. We aren't stupid,' she glared at him.

Zeb made a peace sign and brought out a pen. He crossed out their names on the list as they watched in silence.

'Riva and Adir,' Dalia persisted. 'You checked them out?'

'Let's just say I *know* they weren't in Jerusalem when those killings happened.'

The kidon looked at each other, pondering his choice of words. They seemed to know what that implied. 'We don't work with other country operatives,' Dalia said softly. 'The ramsad must trust you a lot if you worked with those two.'

'Levin and I, we go back a long way,' Zeb offered, and with that, he won them over.

'How can we help?' Carmel leaned forward, staring at the list.

'What do you know about these others?'

A frown creased her forehead. 'You have to understand something ... there will be some of us who think we shouldn't negotiate with Palestine. That everything that's happening is their fault. They started it. Not just Palestine. Iran, Jordan, Saudi Arabia, all the Arab countries. These operatives think Israel should always treat these nations as enemies. There will be others who think both Palestine and Israel need to compromise.'

'Where do the two of you stand?'

'Dalia lost her parents several years ago when Hamas bombed a bus in Jerusalem.' She reached out and grabbed her partner's hand. 'My brother was killed in another suicide bombing attack. Our families have lost a lot.'

'You both think Israel is wrong to negotiate?'

A smile ghosted over her lips. 'Lo,' *no*. She shook her head. 'It's easy to make that assumption. You're wrong, however. We want our country to have a long future. That will not happen unless both sides agree to live as good neighbors. That will only happen with dialogue.'

'How many others think like you?'

'We rarely talk politics when we meet,' Dalia answered. She took the pen from him and added asterisks next to several names. She slid the sheet across to her partner, who made more marks.

Zeb studied the list when they had finished. Fourteen names were marked, all male.

'They think like you?'

'No. Those, they don't want negotiations.'

Chapter 22

—∞∞∞—

Jerusalem
One day after Assassinations

Prime Minister Yago Cantor understood the urgency when he took President Ziyan Baruti's call.

He understood the importance of meeting in person. That was brought home when he had scanned the headlines of the newspapers scattered on his desk in the morning. Some suggested the Palestinians themselves were behind the assassinations. Others demanded that Mossad be held accountable. All of them wanted decisive action from him.

He had asked his aide to make arrangements, and the result was that he was now with Baruti in his office in Jerusalem.

This was an occasion in itself. The two men could count on the fingers of one hand the number of times they had met. Meeting in Cantor's office was a first.

They barely spent any time on pleasantries before diving into details. They could speak freely, since the prime minister had cleared his office. The Palestinian briefed his counterpart on Masar Abadi's threat and on Muhammed Bishara's warning.

'Abdul Masih,' Cantor reflected, 'we have been after him for a long time. We nearly got him last year. He's hunting for you, now?'

'That's what Abadi claims.'

'You have security?'

'Yes, but what good will that be against a killer who is determined? And someone who doesn't care for his own life?'

The Israeli nodded. The best protection in the world couldn't guard against a suicide bomber.

'You're having second thoughts?' he enquired.

'No,' Baruti growled, 'The EQB have always disliked me. They think I am too conciliatory to you. In any case, I cannot be distracted by this. We have come this far. We cannot turn back.' He brought out two files and handed them over. 'The replacements.'

The prime minister flicked through the files and set them aside. 'We should do something for their families.'

'I have already called them and expressed my condolences.'

'Israel needs to do its bit, too,' Cantor pondered for a moment. 'Why don't we make a joint call, right now?'

He called for his aide when the Palestinian nodded appreciatively. Fifteen minutes later they were on speaker to Maryam Razak's parents. It was an awkward conversation initially. The old couple lived in the West Bank and their distrust toward the Israeli was apparent.

'I know how you feel,' the prime minister filled a long pause. 'I promise I will find her killers.'

Even as he spoke, he knew he wouldn't be trusted. *I have to make the effort*, he thought to himself.

The call to Farhan Ba's brother, his only brother, was even worse. The sibling accused Cantor of being a hypocrite and a liar and hung up on him.

'You tried,' Baruti said heavily when the Israeli disconnected. 'That's all you and I can do. Keep trying.'

'Your political position...' The prime minister reminded him, changing topics.

'I need to show a win,' Baruti said. 'That might keep my people quiet as the negotiators work.'

Cantor pondered for a while. The aide came in, freshened their drinks and left silently. In the distance, a police cruiser wailed past, an ambulance following.

'Let's make an announcement,' he declared. 'Today. Saying that in ten days' time, we will make history.'

'Ten days?' the Palestinian's jaw dropped. 'We can't agree to terms in that short a time. This will take months.'

'I know—'

'We agreed we will negotiate first and then declare it.'

'Yes, but with the pressure on you, let's change our approach. Let's say that in ten days, we will announce the outline of a deal that has never been agreed on before.'

'Without going into details?'

'Yes.'

Baruti mulled it over. 'It will certainly buy me time,' he agreed. 'But what about your hard-liners?'

'I will have to deal with them.'

'What do we announce in ten days?'

'We'll see how people react, and if the winds are favorable to us, we will announce our vision.'

Baruti gasped. 'You want to let the world know? So soon?'

'Yes, we don't have the luxury of waiting anymore.'

'They are still out there. The killers. They might strike again.'

'Yes. That is a risk. The negotiators are in a secure hotel. More protected than ever before. Has anyone from your side wanted to back out?'

'No,' the Palestinian admitted. 'I spoke to them before coming here. All of them want to continue.'

'How soon can your replacements arrive?'

'Today.'

'In that case, let's make our announcement in the evening. The discussions start tomorrow. And in ten days, my friend, let's hope we can show the world a new future.'

Cantor's aide set up the press conference later that evening. Baruti made several calls and got the replacement negotiators out of the West Bank. They would be met by an Israeli security team, who would escort them to their hotel.

Avichai Levin was in Cantor's office when Baruti joined them. The Palestinian nodded at him stiffly and made to ignore him, but the ramsad wasn't deterred by his body language.

'Sir,' the director addressed the president. 'I know my agency is the most hated organization in Palestine. You have my assurance on this, however.'

He waved toward a window in the direction of Temple Mount. 'One day, your people and mine will worship at the Dome of the Rock and Western Wall without fear.'

Baruti stared at Levin's back as he left the office. 'I don't trust him,' he confessed to Cantor.

'I understand. However, if there's anyone who can find those killers, it's him.'

The press conference that followed was packed with journalists both local and international. Every reporter was expecting a bland announcement.

What they got took everyone by surprise.

Prime Minister Yago Cantor and President Ziyan Baruti stood shoulder to shoulder and spoke as the world watched.

'In ten days' time, we will be here again. Then, we will make history.'

Chapter 23

———⟨≋⟩———

Jerusalem
One day after Assassinations
Ten days to Announcement

Zeb was still with Carmel and Dalia, going through the names on the list, getting the kidon's assessment of the operators, when the latter rose and turned on the TV in the living room.

The press conference came on screen.

The two kidon watched in silence while Zeb observed their reaction. Initially, the women were astonished.

'If they can stop the hostilities for good...' Dalia breathed.

'We can quit,' Carmel laughed. 'Leave Mossad. Start a new life.' She grabbed her partner's hand and kissed it. Her face darkened in a blush when she felt his gaze.

'We are—'

'Of no interest to me. I mean your relationship...' he gestured vaguely. *I am sure Meghan or Beth could have articulated that better.*

Dalia laughed, kissed her girlfriend on the cheek and disappeared into the kitchen.

Carmel looked at him speculatively and pointed toward the TV.

'That puts pressure on you.'

Zeb knew what she meant.

I was planning on surveilling each kidon. Interviewing them as well. With this announcement, I won't have time for all that.

'This meeting, who I am—'

'It never happened.' Dalia returned, bearing a tray with drinks on it. 'We don't know who you are. Of course, we have heard about Epstein, but we don't know what he looks like.'

Washington DC

President Bill Morgan muted the TV and turned to his visitors. Clare, composed as ever, was seated on a couch.

'You knew about this, sir?' the woman next to her asked.

'Yeah.' The president couldn't help grinning at Alice Monash, who was almost trembling in excitement. 'Yago called me before the conference. Asked my views on what he and Baruti were planning to announce. I approved it.'

'That's why you wanted me here, instead of flying directly to Jerusalem.'

'Correct. I want you to help both leaders in any way you can. The United States is firmly behind them.'

'The hard-liners in the Middle East—they will not like this,' Clare observed.

'They won't,' the president agreed. 'But right now, they don't know what Cantor and Baruti are working on.'

'Those killers are still at large. Alice's presence ... she could be a target.'

'I am aware of that. Which is why we support, but we work in the background for a change. Israel and Palestine are leading these efforts. There are many reasons for that, the main one being optics. The Israeli and Palestinian people should know it is their leaders who made this happen. Not the U.S. That will make it more acceptable.'

'That doesn't change the security threat to Alice.'

'She will be less visible. That should help,' the president replied. 'The Israeli prime minister has promised a crack security detail to protect her. All vetted. I declined his offer. We will be sending our own team with Alice—' He broke off and looked at her sharply. 'Don't you have someone there?'

'Yes, sir. He's working with Levin, to identify the killers.'

'Who is it?'

'Zeb, sir. You met him last year.'

'I remember—'

'Zeb?' Alice's head rose sharply. 'Zeb Carter?'

'Yes.'

'Isn't he the one who—'

'Yes.'

'Sir,' Alice stood up. 'I don't need a security detail. I want Zeb. No one else.'

'Alice, Zeb's on a mission,' Clare protested. 'He can't be distracted.'

'Sir,' the ambassador ignored her and addressed the president. 'Him. No one else. Or I'm not going.'

'Come on, Alice,' the president remonstrated. 'What he's working on is of critical importance. He has to find those killers. You'll be a distraction.'

'From what I've heard of him, he can handle distractions. Sir, I am not going to Israel if Zeb isn't protecting me.'

The president straightened and used the full force of his personality to get her to change her mind.

Alice Monash looked small in front of him. She was a mere five feet, six inches to his six-four frame.

She wasn't cowed by his size or stern look. She returned his stare without flinching.

President Morgan faced a dilemma. Alice was critical to the Middle East peace process. She was accepted by all countries in the region, and her presence was crucial.

He also knew what was behind her insistence on Zeb. There was history.

'Clare?' he sighed in resignation when his ambassador didn't back down.

'I'll ask Zeb,' the Agency's head replied.

'Don't ask him,' Alice interjected fiercely. '*Tell him.*'

'As if we don't have enough problems,' President Morgan threw his hands in the air. 'Make it happen, Clare. And Alice, remember, work in the background!'

Ein Kerem

Navon Shiri turned off the TV and crossed his hands behind his head.

'Ten days,' he said.

'I heard.' Magal didn't look up from his yoga pose. He was stretched down on the floor, face down, his legs bent over his body, his hands clasping them tight, pulling them, stretching and loosening his body.

'Our handler hasn't told us where they are.'

They. The remaining Palestinian negotiators.

'It looks like Maryam and Farhan will be replaced. The

talks will go on.'

Magal grunted with effort. Shiri wasn't telling him anything that he hadn't worked out himself.

'Why don't you stop griping and contact the handler? Ask him for instructions.'

His partner rose and went to his room. He returned with an encrypted laptop and logged into it.

He sent one line.

'Who is next?'

Somewhere in the Middle East

The handler was at his screen when Shiri's message arrived. He had watched the press conference and knew the implications. The killers didn't have much time to carry out the next phase, which was to execute more people.

'I don't know where the remaining negotiators are,' he spoke aloud in the silent room. 'I will find out.'

He sent a reply to Shiri.

'Be patient. Be prepared. Next targets are surviving Palestinians.'

Chapter 24

Jerusalem
One day after Assassinations
Ten days to Announcements

The handler leaned back in his swivel chair and played with a paperweight. He was one of the most powerful people in his country. Many said he was even more powerful than the Supreme Leader, given the organization he ran.

The *handler*. That was how he was referred to in certain intelligence agencies. Long before he had risen to head one of the most feared organizations in the world, he had been a spy chief. He had run agents in the U.S., Israel, and several other Western countries. His operatives had stolen military secrets. They had blackmailed politicians and had infiltrated research and defense organizations.

His career had grown meteorically on the back of his successes, and when the Supreme Leader had offered him his current role, he had readily accepted.

He had been working on this plan for decades. Infiltrating the Mossad. It was necessary to achieve the bigger picture, the grand dream that the leader had, one the handler believed in: destroying Israel and placing their country at the forefront of the Islamic world.

It hadn't been easy, and his planning had fallen apart several times. Until he had found Shiri and Magal. Stone-cold killers. They weren't psychopaths. They took no perverse pleasure from assassination. However, they felt no remorse, either. It was as if their emotion switch was permanently switched off.

Finding such killers wasn't an impossible task. He had many more such people in his organization. What the two had was their unique backstory.

The two men grew up in Jerusalem and had lost family members to Palestinian suicide bombings. They had grown up on a diet of Israeli TV and media that portrayed Palestine as the transgressing party.

They had joined the IDF and been operators in the Sayeret Matkal.

They had been deployed in the handler's country to rescue two Jewish hostages. That was when the man in the room had come across Shiri and Magal.

Ten years ago, he had been interrogating one of the hostages, an Israeli journalist who had written several devastating exposes on the handler's country. He, the handler, wanted to know the Israeli's sources.

He was using aggressive questioning tactics—a couple of live electrical wires attached to the captive's groin—when the door had smashed open. Two masked men burst in, both in black, wielding automatic weapons.

The handler didn't waste time wondering why the security

personnel outside the remote compound hadn't stopped the intruders.

He dived toward his HK416, which was an arm's length away. Simultaneously, he shoved the journalist's chair at the masked men.

That second act slowed the shooters. They weren't expecting the handler to use the Israeli as a shield.

One gunman swung around the captive and dived to the floor when the handler's HK chattered. His rounds went wide. He snatched a quick glance at the second shooter. That intruder was looking to free the Israeli. Neither stranger had shot at him.

They want him alive. I, too, want them, or at least one of them, alive. To see who they are.

The handler pounced on the gunman, who was on the floor, to club him with his HK. He slapped away the intruder's rising weapon with his left hand just as the attacker triggered and a burst of bullets streaked past his face and embedded in the ceiling.

He punched the intruder in the face. Took a blow in the ribs in return. The two men grappled for seconds, both of them trying to gain the upper hand, their weapons momentarily useless as they struggled to get a hold.

Just as the handler felt he was subduing the gunman, a blow struck him on the shoulder. He fell. Lost his weapon. Turned and landed on his left shoulder. Saw that it was the second gunman, who was now supporting the journalist.

'WHO ARE YOU?' he yelled and lunged at the nearest attacker.

The gunman evaded his charge and brought a knee into his groin. The handler collapsed, but not before his nails had dug into the shooter's vest.

It stretched, exposing the attacker's right shoulder, revealing the small tattoo on the fleshy part.

The handler recognized it.

'YOU'RE FROM MY COUNTRY?' he yelled and charged again, trying to unmask the intruder, not caring that he could be shot.

The second gunman struck him again, felled him to the floor and kicked him viciously.

The handler's vision dimmed. He saw the first gunman pull up his vest and stare at him. Then the men left, taking the journalist with them.

The handler was in hospital when he came to, surrounded by his people. He ordered an investigation, which revealed that the two intruders had circumvented the security systems in the compound and had rendered several guards unconscious.

Only a few agencies in the world had such capable operatives. Fewer of those would rescue an Israeli journalist by sending in lethal operatives.

The handler had two organizations in mind: Mossad and Sayeret Matkal.

He got his proof when Israeli media reported the daring rescue of the journalist. It credited the latter organization for the act.

The handler never forgot that night. He was left with two questions.

Why did an Israeli soldier have that tattoo? Why didn't they kill him?

He got his answers five years later, when Shiri and Magal made contact.

Chapter 25

—❧—

Somewhere in the Middle East
Several years before the Assassinations

The handler was in his private club and had just finished dinner when the two men dropped into chairs next to him, flanking him.

The handler didn't recognize them.

'Leave,' he ordered, 'I want to be alone.'

He saw his security detail move toward his table.

Neither man spoke. The one to his left loosened a button on his shirt and pulled it to the right.

The handler froze when he saw the tattoo. The events of that night came back to him in a flash. He had a handgun strapped to his left leg, just above the ankle. Could he reach it in time? He could shout, and that would bring his guards running.

'If we wanted to kill you,' Tattoo smirked, speaking in Arabic, 'you would have died a long time back. We have been watching you. We know your routine. We could have taken you out several times.'

Ty Patterson

'Why are you here?' the handler whispered. 'What do you want? Don't think of kidnapping me. You can't escape.'

'You're a very high-profile target. Our country will benefit immensely if we grab you. Make no mistake, we are capable of snatching you and taking you away. Your men,' Tattoo snorted contemptuously, looking at the security guards, 'are not capable of stopping us.'

'We're not here to kidnap you,' the second man spoke. 'I am Navon Shiri, he's Eliel Magal.'

The handler reached out for his glass of water and drank it. He was buying time. He didn't know where this was going and needed all his wits about him.

He spluttered at Magal's next words.

'We want to work with you.'

The three men spoke at length that night in the private club. No one disturbed them. Everyone knew who the handler was, and the reputation of his organization. The other diners left their table alone.

Magal and Shiri were orphans, the handler learned. They had lost their parents in a Palestinian attack in Tel Aviv when they were six years old.

They were each taken in foster parents in Jerusalem. It didn't take long for Magal's new family to discover the tattoo on his shoulder. They contacted Shiri's folks and the two families tried to research the boys' backstories.

They didn't find much. They discovered that the Magal and Shiri families had migrated to Israel a couple of generations ago and had grown up in Tel Aviv. Magal's father had been a teacher, while Shiri's dad had been a taxi driver. The two boys went to the same school and were firm friends, a relationship that the foster parents nurtured and one that endured as they grew older and joined the IDF.

The handler scrunched his eyebrows at Magal. 'When did you get your tattoo?'

'When I was four. I don't remember much of that time.'

'What did your folks tell you about it?'

'That it was a cool image. Nothing more than that. They didn't tell anything about where they were from.'

'Same with me,' Shiri interjected. 'It was only later, when Magal's foster parents discovered his ink, our folks did their research, that we both found out who we were.'

'How did you feel?'

'Ostracized. The kids in school picked on us. Our folks, the new ones, didn't hide where we were from originally. But we were mentally strong,' he shrugged. 'Our new families taught us to be tough.'

'You are with me because of your origins,' the handler stated in satisfaction, confident that the pull of his country was irresistible.

'No,' Magal replied flatly. 'We identify as Israelis. Don't read too much into our backgrounds.'

'Why are you here, then?'

'You wanted backstories; we told you,' came the reply. 'There's nothing special about them.'

'Other than the country your grandparents came from.' the handler interjected. 'My country.'

'I said we are   Israelis,' Magal shrugged. 'Your country has no meaning for us, other than a hostile target.' He grinned.

'As to why we are here...' Shiri broke off a piece of bread and chewed on it. 'We want to help you.'

That was the second shock the handler received that

night. He stared in disbelief at the two men. They were calm, composed, returning his look with no expression.

'Help me? Do you know who I am?'

'Yes. Why do you think we came to you?' Magal sniggered.

'You just said you're Israelis,' the handler said harshly. 'Your country and mine ... we are hostile to each other. You said it yourself. We want to see you destroyed. I can arrest you and throw you in prison, never to be seen again.'

'You can try.' Magal tossed an olive into his mouth. 'You won't live the night.'

'This isn't a game,' the handler replied with venom. 'You—'

'We came to offer our services,' Shiri waved him to silence, 'not to hear a history lesson. Your country ... maybe it is ours, too.' He pointed discreetly at Magal's shoulder, at the tattoo.

'I knew it!'

'You don't,' Magal said sharply. 'We aren't sitting with you because of any emotional or subconscious ties to your country. We don't think of countries the same way most people do. We are Israelis. It is a fact and nothing more. We have been thinking about this for some time. Of *branching* out. Your reputation as a handler is well-known. You plan well, support your operatives... that's why we are here.'

'And that's enough for you to turn traitor?'

'No. But the money you offer, and the game...' he trailed off. 'Don't go looking for any deep meaning behind our motivations. We aren't carrying any grudge against our country. We are not indulging in some kind of vengeance mission.'

The game. Over the next couple of hours, the handler found that the two operatives loved the clandestine business they were in. The hunt, the chase, the mission, that was what they lived for.

Their moral compass was virtually nonexistent, which made them top-notch killers. That absence of values also was the reason they could switch allegiances so easily. One day they could be working for Israel. The next, they could see themselves working for the handler.

The two men claimed they had been seeking something else, a bigger thrill. They had been drifting from mission to mission until the rescue of the journalist. The handler's presence that night had shaped their desire. And here they were.

Magal swirled the wine in his glass, sniffed it and dropped another bombshell. 'We have both been selected by Mossad. To join their kidon.'

He took a sip and looked over the rim of his glass. 'Are you in with us?'

The handler didn't take long to decide.

He was in.

Chapter 26

—⚬⚬⚬—

Somewhere in a Middle Eastern desert
Several years before the Assassinations

The handler met the two men discreetly a few more times. Learned that the two men *did* seem to have a code.

'We won't tell you of any mission that doesn't affect you,' Shiri announced when they met in a shack at the edge of the desert. 'You won't learn much about Mossad from us.'

'What's your value to me, then?' he countered.

'You'll know of the operations we undertake in your country. We can tell you about anything that's going down against your people that we know of, which might not be much, since Mossad is compartmentalized.'

'Can I use you to conduct my own operations in Israel?'

'Yes.'

'Any target?'

'We'll decide that on a mission-by-mission basis. Now, about compensation and logistics...'

The two men negotiated hard and made the handler agree on an eye-watering sum. The handler, in turn, got them to accept that there would be an initial deposit and the larger payments would follow only after trust had been built.

The logistics were easier to work out. The three of them were well-versed in black-ops. They agreed on a communication protocol. They would use well-known websites such as property-listing portals. The handler would put up a property for sale; the two operatives, posing as interested buyers, would message, using coded language.

'You alone will manage us,' Shiri demanded.

The handler agreed. That had been his plan in any case.

'How come Mossad selected you?' he asked Magal curiously, 'with that tattoo?'

'That helped, actually,' the operator grinned. 'They went through our backstories thoroughly, as you would expect. We aced every psychological test. The tattoo … the ramsad decided it would help us in operations in your country.'

'And what about the psych tests? They must have detected your lack of…'

'Morals? Ethics? We were surprised at that, too. We think those flaws made us more valuable to the agency.'

The handler could see the logic in that. Operatives who weren't driven by ideology or patriotism were rare. He transferred the first payment and they were in business.

The handler suspected a trap, however. Why wouldn't he? Israel had carried out several espionage attacks on his country. Magal and Shiri's approach could be an elaborate ruse by the Mossad to get inside the handler's organization.

Over the next year, he made few demands from the two kidon. He gave them relatively simple missions. Grab an American diplomat and bring him over to his country. Bug the room of the British defense minister, who was visiting Israel.

The kidon didn't ask him for his reasoning. They carried out each operation and reported back when complete. Every mission was clean. Zero blowback.

The handler was impressed and, after a while, gave them more difficult jobs. He also carefully let slip several pieces of sensitive information: intel on his country that would be valuable to the Israelis. Nothing happened. No Mossad, Shabak or IDF team acted on it.

One time, he *accidentally* dropped a file that contained intel on the country's nuclear reactors. It didn't seem like the information reached the ramsad.

After several such traps, all of which the two operatives passed, he gained confidence.

And then the two men told him they were tasked with taking out a prominent politician. A high-flying figure in the handler's country, who was violently opposed to Israel and had significant popular backing.

The handler was in a dilemma. He could prevent the operation and capture Magal and Shiri. That would be a coup for him. However, he was interested in the long term.

Reluctantly, he told the men to go ahead. He would not interfere. The two men looked at him, astonished.

'You realize we will kill him?' Magal asked.

'Yes. Go ahead.'

'Why?' Shiri's eyes narrowed.

'It will consolidate your position in Mossad. Despite all your psych tests, I am sure there will be people who treat the two of you differently, just because your origins are in my country.'

Magal nodded, thoughtfully.

'All I ask is, give me sufficient notice if you're carrying

out other missions in my country.'

The two men looked at each other. Magal nodded again.

'Remember,' Shiri warned, 'we won't know of missions carried out by other khuliyot.'

'I know,' the handler replied.

He didn't tell anyone in his government about the Mossad's mission. He acted shocked when two masked men, on a motorbike, pumped several bullets into the politician and escaped.

MOSSAD ASSASSINS STRIKE!

Headlines in his country screamed accusingly. That agency didn't take credit, but it was a trademark kill.

Years passed. The handler still hadn't used Magal and Shiri for any significantly major mission. There were a couple of reasons for that.

A new ramsad, Avichai Levin, had been appointed and the three men wanted to see how he would treat the two kidon. It turned out the director rated the two operatives highly.

The second reason was infiltrating Mossad's systems. Israel had carried out cyber-attacks on the handler's country several times over the past years. One in particular had delayed the nation's nuclear program.

The handler had been beefing up his cyber capability ever since that attack. He wanted to use Magal and Shiri for a high-profile operation only when he was confident he had sufficient electronic warfare capability.

He used the two kidon without their knowledge when his electronic warfare team was ready. He gave the two kidon an encrypted thumb drive that established secure comms with him. What the two kidon didn't know was that there was a worm in the drive.

The worm spread through their laptops and penetrated inside Mossad's systems. All it did was listen and pass information back to the handler. It had been built by the country's best hackers and went undetected by the Israeli agency's network security.

It worked perfectly. The handler now had eyes on whatever Avichai Levin received or sent. However, he knew that the worm had a limited shelf life. It would self-destruct over a period of time. His cyber team had told him that was the best approach; otherwise they ran the risk of it being detected.

Of course, it still could be found by the Israelis before its window expired. He had to use it to maximum effect while it remained burrowed in Mossad's systems.

The worm gave him a rich trove of information, but it failed in one respect. The handler was desperate for the identities of Mossad's operatives. The worm couldn't find those. It looked like Levin kept those in a different database that wasn't networked. Sure, the ramsad sent emails to his people, but he addressed them by only their first names.

The handler tried to search for people with those names but didn't get far. They were common Israeli given names.

He could ask Magal and Shiri, but he knew what their response would be. They would refuse.

The handler wasn't unduly upset. He could work with the intel the virus yielded. And if he was patient, the worm would deliver.

That opportunity came when he found out about the Israel-Palestine negotiations and the identities of the team members on both sides. He then had the first high-risk, high-profile mission for Magal and Shiri.

'What will killing them achieve?' Magal had asked when

he briefed the two without mentioning the source of his intel.

'It's not the killing, but the reaction,' the handler had replied in satisfaction.

He was more than pleased by how the two kidon carried out their assignment, their first major one for him in Israel.

Somewhere in the Middle East
One day after Assassinations
Ten days to Announcement

They proved themselves, the handler mused as he put down the paperweight and leaned forward in his swivel chair.

He tapped on his keyboard, and his heart beat faster when he read what the worm had discovered: the location of the remaining Palestinian negotiators. It was in an email that Avichai Levin had received very recently.

He had sent the *be patient* message just a few moments ago. Now, Magal and Shiri had their next assignment.

It had to be *executed*—he liked that word—within ten days. Before Yago Cantor and Ziyan Baruti made whatever announcement they were planning.

The handler didn't care that there could be peace in the region. He and the Supreme Leader weren't interested in that.

Their ambitions were higher. The death of a few Palestinians was a small price to pay.

Chapter 27

Jerusalem
Two days after Assassinations
Nine Days to Announcement

Zeb was in Romema early the next day.

He had spent several hours with Carmel and Dalia, getting their input on the male operatives that they had marked: the ones who were hard-line in their views that there could be no negotiations between their country and Palestine.

He hadn't much to go on. While the kidon had told him as much as they knew about each of the men, it wasn't a lot. He had more information on their personalities, and that was about it.

'What will you do?' Dalia had asked him. 'You are just one person … or do you have a team?'

'Just me. And I'll do what I did with you. I need to know where these men have been in the last few days. That's sufficient to clear them. I was planning on interviewing all of them, even you…'

'But now, you don't have time?' Carmel had guessed.

'Yeah,' he had grimaced. 'That announcement isn't helping me.'

'What if we had killed you? On the staircase or later, in the apartment?' Dalia had asked.

'You wouldn't have,' he had replied confidently. 'You would have wanted to interrogate me. See if I was sent by the Tunisian.'

Her smile had been fleeting. 'You're lucky we live together. Most of those men live alone. They might have better security than us.'

'If you have their personal cell numbers, it will help.'

Both women had shaken their heads regretfully. 'We don't give out that information. It so deeply ingrained ...'

'I understand.' He had risen and stuffed the list in his pocket.

'What about us?' Carmel had asked. 'We are clear, I guess. We can resume our mission.'

'You are clear, but no mission for you. Until I check out all the operatives and either clear them or find the killer.'

'Are there any more bugs in our apartment?'

'You removed them all. But you might want to check the dish TV antenna outside. The one above your apartment.'

An indecipherable expression had crossed her face and then her lips quirked. 'You are good, Epstein. Or whatever your real name is. Your investigation ... surely the police, Shabak, they too are investigating.'

'Yeah, but I'm the only one who's looking into the kidon. They are checking out everyone else.'

'I can't believe the killers could be our own.' Dalia had crossed her arms. 'Whatever our personal views, we are highly disciplined operators. I can't imagine anyone will act on their own.'

'That's what I am here to find out.'

'Shalom, Jarret Epstein,' Carmel had wished him, her lips twisting in a bittersweet smile. 'Stay alive.'

Zeb recollected the previous day's conversation as he hurried to a dojo in Romema. Yakov, one of the operatives, trained there. Zeb figured it would be easier to observe him there. *And if the opportunity arises, get a dump of his cell phone.*

He had thought long and hard about a way of exposing the assassins, given the news announcement. He hadn't been able to come up with one.

He was stuck with his original plan. *Check out their past movements. Ideally, get a dump of their cells and laptops. Plant a bug on them. Interview as many of them as possible. Use any and all means possible to ascertain their movements. And even then, what I find might not be conclusive.*

The problem was, there was just him, twenty-eight of the kidon and ten days to apprehend the killers.

Twenty-four, he corrected himself. Riva, Adir, Carmel and Dalia were no longer on the suspect list. *And only nine days left.*

He had thought about calling his friends ... *they'll stick out even if they disguise themselves. They're too tall. The Mossad operatives will make them. Only the twins can pass as locals.*

He could call the sisters, but he was reluctant to do so. They had been grievously injured in their last case, and even though both had fully recovered ... he shook his head unconsciously. No, he would see how far he could progress on his own.

He cleared his mind and focused on Yakov.

The operative returned from Iran, where he had been

conducting a solo recon mission on a military target. He lived in the same neighborhood where his dojo was located, in a one-bedroom apartment.

He was a krav maga expert and spent a couple of hours working out with others, when he wasn't on missions.

Carmel said he's an alpha male. Very competitive. Doesn't like to lose. Has an explosive temper, which he never loses when on missions. And he hates Palestinians.

Zeb saw the sign board and crossed the street. In his backpack were his surveillance gear, weapons and his black gi.

He approached the dojo's entrance and joined a line of members who used cards to swipe their way through the turnstiles.

'I am not a member,' he told the woman behind the counter. 'I want to train for a few hours.'

'We don't take non-members,' she said.

He sighed and made a show of looking irritated. 'Look, I am a friend of Jessy Levitsky. He said I could just walk into any dojo and train.'

The woman didn't recognize the minister's name.

Zeb reached into his backpack and pulled out an identity card.

'You're with the police?' she straightened when she read his credentials, which stated he was Commander Jarrett Epstein.

'Yes.'

'We can make an exception for you, sir,' she reached beneath the counter and pressed a button for the turnstile.

'One more thing,' he told her as he passed through the barrier. 'No one should know I have been here. I can trust you with that?' he asked her, steely-eyed.

'Yes, sir.' She blanched and bent her head down as he walked through.

He felt guilty at going heavy at her, but his role demanded it. *I'll apologize to her when all this blows over.*

The dojo was similar to thousands like it across the world. A large wood-floored training room on which mats were laid out. A gym, a few racquet courts, male and female changing rooms, a seating area and a food and drinks counter, all organized around the central area.

He went to the training room, which had about twenty people in it: some practicing moves, an instructor coaching a group in a corner.

Zeb went to the changing room and checked its occupants. No Yakov. He put on his gi and went back to the central room, barefooted.

He stood to the side and started a light warmup, his eyes searching.

Levin's file on him was clear. He's usually here at seven am, when he's in Jerusalem.

A shout got his attention. Two men, fighting, both of them wearing head and chest guards.

There he is!

The kidon was of average height, five feet, nine inches, with no hair on his head or face, and burning eyes.

He was throwing punches furiously, kicking out with his legs, shouting aggressively whenever he made contact.

His partner had a hard time keeping up with him, and, when he took a nasty blow to the head, raised his hand in surrender.

The two men stopped and removed their headguards. Yakov wiped sweat from his forehead with the sleeve of his gi and cracked a joke. He didn't wait for his friend's reaction. He went to a bag against the wall, grabbed a bottle of water and sipped from it.

He doesn't trust a locker. Smart.

Zeb had moved closer to them and was watching through the corner of his eye.

I need an opening to go through that bag.

'You know krav maga?'

Zeb looked up. Yakov had noticed his interest.

'Yes,' he replied.

'I haven't seen you around.'

'You know everyone?'

'No,' the kidon laughed. 'I don't come regularly. I travel a lot. But, last few days, I have been here. Didn't see you.'

'I am not regular, either,' Zeb replied, thankful that Levin hadn't shared his description with the operatives. Yakov would have been suspicious immediately.

'You want to spar?'

That isn't what I had in mind.

'Maybe it's not for you,' Yakov continued slyly, his alpha-male surfacing. 'I go full contact.'

Zeb hesitated.

'Maybe you're at a lower level,' the kidon said, conde-scendingly. 'It's all right. I'll find someone else.'

'I'll spar.'

'You're sure?' Yakov smiled smugly. 'You saw how we fought. You're ready for that?'

'Yes.'

Zeb knew how he could get to the kidon's bag.

Chapter 28

———∞∞∞———

Jerusalem
Two days after Assassinations
Nine Days to Announcement

Zeb went back to the reception counter and rented protective gear. He returned to the training room, stripped off his gi and put on a loose pair of gym trousers and a tee. A chest guard, head guard, groin protection and gloves completed his attire.

'You might want those, too,' Yakov smirked, pointing at the shin guards and forearm guards on the floor. The kidon wasn't wearing them.

'I'm good,' Zeb replied shortly, the man's arrogance irritating him.

The two men cleared a space for themselves and faced each other.

'Hey, Gal,' Yakov called out to someone behind Zeb. 'Watch us. This is how men fight.'

Zeb half-turned. The next moment, a tremendous blow landed on his chest and sent him sprawling to the floor.

'This is krav maga, buddy,' Yakov chuckled. The kidon

held out a hand and helped him to his feet. 'Anything goes here. You've got to stay alert. Don't be distracted. I thought you said you knew—'

Zeb slapped his hand away and punched his head guard. The force of his blow rocked Yakov's head. His jaws snapped together in an audible click. He yelled in rage and counter-punched furiously.

Zeb ducked and parried, thrust when he found an opening, took a blow to his chest, and countered with a savage kick to the kidon's thigh.

He was breathing lightly, a thin film of perspiration on his forehead when the two men broke off for a moment.

A small group of spectators had gathered around them.

'You know krav maga,' Yakov admitted.

'That's what I said,' and Zeb attacked with blurring speed.

He feinted with his right fist. The kidon bent back. Zeb's left hand shot out straight at his throat. Yakov's hands came up to counter his blow.

Zeb closed in, letting the beast break free and fill him, feeling his fingertips tingle with a surge of power. His right hand moved faster than Yakov could react. He grabbed the operative's tee. His left glove locked around the kidon's left wrist. His left leg kicked the operative's feet out from under him.

Zeb spun on his right heel, lifting Yakov bodily in the air, and brought him down to the mats.

'And that's judo and some other disciplines,' he said.

Yakov groaned and clutched at his right shoulder. His face turned pale, sweat dripping off his face. Zeb bent over him and helped him sit upright. He removed the man's mask and chest guard.

'It's dislocated,' he said. *Just as I planned.*

Men and women crowded over them. An instructor shoved his way through, his eyes angry, his rage directed at Yakov.

'I warned you many times. Control your fighting. One day someone will get hurt. Today, it's you.'

He felt the kidon's shoulder with light fingers. 'I can fix this. It's not broken. Let's take him to the medical room.'

Three men lifted Yakov and carried him away, with the instructor following. A group of onlookers followed them.

Zeb sank to the floor, his back against the wall. To his right was Yakov's bag. To his left was his backpack. He removed his headguard and his gloves. Wiped his face and grabbed his water bottle with his left hand while his right dived into the kidon's bag and searched.

It came out with two cell phones.

He looked around. No one was watching him.

He worked with practiced haste. Removed the required gear from his backpack and hooked it up to one cell. Copied its data. Repeated the move for the second cell.

He had data dumps now. He removed the batteries from Yakov's phone. Standard make.

He replaced them with two identical-looking ones from his backpack. They were batteries, but they were also listening devices.

He had ears on Yakov now.

He stuffed the phones back in the operative's bag and arranged its contents the way they had been. He stowed away his gear, rose and shouldered his backpack.

Went to the medical room where the kidon was now sitting, drinking from a bottle of water.

'You don't fight fair, friend,' Yakov wiped his mouth.

'It's krav maga. There's no such thing as a fair fight. You're okay?'

'Shoulder's back in position.' He moved his right limb gingerly. 'No training for me for a few days.'

'That will affect your work?'

'No,' he shook his head. 'I am taking a break.' He sized Zeb up with keen eyes. 'You're good. The best I have seen in this dojo. Maybe we can spar more often.'

'Sure, if I see you next time. I travel a lot, you do, too. Don't know when it will be.'

Zeb slipped out of the room when the instructor bustled in and hovered over the kidon. He showered after securing his backpack in a locker and changed into his street clothes. He was returning the protective gear at the reception counter when he felt a hand on his shoulder.

He turned. It was the instructor.

'I saw what you did. You slowed down his fall at the last minute; otherwise he could have been hurt more seriously.'

The man looked at him consideringly. 'It was deliberate, wasn't it?'

'Sir,' Zeb laughed, 'I am not that good. I was acting instinctively. There's no way I could have made him land in a particular way.'

'There are people who can make it happen. He needed to be taken down a notch.' He winked and went inside the dojo.

Zeb looked up an app on his phone when he hit the street. Two green dots for Yakov's cells. He looked up Riva and Adir. They were still in Istanbul, a third dot near them, for Hussain.

What's happened to Shahi? he wondered idly. He checked his watch. Nine am.

It'll be one am in New York. He opened a messaging app on

his phone. Two grey dots next to Beth and Meghan's names. That shade meant they were offline. Sleeping. He searched for a reasonably quiet café and found one several streets away.

He placed his order and sent Yakov's phone dumps to the twins. The server returned with his food, coffee with beans on toast. Something light, yet filling enough for a long day during which he planned to check out other kidon.

He was on his second refill when his phone buzzed. Clare.

'Ma'am,' he greeted her, wincing when the quickly swallowed drink burned his throat. 'You're up late.'

'You had a good night's sleep?'

Zeb looked at his phone as if he could see her. It was unlike her to waste time on trivialities.

'Yes, ma'am.'

'Had breakfast?'

'Having it.'

'Then you can digest this. You know Alice Monash?'

'Our ambassador? Of course, ma'am. We haven't met, though.'

'She's returning to Israel. We thought she should have enhanced protection.'

'Good thinking, ma'am.' He guessed who she meant by *we*.

'She turned down our offer.'

'That isn't wise, ma'am. Things are tense here.'

'She wants something better.'

'Like what?' Zeb didn't like where this was heading.

'She wants you.'

Chapter 29

Jerusalem
Two days after Assassinations
Nine Days to Announcement

'Ma'am,' Zeb protested, wondering if he had heard right. 'I don't have the time to play protector—'

'Save it, Zeb,' Clare sighed. 'I argued with President Morgan. Tried to convince Alice. She isn't budging. You'll have to figure something out.'

Zeb pinched the bridge of his nose. 'When's she arriving?'

'Your evening. I'll send you the details.'

He stared blankly when the call ended, unconscious of the smile the waitress bestowed on him, thinking that he was looking at her.

Avichai wants me to find these killers. If they are kidon. At the same time, I'm supposed to bodyguard our ambassador. Does anyone else want me to save the world?

His lips twisted wryly at his feeble attempts to humor himself. He finished his breakfast, deciding to worry later. An operative couldn't let circumstances get the better of him.

He would be at Ben Gurion Airport in Tel Aviv in the evening, to meet Alice Monash. *I might be able to convince her.* In the meantime, he had kidon to investigate.

Eliel and Navon. The two operatives who had offered to meet him when Levin had sent out the Jarrett Epstein email. Their backstory intrigued Zeb. Both raised by foster parents. Their families had come from a different country. The two men identified as Israelis and, if anything, their origins helped them carry out several missions in their grandparents' land. Mossad had deployed them several times in that country, and each time the two had carried out successful missions.

They're two of the best operatives Levin has got. Both proficient with multiple weapons, but Eliel prefers the blade.

Knife work, by its very nature, required a killer to get close to victims. It was messy, brutal, and in Zeb's experience, many of those who used the weapon liked killing.

Nothing of that sort in Eliel's file. Which made Zeb eager to meet him and Navon.

A knife-wielding operative who is as normal as operatives go. Not many of those around.

Zeb found the kidon in a café in the Downtown Triangle of the city. It was an area bounded by Jaffa Road on one side, King George Street on another, and Ben Yehuda Street completing the third side. There were offices, shops, and outdoor cafes in the area. It was a neighborhood that catered to the yarmulke-wearing person as well as more secular office-goers.

The two men had responded quickly when he messaged them and had agreed to meet at the venue he had chosen.

Zeb was disguised as an older person. Thickset in the middle due to the padding and armor beneath his sweater, his face jowly thanks to cheek pads, a heavy nose and bushy eyebrows. His Glock was taped to his right shin, a knife sheathed to his left leg.

Eliel and Navon were seated in a corner, facing the entrance, their backs to the wall. A couple of drinks on their table that they sipped occasionally.

He entered the café and observed them as he joined the line at the counter. The two men didn't talk much. Didn't make eye contact when they did.

They've been a team for a long time. He took his coffee from the server and approached the men.

'Jarrett Epstein?' Eliel rose, asked in Hebrew, when he came to their table.

'Yes.'

He pulled out the empty chair and gestured at the operative to sit. Navon hadn't moved a muscle, his dark eyes flickering as they ran up and down Zeb.

'You got any ID?' he asked, an undercurrent of hostility in his voice.

'No. What about you?' *I can show them my Mossad card, but I want to push back at them. See how they react.*

'Several.' Navon brought out several cards, his lips twisting humorlessly. 'Which one do you prefer?'

'The one that says who you really are.'

The kidon collected his credentials and stuffed them in his pocket. 'Neither of us have that. If you know who we are, you'll know why. How do we know you're Epstein, though?'

'Call the ramsad. Ask him.'

Navon took him up on his offer. He dialed the director's number, his eyes never leaving Zeb. 'There's a man who says he's Epstein,' he explained when Levin came on line. 'You never described him. Heavy. Greying hair. Big nose. Wait …'

He snapped a picture with his phone and sent it to the ramsad.

'Okay,' he said and hung up.

'You're Epstein.' He stowed away his phone.

'That's what I said.' Zeb signaled the server and placed his order. 'That tattoo on your shoulder—' he switched his attention to Eliel, 'why do you still keep it?'

'You know about it … of course you would! The ramsad must have given you our files. It comes in handy. Especially when we are going to that country.'

'And in others?'

'Well, it's not as if I expose my upper body to everyone. It hasn't proven to be a problem.'

'I know how operatives work. Most would erase any marks that could reveal their identity.'

'I won't. That tat is who I am.'

'We've never seen you before,' Navon asked abruptly. 'Which department are you with?'

'Which department do *you* belong to?'

'Navon, stop!' Eliel frowned in irritation. 'He's doing his job. I am sorry,' he said, turning to Zeb and spreading his hands in apology. 'If you've read our files, you'll know we have just returned from Jordan. Our mission was stressful. We haven't decompressed fully.'

'And what operation was that?'

'Tailing Ali Gaber, a colonel in their army.' Eliel's lips curled in a thin smile. He knew what Zeb was doing. Getting the operatives to confirm, seeing if their story strayed from what was in their dossiers. 'We suspect he's running an espionage ring in Israel. Here,' he reached inside his vest and brought out a sheaf of photographs.

A man in either business attire or in uniform, striding through the streets of Amman, briefcase in hand. In a few of the images, Eliel and Navon were in the background. Each image had a time stamp on it.

'How did you get these?'

'It turns out we aren't the only ones interested in Gaber. We spotted another tail. We broke into his apartment. He's an FSB agent. We got those pictures from his camera.'

'So, you've been made?'

'Made by the FSB. We don't know if Gaber knows about us. Even if he does, it's not relevant. We wanted Gaber to know we were shadowing him. His reactions, his behavior, was what interested us.'

Their story matches what's in their files.

'Photographs are easy to fake.'

'Yes, we know. But we have this,' Eliel turned his cell phone to face Zeb and navigated through its menu. 'This is my personal phone. Not a burner. You can see where it has been in the last few days.'

Zeb saw. The kidon had been in Amman all along and had returned to Israel on the evening of the assassinations.

Navon shoved his phone wordlessly across the table. Zeb checked it. Same story.

Eliel was smiling thinly when he glanced up. The Israeli handed him a flash drive. 'Copies of our phone data as well as laptop hard drives. Normally we wouldn't share that with anyone, but the ramsad says you have security clearance.'

'We came prepared,' he continued when Zeb pocketed the device without a word. 'We know how such investigations work. Call me if you need anything else.'

It looks like they are clear. Beth or Meghan can check that phone data and verify if it has been tampered with. I doubt it, however. They wouldn't take such a risk.

Still, he was not ready to cross them off his list just yet.

'Show me your tattoo.'

'Here?' Eliel asked, startled.

'Yes.'

The operative glanced around quickly and pulled aside his vest. The design was small, no larger than a quarter coin. The image was recognizable, too, a revered figure in the country of Eliel's heritage.

'Satisfied?' Navon asked sarcastically when Zeb nodded in thanks.

'Not quite. Who is this FSB man? Did you identify him?'

'Peter Raskov. That's what he calls himself,' Eliel replied, throwing a sharp look at his partner.

'How do you know he's FSB?'

'We didn't. Not then. We relayed the info to the ramsad, who got back to us with his identity.'

'Why is the FSB interested in Gaber?'

'Don't know,' the Israeli shrugged. 'We didn't get that far. The ramsad recalled us.'

'We are done,' Zeb laid a few notes on the table, enough to cover a tip, and rose. 'Don't leave—'

'We won't leave the country,' Navon replied snidely. 'Don't worry. The director's instructions were clear.'

Zeb followed them discreetly but didn't see anything suspicious. The two men went to a grocery store and then headed home to their apartment in Yemin Moshe, a neighbor-hood close to the Old City.

He returned to his room and made another call.

It was time to talk to Grigor Andropov.

Chapter 30

Jerusalem
Two days after Assassinations
Nine Days to Announcement

Grigor Andropov ran a secretive intelligence outfit in Russia, similar to the Agency. While the media and the lay population knew of the FSB, only a few in the intelligence community were aware of Andropov's organization.

'Moy droog!' Zeb winced and held the phone away from his ear when the Russian's voice boomed in his phone. 'You have forgotten me.'

'Grigor, you got to go easy on the vodka, especially this time of the morning.' It was just eleven am and Andropov never drank while in the office, but it was a standing joke between them.

'Where are you, and how did you remember me?'

'Israel,' Zeb answered, knowing the spymaster would have triangulated his location from his call. 'Don't ask why. I need to know about an FSB agent, one Peter Raskov.'

'That's a mess, those killings. I bet Avichai's back is to the wall.'

'I haven't met him, Grigor,' Zeb lied smoothly.

'I hope you find those killers soon,' Andropov said, ignoring him. 'The longer they are out there, the more damage they can do.'

That fox. He's connected the dots just by my presence in Jerusalem and my call.

'Grigor,' he sighed theatrically, 'I don't know what you're talking about. Peter Raskov. Have you heard of him?'

Andropov turned serious immediately. 'No, but then, FSB's got several agents. I don't know all of them. You're sure he's one of theirs?'

'That's what I have been told. I want to know if he is FSB, where he is currently and what he's up to.'

'I'll get back to you. Take care, droog,' his voice turned sly, 'and save the world.'

The U.S. had an uneasy relationship with Russia and the intelligence agencies in the two countries weren't friendly. However, Zeb's friendship with Andropov went beyond national ties. Their bond had been forged over several black-ops missions, and the two kept a channel open, frequently exchanging intel that might help both. It also helped that he had saved Grigor's life on a few occasions.

Zeb logged in to his screen and smiled when he read the message from Levin.

'Thick? Heavyset? You should have given me advance notice. You were wearing another disguise when with Carmel and Dalia. I blindly said yes when Navon called. By the way, I asked you to investigate my operatives. Not damage them.'

'It looks like Mossad's training lacks one vital piece. I did you a favor. I completed that for Yakov,' he messaged back.

'What's that?'

'I taught him manners.'

Levin responded with a string of curses.

Zeb's smile faded when he saw the email from Clare. It had Alice Monash's flight details.

Lands at Ben Gurion at seven pm. Which means I'll have to leave Jerusalem at about five-thirty. I still don't know how I am going to investigate all remaining kidon before the press conference.

He glanced at his watch. Twelve pm. Maybe he could squeeze in another operative before he met the ambassador.

Zeb went with the heavyset man disguise. *Eliel and Navon might inform the other operatives how I look.*

He went out to street level and took a moment to orient himself. Musrara was where he wanted to be. The neighborhood nestled between the Russian Compound, Meah Shearim and the Old City. It had stone streets, some of them embedded with ornate marble designs, houses of differing architecture, modern juxtaposed with the old.

Half an hour later he was at a large grocery store in the neighborhood. He took a metal shopping cart and wheeled it inside, searching the various aisles like other customers.

Levin's files were incredibly detailed. They had the daily routines for each of the kidon when they were off missions.

Meir, the operative Zeb was looking for, visited that particular store every day at noon when he was in Jerusalem. He was one of the few kidon who had a partner, a girlfriend.

Zeb spotted him near the deli counter. Closely cropped hair, watchful eyes, dressed in white tee and loose trousers. A woman beside him. They were eating olives from a sampling plate, their teeth flashing as they conversed and laughed.

I can't do anything here. Not with her around.

No innocents to be involved. That was a rule he rarely crossed.

As Zeb watched, Meir drank from a bottle of water and handed it to his girlfriend. She glugged from it, capped it and tossed it in their basket.

That gave him an idea.

There was no label on that bottle. Plastic, small, nothing distinguishable about it.

He wheeled his cart closer to them and randomly tossed several items into it. Their backs were to him when he passed them, their trolley to his right. He glanced swiftly and assessed the bottle. Yeah, no label. He got an idea of the water level and went to the drinks aisle.

He scanned the shelves and finally found a bottle that looked identical to Meir's. He parked his cart in a corner, went to checkout and paid for his bottle. He went outside and stripped it of its label. Unscrewed its top and drank until the level was close to what the kidon had.

He removed a soluble tracker from his backpack and dropped it in the bottle. Shook it rapidly to dissolve and waited for the water to clear.

He went back inside, retrieved his cart and went to the deli section. Meir and his friend were still at the olives plate, but now were sharing a pastry. Zeb rolled his cart over to theirs and leaned over their shoulder.

'Can you reach that for me?' he asked Meir, pointing toward a slice of cake that was beyond his reach.

'Sure,' the kidon replied and leaned forward. For a moment, Meir and his girlfriend were distracted, which was when Zeb switched bottles.

'Toda,' he thanked the operative. Went to the counter, paid for the slice, and ate it messily.

The couple averted their eyes and strolled away. No one wanted to see a clumsy eater and even hardened operatives disregarded such persons as a threat.

Zeb wiped his fingers on a paper towel and threw it in the bin. He pushed his cart and, as he was overtaking them, burped noisily.

He watched Meir and his companion discreetly as he paid for his shopping. Was gratified when both drank some more water, paying no attention to its container.

Once back in his room, two more green dots appeared on his screen.

He could now enter Meir's apartment when the kidon was away.

Chapter 31

───❧❧❧───

Ben Gurion Airport, Jerusalem
Two days after Assassinations
Nine Days to Announcement

The U.S. military Gulfstream touched down at exactly seven pm and taxied to a secluded part of the airport, the one reserved for celebrities and government dignitaries.

Alice Monash climbed down the stairs, escorted by two men in suits, and entered the airport complex. There were Israeli security personnel present, but no other travelers. She scanned the concourse quickly, her eyes settling on a lean, brown-haired man.

'Zeb?' she went to him.

'Yes, ma'am.' He shook her hand firmly and checked out the suits, who hung back.

'They're returning,' she followed his look. 'The president insisted on sending them along.'

'Don't you have a security detail with you, normally?'

'Yes. Clare must have told you. *You* are my protection.'

It's a long flight from home; she must be tired. But I can't put this off any longer.

'Ma'am, do you want to get some coffee?'

They went to an espresso outfit in the arrivals hall, and with the suits giving them privacy ordered their drinks and made their way to a corner table.

'I know what you're going to say.' She held a hand up when he opened his mouth. 'I am not here to make your job difficult. But, this is the only way I could meet you. Do you know how many times I tried?'

'Clare told me. Daniel, as well.' Daniel Klouse, the national security advisor, was a friend.

'Why were you avoiding me?'

'I wasn't, ma'am,' he protested. 'I've been on various operations.'

'You couldn't get one day to meet?'

'Ma'am—'

'Zeb Carter,' she leaned forward, her eyes intense, boring into his. 'Tom and I, we are grateful that you were there. We know you did everything possible that evening—'

He looked away, memories flooding back.

Five years ago, he had been in Thailand, taking a break from Agency work. Just him and the rugged mountains of the country. He had trekked in the Chiang Mai province of northern Thailand, had spent nights with villagers. TVs and cell phones were extraordinary luxuries for many of them.

Three weeks later he had returned to Bangkok, where he would catch his flight. He had traveled to the city the night before his departure and was exiting Chong Nonsi BTS Station when he heard loud reports from a nightclub.

Zeb knew what gunfire sounded like. His fears were proven true when the venue's doors burst open seconds later and revelers flooded out in panic. Young, many of them teenagers.

'What's happening?' he stopped a runner.

'GUNMEN!' the man cried, 'GET AWAY. THEY GOT HOSTAGES.'

Zeb went inside. He knew it was foolhardy, but he had the element of surprise on his side. The shooters would expect everyone to flee, not for someone to enter the club.

He struggled through the crowd as more reports sounded and screams rocked through the building.

A long corridor, lined with candles and drapes, many of which were torn and lay on the floor. The sound of beats reverberating. It didn't look like anyone had turned off the music.

'How many?' he yelled above the noise, at a tearful woman.

'Two, three, I don't know,' she screamed back. 'Why are you going inside?'

He didn't answer. *Doesn't look like they're stopping the escapees. What's their intention?*

He heard loud voices ahead. The sounds of crying and sobbing, above whatever track was playing. In the distance he could hear sirens wailing.

The corridor opened suddenly to a large, open area. Several bodies on the floor. Motionless. Dark stains. Clubbers jammed at the mouth of the corridor. Struggling to run away. Three men on a podium, holding what looked like AKs. Strobe lights painting the inside in dark colors.

'Surrender...government...' a gunman screamed, most of his words swallowed by the music and the sounds of desperate people escaping.

No coordination among the three, Zeb observed. Two bodies at the feet of two of the gunmen. They were shooting randomly, sometimes at the ceiling, occasionally into the panicked mob.

Even as he watched, a shooter opened fire at the corridor.

Screams filled the air. Zeb dived to the floor, feet stomping over him. He struggled to get his Glock out from its holster and peered between legs. The weapon and several spare mags were standard gear for him, wherever he went.

The shooting stopped. A gunman laughed. Went over to another and high-fived him. The crowd was thinning. Maybe fifty or so left at the mouth, bodies on the floor slowing them down. He wouldn't have any cover once the last of them escaped.

He narrowed his eyes as he counted the ones on the dance floor. Stopped when he crossed twenty. Felt a white hoodie move on the floor and then saw the motion. A woman, by the looks of the dark hair falling over her top. She was raising her head cautiously, looking right at him.

Not at me. At the corridor. Looks unhurt. She must have dived to the floor when the shooting began, playing dead.

Don't, he prayed silently. *Stay there. Stay down. Don't move. They'll shoot.*

A shoe crushed his left hand. He winced, closing his eyes momentarily, biting back his groan. When he looked again, the girl seemed to have stiffened. In preparation for making a run.

The shooters were fifteen yards behind her, talking to one another, laughing. One of them slapping a fresh mag into his weapon. All three AKs pointing to the ceiling.

The woman heaved herself up. Got to her knees. Her movement drew the gunmen's attention. Time seemed to slow.

Zeb flung away an escapee to make room for himself.

Struggled to his feet. Yelled loudly to draw the hostiles' attention. Giving the woman a chance, who was getting to her feet, her face scared, her hair flowing behind her.

Twenty yards to her. Almost the same distance from her to the shooters. Dark, flashing light, not ideal shooting conditions.

He shouted again, challengingly, at the gunmen, as the woman started running. One shooter started training his weapon at her. The two others focused on Zeb, who broke free from the thinning crowd at the mouth.

He took a long step forward. His Glock came up. He triggered a long burst just as his second foot came down. None of his rounds hit. The gunmen flinched. Started diving away. An AK chattered.

'NO!' Zeb roared when the woman jerked, started falling. She was close enough for him to see her wide eyes. He leaped at her, got his left arm around her, firing rapidly at the men, carrying her along with him, crashing to the floor, putting his body between her and the shooters, but not before he felt her jerk again and cry out.

The beast exploded inside him. Zeb fell on his right shoulder. His left leg and hand shot out and trapped her behind him. His right hand rose in a straight line, firing as fast as he could at the shooters. He felt something slam into his chest. Heard someone shouting and yelling. A gunman fell.

Zeb's left hand moved unconsciously, replacing his mag smoothly, firing almost immediately again as another gunman fell.

Incoming rounds above him, some whizzing past his face, his leg trembling as it got hit. Another blow to his chest, and still he didn't stop until a third mag emptied and the third shooter fell.

He moved stiffly, aware that his chest was caked in blood and his right leg was sticky. Turned to the woman, and his insides twisted.

Her back was caked in blood. Her neck was bleeding and, as he reached out, her eyes flickered and she went still.

The police came as he was on the verge of losing consciousness. He was in a hospital when he came to, the next day.

'You're lucky,' a Thai doctor told him. 'Two rounds in your chest, none hitting any vital organs. Your thigh, the round went clean through. It didn't hit bone. You'll recover. It will take time.'

'The woman?' he whispered.

'She died.' The doctor removed his glasses and polished them. 'We heard what you did. The cops,' he nodded sideways, 'they're out there. Waiting. They have questions.'

The cops regarded him suspiciously, initially. *Why would anyone charge toward a terrorist incident with nothing but a Glock? Why was a tourist carrying a handgun in the first place? What connection did Zeb have to the gunmen?*

Clare wielded her juice. She made calls and got powerful people in DC and Bangkok to make more calls.

The police disappeared. Instead, the U.S. ambassador to Thailand appeared. He made arrangements for Zeb's return. He didn't ask any questions and had a single-line answer when Zeb asked him who the woman had been.

Sound returned to Ben Gurion airport. Servers cleared tables next to them. Zeb sipped his tea, forcing himself back to the present, composing himself.

He raised his head and looked at Alice Monash.

'I am sorry,' he whispered, 'I couldn't save your daughter.'

Chapter 32

———— ∞∞∞ ————

Jerusalem
Two days after Assassinations
Nine Days to Announcement

Alice Monash clasped Zeb's hand in both of hers. Her eyes were moist. 'You did everything that you could. Heck,' she laugh-cried, a tear sliding down her cheek, 'you didn't *have* to do anything. You could have been a bystander. You saved many lives that day. My daughter …' she sniffed and wiped her eyes. 'You couldn't do anything more.'

Lauren Monash had been on a month-long backpacking trip to Thailand, her trip paid for by her parents as a twenty-first birthday gift.

Coincidentally, she was to catch the same return flight as Zeb the next day. On her last night, she had gone to the night-club, and there, her young life had ended.

Alice Monash had pulled several strings to learn his identity. The Thai police gave her a name that turned out to be fake.

The U.S. ambassador to Thailand said he had been ordered

to collect a man from hospital and escort him to the airport. He had been expressly forbidden from asking any questions.

'Who gave you those orders?' she had demanded.

'The State Department.'

That department ignored her requests. Months passed, but she didn't give up. She persisted. She had threatened, cajoled and persuaded people until finally, Clare, a close friend, admitted that Zeb Carter was one of hers.

'I want to meet him,' Alice had told her, after letting loose a furious tirade at her.

'He doesn't want to meet.'

Zeb knew the ambassador had moved heaven and earth to get to him. He had ignored her efforts. What could he say to her? That if he had acted faster, if he had shot when he was beneath the crowd, maybe, just maybe, Lauren would have been alive?

'You aren't responsible,' Alice squeezed his hands, seeming to sense his thoughts. 'You can't go down the *could have, should have* route. You can't blame yourself. Tom and I don't. We lost Lauren that night. It has left a hole in our lives that cannot be filled. We have learned to live with it. We want you to put it behind you and move on. And we want to say, thank you.'

'For what, ma'am? I didn't do—'

'You tried,' she said firmly. 'For which we will be grateful forever.'

They sat in silence until one of the suits at the perimeter of the café shifted on his feet. That reminded Zeb.

'Ma'am, I really can't protect you. There is another job that occupies—'

'I know,' she patted his hand. 'This was the only way I could meet you. I made arrangements while on the flight. Our embassy's arranging a security detail for me.'

'Does Clare know? She didn't tell me this change of plans,' Zeb asked, much relieved.

'No,' the ambassador chuckled. 'She didn't tell me your identity. Not for several months. This is small payback.'

Her smile faded. 'You know what's going on here?'

'The peace talks? Sure.'

'You don't know the big picture, do you?'

'Both sides are negotiating a deal, aren't they?' he asked, puzzled.

'Yes, but there's more to it.' She gnawed at her lip and then sighed. 'Zeb, if Clare or Avichai Levin didn't tell you, neither can I.'

She looked at him, worried that he would take offense.

He didn't. He was used to need-to-know. His boss and the Mossad director would have their reasons.

She relaxed when he shrugged. 'I will be spending my days with the negotiating team. Will it be possible for you to escort me from the embassy to their hotel? And back, in the evening?'

'Ma'am, you said you have your detail.'

'I do. I would feel safer if you were around, too. If it helps, I'll be keeping a low profile. This is the Israeli and Palestinian show. We're in the shadows.'

'Low profile? You're the ambassador to Israel!'

'I know.' She laughed. 'This job is always in the spotlight. Well, I'll be trying my best to be as invisible as possible.'

He thought fast. He didn't know where the negotiators were holed up. *Somewhere in Jerusalem for sure. Joining her detail twice a day will crimp my plans. I don't have much time.*

He felt the diplomat's eyes on him and grimaced inwardly. *The negotiators will be in some hotel in the city center.*

Ty Patterson

Shouldn't take me more than an hour in the morning and another in the evening, if I join her team.

'Sure, ma'am, though there might be times I can't make it.'

'You'll give me notice?'

'Yes, ma'am.'

'Can you come with me, now?'

'I'll drop you off at the embassy, ma'am.'

He walked with her through the terminal and out, slipping into close-protection mode. The suits fell in step behind them as they checked out other travelers automatically, looked for signs of danger, exits and shooting angles.

They reached his rented SUV without any incident and, a minute later, they were away from the airport.

Gaza Strip, a couple of hours later

'Do you know where the negotiators are?' Abdul Masih asked.

He was in a small house in Deir Al Balah in the strip, with two other men. Narrow lanes, crowded houses, electricity cables hanging overhead, chimneys and TV dishes sprouting from rooftops marked the Palestinian city.

The men were heavily armed, as was Masih. Outside, children played in the darkening night, but no adult ventured near the house. The sight of menacing-looking heavies loitering outside was enough to deter people.

'No,' one of the men shrugged. 'We have tried hard. Our informers in Jerusalem have no clue.'

Masih stroked his beard. He was lean, gaunt-faced, and had an air of restless energy around him.

He moved from house to house, never staying in one place for more than three nights. He had a core group of men around

172

him always, his protectors, who checked out each accommodation prior to his moving in.

The EQB had built a series of elaborate tunnels that ran
beneath the Israel border and opened into various locations in
Jerusalem and its outskirts.

Tunnel was a glorified name for the narrow passages,
which often weren't more than crawl spaces.

The Al-Qassam militants used those subterranean routes
to infiltrate into Israel and carry out their attacks.

It wasn't easy. The IDF were continually searching for and
closing down tunnels. Sometimes they trapped the militants
inside and collapsed the passages on top of them.

It was a continuous, deadly cat-and-mouse game. Hamas
and EQB teams continually digging new burrows, the Israelis
shutting down those they could find.

'There's something,' Qadir, one of Masih's lieutenants,
spoke. 'One of our spotters at the airport, he has some news.'

'What?' the commander uncapped a bottle of water and
washed his face. He wiped it with the sleeves of his shirt and
drank the remaining liquid, his throat bobbing as he swallowed.

'The U.S. ambassador. She arrived in the evening.'

Masih stilled. His eyes glittered.

'She has gone to their embassy?'

'Yes.'

'Follow her, wherever she goes. She will go to the negotiators. There, we'll find the Palestinians.'

Qadir wiped his palms on his trousers, uneasily. 'If we
take her out, the U.S. will join the Israelis in attacking us.'

'So what?' the EQB leader paced the room. 'Mossad
killed our people. We need to retaliate. If Monash dies …
we have survived for a long time. We'll survive even if the

Americans bomb us.'

'Follow Monash,' he gestured, and his men left the room.

Somewhere in the Middle East

The handler had returned from a meeting with the Supreme Leader. The two men had discussed matters of state, alluding only discreetly to the ongoing operation in Israel.

The leader didn't want details. He didn't care that the handler had pulled off the biggest coup of his career by recruiting Magal and Shiri. He was happy that the two Palestinians had been killed, but he wanted more. He launched into a tirade the handler had heard several times. About the Great Satan, about the Jewish nation, how the West was conspiring with the Israelis to overthrow Islamic governments.

The handler didn't interrupt as the Supreme Leader ranted for half an hour. He put on an expression of agreement and leaned forward as if listening attentively, nodding occasionally. The two men shared the same objectives. *But I can do without the sermonizing.*

The leader finally ended with a demand. When would he see results?

'Soon, sir,' the handler had bowed his head and left.

He logged into his screen when he was back in his office and set up a call with the two operatives to discuss the upcoming mission.

'That hotel address you gave us,' Magal exclaimed, 'It's on Emek Refaim! The same street the other hotel was.'

'Yes. I think the Israelis are getting overconfident,' the handler replied.

'No,' the kidon replied thoughtfully. 'German Colony

has many business hotels. That one will be well protected by police. Entry will be extremely difficult.'

'You're saying it is impossible?'

'No.'

'Today is finished. You have eight days left. Seven, really. You won't be able to do much the day of the announcement.'

'Seven,' Magal agreed. 'What about Raskov?'

'He's under control. If anything changes, I'll take care of it and let you know.'

'What about collateral damage?'

'Don't care. The Palestinians are the main target.'

Ein Kerem

Magal hung up, removed the SIM card from the burner phone, and cut it to strips. He extracted its battery and smashed it with a hammer. They would dispose of the device's remains in a drain. Standard operating procedure.

The two men had moved back to the Ein Kerem safe house after their meeting with Epstein. 'You think he believed us?' he had asked Shiri after their meeting with Levin's investigator.

'Yes. He hasn't followed us. Hasn't tapped our phones. Besides, our cover is tight. The handler has made all arrangements. Peter Raskov will come through for us.'

Magal wiped away all traces of the destroyed phone and looked up when Shiri returned, carrying two plates. Their dinner.

'Do you wonder why we are doing this?'

His partner looked at him, puzzled. 'This? Working with the handler? Killing Palestinians?'

'Yes.'

'How do you identify as?'

'Me? I am Eliel Magal.'

'Are you Israeli? A Jew?'

'I am Eliel Magal.'

'How do you feel right now?'

'Alive.'

'How do you feel during our usual Mossad missions?'

'Mechanical.'

Shiri nodded in satisfaction. Magal had answered his own question. It was simple.

The two men were Israeli but had never felt like they belonged in the country. Perhaps it was due to their early years.

At school, no one had gotten close to them. Their origins, which everyone knew, were an invisible stigma.

Not Israeli, their classmates would snidely whisper as they excluded Shiri and Magal from activities.

That tag, *not Israeli*, followed them into adulthood. Even in Mossad, the previous ramsads and some operatives behaved differently around them. Even though Magal and Shiri were the best in the kidon organization.

However, it wasn't their sense of not really belonging that drove them to work with the handler.

It was simpler.

We live in the dark. We live on the edge.

The relationship with the handler offered them all the edge and darkness they longed for. That defined them. That was who they were. If the world called them traitors, so be it.

They knew what they were doing was considered morally wrong by others. But questions of morality had never bothered them. Patriotism wasn't a word they identified with.

The two men dug into their dinner and made plans for turning live Palestinians to dead ones.

Chapter 33

——∞∞——

Jerusalem
Three days after Assassinations
Eight days to Announcement

Zeb reached the U.S. embassy early in the morning and waited for the ambassador to emerge. He was in standard undercover operator clothing. A tee, over which his Glock was strapped. A jacket. Cargo pants, their pockets filled with all that he would need. Shades over his eyes and a cap low over his head. Backpack over his shoulders.

Alice Monash walked out of the embassy flanked by three men in suits. They were hard-faced, hard-edged, their weapons clearly outlined beneath their jackets. She made brief introductions, only one name staying in Zeb's mind: Bob, who seemed to be team leader for the detail.

The men headed to an armored Mercedes with darkened windows, and one held the door open for her. Zeb climbed in the front and sat next to the driver. The others got in beside the ambassador, Bob on one side of her, the second man on the other. None batted an eyelid at Zeb's presence.

Good. Looks like she's briefed them about me.

The driver got in and adjusted his rearview mirror.

'Where to, ma'am?'

'Beit Aghion, the prime minister's residence.'

They set off, the car moving smoothly, like the finely tuned machine it was.

'You're in the service?' The driver snatched a glance at Zeb when at a light.

'Was. You?'

'Marines. All three of us.'

No further discussion. Forty-five minutes later, the vehicle pulled up in front of their destination.

Zeb climbed out, checked the surroundings and tapped his window.

The two suits got out and surveyed the street before escorting the ambassador inside the residence.

'You hanging around?' the driver asked him.

'Nope. I'll be back in the evening.' Zeb waved a hand and made his way toward Malha, a neighborhood in the southwest part of the city.

It was a brisk hour's walk. It gave him time to review the next kidon he was going to face.

Nachman, thirty-three years old, another operative who had a girlfriend with whom he lived. He was back from Germany, where he had been gathering intel on anti-Jewish hate groups.

When in Jerusalem, he and his partner went for a run at six am. Two hours later, the two walked their dog in the neighborhood. At ten am, the girlfriend went to work in an ad agency in downtown Jerusalem.

I'll catch them as they're returning home, if I time it right.

And if they stick to schedule.

Which reminded him. He searched for a hotel and found one not far from the Jerusalem Botanical Gardens. He ducked inside its bathroom and pasted a mustache above his lips. He made sure it was securely fastened. Don't want it falling off, as it had with Carmel and Dalia.

He applied a fast-acting dye to his hair and colored it black. He inserted the cheek pads, gave one last look, and was good to go.

I need more disguises. I'll run out of ideas soon.

He shelved the thought and picked up his pace.

Zeb's estimate was correct. Nachman and his girlfriend were heading toward a block of apartments when he turned into their quiet street.

The building was made of pale limestone, as many were in Jerusalem. Green vines crawled over its walls, some blooming with flowers. A few cars were visible behind gated entrances.

Zeb reduced the distance to them until he could hear their conversation. The couple made no effort to keep their voices down as they indulged in a playful argument.

The kidon heard Zeb's footsteps and looked back. He didn't seem to sense any threat in the thickset man heading their way. He clasped his girlfriend's hand tighter and pulled her closer.

'Nachman?' Zeb called out.

The kidon reacted fast. He shoved his partner to the left and leapt to the right. He pivoted on his heel to face Zeb, his hand reaching beneath his shirt.

Zeb held up both hands in a pacifying gesture. The girlfriend's eyes were wide, her palm cupping her mouth. She didn't scream, however.

She probably knows what he does.

'Send her inside,' he told the kidon.

'Who are you?'

'She's not part of this.'

'WHO ... ARE ... YOU?' Nachman asked slowly, his voice menacing. 'How do you know my name?'

'Think. Somebody must have told you a stranger would approach *each one* of you.'

Nachman's eyes flickered. He seemed to get Zeb's emphasis. 'Ela,' he told his girlfriend without looking at her, 'go inside. I'll be in, shortly.'

'Ela,' he snapped impatiently when she didn't move.

'Should ... I ... call ... someone?' she asked tremulously.

'No. He's from my office.'

'You didn't recognize him just a minute ago.'

'I work in the same organization, ma'am. We've never met. It's just work stuff that we need to discuss. Nothing dangerous, I assure you,' Zeb butted in, hoping to calm her.

She looked at him quickly and then at her boyfriend, who nodded reassuringly. She took a few steps toward the building, looked back once again and then went inside.

'You are Epstein?' Nachman asked, still crouching, still alert.

'Yes.'

'Show some proof.'

'Proof?' Zeb snorted. 'You think we work in some normal office, carrying a card hanging around our necks? Ask the ramsad about me.'

The kidon called. It was a brief conversation that made him relax.

'You could have arranged a meeting,' he said, leaning against a parked car.

No invite to his house. Doesn't look like I'm his friend. But then, that's to be expected. I'm investigating all of them.

'Did you kill Maryam Razak and Farhan Ba?'

His eyes blinked at Zeb's bluntness.

'No. I was in Germany.'

'Can you prove it?'

'The ramsad knows it.'

'He wouldn't have appointed me if he didn't want to verify every kidon's movements. Don't make this difficult.'

Nachman considered him for a long time. 'I was under-cover ... there will be train ticket stubs from Berlin. Restaurant receipts.'

'Don't mean anything.'

'Airports—'

'You're a kidon.' Zeb laughed mockingly. 'You walked about with your face to the cameras in public places?'

'Ela can confirm.'

'Yeah, that you were away. Surely you didn't—'

'I called her every night. On Skype.'

That stopped Zeb. *Not good tradecraft. Hope he has a good reason for it.*

Nachman had. 'She's pregnant. We found out before I went to Germany.'

That is a good reason.

'That still—'

'She records all our calls,' the kidon hurried to respond. 'She's a little emotional now. They are on her computer.'

That'll do for me. I can trace his location from those calls. But one more data point will help.

'What about your cell phone?'

The operative's brow furrowed as he wondered where Zeb was going with his question. It cleared when he made the connection.

He fished his mobile phone out of his pocket and tossed it at Zeb.

'This is yours?'

'Only Ela knows the number.'

'Not even the ramsad?'

'I have another phone for him.'

The kidon watched as Zeb copied the phone's data. 'You're allowed to do that?'

'The ramsad gave me a free hand.'

Nachman took back his phone, turned it on, checked that Zeb hadn't tampered with it, and slid it back into his trousers.

'I'm clear?'

'I need those Skype recordings. And also, the data on your laptop.'

'That's private.'

'You know how a Mossad investigation works.'

The operative shrugged defeatedly, made a follow-me gesture and led him to his apartment. Zeb waited in the living room while the kidon went to a bedroom. He heard murmuring, and presently Nachman returned with two laptops.

He gestured toward a couch and sat next to Zeb. Powered on his girlfriend's laptop, went through a directory and located the recordings folder.

Zeb extracted a cable and connected his screen to the other machine. He ran a few commands and connected to Werner using his cell phone's signal. He turned his screen away from Nachman and got the supercomputer to analyze the files.

'Do they still have high ceilings and fans in their rooms?' he asked when it returned a location in Berlin. A hotel in the Kreuzberg neighborhood, one that he had stayed at, several times.

'Huh? That hotel? No, they have central AC.'

Correct. They had fans but revamped last year.

He disconnected the machine and reached out silently for Nachman's. The operative handed it over and watched him as he copied the hard drive.

'I am clear?' he asked when Zeb had finished.

'Looks like it. I still need to run more checks on all the data, however.'

'I passed the polygraph, you know. I don't know why the ramsad suspected me. I wouldn't do anything like that.'

'Those tests aren't impossible to beat for trained operatives. You know that. You don't like these ongoing negotiations, do you?'

His head jerked up so fast that Zeb thought he heard a click from his bones.

'You know that?' his eyes hard, challenging. 'How?'

'It is my job to know. Don't forget, you work in Mossad. We keep tabs on everything.'

'So what if I don't like what's happening? I don't allow my feelings to interfere with my work,' Nachman said angrily.

'I never said it was a problem.'

'Then why did you say that?'

Zeb had had enough of the kidon. *I'm sure he's a good operative, but he wouldn't work in my team.*

'You can work it out yourself,' he said shortly and walked out of the apartment.

'It means I had moved up the suspect list?' Nachman called after him.

Zeb didn't answer.

He rolled his shoulder when he reached the street and found a small garden in between buildings. A bench was unoccupied. He claimed it and smiled absentmindedly when a mother looked in his direction.

He opened his screen and sent Nachman's data to the twins. He was reasonably sure the kidon wasn't one of the killers, but the sisters would have final say once they analyzed it.

He clicked on a new message from Beth. The twins had found nothing suspicious on Carmel and Dalia's data dumps. The two women were clear. Yakov was uninvolved, too. His cellphone history put him out of the country.

Zeb brought up the list of male kidons and was perusing it when another mother settled next to him on the bench. He shut down his screen and headed out, aiming to find another quiet spot or a café.

It was then that he got the call.

Beit Aghion

Alice Monash knew she had put a crimp in Zeb's plans by insisting on his presence, even if part-time.

I feel safer with him, she thought as she entered the cool interior of Prime Minister Cantor's residence.

Monash knew Israel like the back of her hand. It was as good as her second home. She knew how volatile the Middle East was, and yet the country and Jerusalem felt very safe.

Those killings had made her jumpy, however. *If those assassins could find where those negotiators were, they could target anyone else.*

She put on her game face when the Israeli leader approached

her with a broad smile.

'Alice,' he beamed, 'It is good to have you back.'

The two were good friends and used first names in private. She hugged him and inquired about him as she followed him to his office.

And stopped suddenly when she saw the person awaiting them.

'President Baruti,' she breathed. 'I had no idea you were here.'

'No one does,' Cantor said, shutting the door, 'other than my security detail and a few cabinet ministers.'

'Is there a problem?' She shook hands with the Palestinian and settled on a couch.

'We don't know,' Baruti replied. 'You have briefed her?' he asked his Israeli counterpart.

'No.'

'What's up?' Alice Monash looked at both of them, still coming to terms with the Palestinian's presence. 'It must be important for such a secretive meeting.'

'Both our governments are nearing collapse.'

Chapter 34

———— ∞∞∞ ————

Jerusalem
Three days after Assassinations
Eight days to Announcement

Cantor's words sucked the breath out of Alice Monash.

She stared at him and then at Baruti, who nodded. 'Tell me everything,' she commanded both men, finally.

'You know we are a coalition.'

She nodded. Cantor was stating the obvious.

'The hard-line wing in my party and some of the other parties in government are putting pressure on me.'

'They want to call off the negotiations?'

'Yes. It gets worse,' he said, rubbing his eyes tiredly. 'They think I am giving in to the Palestinians. There's talk about a no-confidence motion.'

'I thought you had bought time with that announcement in ten days.'

'Eight days, now. That's what we both thought. But this happened almost overnight.'

The ambassador thought swiftly. If Cantor's government

fell, then any Israeli-Palestine discussions were dead in the water. A new government could well be a hard-line one.

'And your problem, sir?' she addressed the Palestinian.

'It is similar,' Baruti answered gravely. 'If anything, my situation is worse. Not many like me in the West Bank or in the Gaza Strip. Politicians think I am soft. The people think I am Prime Minister Cantor's poodle. The only reason I have survived so long in this post is because there is no credible challenger.'

'Don't sell yourself short, sir,' Alice Monash admonished him. 'History will know you as the most visionary leader Palestine has ever known.'

'If I live that long,' Baruti replied sardonically. 'Hamas is making noises. They are saying I am a traitor.'

'How can you be a traitor if you are working for peace?'

'They say I am not taking a hard line against the Israelis. That we should talk only when Prime Minister Cantor produces those Mossad killers.'

'We don't even know if they are Mossad,' the Israeli exploded.

Alice Monash raised a hand to silence him. 'Let the president finish.'

'Masar Abadi called me recently. He threatened me. He said Abdul Masih was gunning for me. Not just me, but he would go after the Israeli negotiators, too.'

'What can I do?'

'Give a press conference. Today. Right after this meeting. Tell the world that the United States fully supports our discussions. And that it is behind our governments.'

'President Morgan has already done that, several times.'

Cantor shook his head. 'Your being here makes a huge

difference. People know you. Your background. Your speech will help me with my coalition. It might help President Baruti.'

'It will,' the Palestinian replied. 'Like the prime minister said, my people too know you. They know you don't take sides. You are a hard, fair negotiator.'

Alice Monash thought about the request. *The president said I should work behind the scenes. This will make me visible. I could be a target for those killers or Masih.*

'I'll do it,' she said. 'Whatever support I can give, I will.'

'Change of plans,' Alice Monash said crisply when he took the call. 'I am still in the prime minister's residence. I will be giving a press conference shortly and then going to the hotel, where the negotiators are. Would like it if you were around.'

Zeb looked unseeingly at the street ahead of him.

There goes my plan of checking out more kidon.

'Press conference?' he asked automatically. 'I thought you didn't want to be in the limelight.'

'There have been developments on the political front. I've got to go. Hope to see you here.'

Zeb quickened his pace. *I wanted to interview a few more operatives today. Now, I don't know.*

He made a swift decision. He looked up the app on his phone. Green dots next to Beth and Meghan's name. *They're still awake?* It was late in the night in New York.

Call me, he messaged the younger sister.

He had walked no more than ten paces when his phone buzzed. An incoming video call.

He accepted it. The twins appeared on screen, Beth in front, Meghan behind her.

They looked at him for a long moment without saying a word.

'What do you think?' Meghan asked her sister. 'Is it an improvement?'

'He'll have to try harder. He won't get any calls for modeling photoshoots. Not looking like that.' Beth replied, dismissively.

Zeb realized he was still in his Epstein disguise.

'Why are you still up?' he asked.

'Saving the world is a twenty-four-hour job,' Beth replied solemnly.

Snark. The twins hadn't invented it, but they sure had perfected it.

'We don't have any ongoing missions.'

'There's always a bad actor somewhere who needs to be—'

'We'd been to a bar,' Meghan said, flicking her sister's ear to shut her up. 'Mark and a few friends of his. Us. We just returned.'

Mark was Beth's boyfriend, an NYPD detective who had followed her to the city when she and Meghan had relocated from Wyoming.

'What's up, Zeb? You missing us? Is that why you called?' Beth smirked, batting her eyes at him.

'I need your help.'

The sisters fell silent. Beth looked at Meghan, who shrugged.

'What's that again?'

'I need you here.'

Beth inserted her finger in her ear as if to clear it. She shook her head. 'We can't hear you. Can you be louder?'

'I. Need. Your. Help. Can. You. Get. Over. Here?' Zeb said slowly and clearly.

'Sis, are we recording this?' she chortled. 'This hasn't happened before, has it? Zeb asking us—'

Meghan punched her lightly on the shoulder to keep her quiet. Worry on her face as she leaned closer to the screen.

'Did something happen?' she asked.

'I have less than eight days to go through all the kidon,' he growled in frustration. 'On top of that, I have protection duty as well.'

'Protecting whom?'

'Alice Monash.'

'Our ambassador?'

'Yeah. In fact, I'm heading to meet her right now.'

'We'll leave right away.'

Just like that. As if Jerusalem was a couple of blocks away from their office in New York. *This is why they're so good. Why our team revolves around them.*

Zeb felt a surge of pride in the sisters. They had been running a web-design agency when he first met them. He had saved them from a bunch of assassins. Something had changed in them after that incident. They had sold their business and had come to New York. They had badgered Broker and him to let them join the Agency. Zeb had refused, initially. The covert outfit wasn't a place for civilians. Or so he had thought.

The twins didn't give up. They persisted until Broker caved in and persuaded Zeb to try them out.

From then to now, they've changed a lot. Zeb shook his head unconsciously in admiration.

'What's that mean?' Beth broke in with exasperation. 'Why're you shaking your head like that?'

'Nothing.' He suddenly remembered. 'Weren't you and Mark planning a vacation?'

'Phooey! That can wait. Meghan's gone to call the Gulf-stream. We'll be there soon. To save your ass.' She hung up before he could retort.

He caught a reflection of himself in a store window. He was grinning foolishly. He erased it and hastened toward Beit Aghion.

Zeb reached the prime minister's residence just as Alice Monash took questions from journalists. She was on the lawn, behind a podium, Prime Minister Cantor behind her, to the side.

Reporters and TV crews were seated or hanging about. A crowd of people were gathered in the street. Tight security.

He watched from a distance, could hear fragments of her answers.

The United States supports these talks ... Historic ... Announcement in eight days ...

He spotted a suited man in shades. Part of her protection detail. He wasn't looking at the ambassador. He was checking out the street, passersby, buildings in the distance.

Zeb was reassured. *Looks like the suits around her know their job. They aren't run-of-the-mill heavies.*

Prime Minister Cantor made a few concluding remarks and ended the event. It took another half-hour for the lawn and the street to be cleared and yet another half-hour for the ambassador to emerge from the house.

She was surrounded by the three suits, who walked her swiftly to her vehicle.

Zeb approached them. He was fifty yards away when the protection detail reacted.

'STOP!' one man commanded, his hand going inside his jacket.

Zeb stopped. Cursed himself inwardly. *I should have removed my disguise.*

'It's me, Zeb Carter,' he raised his hands. 'There's a reason for this,' he looked down at himself.

The suit's hand moved deeper inside his jacket. His partners hurried the ambassador into her vehicle. One of them slid inside next to her; the other returned to provide backup.

'Come closer,' the first man said, 'slowly.'

Zeb approached the two men. A small crowd of people was gathering nearby. The police officers outside the prime minister's residence were breaking away from their discussions and heading toward them.

'I am in a disguise,' he told the two men softly. 'I'll explain when we are inside the vehicle. Don't take my name here.'

The first suit jerked his head at the other. That man approached Zeb cautiously, staying out of his partner's firing line.

He caught hold of Zeb's mustache and pulled at it hard. It started coming off.

'It's him. I recognize him, now.'

'You're sure?' his partner asked.

'Positive.'

The first suit relaxed. 'Let's go. The ambassador's running late.'

Zeb opened the passenger door at the front and occupied his now-usual seat. He removed the pads from his cheeks. The mustache followed. He swiveled to face Alice Monash, who raised an eyebrow.

'There's a reason for that?'

'Yes, ma'am.'

'You had us worried for a moment. Bob,' she pointed at

the first suit, who was behind her, 'was ready to open fire.'

'I can imagine. Where are you off to now?'

'To meet the negotiators from both sides.'

The driver gunned his engine and was preparing to drive when Zeb felt it.

The faint ping from his inner radar.

His senses, finely tuned in combat situations all over the world, alerting him.

Someone was watching them.

'STOP!' he ordered.

Chapter 35

Jerusalem
Three days after Assassinations
Eight days to Announcement

The driver slammed his brakes.

'What? What's up?'

Zeb held his hand up to silence him. He was looking straight ahead, trying to get a hang for his *feel*.

What he had wasn't really a radar, of course. It was a survival instinct, one that predators in the jungle had. Battle-hardened operatives, those who spent long spells in hostile territory, had it. A warning that they weren't alone, were being observed, or were in danger.

'Carter, we're running late,' Bob said impatiently from the rear. 'Why did you stop us?'

Zeb didn't reply. He was scanning the area in front of them. A stronger than usual police presence on account of the press conference. Traffic returning to normal. Onlookers dissipating away. No parked vehicles in sight.

He turned his head slowly. No one could see inside the

vehicle, but sometimes sharp movements gave themselves away.

'Carter!' Bob repeated.

'Bob, quiet,' Alice Monash stopped him, steel in her voice. 'I trust Zeb. Leave him be. My schedule can afford some delays.'

Zeb ignored all of them. Focused on two vehicles that appeared in their rearview mirror, one behind the other. A Toyota at the front. Its blinker came on as it swung around their Mercedes and sped away. It, too, had dark windows, but he thought he saw two shadows inside.

The second vehicle was empty. He craned his head to look out of the rear window. Everyone copied his move.

'You saw something? Someone?' Bob asked, his tone conciliatory.

'I felt something. Like someone was watching us.'

He met Bob's eyes and saw something flicker in them. Something like respect.

'You've been in the field long?'

'Yes … let's go. I think whoever it was has gone. It could have been a false alarm as well. It happens sometimes, in crowded areas.'

The ambassador's eyes were curious, but she made no comment.

'Let's do this. Let's do an evasive maneuver, however. Ma'am, where are we heading? Which hotel?'

Alice Monash gave them the name.

I know where it is. Not far from where the attacks happened. Good hotel. Great security.

'That name doesn't leave the four of you,' the diplomat warned. 'You know the reason.'

They knew.

'Ma'am, won't people recognize this vehicle?' Zeb objected.

'I am not sure if you noticed, Zeb.' There was a smile in her voice. 'It has Israeli plates. It is registered to a local politician who is opposed to the prime minister. We'll be parking at an adjacent hotel.'

He turned around to look at her, confused.

'That hotel and our target have a common wall. A while back, a passage was made between the two. Conference rooms in each hotel on the ground floor on either side of that opening. Both rooms are situated at the back. Not much traffic to them. All that is why that hotel was chosen.'

'That must be public knowledge.'

'Not many know. At least, that's what the prime minister tells me. In any case, both locations are crammed with police. Every resident has been checked out. The negotiators are on a floor of their own. Access to it is blocked. Various security measures are in place. I think it's safe.'

'What about the entrance, the driveway?'

'Those are separated by a waist-high wall. Relax, Zeb. The police have checked it out. They approved the hotel and our deception.'

Zeb turned back to the front. *It's not my place to pick locations. If the Israelis are satisfied, I am good.*

The driver swung out. He drove randomly, circling back every now and then. He passed through red lights at will, often overtaking on the wrong side.

Zeb didn't spot any tails. Neither did any suit, and after an hour, they headed to their destination.

'Do you think they spotted us?' Masih asked his driver. His heart was thumping, his palms sweaty, yet his face was expressionless, as was his voice.

He and the driver, one of his most trusted shooters, were in the Toyota. The vehicle had diplomatic plates that they had stolen from one of the parked vehicles around the prime minister's residence.

He had infiltrated into Israel the previous night, after hearing that more tunnels had been destroyed by the IDF. He hadn't wanted to risk being stranded in Gaza if all passages were blocked.

He and his men had moved in the darkness of the night and had sought cover in their safe house in the Old City. And then he had taken over tailing Alice Monash.

The two men had mingled in the crowd around Beit Aghion and watched the conference. This was a recon mission. Opening fire in the midst of tight security was suicidal. Abdul Masih harbored no such notions. He left the suicide bombing attacks to his juniors.

No, this was just surveillance, to see how well protected Alice Monash was and to see where she went after the conference. Masih was hoping she would lead him to the negotiators.

He had expected the ambassador's vehicle to drive away immediately. It hadn't, and that had raised his suspicions.

'We'll have to follow her tomorrow,' Masih said, slamming his palm against the dash in frustration. 'From the embassy.'

'Is that advisable?' the driver asked, concerned. 'There will be tight security around the place.'

'The Israelis and the Americans haven't caught Abdul Masih in these many years,' the terrorist boasted. 'They won't, now.'

Magal and Shiri were more careful. The two men had split up and were hunkered down in two off-duty cabs on Emek Refaim. The presence of their vehicles wasn't unusual. There was a long line of cabs on the street, waiting to serve the patrons of various hotels. They had papers to back their identities; their covers were tight.

Magal was at the front, pretending to read a newspaper, while Shiri was several vehicles to the rear, shades over his eyes, snoozing.

Magal noticed a vehicle with darkened windows arriving in the hotel next to their target. He didn't pay it much attention, since they were casing the place where all the negotiators were staying.

He couldn't control his gasp when Alice Monash stepped out and was immediately surrounded by three suits.

'What?' Shiri asked in his earbud.

'The American ambassador, at your ten.'

'What's she doing there?' his partner asked incredulously, after a while.

'No idea.'

'She must be here to meet both teams. Why else would she be here? But they're in the neighboring hotel. Not this one.'

'No idea,' Magal repeated, watching the woman disappear into the interior of the establishment.

'We've got the right one?'

'Yes.'

'Has the handler given us the wrong address?'

'His intel has never been wrong before.' Magal's voice was tight. They had been making an attack plan for the hotel based on their surveillance. However, if the negotiators were in the adjacent … 'Let's see when she leaves. She might be here for another meeting.'

Shiri grunted unconvincingly.

There was movement from within the diplomat's vehicle even as they watched. A tall man climbed out, brown-haired, clean-shaven. He stood relaxed, one arm on its roof, as he looked around.

A hundred yards separated Magal from the stranger, but even through the distance, the kidon felt the man's stare as he checked out every vehicle on the street.

The agent's lips barely moved as he voiced the thought in his head.

'Who's this man?'

Chapter 36

———— ∞∞∞ ————

Jerusalem
Three days after Assassinations
Eight days to Announcement

Zeb didn't sense any danger when he scanned the street. There was a taxi line outside, on the street, all of which had been checked out by the Israeli police. A steady stream of cars arrived in both hotels' forecourts, which, as the ambassador had described, were separated by a waist-high wall.

Discreet, armed security was present in front of both establishments, as was the case with every hotel on the street.

Every guest in both hotels had been investigated as well. No danger there. Armed guards prevented unauthorized people from going to the rooms where the passage was.

Zeb had messaged Levin on the drive, asking him about Monash's revelations about the hotels.

'*She's correct,*' the ramsad had replied. '*Security is good. I am confident no hostile can enter either place.*'

Zeb had no reason to doubt the director. Still, he watched, allowing his unconscious mind to absorb the flow of vehicles, letting his instincts warn him if there was any danger.

His radar stayed quiet.

The ambassador stepped out of the decoy hotel several hours later, when shadows were lengthening. He held the door open for her and was the last to climb in.

'Everything's good?' he asked Alice Monash.

'Yeah,' came the satisfied reply. 'I gave a pep talk to both teams. Boosted morale, especially that of the Palestinians. Looks like we are making progress.'

They drove back to the embassy, using circuitous routes again. The ambassador stayed back in the car when they arrived and signaled to her detail to leave her alone with Zeb.

'Your friend, Levin, is under pressure.'

'I know,' he replied.

'You know about this unit Cantor has put together?'

'Yeah. Avichai told me.'

'I got a call from the prime minister. He had wrapped up a meeting with the unit. He had also met Levin, Shoshon, Levitsky. The investigation hasn't made any progress.'

That was news to Zeb. He had been so focused on the Mossad kidon that he hadn't caught up with Levin. *Other than to exchange messages on various kidon.*

'Cantor's cabinet is rounding on your friend. They want the prime minister to allow Shabak to investigate the kidon.'

'That would put at risk—'

'I know.' The ambassador blew out a tired breath. 'Cantor knows, too. The other ministers have asked for Levin to be replaced, too. The prime minister has stood his ground. For now.'

Not for long, though. It is a coalition. He can't withstand political pressure forever.

'What about Levin? How did he react?'

'He didn't. That man has ice-cold nerves. Cantor said he just smiled and made no comment.'

He's counting on me, Zeb thought bleakly. He looked at the clock on the car's dash. Seven pm.

There was time to check out a few more kidon.

Chapter 37

—∞∞∞—

Jerusalem
Three days after Assassinations
Eight days to Announcement

Zeb headed back to his room and changed into another Jarrett Epstein disguise. A lean, deeply tanned, mustache-sporting and shades-wearing man. Just like thousands of Israeli men on the street.

He took one look at the kidon files and decided to approach Yonah, Osip, Danell and Uzziah. The four men had returned from Britain, where they had been surveilling an anti-Jewish hate organization. *Danell was in an accident the day before the killings. A collision with a scooter. He has a broken collarbone.* The Mossad files had hospital records for him. *That eliminates him, but what about the others?* He chose Yonah randomly as the next kidon to investigate and looked up where he lived. *He's not far, but I need to change hotels. I've been at the current one for too long.*

He checked for messages from the sisters. A long one from Meghan with a lot of technical details, summed up in a few lines. Nachman was clear. His Internet calls were conclusive. He was in Berlin when the assassinations went down.

Eliel and Navon were good, too, the sisters confirmed in the same message. *I still have to hear from Andropov.*

He looked at his messaging app. The twins were greyed out, with a new status message. *In transit.* Flight distance from New York to Tel Aviv was about eleven hours if one flew commercial. Ten, if one was using private aircraft, which the twins were. Four more hours for transit to and from both airports. *Sometime early in the morning,* he decided. That's when he would have more support.

He checked out of his hotel and found another one in Talbiya, which was half an hour away from where Yonah lived. It was suitably anonymous, had a room on the ground floor, had a rear exit. His room had a window to the street and a sturdy door. *Everything that I want.*

He walked briskly from his new accommodation toward the kidon's apartment. It was on the first floor on a quiet street. Large windows on side walls, none of them overlooking the main thoroughfare. Zeb looked left, then right.

An amorous couple passed him, whispering in each other's ears. He let them disappear in the darkness and entered the building. No one in the lobby to stop him. He took the concrete stairs two at a time and reached the first floor.

Four doors on it, four apartments. Yonah's was to his right. *Direct approach. I'll just knock, ask him and play it by ear.*

Zeb discarded his plan when he went to the door and heard faint voices from within. *He's got company?*

He checked the bottom of the door. Yeah, there was a thin sliver of light, indicating a gap between door and floor.

He removed a cable camera from his backpack—a thin,

flexible, plastic-sheathed wire that had a miniature camera at one end and a phone jack at the other. He slid the lens underneath the door and plugged the other end into his cell. Images in high definition appeared instantly, the camera drawing its power from the phone. Four men, seated around a table, cards in hand, a bottle and glasses beside them. Yonah, Danell, Osip and Uzziah, all of them under one roof.

Zeb stowed the camera back, slipped his cell into his pocket and inspected the door. Wooden, sturdy. A lock that seemed easy enough to pick. There could be deadbolts inside.

He decided to try his luck and brought out his burglar kit. It had master keys, picks and various levers. He tried several keys and, when none worked, used other tools, working with controlled haste, paying attention to the sounds within and to those on the floor.

The lock gave with a soft click. No change to the laughter from inside. Zeb tried the door with soft hands. It opened a crack.

He frowned. No bolt? No chain? No other security? Either Yonah was supremely confident of himself or this apartment was purely a transient one.

He pushed the door cautiously and, when a burst of conversation broke out, risked a peek. The men were inspecting their cards, none of them paying any attention to the door.

He was halfway inside when Yonah's head rose. The expression on his face was almost comical when he regarded the stranger in the apartment.

'Who are you—' he began.

Osip and Uzziah reacted fast. They rolled off their chairs, one operative diving toward a bag on the floor, the other hurling something at the intruder.

The missile, a dinner plate, shattered behind Zeb, who dived to the floor, rolled to his left, his Glock rising to cover Uzziah. *He's quicker than the others. He's the threat.*

'STOP!' he commanded, his weapon covering the kidon.

The Mossad men froze. None of them had produced a gun yet, and they were smart enough to know they could not out-move a bullet. *Not without at least one of them getting hurt. Or killed.*

'Who are you?' Uzziah asked roughly, his eyes hard.

'Jarrett Epstein. You must have heard of me.'

They had, by the quick exchange of looks between the operatives.

'You come in like this?' Uzziah snarled. 'You couldn't have requested a meeting?'

'And miss this reception?' Zeb rose slowly and holstered his gun when the operatives made no further hostile moves.

He approached the table and occupied an empty chair. Gestured at the kidon to seat themselves.

'Which one of you killed the Palestinians?' he asked them.

'None of us,' Uzziah reacted angrily. 'How do we know you are Epstein?'

'Call Levin,' Zeb replied. 'Check me out.'

The operative was reaching into his pocket when Danell stopped him. 'Who else would it be? No one else knows Epstein's name. You considered knocking?' This was directed at Zeb, with a tilt of the eyebrows.

'What would be the fun in that?' Zeb retorted, liking the operative immediately. Of the four kidon, he alone sat relaxed, an amused look in his eyes. 'Your friends are right, though. You should confirm who I am with Levin.'

'I'm good friends with Carmel and Dalia,' the operative

waved a hand nonchalantly, 'unlike these three. They gave me a heads-up. That you might come calling. Nachman, too. Though their descriptions,' his teeth flashed, 'are quite different from how you look.'

'You know how it is in our business.'

'We do,' the kidon nodded. 'None of us killed those Palestinians.'

'Speak for yourself.'

'I'm speaking for my friends, too. They were with me at the British hospital.'

'There's no record of that. Nothing in their files. Or yours.'

'There wouldn't be. We wanted to minimize any mention of their presence.'

'Your word isn't proof, however.'

'Check the hospital's security cameras,' Danell grinned. 'We tried to delete the footage, but we couldn't hack into their system. I am sure if you ask politely, the British will hand over the relevant clips.'

'Why isn't this in your reports?'

'Because the ramsad asked them,' the kidon nodded at his friends, 'not to be at the hospital. They disregarded his orders.'

'I'll have to tell Levin.'

'I know. It doesn't matter now,' Danell laughed, 'I think the ramsad has a lot more on his plate than blowing his top at us.'

Chapter 38

Jerusalem
Three days after Assassinations
Eight days to Announcement

Zeb left Yonah's apartment half an hour later, after copying the phone and laptop data of each kidon. He sent the large file to the twins as he walked and shot a message to a contact in MI6. The British agency would be able to get the hospital's video data. *If that corroborates, and no reason why it shouldn't, these four operatives are clear, too.*

Nine pm. He grabbed a baguette sandwich from a street vendor and wolfed it down in front of an electronics store. The TV in its window was playing a news channel. Talking heads speculating what Prime Minister Cantor and President Baruti would announce in a few days.

The scene cut to one of Alice Monash addressing the crowd at Beit Aghion. That was followed by file photos of Avichai Levin, Levitsky and Shoshon. The TV host and her panel hotly debated the lack of progress in the investigation.

'Levin must go. It is clear Mossad is behind those

assassinations. There is a government coverup, which is why no suspects have been identified,' a guest, a Palestinian, stated. The TV audience, a predominantly Israeli one, burst out at that.

This is how it will go down, Zeb thought as he turned away and drank from a bottle of water. *Palestinians and Israelis even more entrenched in their positions.*

Unless Cantor's task force can prove conclusively that Mossad wasn't involved.

Or I do.

He brought up the GPS app on his cell and checked the various green dots on it.

Meir wasn't at home. Zeb looked at the kidon's location.

He's at a cinema.

Zeb had been on his feet ever since he left his hotel in the morning to meet Alice Monash. The continual switching from investigator mode to bodyguard was taking its toll on him. He was tiring. He was aware an operative lost his edge in such conditions.

I don't have a choice.

He made his way to Meir's apartment.

Moscow, That Evening

Andropov slammed his phone down and scrunched his face in disgust. Getting intel on Peter Raskov was proving to be surprisingly difficult. He was an FSB agent, that much the spymaster had found out. However, he hadn't been able to get anything more on the agent.

Where is he? What's his mission? Who is his handler?

He prided himself on keeping track of every Russian

operative, whichever agency they belonged to. He had discovered that Raskov wasn't in his system. That had been the first cause for his irritation. He then had found that none of his usual sources knew anything about the operative. That not only angered but also intrigued him.

Just who was Peter Raskov?

He made more calls. Met the directors of other covert agencies to see if they knew anything about a mission in Jordan. No one had any information.

He drummed his fingers on his desk and reached a decision. Calling the FSB director was a last resort. However, if Zeb needed help, Andropov would go to the Kremlin if that was needed.

He made the call.

Somewhere in the Middle East

It was the handler's turn to grimace. Magal and Shiri had sent him a photograph. That of the stranger standing beside the American ambassador's vehicle. But that man didn't seem to exist. Not in any of the agency systems that the handler had hacked into.

No such person in Mossad. FSB didn't have anyone who looked like him. It wasn't just the Israeli agency that the handler had penetrated when his people had developed their cyberattack capabilities. The Russians, the Germans—heck, even the Chinese. He hadn't gone after the U.S. and UK, however. Not because he thought they couldn't hack into MI6 or American systems, but because, if discovered, his entire capability would be nullified.

Those two countries would detect his viruses in little time, would erase them, create defenses and would then share those with their allies.

He smoothed his beard and looked at his reflection in the polished surface of his desk. He looked the part. The head of a ruthless and feared agency. But his looks didn't reassure him just then.

This new person was obviously an American. Who else would ride in Alice Monash's car? But why was he there?

He perused the dossiers his agency had of all U.S. agents. No file photograph matched that of the stranger. He cursed in disgust and turned off the screen. He was overreacting. Why did it matter if some unknown person was with the ambassador?

It wouldn't affect what he was working on.

Which reminded him.

He shot off a message to Magal and Shiri.

When will you attack?

Somewhere in Jerusalem

Abdul Masih ripped a piece of bread, dipped it in olive oil and stuffed it into his mouth as he pored over a map.

He was in their safe house, a small residence in the Muslim Quarter in the Old City. Three of his trusted lieutenants were with him. Outside, more of his men were spread out, some at the entrance and exit of the narrow street. Those would warn him if any police or IDF personnel made an entry.

'How do you know it is that hotel?' he asked, stabbing his finger on a red circle on the map.

'She visited it. One of our informers entered it as well and saw heavy security. He—'

'He wasn't spotted, sayidi,' his lieutenant clarified hurriedly.

'Good. Did he see where she went?'

'There's a corridor that goes to conference rooms. There were many guards. He didn't see where exactly she went from that corridor.'

Masih pursed his lips as he examined the map silently. Emek Refaim was a busy street. The previous attacks were practically a stone's throw from the circled hotel. Why would the Israelis move all negotiators to another one so close by?

Because no one will think the talks are happening practically next door.

He nodded unconsciously and glared at his lieutenant, who smiled as if he was being complimented.

'What's the plan?' he barked.

His man faltered. Plan? That was for the sayidi to make, wasn't it?

Masih growled in anger at his silence and looked at the others. They turned away.

'I have to do everything,' he grated. He bent down and studied the map again. The street was broad, but getting away would be difficult. The Israelis would have a heavy presence and at the first sign of trouble, would block all escape routes.

Unless ...

'Do we have any suicide bombers here? In Jerusalem.'

'Yes, sayidi. Lots of them, ready to die for the cause.'

'Do we have fighters? A dozen or so?'

'Yes, sayidi.'

'They will die.'

'They are ready for it.'

Chapter 39

—⁓∞⁓—

Musrara, Jerusalem
Three days after Assassinations
Eight days to Announcement

Abdul Masih was the furthest thing from Zeb's mind. He was breaking into Meir's apartment when the terrorist was enquiring about suicide bombers.

Getting entry into the building hadn't been a problem. The residential complex didn't have a concierge, nor did it have security of any kind.

With his ball cap pulled low over his face, Zeb raced up the stairs and reached Meir's fifth-floor apartment. He inspected the door and spotted the discreetly mounted security camera.

Can't risk picking the lock.

He took the stairs, climbing rapidly until he reached the landing on the twelfth floor, and took a door that opened on the roof.

A water tank in one corner. Air-conditioning equipment. Solar panels. No other human.

He peered over the parapet that ran all around. Luck

favored him for a change. The Mossad operative's apartment was at the rear of the building and overlooked its parking lot. Which happened to be quiet at that time of the night and was dark.

He extracted a climbing rope from his backpack and secured one end to the tank. Donned gloves and slithered down the side of the building. He slid down the eleventh floor, tenth; kicked hard and jumped to the right when a bedroom window opened on the ninth floor and a head peered out. He remained motionless, a dark figure against the wall, his feet braced against the building, his palms wrapped firmly around the rope.

The head, a woman, called out querulously in the night. A voice replied from somewhere beyond the parking lot. The resident cursed, retreated and slammed the window shut.

Zeb resumed his approach. He stopped when he reached Meir's window. No curtains inside. He looked around and upwards and downwards. He was alone in the night. He peered cautiously through the pane and saw only his reflection. He brought out a palm-sized flashlight and aimed it at the room.

Bedroom. A double bed. A floor-to-ceiling wardrobe. A door at the far end. No alarms visible. He clutched the flashlight between his teeth, drew out his blade and jammed it beneath the sill. There was give between the window and its frame. Sufficient enough for him to use his burglar toolkit and open the window.

Moments later, he was padding across the room, after confirming there were no intruder alarms or cameras. He searched the room swiftly. No phone. There was a laptop on a side table, but it was password-protected. That wasn't a deterrent. He inserted a thumb drive in its port. The program on it would force the machine to perform certain commands and yield its files. Zeb knew how it worked; the twins had explained it to him in excruciating detail. *Hopefully Meir hasn't encrypted his files.* Werner could crack those, too, but it would take longer.

He searched the rest of the apartment while the thumb drive did its work. There was another bedroom that seemed unoccupied, a living room that also doubled as a dining room, a kitchen, bathroom. The apartment was comfortably furnished, pictures of Meir and his girlfriend adorning the wall. No files of any kind. No concealed safe, not that he could detect. *There must be one for his passports, weapons. Or he has a locker somewhere else.* He didn't find another phone.

He planted listening devices in the apartment and, when the thumb drive stopped flashing, removed it and stowed away the laptop in its original position.

One last look around the apartment and then he was out of the window, climbing back to the roof.

Forty-five minutes later he was on the street, with no proof that the kidon was either innocent or the killer. He hoped the thumb drive would have something.

One hour later, Zeb was in his hotel room, fresh after a shower. He sent the files to the sisters and crashed on his bed.

He woke up in the morning to find a Glock pointed at him.

Chapter 40

—⊱⊰—

Jerusalem
Four days after Assassinations
Seven Days to Announcement

Behind the Glock were two pairs of green eyes. One mirthful, the other steady. Beth and Meghan Petersen. One impulsive, the other analytical.

Something deep inside Zeb settled on seeing them. He had always been a loner. He still was. However, the twins, just by their presence and their enthusiasm, had reshaped him to a large extent. He no longer felt isolated, strange, when he was with his friends. With them around he felt … grounded.

He also felt relief. Now that the twins were with him … *we can work faster together.*

'How did you find me?' he stifled a yawn and pushed the weapon away.

'It wasn't difficult,' Beth chortled, holstering her gun. 'We figured you would be in some place central. Not more than an hour or ninety minutes away from the furthest Mossad operative. Close enough to the embassy, too. We zeroed in on various hotels, shortlisted thirty and approached them.'

'The people at the desk gave me up, just like that?' he asked, startled.

'This,' Meghan produced a Mossad ID card, 'carries a lot of weight in Israel. And when Beth fluttered her eyes ...'

'I used a false name. I was in disguise!' he protested.

'Well, they gave us a list of rooms that had single occupants, described them in general, and that was our starting point.'

'How long have you been knocking on hotel doors?' he asked suspiciously. *Did I let slip somehow where I was staying? They could have tracked my phone, but I turned it off. And I am not wearing clothing that has GPS tags.*

'Two hours. We got lucky,' Meghan admitted, running her fingers through her hair. 'This was the third hotel we approached, and yours was the second room we picked.'

Zeb shook his head in disgust at himself. He normally would have woken up at the slightest noise, alert at any sign of intrusion.

I must have been exhausted.

Three cups of steaming coffee were on the small table in his room when he returned from his shower.

Beth and Meghan were seated shoulder to shoulder, their screens running.

'Bring us up to speed,' Beth ordered. Work mode. No joviality.

He broke it down for them succinctly, right from Kadikoy, even though they knew parts of it.

'Riva and Adir, Carmel and Dalia, Yakov, Nachman, Danell, Yonah, Osip, and Uzziah, Eliel and Navon ... those are the only ones we are confident of. Who had no role in the killing,' she summed up.

'Correct. Meir … You got anything from his files?'

Meghan's fingers danced over her keyboard as she shook her head. 'Encrypted. Werner's working on cracking them open. It's also listening to those bugs you planted in his apartment. Searching for keywords. Nothing so far. Meir and his girlfriend have been talking domestic stuff.'

'Out of twenty-eight kidon, we have crossed out twelve,' Beth sipped her coffee and swiped her tongue over her lips. 'Sixteen operatives yet to be cleared. Of the fourteen men Carmel and Dalia identified, six remain.'

'Correct.'

'Just because those men are opposed to what's happening, doesn't mean any of them … The ones not on Carmel and Dalia's list also can be—'

'I know. It is a matter of priorities, however.'

'We've been thinking about this,' she nodded, accepting what he said. 'The time crunch and all that.'

'Someone's got to do that, you know,' Meghan interrupted wickedly, 'thinking, I mean.'

Zeb put on a stoic face, though he was finding it hard not to smile. 'And?'

'You meet the operatives. All day today. One at a time, or in a group, however you want to play it. Beth and me, we'll break into their apartments and see what we can uncover.'

Zeb emptied his cup, collected the twins', and went to the kitchenette to rinse them. *It might work. Interviewing the kidon will not necessarily prove anything. But this two-pronged approach will lead us to something. Faster.*

'Let's do it.'

'Great,' Beth bounced in her seat. 'Start off with Abraham

and Mattias. Their apartments aren't far. Half an hour away. A brisk walk, for us. Might be longer for you, given that you are old.' She tossed him his cell, the Jarrett Epstein one. 'Set it up.'

Beit Aghion

Prime Minister Yago Cantor was having a breakfast meeting with Jessy Levitsky, Nadav Shoshon and Jore Spiro. His morning was already turning sour with the lack of progress.

'We have some of the finest intelligence agencies in the world. And what have we to show for that?' He speared toast viciously with his fork and chewed angrily. 'Nothing. Why is that?'

'Prime Minister, it's just four days from—' Levitsky began, at which the leader sighed.

'I know, I know, Jessy. It's just that ...' He composed himself. 'Tell me what you have got.'

Cantor had appointed the minister to liaise with all investigative bodies, including the task force he had set up.

'The weapon was a Galil Mar,' Levitsky outlined crisply. 'Ballistics confirm that, but we have not found it. Unfortunately, those rifles aren't hard to get. We have some cell phone footage of two men getting out of a VW and into a Toyota. We got lucky with that. A tourist was filming randomly and caught them.'

Cantor leaned forward. 'Who are they?'

'We can see only their backs,' the minister replied dispiritedly. 'The men are average sized, dark hair ... not much for us to go on. Thousands of people have sent their cell phone clips. We are going through them all. It will take time.'

'How did they know where those negotiators were?'

'We don't know.' An awkward silence followed. The minister didn't need to state that if the killers were Mossad operatives, they could have gotten access to inside knowledge.

'What of the task force?'

'Shabak has cleared several Mossad agents,' Levitsky glanced sideways at Levin, who remained unperturbed.

'Several, not all?'

'That's correct, prime minister.'

'Avichai, what have you got for us?'

'I have sixteen kidon yet to be cleared.'

'Sixteen out of how many?' Shoshon challenged. It was no secret that the Shabak director didn't like Mossad's preferential treatment by the prime minister and the media. Cantor had explained to him several times why the counter-intelligence agency needed to operate in secrecy. His reasoning fell on deaf years. He had thought about firing Shoshon, however, the director was good at his job.

'Sixteen remain; that's all that matters,' Levin replied urbanely.

'That's a large number. We don't have much time.'

'I know. We are working as fast as we can. Such investigations cannot be rushed.'

'If you throw more people at it ...' Shoshon's eyes narrowed. 'Wait! Are you investigating yourself?'

'I have an experienced agent checking them out.'

'Just one?'

'One is all I can trust.'

'He's not from Mossad, is he?' the Shabak director smiled knowingly. 'Who is he?'

'He's good,' Levin replied shortly. He turned to the prime

minister with a questioning look, as if to ask, *is this going somewhere?*

Cantor took the hint. 'Avichai, you know what we are up against. It is vital we find the killers before our announcement.'

Spiro stirred in his chair. 'What happens if we don't?'

'We might not be able to make that announcement. Our government might collapse. You have heard of the no-confidence rumors?'

Heads nodded around the table.

'They are true,' Cantor confirmed. 'And on top of that, if more killings happen and Mossad is blamed—'

'Our country may not exist,' Levin completed, softly. 'A war will inevitably break out.'

Chapter 41

———❦———

Jerusalem
Four days after Assassinations
Seven Days to Announcement

Avichai Levin broke the brooding silence that followed his words. 'Prime Minister,' he stated firmly, 'I can't guarantee I can prove my kidon are innocent or are involved by that deadline. However, there's a way we can build confidence in the coalition partners.'

'I am listening,' Cantor replied.

'Take the American ambassador's help. Her speaking outside Beit Aghion made a difference. The opinion polls showed a slight increase in support for you.'

'I am aware of that. What more can she do, however?' the prime minister ground out in frustration.

'Lots, Prime Minister. Arrange meetings for her with your coalition partners. Get her to convey that America is firmly behind you. She has to state that calling off the negotiations is not an option, regardless of who the killers are. Talk to President Baruti as well. Arrange Alice Monash to have similar discussions with his party and political partners. Believe me, her presence and her message will make a significant difference.'

Yago Cantor stared unseeingly at his ramsad as he considered Levin's words. He had been in his position this long because he considered politics to be one enormous game of chess. And he had few equals in the political maneuvering such a game required. *Levin is right. I should have thought of it earlier.*

'That's a good idea,' he nodded. 'Let me work on it. Can you stay back, Avichai?' He signaled the end of the meeting and waited for the others to leave the room.

'Avichai,' he crossed his arms behind his neck, a ghost of a smile behind his lips. 'What I said earlier … you *do* have a career in politics. It comes naturally to you.'

His face turned serious. His hands dropped to his sides. 'We still need to find those killers. If they are Mossad—'

'I know. My house will need to be cleaned up.'

'This man you have appointed … he's good?'

'The best, prime minister.'

'From which agency?'

'He's not from our country.'

'U.S.' Cantor worked it out quickly. 'There's no other country you would trust.'

'Correct, sir.'

'Do I know him?'

'You have met him, prime minister. It was some time back. You won't remember him. I can't say more.'

'You trust him?'

'He found my daughter's killers, Prime Minister,' he said, simply.

Moscow

Andropov's call with the FSB director hadn't yielded much. All he got was that Peter Raskov was an agent, which he had known in any case. *Zeb wanted to know where he was, as well.*

The spymaster brooded for a moment and then yelled, 'Yuri!'

'Peter Raskov,' he told the flunky, one of his best hackers, when he arrived. 'He's FSB. Find out where he lives.'

'He should be in our system.'

'He isn't,' Andropov replied testily.

Yuri's face glowed. A challenge. He loved those.

'You want this yesterday?'

'Yes,' the spymaster glared at him, and the man disappeared.

Ein Kerem

'We go as who we are?' Navon looked at the map of the hotel spread out on the dining table.

'Yes,' Magal replied. 'We are Mossad operatives. We have been cleared by Epstein. No one will stop us. Once inside the hotel, we find out where the negotiations are happening, check out the security, and then we'll make our plan.'

The handler had confirmed that his intel was correct. The negotiators were in the hotel to the right, not the one where they had spotted the ambassador.

The two kidon had figured out that either the two hotels were connected in some way and the one on the left was a decoy, or Alice Monash had another meeting in the other establishment.

'Tomorrow?'

'Tomorrow. I'll let the handler know.'

They didn't consider disguises or cover stories. They were working to a plan the two had agreed on, a long way back. This would be their last job for the handler. It wasn't that they didn't enjoy it or had fallen out with him.

The heat on Mossad after the killings will be too high. Every agent will be under a microscope. Chances are good we will be found.

No, Magal shook his head unconsciously. *It's best we disappear after killing those remaining Palestinians.*

Eliel Magal and Navon Shiri would no longer exist. They had worked out a new career path for themselves. The two would turn into international assassins. That career move would provide them with all the darkness and edge they wanted.

They would be international criminals, wanted by the world's agencies. Magal shivered in anticipation. Yes, that was the right move. They would work as a team, taking jobs from whomever bid the highest.

It was time to branch out on their own.

But first, they had to finish the Palestinians.

Somewhere in Jerusalem

'You have the suicide killers lined up?' Masih asked his lieutenants.

'Yes, sayidi. Four of them.'

'The car is ready?'

'Yes. A Peugeot, packed with explosives.'

'Those men know the route?'

'It is easy. Down Emek Refaim. The hotel cannot be missed. It is to the right. They will blast through the security cordon, firing as they drive. They will smash through the glass doors. There are just three steps, which the car can easily climb. Once inside, they will detonate the explosives.'

Masih nodded approvingly. He had come up with the plan after further recon on the hotel. There was too much security, outside and inside, for him to risk himself.

No, he had told himself. *Let the suicide killers take out as many as possible. The Israelis will evacuate the hotel. They will escort the negotiators to vehicles in the basement car park. Once they exit the hotel and reach the street ...* he smiled in satisfaction.

He would be at street level. In an ambulance, wearing an EMS worker's uniform. He would be in the right vehicle in the right place at the right time.

Of course, no other ambulance in Jerusalem carried a grenade launcher.

Chapter 42

—✺—

Talbiya, Jerusalem
Four days after Assassinations
Seven Days to Announcement

Zeb was with Abraham, in a café not far from his hotel, in his Jarret Epstein disguise. The kidon was part of a three-person khuliyot that had been in the U.S. when the assassinations happened. Or so their mission report stated.

The other operatives in the team were Mattias and Cale.

Zeb had introduced himself when the operative arrived and had waited while Abraham went through the drill of calling Levin and confirming his identity. He had engaged the man in small talk, to get him comfortable before starting with hard questions.

'Everything is in my report.' The kidon scratched his stubble and looked away from Zeb's steady gaze.

'I know. I read it. I have to ask you these questions, however. It is how investigations work. You were tailing a Russian arms dealer in New York?'

'Yes. Mattias, Cale and me. Groshky, the Russian, has

sold arms to Hamas in the past. We have tried to catch him in the act but failed. We thought he was in New York for another deal, which is why we were following him.'

'When did you hear about the assassinations?'

'That evening. We turn cell phones off when we are on a mission. We checked them at our hotel, caught up on the news, and by then, the ramsad had recalled us.'

He scratched his neck and fidgeted in his chair, not making eye contact.

His behavior doesn't mean anything. Some of the best agents I know don't look directly at another person.

'New York to Tel Aviv is about twelve hours. You could have come the previous day, killed those Palestinians, stayed back in Jerusalem and shown up as if you just landed after Levin summoned you back.'

Abraham stiffened. 'What are you implying?' he barked, meeting Zeb's eyes for the first time.

'That you could be the killer. Just because you were in America proves nothing.'

'I am sitting here,' Abraham hissed through gritted teeth, 'just because the ramsad asked me to cooperate with you. That doesn't mean I have to listen to wild accusations. I did not kill—'

His hand shot to his pocket and brought out his cell phone. He looked at it, his brows drawing together in astonishment.

'I have to go,' he rose abruptly and walked away without a backward glance.

'Abraham—'

'Later,' the kidon shot over his shoulder and broke into a run.

Zeb stared at him, puzzled. He waved the approaching server away, still wondering. A sudden premonition hit him.

He checked his cell phone. Brought up his GPS tracker app. Narrowed his eyes when he saw the green dots for Beth and Meghan moving rapidly.

Too rapidly. As if they were jumping … or fighting!

He swore under his breath and broke out into a run, following Abraham.

The plan had been simple. Zeb would interview Abraham while the sisters broke into the kidon's apartment. They would bug it, make copies of his computer's hard drive and make clones of any cell phone they found. Zeb would ask him for his personal device and, if the operative carried it with him, make a copy of it. They figured the overt and covert operations, working in tandem, had a better chance of either clearing operatives of identifying suspects.

The plan was good. Abraham lived alone and was single, so there was no danger of encountering a partner in his apartment.

The sisters, wearing jeans, jackets and trainers, entered Abraham's building. Once they reached his floor, unchecked by any person or security system, they looked for security cameras. They found none.

They pulled on thick, dark vests over their jackets and masks over their faces. They looked the way they wanted to be seen, as burglars of indeterminable gender.

Meghan picked the lock while Beth kept watch. They entered noiselessly and surveyed the apartment. Simple, almost spartan. A wicker chair in one corner, a glass coffee table that had the remains of dinner on it, cane furniture to another side. A TV on the wall next to the door, playing a news channel, sound muted.

They broke off, Meghan going to one bedroom to the left, while Beth took the kitchen and the other rooms to the right.

They were fifteen minutes into their search when a fist pounded on the door.

'Abe!' a voice called out from outside.

Meghan rushed to the living room and looked across at her sister. They weren't anticipating visitors. Levin's notes on Abraham were clear. The operative was a loner, and visitors to his apartment were very rare.

Zeb said he would keep the man occupied for at least an hour. The thought raced through Meghan's mind as she considered escape options. The apartment was on the third floor, one window facing the street, the others looking over an inside yard.

Busy time of the day. Traffic and pedestrians outside. Can't go out of the street window. They didn't know the building's layout and couldn't risk scaling down to the courtyard.

'Abe!' another voice yelled and the door shuddered as fists pounded on it.

'Hide!' Meghan whispered and was ducking back to the bedroom when the door opened.

Two men framed in it, their laughter dying away, their eyes squinting at the masked figures in the living room.

Mattias and Cale. She recognized them immediately.

Something flew from Mattias's hand straight toward her. She ducked instinctively, and the wine bottle that he had thrown crashed into the wall behind her. Before she could recover, the kidon was on her, smashing into her ribs. She went down, catching a glimpse of Beth and the other operative grappling furiously.

They reacted so fast, she thought dimly as she tried to

evade her attacker's blows. *They would. They're Mossad.* She couldn't risk calling out to Beth. *Nor can we allow ourselves to be unmasked.* They wanted to maintain the cover that Epstein was operating alone.

Mattias jabbed at Meghan's neck. She jerked her head away at the last minute but wasn't fast enough. His knuckles dug deep in her throat, dimming her vision, leaving her breathless.

And with that came rage. She and Beth had trained with the best. She wasn't going to allow a kidon to beat her.

She twisted her hips to throw him off-balance and gouged an elbow deep into his side. His teeth were bared as he struggled to get his fingers under her mask and rip it off.

She met his hard eyes and widened her eyes and smiled. He faltered for a fraction of a second. She headbutted him viciously, breaking his nose, and with another furious gouge to his ribs threw him to the floor.

Meghan went on the attack, raining blows on him, risking a swift glance to see that Beth was holding her own against Cale. *We need to overpower them and knock them out. We can then get away.*

The hard edge of her palm slammed into Mattias's neck. The kidon reacted by rearing his legs up and slamming his knees into her back. She fell forward but didn't ease her hold over him.

She had drawn her fist back, aiming for his neck, when something slammed into her and sent her sprawling to the floor.

Chapter 43

———∞∞∞———

Jerusalem
Four days after Assassinations
Seven Days to Announcement

Zeb raced through the streets of Jerusalem, swerving around tourists, shoving away slower-moving pedestrians.

Someone else must have been in the apartment. Or arrived when the twins broke in.

Abraham had a start of just a few minutes. There! Zeb could see the kidon's back. He was running swiftly, a hand cupped to his ear.

Calling whoever is in the apartment? Getting reinforcements?

Zeb leaped over a crouching mother, who was tending to her baby. Felt her startled glance. Called out a hasty *sorry* and powered forward. He had to reach the operative before he altered the equation in the apartment. *That's assuming the sisters haven't been overpowered.*

He checked his phone. The green dots were still moving rapidly, randomly. *They're fighting.*

Abraham turned left. Zeb followed a minute later. A quieter street. Less obstruction. He could move faster. A right, and another right, and then the kidon disappeared into a building's entrance. He was so focused on his task that he didn't hear Zeb, nor did he sense his follower.

Zeb entered the building. Empty lobby. The elevator was rising. He took the stairs. Left hand on the balustrade to guide him initially, two steps at a time.

First-floor landing reached. Empty. He carried on, listening intently for shouts or gunshots. He heard none. He lost speed when he removed his backpack, unzipped his jacket and put it back on inside-out, so it was now a different color. He drew out a mask from his backpack and pulled it over his face. *Hopefully that'll be enough to fool Abraham that I am not Epstein.*

He slowed further when he reached the third floor. Opened the landing door carefully. No one visible. Entered it and then burst into motion when he saw the kidon's apartment was open.

He took everything in instantly.

Yells of rage from men. Meghan on the floor, Abraham and another man over her. Beth had her right hand around the neck of another man, who was raining blows on her with his free hands. Both women masked. Neither making any sound. Abraham moved. His hand drew back to punch Meghan's face.

Zeb drew his Glock with blurring speed. He shot over Abraham's head, the report echoing in the apartment. Everyone froze.

'Move away,' he ordered gutturally, deepening his voice deliberately.

The three kidon—he recognized the other two attackers—looked at him. They didn't move.

He fired again, this time aiming just over Abraham's shoulder. '*MOVE!*'

The operative got up and stood to one side. Mattias joined him. Beth released her attacker and pushed him away. The sisters kept clear of his firing line and came to his side.

'Who are you?' Abraham asked menacingly.

'Go to the bedroom.'

None of the operatives moved.

'You can't outrun a bullet,' Zeb grated.

The kidon remained where they were.

Zeb shot Abraham in his left thigh. The operative cried out in shock and anger, jerking from the impact. His friends grabbed him as he started falling and dragged him to the bedroom.

'Shut the door.'

They radiated hostility as they obeyed him.

The next moment, Zeb and the sisters were out of the apartment, slamming the door behind them.

They took the stairs, leaping down swiftly, two at a time. None of them speaking as Zeb holstered his weapon. They reached street level, zigged and zagged through passages, people scattering out of their way, cries of alarm following them.

They reached a crowded market and slowed. Used the cover of a van to pull the masks off. Zeb nodded in the direction of a few restaurants. They went to separate establishments and into their restrooms.

They emerged ten minutes later wearing no disguise. The sisters had changed their jeans and tops; Zeb was wearing a different jacket.

They seated themselves in front of a restaurant, under an umbrella, and while Beth drew out a map of the city, Zeb placed their order.

Three tourists, taking a break for a drink while deciding which historical attraction to visit next.

'What happened?' Zeb asked, when the server placed their order and left.

Meghan's lips quirked wryly, 'Mattias and Cale happened. They had a key. They saw us and went on the attack.'

'Abraham … you,' Beth slid her shades down her nose, 'how did that happen?'

'He got something on his phone and took off suddenly. He didn't say why.'

'A call?'

'No. Must have been some security alert. Something you didn't spot.'

'Nope,' Meghan replied confidently. 'We were careful. His apartment was unprotected. Which reminds me,' she reached into her pocket and brought out her cell phone. Her eyes glinted in mischief as she brought up an app and put the device on speaker.

'*Who were they?*' a voice asked angrily.

Abraham! Zeb recognized his voice immediately. 'You bugged him?' he asked in surprise.

'Yeah,' Meghan chuckled, and paused the recording. 'There was one moment when my hand got caught in my jeans pocket. I used that opportunity to slip out the bug and insert it in his back pocket.'

'And I have this,' Beth said triumphantly, as she fished out a cell phone and placed it on the table. 'Cale's. It was on the floor. Must have fallen when we were fighting.'

These two are something. Zeb shook his head in amazement. 'What can I say!'

'A lot,' Beth grinned. 'That you need us. Without us you are helpless. Shall I keep going?'

He raised his hands in surrender and nodded at Meghan. She pressed play.

'*How do we know?*' a voice replied to Abraham, equally angry. '*They were masked. We weren't sitting around chatting.*'

'*Did they say anything?*'

'*No.*'

'*Did Groshky make us? In America? Could he have sent people after us?*'

'*It is possible. But we were careful and he would have to move very fast. No, this felt like a burglary,*' the same voice replied. '*Let's get you to a hospital.*'

'*No need,*' the other kidon spoke. '*The round grazed his thigh. It is a shallow wound. We go to the hospital, there will be unnecessary records. We can treat this at home.*'

'*That okay with you, Abraham?*'

'*Yes. It hurts, but not that much. I was angrier that he shot me. We need to find out who these three were. The ramsad needs to know as well. Where did that third person come from?*'

'*They must have posted a lookout. He saw you coming and followed you.*'

'*We should search the apartment. See what's missing. They could have planted bugs.*'

'*I don't think they had time. From their reaction, we had caught them soon after their entry.*'

'*I agree with Mattias. They didn't have time. We'll search in any case, but I am sure we will find nothing. He's right about the burglary, too. That shooter, he could have killed us. He didn't.*'

Zeb looked up when he felt the sisters' eyes on him. He nodded. The last speaker had been Cale. They could now put names to the voices.

There were sounds of movement. Metal clinked. Abraham groaned.

'They're cleaning his wound,' Beth murmured.

'How did your interview go? With Epstein?' Mattias asked.

'I don't know why the ramsad wants this man to interview us,' Abraham replied angrily. 'Why would we kill those Palestinians? Besides, he polygraphed us. What more does he want?'

'He is doing his job,' Cale said sharply. 'If I was in his position, I would do the same. If there's a traitor in Mossad's ranks, he needs to be found. By any and all means.'

'I thought you didn't like these negotiations,' Abraham goaded.

'Yes. Neither do you nor Mattias. I am sure the ramsad knows our views. Since Mossad does regular psych evals on us, we must be at the top of the possible suspects list.'

'You seem to be okay with this Epstein's interviews.'

'I am. So should you be, and any other kidon. The sooner he finds the traitors or clears all of us, the better for all of us.'

'What did Epstein ask you?' Mattias broke in, playing peacemaker.

'He said Tel Aviv was just twelve hours away from New York. I could have come the previous day, killed the Palestinians—'

'The three of us were together the day of the killings.'

'That's what I am angry about,' Abraham exploded. 'It is in our report. Each one of us is the other's witness. We aren't the killers.'

'What would you do in the ramsad or Epstein's place?' Cale asked. 'Would you believe the report? Or carry out an independent investigation?'

A long silence fell, broken only by the sounds of breathing and movement.

'What else did he ask?' Mattias resumed.

'I left.' Abraham was clearly embarrassed. 'I remembered you and Cale were coming over.'

'You left Epstein just like that?'

'Yes.' An awkward silence fell.

'What's going on here?' Cale asked, perplexed.

Mattias sighed, 'You might as well know, now. Abraham and I were planning a surprise party for you. Happy birthday, buddy.' There was the sound of palms smacking. 'Abraham was to arrange a cake. Clearly, he forgot.'

'I did,' Abraham admitted.

Zeb reached out and hit pause.

'That's why he bolted from my interview.'

'Yeah. That ...' Meghan pointed to her phone. 'That recording clears them, right?'

'It does. I'll still go through the motions of the interview. It'll be interesting to see what Abraham says when he meets me again.'

His phone buzzed. He checked the number and took the call.

'Yes, ma'am?'

He listened for a moment and nodded. 'I'll be there.'

'Alice Monash, the ambassador,' he told the sisters, who were regarding him quizzically.

'She wants to meet.'

Chapter 44

Jerusalem
Four days after Assassinations
Seven Days to Announcement

'We're not leaving your side,' Meghan insisted as she and Beth hurried along with Zeb.

He had asked them to look into other operatives they could investigate while he met the ambassador. The twins had refused point-blank. Beth had held up her screen when he pointed out that they could research the kidon while he was away.

'You have a knack of getting into trouble without us,' she had said, winking at him.

He gave up trying when he looked at Meghan and heard her response.

'What does she want?' the older sister asked, matching his pace.

'No idea. I didn't meet her today to escort her to the hotel. Maybe that upset her.'

'Ha!' Beth snorted in disbelief.

The sisters hadn't met the ambassador but had heard of her. They knew she wasn't that petty.

'Zeb?' Meghan raised her hand to get his attention. 'What happens if we don't clear all the Mossad operatives before Cantor and Baruti's press conference?'

'Bad things, for sure,' he replied grimly. 'Regardless of what's declared, hard-liners on both sides will say each leader let their country down. Cantor or Baruti, even both, could lose their governments.'

'If that happens, any announcement would be meaning-less,' Beth panted as she skipped to keep up with them.

'Yes. And I think rioting would break out … that would apply more pressure on the two countries, until one or both took a step back.'

'That doesn't make much sense,' Meghan argued. 'What if the two announced a breakthrough peace deal?'

'There *were* negotiations between the two countries previously.'

'Five years back? Facilitated by our then secretary of state?'

'Yeah. There was hope, then. Despite world support, those talks collapsed and then there wasn't the backdrop of assas-sinated Palestinians. Look around you,' he said, pointing to a group of Israeli protesters holding placards condemning the prime minister. 'This region is on the brink of war. Each day, an Islamic nation makes a statement. That Israel should produce the killers or accept the consequences. In the Middle East,' he ran his fingers through his hair in frustration, 'you don't negotiate with the other party. You negotiate with history and your perception of it.'

'Cantor and Baruti want to rewrite history. That's all I can say.' Alice Monash looked at them from her rear seat.

They were sitting in her car, in Beit Aghion's car park. She had hugged Beth and Meghan when Zeb introduced them as his co-workers, saying, 'I'm glad you're here. Someone needs to watch his back.' At which the younger sister had smirked.

Her ambassadorial mask had come on when Meghan had pressed her for details on the press conference.

'You called us, ma'am?' Zeb reminded her. He knew prying any details out of her would be unsuccessful. He had tried.

'Yes. You know the nuclear scenario—'

'Not finding the killers in time? Yes, ma'am. We were discussing it on the way here.'

'Prime Minister Cantor thinks he has a way to defuse the situation if that happens.' She smiled slightly. 'It was your friend Levin who suggested it, in fact.'

'What's that?'

She took a deep breath. 'I will talk to all his coalition partners. Especially the hard-liners. I will also go to the West Bank and similarly convince them, too.'

'They will be convinced?'

Her tone hardened. 'The United States is fully behind Cantor and Baruti. The two countries have no choice but to progress the negotiations. There is no alternative. The U.S. would not like it at all if the coalitions in both countries collapsed. I am convinced the various parties will listen to me. They will put off their saber-rattling. We are a powerful ally to have.'

'And an enemy to be feared,' Beth said.

Zeb looked away, thinking. Faint sounds of traffic came

through the toughened windows. An armed guard walked past, giving their vehicle a long look.

'It could work,' he said, finally.

'And that's the reason I called you. You don't need to escort me from the embassy tomorrow. I will be at the Knesset all day. However, I would like it if you were there at the hotel in the evening.'

'We'll be there, ma'am.'

'And Zeb?'

He paused as he was climbing out of the vehicle.

'It will be better if you find something before the announcement.' 1

They went back to Zeb's hotel, where Beth and Meghan also got rooms. They gathered in his, with the twins getting to work immediately. Screens on the small table, steaming coffee mugs, headsets over their ears.

Zeb texted Abraham to set up another meeting.

Busy today, the kidon replied curtly. *Tomorrow*.

He reached for Meghan's phone and played the bug's recording. It continued for several more minutes from the last pause and then ended abruptly on a *'What's that?'*

'They were going to discuss it sooner or later,' Beth shrugged. 'I checked Cale's phone. He *was* in the U.S. Nothing on his cell. Texts to his mother in Tel Aviv, various messages to friends, including one on-and-off girlfriend.'

'Meir's files.' Meghan held a finger up to silence her sister. 'Werner has decrypted some of them. Details of a house purchase, mortgage, car loans, financial records. All that seems to fit into his earnings. No irregular payments.'

'You can access his bank records?' Zeb's eyebrows raised.

'All his bank statements are on file. He might have other accounts, but these are clean.'

'We can't—'

'I know. He's still a suspect. Why don't you interview Cale and Mattias today? We'll check out the houses of other operatives.'

That's what Zeb did.

Somewhere in the Middle East

The handler was restless. He knew Magal and Shiri were going to check out the hotel tomorrow. He had tried cautioning them but had been met with cold silence. Which was message enough. They were the operatives, not he.

No, that wasn't the reason he was restless, however. Peter Raskov was troubling him.

He had turned the FSB agent a while back. The Russian kept feeding him useful intel in return for large contributions to a Swiss bank account. It was a mutually beneficial relationship. One that became very significant when Raskov turned up in Amman, too, tailing Gaber.

The handler reacted swiftly when he learned of Raskov's involvement. He called the Israelis and told them about his plan. Gaber could be their alibi. They agreed.

His next call was to the Russian, and after a little convincing and a lot of cash, the FSB double agent was on board.

It went down like clockwork. Magal and Shiri reported that Epstein, the Israeli investigator, had bought their stories. Raskov's photographs had helped.

The Russian had scented his opportunity, however. He demanded more money and threatened to go to Mossad if the handler didn't deliver.

The handler didn't like threats. He made his decision. Raskov had outlived his usefulness. He had to be taken out.

Problem was, who would do it? His own teams were busy, in different countries.

He fingered his paperweight again and thought through his various options.

There was only one that would deliver a quick result.

He didn't like making the call, but he had to.

Magal answered his call.

'There's a problem,' the handler said.

Chapter 45

─────◦◊◊◦─────

Jerusalem
Five days after Assassinations
Six Days to Announcement

Zeb's interviews with Cale and Mattias the previous evening had been straightforward, and he didn't spend much time with them. They had cleared themselves inadvertently, courtesy of Meghan's bug.

He had also had the chance to interview three more kidon: Iram, Gabe and Sinon, all three members of the second khuli-yot that had been in the U.S.

He met them together, spent an hour with them, throwing questions at them, and then spent an hour each with them separately. Four hours of interrogation, out of which he got vehement denials that they were the killers.

He also got copies of their laptop hard drives. He didn't get their cell phone data. Gabe and Sinon told him they didn't have personal devices. That they used the Mossad phones for their private use, too. They readily handed over those devices.

Iram said his was back at his apartment. He would make a

copy of its data and send it to Epstein. He smiled as he spoke, knowing why his interrogator wanted the copy.

Beth and Meghan checked out the apartments of all three while Zeb was questioning them. Gabe's was in Talpiyot, Iram's was in Tel Arza, and Sinon's was in Nayot.

The sisters had to crisscross the city to investigate the residences and as a result didn't have time to break into them. They did plant surveillance cameras outside, however.

The day had ended with question marks remaining over the three men and Meir. Meghan hadn't been able to crack open all his files.

'Why not ask them directly?' Meghan regarded Zeb over her glass of juice. 'Ask all the remaining operatives to submit their personal cell phones.'

They were gathered in Zeb's room again. Breakfast, which was sparse. A few slices of bread, bacon, juice. They had a busy day ahead and none of them wanted to indulge in a full spread.

'We can.' Zeb buttered a slice. 'The problem is, if any of them are the killers, they would have anticipated such a move. They'll provide a fake phone and we'll have no way of knowing. Which is why I was breaking into apartments.'

'Now,' he shrugged, 'we are running out of time. Let's do it. Ask them to send their cell phone data. And break into their apartments as well. I have asked Meir to meet me today. We can start with him.'

'Werner's found nothing on any of them. Nothing incriminating.' Beth swallowed quickly and went into a coughing fit. 'Which proves nothing, I know,' she continued when she had recovered. 'However, our best case might be to go back to Levin with a probability, based on what Werner's found, what's in their laptop files …'

'Yeah, that's what I was planning to do—'

His phone rang. Alice Monash.

'Yes, ma'am?'

'I need some dirt on Jaedon Haber. And I want you at the Knesset.'

Knesset

Zeb took fifteen minutes to reach Givat Ram, the neighborhood where the Israeli legislature was based. He had left as soon as he got the ambassador's call.

'There go our plans,' he had told the sisters with a wry smile. They were already busy, heads down, looking into Jaedon Haber once he had relayed the ambassador's instructions.

'You know why she wants this? And why she wants you? She didn't mention any politician yesterday,' Beth enquired.

'No. She doesn't speak much on the phone.'

Zeb knew Haber was the leader of One Israel, a political party that was in the coalition with Prime Minister Yago Cantor. He didn't know anything else. *No doubt Beth or Meghan will enlighten me.*

Operatives had to adapt to changed circumstances. That's what Zeb and the sisters did on receiving the ambassador's call. The twins would look up Haber and get back to Zeb. If time permitted, they would check out the apartments of all the remaining kidon while Zeb met with Alice Monash. As for Meir, he would have to be rescheduled.

Zeb paid off the cab and looked up when a whistle caught his attention. Bob, from the ambassador's security detail.

255

Zeb spared a moment to admire the imposing rectangular building of the Knesset and then hurried over to join the American.

'She's waiting inside,' Bob said, jerking a shoulder at the legislature. 'Here,' he handed Zeb a card dangling off a lanyard. 'You're good to go. Security cleared. Don't ask me how she managed that.'

'Do you know—'

'Nope,' Bob replied and gestured at Zeb to proceed toward the security hut.

The ambassador was waiting for him in a small room in the interior of the building. She looked at him expectantly when he entered, as Bob stationed himself outside.

'You've got—'

'Zeb?' Meghan, over his earpiece, her excitement apparent. He held a finger up to excuse himself.

'Yeah, go on,' he answered in a low voice.

'Haber's uncle, his father's brother, has a real estate business in New York. He was accused by his competitors of illegal business practices. Money laundering as well. The FBI looked into it but nothing came to light. Those same competitors said Haber, the uncle, had bought off the investigators.'

'Keep looking.'

'Gotcha.'

The ambassador smiled grimly when Zeb conveyed the information. She caught his arm and led him out of the room.

'What's this about, ma'am?' Zeb slowed so she could keep pace.

'You have heard of Haber?'

'Just that he's the prime minister's ally.'

'He is that. He's also bitterly opposed to any negotiations with Palestinians. He regards them as the enemy and says, as long as Palestine is around, Israel will be at war.'

'He's a hard-liner?'

'Very. Unfortunately, he also wields substantial power. His party has eleven MKs, Members of Knesset. He has threatened to withdraw support to Cantor if the prime minister doesn't stop these negotiations.'

'What's all that got to do with me?'

''I am meeting him right now. To show him the power of the United States. I had a call with the prime minister in the morning. He said mere threats, which is what I was thinking of, wouldn't work. That's why I called you.'

'I got that, ma'am. I get why you need dirt on him, but why me?'

The ambassador laughed. 'You, Zeb Carter, are the FBI's Special Investigator, looking into the Haber family's suspected money laundering.'

Chapter 46

⸙

Jerusalem
Five days after Assassinations
Six Days to Announcement

Jaedon Haber was short, stocky and white-haired. His black suit fit him poorly, but he didn't seem to be one interested in sartorial elegance. He wasn't a man who stood still. He paced, he waved his hands, he grimaced.

'Ambassador,' he greeted Alice Monash with a firm shake of the hand, 'it is an honor to meet you.' His belligerent voice indicated it was anything but an honor. He ignored Zeb; clearly, anyone who looked like an underling was of no interest to the politician.

Alice Monash greeted him and began to make small talk. The politician wasn't interested. He cut her off with a shake of his head.

'You asked to meet me, Ambassador, at short notice. Can we get down to it?'

'We can,' she said, and just then the door opened to admit Prime Minister Yago Cantor.

'Yago, I didn't know you would be here.'

'I wasn't expecting to be, Jaedon, but when Alice summons, who am I to refuse?' He shook the ambassador's hand and cast a quizzical look at Zeb.

'If you're here to persuade me to support the prime minister,' Haber snapped, his brows twitching angrily, 'you have wasted your time, Ambassador. I intend to table a no-confidence motion in—'

'Jaedon, surely we can talk—' the prime minister interrupted.

'Talk!' the One Israel leader flared. 'That's what has gotten us to this state. If you hadn't initiated those talks, those Palestinians wouldn't be dead.'

'You want us to keep fighting with them? With our neighbors? Forever?'

'They're the ones who are bombing our people.'

'Enough!' Alice Monash's voice was steel. Her eyes flashed dangerously. 'Haber, these negotiations will proceed whether you like them or not. The United States supports them fully. So do the British, the French and numerous other governments.'

'In that case, this government will fall. I have enough support to enable that,' the party leader said, wagging his finger menacingly.

'You won't.'

'Who's stopping me?'

'I am. Or rather, the FBI. This man,' the ambassador nodded her head in Zeb's direction, 'is investigating your family. They believe you and your uncle are laundering money. You stifled a previous investigation. If you persist—'

'LIES!' Haber thundered. An aide poked his head into the

room and withdrew it hastily when four heads turned in his direction. 'My uncle runs a clean business. You are misusing your position, Ambassador, with these threats. I will write to the president immediately. I will ask him to remove you from your position.'

'*Zeb*,' Meghan whispered. '*We have found an account in the Caymans. Connected to the Habers. We haven't checked the money trail in and out of it, but it looks shady.*'

'Mr. Haber,' Zeb uttered his first words since entering the room.

Everyone fell silent and looked at him.

'This number mean anything to you?' he recited a ten-digit figure.

The One Israel party leader blanched. His fingers trembled.

'You and your uncle are signatories to that account. You should have covered your trail better.'

'How did you—' Haber started to bluster.

'Enough,' Zeb said coldly. 'You're done talking. It's time to listen to the Ambassador.'

An hour later, Alice Monash and Zeb were alone with the prime minister in another room. Cantor looked weary and yet relieved as he sipped the coffee an aide served them.

Haber had heard the ambassador out and nodded just once before leaving the room, a broken man.

'I can't thank you enough, Alice. One Israel has been a thorn in my side for quite some time. But it isn't the only one. You need to work your magic with my other coalition partners and then do the same with President Baruti's.'

'One win at a time, Yago.' Alice Monash raised her cup in a silent toast.

'How did you wrangle that?'

'I didn't,' she replied drily, 'the FBI did.'

Cantor looked at Zeb, who was leaning against the wall, arms crossed on his chest.

'FBI, huh? What's your name, agent?'

Zeb straightened and grabbed the card dangling from the lanyard. *Rookie mistake. I should have looked at the name the ambassador made out for me.*

'Tom,' Alice Monash spared him his blushes. 'Special Agent Tom Brown.'

'Tom Brown,' Cantor's eyes twinkled. 'That's an original name. I have to say, Alice, I haven't come across any FBI agent looking like him.'

He's right. I'm wearing jeans and a jacket.

'Especially one who speaks Hebrew like him. Like a native of Israel.'

He kept looking at Zeb, his gaze sharpening. 'Agent Brown ... you must know Avichai Levin well.'

'Levin, sir? I don't know anyone by that name.'

The prime minister looked at him with hooded eyes and nodded to himself once. 'Now I know,' he said mysteriously and turned to the ambassador. 'When are your next meetings, Alice?'

'Right away. We need to get going.'

It was nearing five pm by the time they headed back to the hotel. They had met two more leaders, and with each of them, the ambassador had been firm. Their parties needed to support the prime minister, or else face the wrath of the United States. Both leaders had caved in without Special Agent Tom Brown needing to speak a word.

'The next one won't be this easy,' Alice Monash told Zeb

as they turned into the hotel's drive. 'We'll be meeting Omet Zeev, leader of the Jewish Party of Israel. I'll need you to find anything you can get on him.'

'Ma'am, you didn't need to come to us for this. There are enough agencies back home to help you.'

'Yeah. But none who will work this fast. And none whom I know so well.'

Zeb didn't reply. He knew Clare and Alice Monash were good friends. *In any case, Clare has asked me to help her. Directive from the president.*

'Wish me luck, Zeb.' The ambassador stepped out of the vehicle and adjusted her suit jacket. 'The negotiators are nervous. They follow the news. They know the political situation in both countries is tense.'

'Sweet-talk them, ma'am. If that doesn't do the job … Special Agent Tom Brown is available.'

'Is everyone in place?' Abdul Masih asked. He was in his ambulance, heading toward the hotel. His lieutenant was next to him, the grenade launcher in the rear.

'Yes, sayidi,' came a voice over his cell phone. 'You give the signal and the suicide bombers will drive. The fighters will follow.'

'How many of them?'

'Four in the car. A dozen gunmen.'

'Remember, both teams have to act only on my signal, not before.'

'They will, sayidi.'

Magal parked their car between a Ford and a Peugeot. He stepped out and joined Shiri on the pavement. Both were in disguise. Long hair falling to their shoulders, colorful shirts over jeans, padding in their cheeks and around their waists. They didn't look anything like lean Mossad operatives.

The two looked at the hotel. They could see a few armed guards outside, as was the case with all hotels on Emek Refaim. From their earlier surveillance they knew more security would be present inside.

If the handler's intel is right.

'It will be,' Shiri replied, and only then realized he had spoken aloud.

The two men walked quickly without drawing attention to themselves. They scanned the various vehicles on the street, both parked and rolling. No one looked at them.

An ambulance jostled behind a bus and parked behind another hospital vehicle. A car door opened and slammed shut somewhere, the sound loud.

'He's there,' Shiri spoke from the side of his mouth. 'That man we saw with the ambassador.'

Magal looked in the direction his partner was discreetly pointing.

Yes, there he was. The American, if he was that. Leaning against a vehicle, talking to someone inside, hands crossed across his chest, facing the hotel.

'Should we proceed?' Shiri asked.

'Yes, we should go.'

'Go!' Masih shouted in his cell phone.

Chapter 47

---ᐤᐤᐤ---

Jerusalem
Five days after Assassinations
Six Days to Announcement

'We're behind you, third car in the line,' Meghan directed Zeb. She and Beth had rented an SUV and driven to the hotel to meet him there.

A Range Rover. Good choice. It would be noticeable but was sturdy and would withstand wear. *Not that I am expecting any action.*

Beth saluted him from the passenger seat and bent her head back to the screen on her lap. It was always that way. Meghan drove, Beth the passenger.

'You got any kidon work done?' he leaned in through the window and fist-bumped Meghan.

'Not much,' she grunted in disappointment. 'Your last request, to find something on Omet Zeev, took time. We didn't find much on him. A few bank accounts in a few places. But he has a mistress,' her eyes danced. 'In Tel Aviv. He visits her every week.'

'That will be useful,' Zeb said automatically as he scanned the lines of vehicles. All but the Range Rover seemed to be empty. *No, that ambulance there. Movement inside it.* He shrugged. An EMS vehicle was of no use if it was unattended. *The police will surely have checked it out.*

'You're expecting trouble?' Beth sensed his unease.

'Nope. But I wish the ambassador stopped coming here. There are too many targets under one roof in there.'

I don't like this location. The two hotels have a common carpark, which is okay. It is in the basement, which is good. But the entry and exit are on the same side as the street entrance.

A dark opening to the right of the negotiators' hotel was the parking lot's approach.

'As I was saying,' Meghan drawled, 'on the other operatives: Werner cracked all of Meir's files. It turns out he has location-tracking activated on it and carried the machine with him on missions. He's clear, too.'

'I'll still talk to him.' Zeb was still looking at the hotel, the street, traffic, taking in security arrangements.

Two men strolled past him, their heads bent, turned away from him. He stifled a smile when he noticed their shirts. *It's not Hawaii. But what do I know about current-day fashion?*

Three armed guards were at each hotel's entrance. There was thick evening traffic on Emek Refaim. Office workers heading home.

'You're wearing armor?'

'Always.' Beth shut down her screen and looked at her sister, who raised her shoulders and shook her head. Zeb's disquiet was rubbing off on them.

It was a faint tickle at the base of Zeb's spine. A premonition. Over the years he had learned to pay attention to it.

Often, it turned out to be nothing. But on a few occasions, it had meant the arrival of a hostile presence.

Can't spot anything off here. I am jumpy. And tired. Nothing more than that.

An engine revved in the distance. *Some car enthusiast.*

He watched as the car came racing down Emek Refaim, finding gaps in traffic, squeezing through it. French make, dark windows, the windshield reflecting light, preventing him from seeing who was inside. He could make out heads bobbing inside.

Looks like three or four people.

He and the twins were to the left of the hotel's entrance. The car was approaching them, no flashers lighting up. He turned his attention away and leaned against the Range Rover, crossed his arms.

'You want to hear a joke?' Beth attempted to lighten his mood.

'Go on.'

The car roared. It overtook a slower moving vehicle, dangerously. Angry honks sounded. Curses flew in the air.

It didn't go straight on.

It turned in to the hotel, tires squealing.

The security guards straightened. A doorman came running out, hands outstretched. He went down, his body jerking when an assault rifle appeared in the vehicle's window and chattered.

Zeb's breath escaped him in shock. He stood motionless for a moment, watching the car race toward the entrance. The three armed men at the glass doors fired and then went down as more rifles burst from the car and shot at them.

'Follow me.' He snapped out of his shock, training and experience taking over.

He knew what the occupants of the car planned. It came out of a Middle Eastern terrorist's textbook.

He sprinted toward the hotel on the left, drawing his Glock out.

'Get away,' he yelled at the men in the flowery shirts and fired at the vehicle.

The car kept going. It shuddered and rattled as it climbed the steps, but didn't stop.

Zeb heard footsteps behind him. Snapped a quick glance behind. The sisters, faces intent, sprinting.

Screams from the street. Yells and shouts.

That's Arabic! He spun on a heel and his gut clenched.

About a dozen armed men had exploded out of parked cars. They were in long, loose robes, all chanting, turning their weapons to the hotel, firing indiscriminately.

A car packed with explosives—he was sure of that—behind him, killers facing him.

Sight was action.

The sisters fanned out, clearing his firing line. They kept shooting at the car, still running toward the hotel.

Zeb snapped several shots at the oncoming gunmen. Two fell. Some turned their attention toward him and the sisters, but the majority were firing at the hotel's glass doors, murderous rage in their eyes.

Zeb ducked when a round whizzed past. He swerved and ran toward the wall separating the two courtyards. The sisters followed him.

He leapt across the divider, lost his balance and fell.

And that saved him. A round smacked into concrete, passing through the air he had occupied. He rolled and kept moving. And then he was up, running toward the dark entrance of the parking lot.

'Why there?' Meghan yelled.

'*That's where the ambassador, the negotiators will be evacuated.*'

Yells behind him. He took a long step, whirled in the air to look back, saw a few shooters follow, snapped off shots and then he was landing, gathering his balance and dashing toward the cover of the car park.

It was darker inside. Ceiling lights casting a glow. Several vehicles. All seemed empty.

Meghan and Beth separated. Took positions. One sister behind a concrete pillar, the other crouching behind a vehicle. Aiming, shooting down the approaching terrorists.

Zeb moved from vehicle to vehicle, checking that each one was empty. There was a door to the elevators in the distance. It burst open even as he watched. Two armed men burst through. They spotted him, raised their weapons.

'MOSSAD,' he shouted instinctively in his command voice. 'You are police?'

'Yes.'

'What's the situation.'

A loud *whump* silenced them all.

The building shook. The ground trembled. Cars shuddered, their alarms going off. Dust fell from the ceiling. A chunk of concrete loosened and fell on a car.

Zeb looked back at Meghan. Her eyes were dark, haunted. As was Beth's.

They all knew what had happened.

The car bomb had exploded in the adjacent building.

A very powerful one. Even this hotel shook.

'Keep watch outside,' he told the sisters. 'You,' he directed the guards. 'keep that door open. Stand on either side of it. Any hostile shows, shoot without question.'

They nodded, accepting his orders without question.

'You have radio contact with the other security personnel?'

'Lost it a few moments back.'

'Go!'

The officers positioned themselves next to the elevator's entrance.

Zeb thought quickly, working out threat vectors and defense positions. The negotiators would be well protected, as would the ambassador. There would be contingency plans for just such an event. Security teams would bring them to the parking lot and exfil would be by armored vehicles.

Or so I hope.

He checked his cell phone. No signal.

'Beth, Meghan, you have enough mags?'

'Yeah,' the younger sister replied, 'enough to last a war.'

'Injuries?'

'Nah. We can outrun a bullet.'

'You came close, didn't you? To catching one,' Meghan asked in concern.

He didn't reply. He went to the entrance and peered out. No movement. Three fallen bodies, not far away.

The cops will be coming soon. IDF teams as well. Those fighters have no chance. What if, he turned cold, *they don't find the negotiators in that hotel? And they won't. Unless they know about the passage.*

They'll take hostages, he answered himself. *They might shoot indiscriminately.*

Or they might know about that passage. There would be a firefight in any case.

'Cover me,' he told the sisters and crouched low, running toward the bodies.

He grabbed their weapons and mags. He was turning back when a head popped over the wall.

Hostile!

No time to aim.

He threw himself down on his back and sprayed rounds. The head disappeared.

A barrage of fire came from behind him, pinning down the attacker, if he was still alive.

He got to his feet again, gathered the weapons and raced back to safety.

The weapons were AKs. In good condition. A spare mag with each shooter.

Meghan took one, inspected it. 'Zeb, this could be Mumbai all over again.'

Terrorists had taken over downtown hotels and buildings in Mumbai a few years back. They had shot several residents and had finally been overpowered in a shootout with cops and local SWAT teams.

Those incidents had made every law enforcement and counter-intelligence agency in the world reassess its security measures.

'I hope not.'

'*Someone's coming!*' a guard warned.

'Don't show yourself. Don't shoot unless I say so.'

They accepted his words without question.

'You,' he told the sisters, 'remain here. It's possible there could be more shooters outside, to catch us in a pincer movement.'

He ran toward the elevator. Took cover behind a vehicle

and signaled for the two guards to follow suit.

There was the sound of clattering footsteps. Screams and shouts. Indistinct orders being shouted.

Several armed men appeared. All in Israeli uniform. Behind them were a bunch of people. Panic in their faces and voices.

Zeb waited a beat. Motioned for the guards to stay quiet.

Twenty-five civilians, he counted rapidly. Ten guards. Five in front, five at the rear. He searched in the dimmer light, and his heart leapt when he spotted Bob, his two partners and, next to them, Alice Monash.

He stepped out from cover. Raised his hands immediately when guns trained on him.

'I AM WITH THE AMBASSADOR,' he said in Hebrew.

'Zeb!' Alice Monash cried out in relief. 'He's with me,' she told the Israeli security detail.

'You said you were Mossad,' the elevator guards looked at him suspiciously.

'I am not the enemy,' he thundered. 'Are these the negotiators?' he asked the nearest guards.

'Yes,' one man spoke, evidently the team leader, who clearly agreed with him that it wasn't the time to discuss who he was. If Zeb wasn't pointing a gun at them, he wasn't hostile. 'And some residents. What's the scene here?'

Zeb broke it down to them quickly. Several negotiators cried in alarm at his account.

'You will be safe,' he told them, injecting authority into his voice. He repeated the same message in Arabic. 'I guarantee it.'

'You have vehicles for them?' he asked the leader.

'Yes, and evac locations.'

'Move!'

Bob and the American security team escorted the ambassador to their vehicle. The negotiators and the residents went to six vehicles.

'You two,' Zeb pointed to the elevator guards, 'get in those vehicles.'

That way there will be two to each vehicle.

'Let the ambassador go first,' he told the team leader, who stared at him and then nodded.

'Ma'am, your vehicle will lead.' He ran to the ambassador, who lowered her window.

'No, let them—' Bob protested.

'Bob. Zeb's right.'

'Ma'am, there could be more attackers outside. We'll be the first to be hit.'

'Go!' she ordered, her lips compressed, her face white. 'Zeb, get in. Get Beth and Meghan, too.'

'No, ma'am. We'll run outside. Just in case.'

He darted away, ignoring her shouts and Bob's yells.

'Let's go,' he told Meghan and Beth.

They followed without a word, knowing instinctively what he was planning.

The three of them headed out of the parking lot, walked up the inclined driveway, weapons ready, eyes scanning the street. Sirens were wailing in the distance; armed officers had turned up and were clearing the street.

Zeb waved to the ambassador's vehicle.

It nosed out of its shelter, headlights turned on. Behind it, more lights as the other vehicles followed.

No attacker showed. An IDF man stood in the center of the street, waving at them to come through.

Zeb moved to the right, the sisters followed, allowing the vehicles to pass.

Alice Monash's vehicle reached street level, started turning left.

The door of the ambulance opened, the one Zeb had noticed. It was hundred yards away to the right.

A bearded man stepped out in EMS uniform. Another jumped out and joined him. Zeb looked at their hands. Clear.

He looked back at the vehicles, which were still moving slowly, the ambassador's ride completing its maneuver.

Something bothered him. A car honked in the distance. Sirens grew louder. And then it came to him in a flash.

Why aren't those EMS men rushing to the hotel? There must be enough dead or wounded around.

His head snapped back.

Saw both men reach inside the vehicle.

The leaner, taller one brought out something long, tubular. Zeb's eyes flew to his face.

Recognition flooded. *Abdul Masih!*

'INCOMING!' he roared a warning.

He threw himself to the ground just as the second man started firing at the vehicles.

The EQB leader started raising the launcher to his shoulder.

Zeb fired the AK. His first rounds flew wide.

The second terrorist brought his weapon downwards to bear on Zeb.

Stone chips flew at Zeb. Something grazed his cheek.

Slow down. Masih matters. Forget the other shooter.

He slowed down his breathing. Blanked out everything but the terrorist leader and his launcher. Ignored the sisters' shouts and the shooting that commenced. Everything else was white fog.

Through it, he sensed rather than saw the second gunman fall back after rounds slammed into him.

Zeb didn't pay attention.

His attention was fixed solely on Masih, who gripped the launcher firmly, steadied it and took aim.

Zeb sighted. Something slammed the side of his head. His head jerked back and something warm and wet trickled down his face. He blinked and sighted down the rifle again. He was alive. That was all that mattered.

He focused on Masih. Took a breath and let it out slowly.

The terrorist braced himself, his eyes narrow, his lips parted in a feral smile. He, too, was singularly intent on firing, ignoring the rounds aimed at him.

Breathe in.

Breathe out.

Zeb triggered at the bottom of his respiratory cycle. And this time his aim was straight and true.

Abdul Masih fell back, his body jerking spasmodically as Zeb's rounds punched into him. The grenade launcher clattered to the ground.

Sound returned, though indistinct. The world returned, slowly.

IDF personnel flooded the street. Someone hauled him up. A voice spoke urgently. He shook his head.

It repeated. He blinked rapidly. It was Meghan.

'Are you okay?' she touched his temple, her palm red, wet, when she drew it away. 'You are bleeding.'

'The ambassador?'

'She's safe. Everyone's safe.'

'*Zeb!*'

Avichai Levin came running, his face lined with worry and anger.

'It was EQB. All along, it was them. Not Mossad.'

Chapter 48

———— ✤ ————

Jerusalem
Five days after Assassinations
Six Days to Announcement

'You're hit.' Levin snapped his fingers and EMS personnel hurried across.

'A gash.' Zeb felt his temple gingerly. It hurt. He had been injured far worse. He would live. A medic clicked his tongue and started cleaning the wound. 'That's Masih?'

The ramsad followed his gaze, at the body of the man Zeb had shot. IDF and police officers milled around it, several crouching. The grenade launcher had been taken away to a military vehicle.

'That's him. Identity confirmed. The second man is Alam Qadir, the second most-wanted man in Israel. His lieutenant. Beth and Meghan shot him. They couldn't take out Masih; you were in their way.'

A chopper flew overhead, low, drowning out their voices. Zeb squinted up and saw the bird was a military one, shooters leaning out of it, searching, alert, ready. He spotted a couple

277

more in the distance. He lowered his gaze, became conscious of the ambient noise. Sirens blaring, officers barking orders, crying and screams, police and military officers thick on the ground, herding away civilians within the perimeter they had set up, keeping out curious onlookers. TV vans had rolled up; they, too, were kept outside the cordon.

It looked like a war zone.

It is war, he thought bleakly.

'Zeb!' Meghan brought him back from his thoughts. Beth was beside her. Both of them pale, their eyes wide. Beyond them, the negotiators' vehicles were tightly bunched and parked on the street, surrounded by a ring of grim-faced IDF personnel who looked as if they would shoot first, ask questions later.

'I'm fine,' he replied. 'It's nothing.'

'Not that wound,' the elder sister snapped and pointed to his leg.

Only then did he become aware of the throbbing in his left thigh. He looked down to see his jeans soaked in blood. Another medic crouched and inspected it.

'A flesh wound,' she said. 'You got lucky. The round grazed your leg, took some flesh, but it's nothing serious. We'll clean it, dress it. You might limp for a few days, but you'll be fine.'

Zeb leaned against the nearest vehicle and let the EMS staff work. 'You and Beth?' he asked softly.

'Unhurt. As good as new.' Her attempt at humor fell flat.

'If he had fired ...' Beth looked at the fallen EQB leader and shivered.

'He didn't,' Levin said decisively. He read the speculative look on Zeb's face. 'They,' he nodded at the bunch of police officers who were speaking through the lowered window of one of the vehicles, 'are taking statements from the occupants of each vehicle. Shouldn't take long. Once done, they'll be driven to a secure location. Care to tell me what happened?'

Zeb narrated the events, the sisters chiming in. The medics attending to him gaped, slammed their jaws shut and nodded their heads in assent when Levin barked, 'This remains confidential.'

'Those IDF men at the elevator. They came close to shooting you,' the Mossad director said grimly.

'I know. How many?' He voiced the question he had been dreading to ask.

Levin understood. His voice was like sandpaper. 'Eighteen civilians dead. Dozens injured. Body count not complete.'

'The terrorists?'

'All dead, those who were in the car. Seven others killed. Five in custody, of whom two are critical.'

'Where are they? The ones who are alive?'

'Some place where they will never be heard from again.'

They drove away half an hour later, following the convoy of negotiators' vehicles. They were in Levin's vehicle, his security men in the front. The ramsad was continually on his cell, listening, giving instructions.

He broke away momentarily when the ambassador's ride separated and headed to the embassy. 'Follow it,' he told his driver, and got back to his calls.

Bob rounded on Zeb once they were inside the building.

'You,' his finger shot out, 'put the ambassador at risk. Her vehicle should have been in the middle.'

'You aren't looking at the big picture.'

'I'm here to protect Ms. Monash,' Bob snarled, thrusting

his face against Zeb's.

'Bob!' Alice Monash voice's cut like a whip, 'Zeb did the right thing. If my vehicle had been fired on … that was a risk I was prepared to take. Maybe you didn't notice, but Zeb, Beth and Meghan were on foot. Way ahead of any vehicle. *They* would have been the first to be shot at. The first to be killed.'

Bob stayed where he was, his eyes burning in anger until Zeb shoved him away and went searching for a shower.

An hour later they were back in Levin's vehicle. Freshly showered, wearing clean clothing that the embassy had miraculously procured for them.

No Bob or his team. Just the four of them, the Mossad director and his security team.

'Avichai, where are we going?' the ambassador broke the silence.

'Beit Aghion.'

'The negotiators?'

'At an IDF base in the Negev desert. They can't be more secure.'

'Why weren't they based there in the first place?'

'Optics and perception. Palestine looks at Israel as a heavily militarized state. Conducting peace negotiations in an army camp … will not build a lot of trust.'

They drove through streets that had a very visible military presence. Groups of soldiers watching traffic go past, occasionally stopping cars and questioning their occupants.

'We don't know if any of the EQB men got away,' Levin answered an unvoiced question. 'Or if there are more active cells.'

'I thought Masih was in Gaza.' Zeb stretched his legs and winced when his thigh flared in agony. He caught sight of himself in the rearview mirror. He looked gaunt. His temple had been stitched; the wound was looking ugly. He had stopped the medics from applying a dressing, despite their protests. He didn't want anything around his head.

'There are tunnels,' the ramsad said bitterly, 'between Gaza and Israel. They keep digging, we keep closing the ones we find. He must have crawled through one we hadn't detected.'

'How did he know which hotel to attack?' Beth asked.

'Beats me.' Levin lowered his window when they arrived at the prime minister's residence. He showed his credentials and waited for the security personnel to complete their inspection.

Zeb lingered, along with the sisters, while Levin marched inside with Alice Monash. The director sensed their absence and turned around.

'Zeb—'

'We'll wait in the vehicle.'

'No,' he beckoned them. 'I brought you here for a reason.'

Levin took them down a hallway and nodded at a security guard outside a door, who opened it for them.

Prime Minister Yago Cantor waved them inside and waited for them to seat themselves.

'Let's start,' he said grimly.

Somewhere in the Middle East

The handler watched the Jerusalem scenes unfold on his TV, in shock. Of all the outcomes he had planned for and imagined, this wasn't one. He knew Magal and Shiri weren't involved. They were going to check out the hotel but hadn't gone through with the plan.

A TV chopper was hovering above the hotels, broadcasting live footage of Emek Refaim. A host in the studio added commentary and brought in experts.

'No one knows who the attackers are,' a talking head reported. 'The entire area is sealed. No journalist is allowed to go inside the perimeter. All cell phone signals have been blocked. The government isn't commenting.'

'There are some rumors that the negotiators were in one of those hotels.'

'I have heard those, too, but until we receive official confirmation, all this is speculation.'

More experts arrived and gave their views; some claimed that Hamas had struck, others said the attack was related to the Palestinian killings.

That gave the handler an idea. He logged into a fake social media account and posted a tweet.

MOSSAD STRIKES AGAIN. ATTACKS PALESTINIANS' HOTEL.

Over the years his cyber team had created hundreds of bots to spread fake messages. Those accounts kicked in now. They retweeted his message in rapid succession until it started trending on social media.

Ein Kerem

Magal and Shiri watched the coverage in silence. They had left the scene the moment the American had shouted at them. They, too, knew what would unfold once the car headed to the hotel. They had felt the ground move when the car bomb exploded.

'Who do you think it was?' Shiri mused, 'and did they get the negotiators?'

Magal didn't reply. He channel-surfed but found that every station was showing the same footage. 'The Israelis have clamped down on news,' he said finally. 'They'll release a statement when they are ready. And when they have come up with a story that suits them.'

'Where does this leave us?'

'We'll have to wait and see.'

Shiri's face darkened. He knew what that meant. Chances were high that they would have to act only on the day of the announcement. They had discussed that eventuality, too. It would be extremely risky but not impossible. There wasn't any security setup that couldn't be breached. At a cost. Magal and Shiri knew what price they were prepared to pay—anything that didn't involve their dying was an acceptable risk.

Magal's phone buzzed. He checked it: a text from an unknown number.

'It's the handler.' He showed the message to Shiri.

You cut short your sightseeing trip?

Yes, Magal replied. *It wasn't safe.*

Did you manage to see any attractions?

Not in enough detail. We'll have to go another day.

You can visit that other attraction until the security issue resolves.

Shiri frowned. 'What does he mean?'

'He wants me to take care of Peter Raskov.'

Chapter 49

---ꝏꝏ---

Beit Aghion, Jerusalem
Five days after Assassinations
Six Days to Announcement

'Who are these people?' Levitsky stared at Zeb and the sisters as they sat next to the ambassador.

'They are with me,' Alice Monash replied, not elaborating.

'I understand, Ambassador, but what are they doing here? Yago,' he looked for support from his leader, 'This is an internal meeting. We have allowed Ms. Monash to sit in, but surely—'

Cantor's jaw flexed as he glared at his minister. 'That's FBI Special Agent Tom Brown,' he gestured at Zeb. 'I met him earlier. He helped us in my discussion with Jaedon Haber. You know what that leader was threatening. The two ladies are the ambassador's aides. We have far bigger problems—'

'Yago,' Levitsky interrupted. 'I think this is highly unusual. We are discussing highly confidential state matters that not even the entire cabinet is privy to—'

He jumped when Cantor slammed his palm on the table.

'Jessy, I am still the prime minister of Israel. I will decide who comes into my residence and who sits in my meetings.'

Levin cleared his throat in the awkward silence that followed. 'Only the prime minister and Nadav know this. It is not something that will be disclosed to the public and should not be discussed outside this room. Brown and the two ladies took down Abdul Masih and Alam Qadir.'

Levitsky's jaw dropped. His eyes bulged and he stared at Zeb, Beth and Meghan, hostility disappearing from his face. Jore Spiro looked on with a thin, enigmatic smile on his face, as if he knew who Zeb was.

He might know, Zeb thought. *I met him several years back, on a mission when he was an active soldier.*

'You shot him?' the minister for public security whispered.

'The prime minister is right,' Zeb replied noncommittally, 'there are more important matters to discuss.'

'How did Masih know which hotel to target?' Cantor growled when Levitsky dropped the matter. 'How did he assemble people so quickly? What story do we tell the people?' A muscle in his jaw flexed. 'You have seen what's being discussed on social media. People are saying Mossad is behind the attack. I have a press conference in another hour. I need something to tell the people.'

'About the hotel, it's too early to say, Yago,' Spiro answered. 'The police are looking into the security camera footage. They are questioning everyone in the vicinity of the attack. IDF teams are canvasing the entire neighborhood.'

'Was there a leak?'

'That is a possibility—'

'There was no leak.' Heads swung toward Zeb at his emphatic reply. 'I know what happened. Masih followed the ambassador's vehicle. He put two and two together and made his plans.'

'You know this for certain?' There was a question in Levin's eyes.

He's wondering if I kept something from him.

'I'm reasonably sure.' He launched into a quick account of how he had felt after the ambassador had given her speech.

'You didn't spot anyone then?'

'No. But it wouldn't be hard for Masih to organize surveillance without being detected.'

'We didn't know he was here? Masih?' Cantor asked Levitsky.

'No, Yago.'

'We had the same intel, Prime Minister,' Levin backed up his ministerial colleague. 'That Masih was in Gaza. As to your second question, it wouldn't be difficult for him to get suicide bombers and gunmen.'

'What about my third?'

The ramsad leaned back. What story to spin was a job for politicians.

'Why don't we tell the truth?' Spiro suggested. 'That EQB was behind these attacks.'

'I can do that. But questions will arise about the previous attack. We haven't made much progress, have we?'

'No, Yago,' Levitsky admitted.

'Sir,' Levin hunched forward, 'If I can suggest?'

'Go ahead.'

'Why not claim the EQB is a suspect in the previous killings?'

Sounds of surprise echoed in the room.

'Why would the EQB kill Palestinians, Avichai?' the prime minister asked, puzzled.

'To put us in the position we are in. We are questioning our own organizations, searching for traitors. We don't know whom to trust within ourselves. Sir, there's someone smart behind these killings. Someone very smart, who knows how to use social media to their advantage. Look what's trending now. We know for sure that Mossad operatives weren't involved in this latest attack, yet we are on the backfoot.'

'You want us to play their game,' Cantor nodded, understanding dawning in his eyes. 'Nullify the misinformation they have sown. It will also buy us time.'

'More importantly—'

'Yes, Avichai.' The prime minister managed a smile despite the gravity of the situation. 'It will help us manage the coalition partners. EQB is a good target to blame. It will help President Baruti, too. He has long condemned EQB.'

'Those killers are still out there, though,' Shoshon reminded everyone. 'The ones who killed the Palestinians.'

'And they need to be found. I think they will be thrown off-guard by my statement, wondering what we are playing at … which is what Avichai wants.' He glanced at his watch and rose, his cue for ending the meeting. 'I have several calls to make. Presidents Morgan and Baruti, the British prime minister … Avichai, Alice, can you stay back? Agent Brown, you too, and the ladies.'

He clasped Zeb's shoulder when the others had left the room. 'Agent Brown, I cannot thank you enough—'

'Stop right there, sir. No thanks are needed. We happened to be at the right time and place. That's all.'

'That's not all. Avichai and Nadav briefed me on exactly what went down. You and the sisters,' he looked at the twins warmly, 'had the presence of mind…' he trailed off when he sensed Zeb's embarrassment. 'I hope you know how grateful we are.'

Zeb nodded.

'That other matter?'

'Which one, sir?'

'Finding who the Palestinians' killers are and clearing Mossad.'

Zeb shot a look to Levin, who shook his head imperceptibly.

He hasn't revealed my identity.

'Sir, I'm with the FBI—'

The prime minister silenced him with a raised hand. He looked like he hadn't slept in hours and had come off several crisis meetings. Despite that, there was a glint of humor in his eyes.

'We can drop the pretense, Zeb Carter. Avichai said I had met you a while back. He also said I wouldn't remember you. I didn't, but when he said you had found his daughter's killers … I did some checking of my own and made some calls.'

He sobered quickly. 'Let me know if there is anything you need in your investigation. Avichai's suggestion of blaming the EQB will buy us some time. But not for long. Journalists will ask questions. People up and down the country will, too, once heated emotions have cooled down.'

Zeb looked at him. *Unassuming* was a word commonly used when describing the prime minister. *Shrewd* and *master strategist* were others.

It struck Zeb like a lightning bolt as he stood there with Beth and Meghan beside him, Alice Monash next to Levin.

I know what these negotiations are about. I now know why the secrecy. Why Baruti and Cantor are playing it so close to their chests. Why even Clare didn't tell us.

Cantor seemed to read his mind. 'You know what's at stake.'

'I do, sir.'

'What was that about?' Levin whispered to Zeb as he walked them out. 'You and the prime minister seemed to have a moment.'

'I think I know how to draw the killers out.'

The ramsad stopped abruptly and grabbed Zeb's sleeve. 'How?'

'We'll arrange a welcome for them.'

Chapter 50

───❦───

Ein Kerem, Amman
Six days after Assassinations
Five days to Announcement

Magal left early in the morning armed with nothing but his
backpack. It contained toiletries. No weapons. Identification,
showing that he was a businessman, was in his wallet.

He and Shiri had stayed up the previous night and watched
the news in fascination. Yago Cantor had come on TV several
hours after the hotel attack. He had stated that the EQB was
responsible for the suicide bombings. That Abdul Masih and
Alam Qadir had been killed during the shootout. The prime
minister declared that the terrorist organization was also
behind the Palestinians' assassination and that Israel would
hit back at anyone who threatened its security and peace.

He ended up with declaring that while the hotel attacks
weren't related to the negotiations with Palestine, those
discussions were going ahead smoothly.

He took questions from journalists and in every answer

blamed EQB for the spate of recent killings. He denied that the negotiators were in the affected hotels. A dogged reporter said a fleet of armored vehicles had been spotted leaving the scene. He asked who its occupants were. 'You want me to tell you who was in every car on Emek Refaim?' the prime minister had responded sarcastically. That had brought a titter of laughter.

'Clever,' Shiri murmured, 'EQB is responsible for everything. That takes the heat away from them.'

Social media was already responding. The terrorist organization had replaced Mossad as the trending topic.

'You think they believe it?'

Magal shrugged. He didn't know what to believe. He exchanged a flurry of messages with the handler while Shiri looked on. 'He, too, is confused. Doesn't know why Cantor is adopting this strategy. Said he will try to find out.'

'What do you think Epstein will do now?'

'Let's wait and find out. If he continues the investigation, then Cantor's statement was a ruse.'

Magal took a cab from their apartment to Beit Shean, a historic city in the northern part of Israel, standing at the convergence of the Harod and Jordan valleys. That location made it one of the gateways to the neighboring country.

The taxi ride took a couple of hours. Not much traffic on the road, but the military and police presence were unmissable. His cab was stopped a couple of times, and he was questioned. His credentials were checked and they were waved on.

He made a checklist as the cab drove on.

Find where the negotiators are. That's for the handler to discover.

Find a way to infiltrate that location. That shouldn't be hard. He and Shiri would offer their protection services to the ramsad.

Then make plans.

That was the hardest part.

Magal was reasonably sure that the Israeli and Palestinian teams were in an IDF base. There was no other location that could be more secure.

Attacking such a camp from inside isn't impossible. But what about getting away?

Let the handler discover the location. We'll then figure out a way.

He cleared his mind and focused on Peter Raskov.

The taxi dropped him off on the Israeli side of the border, where his passport was checked, his story listened to. Several calls were made as hard-eyed guards checked him out. One of them finally waved his hand and Magal was free to go.

He received similar treatment on the Jordanian side, with the difference that his passport was stamped. That didn't bother him. *It's a fake passport.*

A line of taxis awaited on the other side of the border, standard practice at border crossings in Israel.

'Amman,' he told the bearded cab driver, whose eyes lit up. It would be a minimum two-hour drive. Money to be made.

Magal reached the Jordanian capital at eleven am. He had slept for most of the ride, and when he stepped out of the cab, he was refreshed, good to go.

The taxi dropped him at Jabal Amman, downtown, where he wolfed down a meal at a food truck. He washed it down with water and set off toward Abdoun. Shades and a cap over his head to combat the heat, and a brisk forty minutes later he was in the most affluent neighborhood of Amman.

It was where embassies were located and diplomats resided. He knew where Raskov lived from their countersurveillance. A gated, three-bedroom house bordered by thick vegetation, not far from Abdoun Circle.

Magal passed the house twice. It didn't look occupied. He leaped over the small gate on his third approach and ducked behind the bushes. No car in the garage. Windows shut, which was normal given the heat. However, no sound from the air-conditioning equipment.

He crouched low and darted to the rear of the house. Peered through several windows. The house looked empty.

He checked the rear door. No visible alarms. It took a minute to break through the adjacent window and enter the house.

No questioning shouts.

He went to the kitchen. The sink was empty. The tap looked like it hadn't been used in a while. He grabbed a knife from its stand and checked out the rest of the house.

It took him only twenty minutes to confirm that Raskov no longer lived in the house.

He returned to the kitchen and poured water into a glass as he made a call to the handler. He was using a burner phone, but it still was a risk.

Can't be helped.

'He isn't here.'

The handler didn't reply for several moments. 'He might have returned to Moscow.'

'How urgent is this?'

'Very.'

'It will affect the plans.'

'Those are already affected ... by the other developments. Can you go to Moscow?'

Magal calculated swiftly. The Russian capital was a four-hour flight away. He knew there were evening flights from Amman. *If I catch the first one, I will be in Moscow by midnight. Which will work, because chances are good Raskov will be home. I can be back in Jerusalem tomorrow.*

'Do you have an address?'

'Yes.'

'I can go.'

Moscow

Grigor Andropov hadn't made as much progress on Raskov as he wanted. He had to depute the hacker on another mission: finding the money trail of a Russian Mafia boss who was suspected of smuggling nukes. That took priority over an FSB agent. His attention was brought back to Raskov when he heard about the attacks in Jerusalem.

Zeb. This may or may not be connected to Raskov. He felt guilty at not helping his friend.

'Yuri,' he shouted.

The hacker came running.

'Where does Raskov live?'

'You called me off that assignment,' the flunky protested. 'You put me on another job.'

'Don't you multitask?' Andropov roared.

Yuri disappeared, shaking his head at the injustice.

It was an act. The Russian spymaster made out like he was a tyrant, and his staff behaved as if they were terrified of him. The reality was, Andropov's employees revered him.

Jerusalem

'I need a hotel which can be destroyed,' Zeb told Levin.

They were in an anonymous Mossad office in the city. Zeb on one side of the table, the ramsad on the other, flanked by Alice Monash. The ambassador had insisted on knowing what his plan was when she heard his mysterious comment the previous day. Beth and Meghan were where they wanted to be: by his side, on their screens, working with Werner, going through the footage of the previous day's carnage.

Levin pursed his lips as the ambassador gasped. 'Destroyed? Just what do you intend to do?'

'If Mossad has traitors, they'll be very careful. After yesterday.'

'Agreed.'

'We have to assume they, whoever the killers are, still want to kill the remaining Palestinians.'

'Yes.'

'Let's make it easy for them. Let's tell them where they are.'

The ambassador looked uncomprehendingly at the two of them and then at the sisters.

'That's the way he is, ma'am,' Beth said helpfully. 'He comes up with these outrageous ideas. Like reducing a hotel to rubble.'

'Hotels. Especially them. Something about their glass fronts makes him want to crush them,' Meghan piped up.

'You see who I have to work with?' Zeb told Levin.

'I can take them off your hands,' Levin offered. 'I would love to have them in Mossad.'

Meghan nudged Zeb in the direction of the ambassador,

who was staring at them glassy-eyed and slack-jawed.

'You'll arrange to leak that the negotiators are at this hotel,' he carried on, seriously. 'I'll take the fifteen kidon, the ones we are sure of, into confidence. They, along with the three of us, will set a trap.'

'Whoever turns up will be the killers,' Levin nodded his head. 'You need those fifteen because they could recognize the killers, if they are Mossad.'

'Correct. And we could do with their presence. More security.'

'That easy?' Alice Monash collected herself, 'Surely you need more to make it look realistic. A military presence, police. Coming and going.'

'You're right, ma'am. But I can't risk any more casualties.'

'Those operatives, they are risking their lives, aren't they?'

'Yes, ma'am,' Levin answered for Zeb. 'But they'll volunteer. It's in their nature.'

'Why can't you ask for volunteers from the police and the army?'

Zeb looked at the ramsad, who fingered his cell. 'We'll get volunteers. I am sure of that. The trick, as Zeb said, is to reduce collateral damage. Let me work on that. I can get you the hotel, too. There's one near the International Convention Center. Its management owes me.'

'They'll be okay with it being damaged?' Alice Monash asked dubiously.

'They owe me, ma'am,' Levin emphasized.

'I will be there, too,' the ambassador stated.

Zeb choked on the water he was drinking. 'Ma'am?'

'You heard me. I can come and go at the hotel, just as I was at yesterday's. That will build credibility.'

'Ma'am, that's a bad idea. We don't know who will attack and how. Having you there—'

'She'll be protected,' Levin said, supporting the ambassador's idea. 'She'll have a ring of kidon around her. I like her suggestion.'

'But—'

'It's agreed, Zeb,' Alice Monash smiled sweetly at him. 'I'll be there. In fact, the other party leaders that I am meeting … I will call them to that hotel.'

'I thought you were going to Palestine, ma'am.'

'That won't be needed. Not with what happened yesterday. Baruti has managed to bring them together. However, more work needs to be done on Cantor's allies. Work on your plan. Tell me when to start going to the hotel.' And with that, she left the room, leaving Zeb staring at the door in bemusement.

'You haven't worked with her before, have you?' Levin chuckled at the expression on his and the sisters' faces.

'No. This is the first time.' He scratched his cheek absentmindedly.

'We know her well. She has a reputation for being a very hard negotiator and getting what she wants. You just saw why.'

Zeb stretched and tested his leg. It ached, but it wouldn't hamper any swift movement. His temple had settled to a dull throb that the medics had promised would disappear in a few days.

'When do you want me to release that hotel's details?'

'Today. I think any attack will come the day after tomorrow.'

'Because?' Beth tapped a pen to her lips.

'Because Avichai will also let slip that on the fourth day the negotiators will be moved to an IDF base.'

'You seem to be looking forward to this showdown,' Levin said with a half-smile.

'I am. Those killers, whoever they are, are good. Very good. They haven't left any trail for us.'

'If they are kidon,' the ramsad replied, 'they are the best.'

Chapter 51

Jerusalem
Six days after Assassinations
Five Days to Announcement

'I am Jarrett Epstein,' Zeb announced to the kidon assembled in the room.

Riva and Adir had returned from Istanbul and were in the front row. They looked at each other but didn't speak. They hadn't known him as Epstein.

Carmel and Dalia were beside them. Nachman, Yakov, Danell, Osip, Uzziah, Navon, Abraham, Mattias, Cale and Yonah, they were all present, some lounging in chairs, some leaning against walls. Meir wasn't there because Zeb hadn't interviewed him formally.

I want to make eye contact with him before clearing him.

Fourteen kidon, Zeb and the sisters and Levin, in the same office that the ramsad had taken them to earlier in the day. It was evening. Levin had returned to his office after their meeting to make arrangements. He had secured the hotel. He had leaned on a junior minister, who had slipped up in a TV interview and revealed the new location for the negotiators. The ramsad had then requested the kidon to assemble for an urgent meeting.

The operatives didn't react to Zeb's announcement. They looked at him, considered the sisters, and then turned to their director, who remained blank-faced.

'You have seen me differently. This,' he gestured at himself, 'is who I am.'

'I don't even know you as Epstein,' Yakov glowered. He had reacted with a start when he had entered the room and seen Zeb but hadn't said anything then. 'Is that your real name?'

'You're going to be a problem?' Zeb looked at him pointedly.

The kidon flushed and settled back in his seat.

I need to win their confidence.

'Epstein is not my real name. I am Zeb Carter. I've known Avichai Levin for a long time, and when the first killings happened, he turned to me.'

Because he wasn't sure which kidon he could trust. The words, unspoken, hung heavy in the air. Feet shifted on the floor; a few operatives darted glances at their neighbors.

'Beth, Meghan,' he looked in the direction of the sisters. 'The three of us are a team. We have been investigating all of you the last few days. You are clear.'

'We could have told you that,' Yakov said sullenly.

'Yes, and many of you did. Pointed out that you had passed the polygraphs. If you were in the ramsad's position, would that be sufficient?'

The kidon remained silent.

'I am sure we all accept you had to do what you did … even though we didn't like some of the methods,' Carmel said as she crossed her legs, her calm voice helping defuse the tense atmosphere.

'I wouldn't have liked it if I was investigated in that manner,' Zeb admitted and saw a perceptible lowering of shoulders.

'Let's move on,' he said crisply. 'Any of you know where the negotiators are?'

'The Jerusalem Galaxy,' a voice shouted from the back. 'It's all over the news.'

'Correct. Some bureaucrat wasn't tightlipped enough. The Israeli and Palestinian teams will be there for three days, and on the fourth, they will be taken to an IDF camp.'

'If the first killers were Mossad kidon,' his eyes swept over the operatives, 'we think they will strike on the third day. The day after tomorrow.'

Silence.

'You said *first* killers. I thought they were EQB.' Dalia leaned forward curiously. 'That's what the prime minister said yesterday.'

'Guess why he said that?'

Carmel swore colorfully and loudly when the implications sank in. 'We are still suspects,' she said bitterly.

'Some of you, yes. But the investigation is wide-ranging. I am the only one who is focused on the kidon. Other agencies are involved as well, looking into other aspects.'

'That doesn't make me feel better.'

'I understand. But I think you can guess why you are here, now.'

'You think we'll recognize whoever comes,' Riva's fingers unconsciously drifted toward her shoulder holster.

'Yes, if they are kidon. And your presence has an added benefit. Extra security. Any questions so far?'

Yonah raised his hand. 'What if they *are* kidon? Someone we know?'

'We want them alive if that's possible.'

'That may not be feasible.'

'A dead traitor is no loss to me,' Levin's words said coldly. No further questions were asked on that matter.

They made plans until late in the night. The operatives organized themselves into khuliyot, each team taking on a security aspect. Carmel, Dalia, Riva and Adir teamed up. Their focus was the entrance to the hotel and the lobby. Yonah, Danell, Uzziah and Osip looked into the rear. Yakov and Nachman, the floor where the negotiators would be. The remaining kidon broke down the rest of the hotel and assigned themselves to various tasks.

Zeb watched silently, along with Levin and the sisters. He flashed a glance at the twins and sensed they were impressed. It was the first time they were witnessing kidon work in this manner.

After a hasty dinner break, takeaway from a nearby restaurant, the teams presented their plans to Zeb and Levin.

'There will be other agencies involved,' Levin said after hearing his kidon out. 'IDF, police. We will need to coordinate with them.'

'You have brought your go bags?' Zeb asked them.

'Yes,' all replied in unison.

'You'll move to the hotel right away. Occupy your positions. Security teams are fitting extra cameras on the various approaches and exits to the hotel. Those feeds will go through a facial recognition program. You will check out anyone who looks like a kidon.' He broke off as a thought crossed his mind. 'Drones.'

'Drones?' Levin frowned.

'Yes, stealth drones. They need to go up from right now until the relocation to the IDF camp. They need to cover a wider area, surrounding the hotel. They should record vehicles, pedestrians, everything they can look at.'

'Drones,' the ramsad repeated. 'What can I offer the three of you? To join Mossad?'

They broke up after a couple of hours, the kidon departing to the Galaxy. Zeb caught Navon's sleeve. 'Where's Eliel?'

'He had to go to Haifa. His foster mother is in critical condition. I thought he messaged you.'

'He didn't.'

'He told me,' Levin overheard and stepped in. 'His mother has been suffering for a while. He said he will return tomorrow.'

Moscow

Magal hailed a taxi when he landed at Domodedovo Airport. 'Kuntsevo District,' he told the driver and rattled off Raskov's address.

He brought out his cell phone and saw that he had several missed calls. Shiri.

'Yes?' he asked when he returned the call and his partner picked up.

'Zeb Carter?' he lowered his voice and switched to Russian. He didn't want the driver to remember a Hebrew-speaking passenger. 'I haven't heard of him. Describe him.'

'No,' Magal shook his head. 'I am sure we haven't come across him.'

He kept listening as Shiri broke down the night's developments in Jerusalem.

'You can check the hotel from inside. Make an escape route for us. See if you can assign yourself to that particular floor. This can work,' he said excitedly.

'We need a distraction,' his partner pointed out. 'The two of us alone cannot deal with all the kidon inside. There will be police and IDF as well.'

'I know. I will get the handler to arrange that.'

He hung up and called the handler.

'Look into one Zeb Carter. He is Epstein. His is the photo-graph we sent to you. American operative.'

He repeated Shiri's information, hearing a faint scratching from the handler's end. *He's taking notes.*

'We'll take the Palestinians out. We have this opportunity. However, we need something.'

'What?' the handler asked.

'Killers. Expendable ones. As many as you can muster in Jerusalem.'

Magal stepped out of the cab ninety minutes later. He paid the driver and watched him leave. He destroyed the burner phone and dropped it in a sewer. He unwrapped a new one from his go-bag and powered it up.

Raskov lived in a multi-floor apartment building next to a park. It was dark, deep in the night, but there were a few strollers, one couple, a dog walker.

Magal nodded at them, pulled his collar tighter around his neck and went inside the building. Entry was buzzer-controlled. He pressed several buttons randomly until an irritated voice squawked and the door clicked open.

A small lobby. An elevator bank in a corner. Magal checked out a door that opened to the stairwell.

He started climbing.

Raskov was half asleep on his couch, the TV flickering silently, playing a soccer match. He was tired. He had returned from Amman, and since then he had been drowning in paperwork. He hadn't reported the presence of the Israelis to his superior. There was no need to. The handler had acceded to his demands.

He heaved himself upright and staggered to the bathroom. He returned, wiping his hands on his jeans, and grabbed the half-empty beer bottle on the table.

He put it to his mouth and drank deeply, wondering if he could squeeze the handler for more money.

And then his front door opened.

His jaw dropped as the sliver of light at the entrance widened and a shadowy figure slipped inside.

He wasn't an FSB agent for nothing, however. He reacted fast. He threw the bottle at the intruder. Didn't wait to see it land. He rushed to his bedroom, where his revolver was.

Magal ducked the incoming missile easily. He'd had no time to plan a covert entry and had decided to come in through the front door. As luck would have it, Raskov was right there, in the living room.

He followed the Russian, saw an open door to his left. The kitchen. A few seconds was all it took to arm himself with a knife.

The blade felt good in his hand. It had a sharp edge, was well-balanced. It put him in the right frame of mind.

For killing.

Chapter 52

Ein Kerem
Seven days after Assassinations
Four days to Announcement

Shiri hefted the snorkeling gear in his hand. It was heavy. He had an explanation if anyone asked him about it.

The hotel had a renowned swimming pool that was deeper than most in similar hotels. Shiri was learning snorkeling. He would practice during his downtime. He was confident his answer would be bought.

It is in the delivery. Confidence, eye contact, no muscle twitches. He and Magal were experienced liars. They needed to be, for the business they were in.

His partner had called him in the night, when he was en route from Moscow. 'It's done.'

'Clean kill?'

'Yes. No traces of me.'

Shiri had sighed. 'You used a blade, didn't you?'

'Yes, so what?'

'It's like a signature, Eliel. We have discussed this several times.'

'Yes, but no one is going to connect me to Raskov.'

Shiri had dropped the matter. He could sense his friend was high from the killing. He wouldn't be open to reasoning.

'The handler has arranged about a dozen shooters. In Jerusalem,' Magal told him.

'So quickly?'

'Yes. Looks like he has such assassins in many countries. He has given me the contact of the team leader. Did you study the hotel's plans?'

'Yes.'

'You saw the water tank on the roof?' Magal interrupted him.

'Yes.'

'Great. That will be our escape. Get snorkeling gear. Get explosives. I will explain when I reach there.'

'Don't need them. The explosives. The IDF personnel have them. I know where they store them.'

Shiri caught a cab to the Jerusalem Galaxy with his extra gear.

Jerusalem Galaxy

By seven am, all the kidon were up, dressed in casual clothing, earbuds in place, weapons discreetly holstered, roaming in their locations. A few had gone back to their apartments early in the morning to bring extra gear they would need.

The previous night, Zeb had assigned Carmel to be the overall team lead for the Mossad operatives. He and the sisters watched as she had briefed every operative and assigned sectors to each one of them. These were different from what each one had in the planning.

The Galaxy had twenty floors, each with a balcony that overlooked the lobby. The guest rooms started from the third floor, which was where Zeb was.

He watched from his vantage position as Carmel moved across the floor and talked briefly with Navon, Riva and Adir. The three of them, along with Eliel when he returned from Haifa, would be responsible for eyeing every visitor to the hotel.

The female operative moved on and met with her counterparts from other agencies. She spent a few minutes with a tall man with bristling grey hair: Moshe Abhyan, the IDF colonel who was the overall commander for the security operation.

Zeb had introduced himself and the twins and had come away impressed. The man knew his job. Equally important, he wouldn't interfere in Zeb's setup. All was good so long as there was coordination between the various cogs in the security machine.

The Galaxy continued to function as normal. Or as normally as feasible. It received guests, checked them out, hosted various events in its conference rooms. The only changes were the highly visible presence of armed guards and the lockdown of two floors.

What only Zeb, the sisters, Levin and a few others knew was that the *guests* were all IDF personnel. All of them had been stationed abroad and had been recalled for just this mission. They were aware of the risks and had volunteered.

The fifth floor was where the twelve negotiators met and conducted their day-long discussions. That floor was guarded by an elite unit composed of police and IDF personnel. No kidon was allowed to go deep on that floor. Food and drinks were served by guards from that unit.

The twelfth was where the negotiators had their rooms. The Galaxy had cleared the floor of all other guests, and this, too, was similarly guarded.

Zeb felt a presence beside him: Beth, and behind her, Meghan. 'All set?'

They both nodded. They were in the hotel's basement, where the hotel's offices were. The sisters had set up shop adjacent to Abhyan's command room. It had secure lines, racks of servers, monitors that viewed every floor of the hotel, and personnel eyeing every feed.

Werner didn't require a giant server. It was present in the various devices the twins had and sent alerts if it flagged any anomaly.

So far, Werner had remained silent.

'I am not happy.' Meghan gripped the polished brass rail and leaned forward to get a better view of the lobby.

'She's been griping about this all day,' Beth smirked.

'All day? It's not even eight am.'

'Griping about what?' Zeb interrupted before the argument escalated.

'She thinks we should take Carmel into our confidence.'

'It's not fair, Zeb,' Meghan's eyes flashed. 'We should tell all of them. If you didn't trust them, you shouldn't have involved these fifteen kidon.'

'I agree.'

Her jaw dropped. Beth looked at him, openmouthed. Neither sister had expected him to cave in so easily.

'We'll tell Carmel. But no other kidon. She will understand. I think they will, too. *Need to know.* The fewer people who know, the more chances our trap will succeed. If they don't,' he shrugged, 'it's Levin's problem.'

'She might tell Dalia,' Meghan said after a pause, as she worked out his reasoning.

'Her privilege. I trust the two of them without reservation.'

'We do, too,' Beth proclaimed. 'We like them, in fact. Riva, too.'

'When will you tell them?'

'Now,' Zeb pointed to an armored vehicle that had driven up to the hotel.

Alice Monash stepped out of the vehicle and was immediately surrounded by Bob and his team.

'We'll take it from here,' Zeb told the protection leader. He shook hands with the ambassador and introduced Carmel, who had followed him, to her. The diplomat smiled at the sisters and walked inside the hotel.

Zeb led her to an elevator manned by a guard.

'Fifth,' he told the man.

The kidon waited outside. Pressed the button to shut the doors when everyone was inside.

Zeb jammed his leg between the sliding panels. 'You, too,' he told her.

Carmel looked at him quizzically for a moment and then joined him. Her eyes swept over the ambassador and the twins. Spotted the barely concealed smirk on Beth's face.

'Something's up?' she asked Zeb.

'You'll see,' Beth chortled.

They arrived at their floor and the entourage moved swiftly on soft carpet. Two guards outside a conference room.

'Just two guards?' Carmel looked surprised.

'Two are enough.' Beth couldn't suppress her grin.

The security personnel straightened and nodded at Zeb,

who pulled open a door and ushered his companions inside.

Six men and women were seated around a large, oval table. They were in IDF uniform. The remains of a hearty breakfast were beside each one of them. All of them were playing cards.

'Join us?' one woman flashed a smile at Zeb.

Carmel stood, stunned. She looked uncomprehendingly at each soldier, at the ambassador, the sisters and then at Zeb.

'What's this?' she whispered.

'The negotiators are at an IDF base.'

She grabbed a vacant chair, occupied it and composed herself rapidly.

'This was part of the trap.'

'Yes.'

'The ambassador?'

'I had to be here,' Alice Monash said, gripping Carmel's forearm reassuringly. 'To make it look real. This was Zeb's idea—'

'Actually, ma'am,' Meghan drawled, 'it was ours. Zeb likes to take credit.'

'*Their* idea. Beth and Meghan Petersen's, in case you have any doubts,' the ambassador said, bobbing her head in acknowledgment. 'This room was supposed to be empty as per Zeb's plan. The sisters thought it would be better if it was occupied. By IDF soldiers.'

'Why didn't you tell us?' Carmel's face tinged pink in anger.

'You can guess why,' Zeb answered. 'The trap has to be good for it to be believable. There's more. You have seen guests in this hotel. They are IDF soldiers. Many of the hotel staff have been replaced by military personnel. In fact, the hotel is almost empty. These *guests* are coming and going, wandering around, to give the impression the Galaxy is busy.'

Carmel's knuckles whitened. Her lips thinned.

'I have fourteen kidon,' she hissed, 'who think the negotiators are here. They are willing to risk their lives to catch the killers. You concealed all this from us!'

'Your operatives wouldn't risk their lives if this room was empty? If they knew everything?'

That floored her. She grabbed a bottle of water and drank it. Wiped her lips and looked away for several moments. The soldiers carried on with their game, ignoring the byplay.

'You are right,' Carmel accepted. 'I overreacted. I am sorry—'

'Hey,' Meghan caught her shoulder. 'Don't say that to him. He's a mean, selfish guy.'

That brought smiles all around.

'We are good?' Zeb asked her.

'We are.' Carmel stood up, her game face coming on. 'Ma'am,' she addressed the ambassador, 'I guess you'll join these *hard-working* people at their game.'

'You're just jealous,' the female soldier ribbed her. 'Zeb, can you work it out with our general? We would like a permanent posting here.'

'I guess I shouldn't be telling any of the kidon about this,' Carmel murmured when she left, along with Zeb and the Petersens.

'That's right.'

'Dalia, too? We don't have secrets between us.'

'Tell her.'

Moscow

Grigor Andropov was angry. No, he was incensed. He controlled it well, however. He had arrived at Peter Raskov's apartment an hour back. Only to find it flooded with police.

A neighbor who had the habit of sharing a morning coffee with the FSB agent had called them when the Russian didn't answer his door.

Andropov had flashed his credentials to the officers at the door and gawped at the scene when he entered the apartment.

Peter Raskov was clearly dead. His manner of demise was horrific, however. He had been slashed. Neat cuts across his body, as if the killer wanted to inflict the maximum pain.

'Who did it? Any clues?' Andropov asked a policeman.

'Nyet. The *ublyudok* is good,' the officer swore. 'The apartment is clean. No one saw anything or heard anything.'

Andropov knew the FSB agent could have been killed by anyone. It could be a simple burglary gone wrong. Or a foreign agency targeting the Russian.

It could also be someone who knew I was enquiring about Raskov.

'Here,' he gave his card to the officer. 'Keep me in the loop.'

'Everything goes to my commander.'

'I'll take it from him as well. But I want to hear from you first.'

The officer looked at the title on Andropov's card and nodded slowly. It never hurt to have friends in high places.

'Da,' he agreed.

Jerusalem Galaxy

'What?' Zeb turned away quickly and moved to a corner of the lobby.

'Raskov is dead.' Andropov sounded weary on the call.

'Cut by a knife. Killer and weapon not found.'

Zeb didn't reply immediately. His mind raced as he tried to work out what this killing meant. Where it fit in the jigsaw.

'You there?'

'Yeah,' he replied and straightened his shoulders when he saw who was walking through the Galaxy's entrance. 'Let me know what you find. I gotta go.'

Eliel had arrived.

Chapter 53

———— ⟡ ————

Jerusalem
Seven days after Assassinations
Four days to Announcement

Magal had reached Jerusalem early in the morning. He was surprisingly refreshed. He had slept on the flight from Moscow to Amman and then through the lengthy taxi rides.

It's probably the high from the killing as well. But I can't tell Shiri that. He'll blow a fuse.

He had freshened in a canteen's bathroom and then headed to Romema, where he sat across from a swarthy man who had introduced himself only as Karim.

Magal compared the man to the picture on his cell, sent by the handler. He asked him a few key questions and checked the answers against the handler's message. Karim passed.

There was a final security question. One that he hadn't agreed on with the handler.

'Give me your cell phone,' he told the man.

Karim hesitated.

Magal leaned forward till his jacket opened wider. His gun

was visible to the man opposite him.

'This isn't negotiable.'

'It isn't what I agreed with our common friend.'

'You'll agree with me now.'

Karim reluctantly handed over the device. Magal swiped through it rapidly and checked the call log. All of them to a number in the Middle East. No other calls. *It's a burner phone.* He called the number. It rang several times.

'Why are you calling me?' the handler picked up angrily. 'You're supposed to meet the man in Jerusalem.'

'This is the man in Jerusalem,' Magal replied. 'I wanted to check that Karim is who he says.'

'Satisfied?'

'Yes.'

'How many men do you have?' he asked the swarthy man as he ended the call and drew out a burner from his go-bag. He simultaneously palmed a spare battery.

He called his cell from Karim's and hung up when his phone rang. 'Now you have my number. And I have yours.'

He reached across to hand over Karim's device. Fumbled while doing so, and it fell to the floor and slid under the table. Magal swooped before the other man could react. He kneeled on the floor and switched batteries swiftly. He got up and handed the cell back to its owner.

Karim didn't look suspicious. Accidents happened. He took his phone, checked that it worked and pocketed it.

'Fourteen,' he said, answering Magal's question. He half-turned toward the back of the eatery. Three men sat at a table, drinking coffee, talking occasionally, the way long-time friends do.

'Your men?'

'Yes,' Karim replied. 'Eleven more.'

'They can shoot?'

'Very well.'

'Criminal records?'

'None of us are known to police. We wouldn't be in Israel this long if we were.'

'You can get rocket launchers?'

'Yes.' Karim didn't blink. 'Won't be the best in the market.'

'As long as they can be pointed at a building and shot.'

'They will do that.'

Magal was once again impressed by the handler's network and resources. The man had never let the kidon down, either with his intel or his logistics support.

Still, taking on contractors at such short notice wasn't something he was comfortable with.

But we don't have a choice. The negotiators will leave for the camp in two days.

'Many of your men will die.'

Karim smiled unpleasantly. 'That is part of the job. What is your plan?'

Magal told him.

'When is go?'

'Today. Evening.'

That surprised the man. He chewed his lip and drummed his fingers on the table.

'Is there a problem?'

'No ...' Karim finished his drink and stood up. 'The rocket launchers. I will need to leave right now if you want them by evening.'

'Attack when I give you the word.'

'Yes.'

Magal circled the Jerusalem Galaxy in a taxi, wearing his cap low over his head. He checked his cell and saw the green dot for Karim. The battery he had inserted in the man's phone was both a tracker and an explosive device. Magal would set it off at the right time. Karim couldn't live. Not after seeing his face.

Magal, too, had studied the hotel's plans. He recollected all that Shiri had told him.

With that amount of security, Shiri and I will have to use our insider status.

He grinned suddenly. He loved the challenge. He knew his partner would be feeling the same, too. It was possible that both would die that evening.

But if they pulled it off ... heck, there would be a long list of callers once they became international assassins.

He got the cab to drive to the rear of the hotel, and as they were driving down the street a kite, high up, caught his eye. He tried to see who was flying it, but there were too many structures in the way.

His eyes lingered on the Galaxy's roof and that of another hotel across the street from it. *About two hundred feet across. The negotiators' hotel is taller. It could work!*

'Let's go to that hotel,' he told the driver.

Forty minutes later, he emerged, satisfied. He had rented a room on the second hotel's highest floor, facing the Galaxy. He would have to make one more trip to leave some gear in it, but his escape plan was ready.

His attack was already mapped out. It drew heavily on surprise and diversionary tactics. Now that their getaway was sorted out, all that was required was Carmel's cooperation.

She needed to be amenable to a particular request.

Chapter 54

Jerusalem Galaxy
Seven days after Assassinations
Four days to Announcement

Zeb stuck his hand out and greeted Eliel. 'You know me as Epstein.'

'That man we met looked very different,' the kidon said, smiling. 'Navon told me about you. Carmel, too.' He lowered his large backpack to the floor and flexed his shoulders.

'You're American?'

'Yeah,' Zeb drawled deliberately.

'You speak our language better than most natives.'

Zeb shrugged. Eliel was fishing, but he wasn't taking the bait. No Mossad operative would ever know who he and the sisters worked for. *We might tell Carmel and Dalia, but no one else.*

'How's your mother?'

Eliel's face darkened. 'She doesn't have much time ... I might have to go suddenly if—'

'Sure.' He turned when a voice greeted them. Carmel,

approaching rapidly.

She punched Eliel lightly on the shoulder and, after a quick nod to Zeb, led the kidon away.

'I have a favor to ask,' Magal told his team leader after she had finished briefing him.

'Go ahead.'

'Can you reassign Navon and me? To the roof? I think you have someone else there, don't you? After all that's happened at home,' he put on a melancholy expression, 'some fresh air will do me good. Up there,' he pointed upwards, 'will help.'

Carmel patted his forearm sympathetically, 'Of course. That won't be a problem.' She turned her head away and spoke rapidly in her mouthpiece. 'Navon's coming,' she said when she finished. 'You're clear to the roof.'

Shiri came presently and hugged his partner briefly.

'You can show him around the hotel?'

Navon nodded.

'Not the fifth floor. You know the rules.'

'Yes, boss,' Navon grinned cheekily.

'What's with the fifth floor?' Magal asked curiously.

'We can't go deep in the hallway. IDF is protecting it,' Shiri said as he led him away.

'What's the plan?' Shiri asked an hour later. They were on the roof of the Galaxy, just the two of them, their backpacks on the concrete surface.

Magal enjoyed the Jerusalem view for a moment before replying. He could see light reflecting off the Dome of the Rock in the distance.

'Where are the drones?'

'Well below us,' Shiri assured him. 'There are a few choppers,' he pointed to the sky, 'but their focus is on street traffic.'

Magal looked around them. The roof was flat, with a five-foot-high parapet running all around. The water tank they had discussed was to one side. Pumps, fans and several pieces of mechanical equipment were bolted by its side. A large, painted circle was in the center. A helipad. The approach to the elevator room was through a raised structure that had a door. No security to it. A simple twist-and-push handle mounted on it.

He touched Shiri's shoulder and took him to the side. 'How far away is that hotel? Its rooftop?' he pointed to the one he had checked out.

'One-fifty, two hundred feet?' Shiri squinted.

Magal leaned over his backpack and unzipped it. He brought out a lengthy coil of nylon rope and a crossbow. Two pulleys followed, as did several belts and harnesses.

'That's our escape.'

'We'll zipline?' his partner caught on quickly, his eyes dancing.

'Yes. I have booked a room. That one, there in the middle.' He pointed. 'I have left weapons and disguises in it.'

'What kind of disguises?'

'Police. We will leave the room as two uniformed police. No one will question us. Now, tell me about the blind spots.'

Shiri told him.

The hotel had security cameras on all floors, however they were mounted deep into the hallways.

'So, the elevators are covered but not the areas on either side of their doors?'

'Yes,' Shiri confirmed. 'They start from the first rooms to

the left and right, which are twenty-five feet away.'

'No cameras in the staircases?'

'No. There are IDF people at the entrance door of each floor.'

'How many?'

'Three. And there are two standing outside the elevators on each floor. You saw them. No one at the roof, though. We are the security, here.'

'What about the fifth floor? How much security there?'

'You mean at the conference room? Two.'

Magal stopped so abruptly that Shiri bumped into him. 'Only two?' he asked incredulously.

'That's what Carmel told me. And I didn't see any more when she and I stepped outside the elevator. But don't forget the two at the elevator and the three on the stairs.'

Magal scratched his chin as he thought rapidly. 'I would have thought they would have more IDF or police on that floor. Carter isn't in charge, is he?'

'No. Not Carmel, either. Moshe Abhyan is. He's an IDF commander. He's on our comms channel.'

'They must be figuring on taking out the assassins on the ground floor. That's why there are barely any guards on the fifth.'

'That's what I figured. The twelfth floor has a similar setup. Three outside the elevators, a roaming patrol of two on the floor and three inside the stairs.'

'How many guests in the hotel?'

'I haven't found that out. Carmel didn't know, either. I checked with the other kidon. No one knew. But there's a constant stream of people in the lobby.'

'I saw that.'

'I have been patient,' Shiri burst out when Magal pinched his nose and kept quiet. 'I didn't even ask you about Moscow. You have some plan here? How we'll tackle all that security *and* take out the Palestinians *and* get away safely?'

Magal couldn't help smiling at his friend's outburst. 'We can't go against all these IDF and police personnel.'

Shiri slapped his palm against his thigh in frustration. 'I thought you were working on something!'

'Patience,' Magal grinned wider. 'I said we can't take them on. Which is correct. There are too many of them. However, we won't need to.'

'Those fighters? The ones the handler arranged?'

'Yes, they will help, but not in the way you think.' Magal glanced at his watch. It was twelve pm. 'Come on. I'll explain as we work.'

He shoved the zipline equipment and the crossbow beneath the tank. He removed an AK from his backpack and added it to the pile on the roof. He then lugged his bag and gestured at Shiri to follow suit.

The two men went to the elevator room, to the concealed door in it, and went down the stairs. They nodded at the IDF men on the nineteenth floor and similarly greeted all the guards they encountered as they moved down.

There were two flights of stairs between each floor, with a landing in between flights. No security team had sight of another, even if they leaned over the railings. That suited the two kidon.

'Making him familiar with the layout,' Shiri told the three soldiers at the fifth floor. Carmel had let all the personnel know that Magal was joining the team; that ensured they encountered no awkward questions.

Magal opened the door to the fifth and peered out. The two guards at the elevator stiffened, then relaxed when they recognized him. He looked down the hallway and waved at the two in front of the conference room. They waved back.

'You've seen the negotiators?' he asked Shiri when they were back on the stairs, in between the fourth and fifth.

'No one has. They are escorted from the twelfth to the fifth by IDF. They have their own elevator. The American ambassador comes every day, however. She joins them in the morning and leaves in the evening.'

He watched Magal remove several smoke bombs and hide them beneath a fire hose box. His partner added two flash-bangs and a small amount of explosive to the bombs.

'That's your plan? Take them all out? I thought we were only interested in the Palestinians.'

Magal connected a remote detonator to the bombs and synced it to his cell. Satisfied, he looked up. 'We will use the handler's men to create panic. What will happen when the hotel is under attack?'

'Evac procedure,' Shiri responded automatically. 'The guards will bring the negotiators out. Surround them and take them down these stairs. Which is why we are on the fifth floor. It's not a long way down to the basement. And this time, there's no chance of a surprise attack by someone like Masih. The entire street has IDF and cops, some in uniform and some in plain clothes.'

'When they are on the stairs,' Magal pointed to the red box that housed the hose, 'I'll detonate those.'

Shiri's eyes widened when Magal finished briefing him.

'It will work,' he said in a hushed voice.

'Of course, it will,' Magal scoffed. 'We have the element

of surprise. No one is expecting us.'

'We may not be able to take out all the Palestinians.'

'We don't have to. We need to kill just a few, not all six.'

'The handler—'

'Is not here,' Magal interrupted him irritably. 'We can't kill them all. We aren't going to risk our lives on this mission.'

Shiri chewed his lip as he looked up the stairs, past the three soldiers there, toward the door. He let it unfold in his mind, how it would go down.

Magal and he would race down from the roof at the first signs of attack. '*Nothing up there*,' he would yell over his comms. '*We're going to the fifth to provide more support.*'

He knew Carmel and Abhyan would remonstrate, would ask them not to leave their positions. They would ignore those commands.

'*Are they here?*' he would gasp at the guards on the negotiators' floor.

'*No. Floor's clear. Stand back!*' a guard might cry out. '*Negotiators coming.*'

Shiri would help him hold the floor's door open as the Palestinians and Israelis surged inside, with IDF soldiers at the front and rear.

'*Go! Go! Go!*' he would yell as the hotel shook and shuddered and sounds of firing echoed.

'*You too!*' he would tell the three guards when the crowd was descending down the stairs. '*Magal and I have got this. Get them to safety.*'

The guards might argue, but just then, his partner would detonate the explosives.

'*Boobytrap!*' he would yell, and he was sure that would be

enough incentive. *'Take them away!'*

Distance would open up. There would be shouting and screaming and swearing. No one would be looking at them.

Magal would fire at the soldiers in the rear and then at the Palestinians—whose details the handler had sent.

Shiri had seen his friend work with a gun. He hadn't seen a better shot maker. Magal could take out the soldiers and a few Palestinians, even through the smoke and panic.

They would have just a couple of seconds, however, before the soldiers at the front looked back.

Shiri would fire a burst at the door and push against it as if there were shooters on the other side.

'Move!' he would yell. *'Magal and I will keep them at bay. For as long as we can.'*

Magal and he would race to the roof as soon as the soldiers and survivors were out of sight.

'Keep a watch,' they would yell at the guards on each floor. *'We've been breached. The stairs could have explosives. Magal and I will check, upwards.'*

The comms channel would be flooded with noise. There would be multiple orders, and with their inputs, there would be confusion.

Enough time for them to reach the roof and zipline away to the neighboring hotel, where they would change into their police uniforms and rush out to the street to support the security personnel.

'Let's do it,' he told Magal.

'There's one more thing.'

'What?'

'It's not happening tomorrow.'

Shiri had had enough of suspense and surprises. He gripped his friend's shoulder tightly and snarled, 'When?'

'It's going down today. In a few hours.'

Chapter 55

———∞———

Jerusalem Galaxy
Seven days after Assassinations
Four days to Announcement

At two pm, Zeb was at what was now becoming his familiar location. Hunched over the balcony rails of the third floor, looking down at the lobby.

'How do you think it will go down?' Meghan approached from behind and joined him.

'I have no clue,' he admitted. 'I don't think the killers will replicate Masih's attack. Abhyan has prepared for that. A stealth approach … frankly, there are so many soldiers and police around that I can't see how they could carry out an attack.'

'What if it nothing happens?'

'Then we are back to square one. Anything on the screens?'

'Nope,' Beth sidled up next to him and mimicked his posture. 'There's enough on social media to reinforce the message that the negotiators will be moved the day after tomorrow. If the killers are checking the hotel out,' she blew hair out of her face, 'we haven't found them.'

'No strange vehicles? No repeat passes?'

'Oh,' she snorted, 'there are enough of those. This place has turned into a visitor attraction. Cabs have circled the hotel several times. A few tour buses have swung this way as well. We have been able to eliminate most such vehicles. A few cabs remain. They aren't able to confirm their passengers' identities.'

'They could be—'

'Yeah. Abhyan's people are checking.'

Carmel arrived, along with Dalia. 'I have reassigned all the kidon. The majority are around the lobby and ground floor. Eliel and Navon are on the roof.'

'Makes sense,' Zeb nodded. 'The drones will warn us of any attack from the top. How are they feeling?'

'Bored,' Dalia laughed. The smile faded away fast. 'They don't believe any kidon could be the killer.'

'I hope they are right.'

Carmel nodded gravely. 'I hope so too.'

Levin will have to rebuild Mossad if it turns out his kidon have gone rogue, Zeb thought bleakly. *That's assuming he still has the job.*

'Tell them,' Dalia hissed, nudging her partner.

Meghan looked at her and then Carmel. 'Tell us what?'

The team leader's cheeks burned, 'I ... we ... Dalia and me, we plan to get ... once this is over ...' her voice trailed off.

Zeb frowned when Beth launched herself at the kidon and hugged them. 'You two ...' he struggled to make sense of Carmel's words. *Just what does she want to say?*

Meghan rolled her eyes, 'That's just like him. Late on the uptake as always. They're engaged, Zeb!'

'Yes,' Dalia's eyes sparkled. 'We've had enough of living in the shadows.'

'Does Levin know?'

She shook her head. 'No. You are the first. We'll tell him—'

Zeb wasn't paying attention. He was looking at the Galaxy's entrance, where a car was turning up. It was some distance away, but he could see it was packed.

He started moving unconsciously toward the stairs, his sixth sense warning him.

The vehicle's doors opened. Bodies fell out.

'ATTACK!' he roared in his comms unit.

He burst into a sprint, Carmel and Meghan ahead of him, Dalia and Beth a step behind.

Rifle fire broke out as they clattered down the stairs.

'Everyone at their positions. Be prepared. Hostiles on the radar,' Abhyan announced calmly.

Once in the lounge, Zeb dived toward the concierge's desk. Sandbags were piled behind it to provide protection from incoming rounds. Small holes had been carefully bored to enable sight and shooting windows.

'In position,' Carmel checked in. Dalia followed.

'We're on the screens,' Meghan told Zeb. 'One vehicle in the driveway. Gunmen inside the car. No other vehicle nearby.'

Zeb peered through the eyehole. IDF soldiers were firing at the vehicle, tearing it to ribbons. There was returning fire, but it was sporadic.

Those shooters didn't have a chance. Surely, they knew that. Unless ...

Something slammed into the hotel, making it tremble. The lights flickered.

'ROCKETS!' he yelled. 'That first car was a decoy.'

'Copy,' Abhyan acknowledged. 'Screen report!'

'A bus,' Meghan's voice was momentarily drowned as

another missile crashed into the hotel and the intensity of firing increased. Glass shattered.

'More shooters behind that bus,' the elder twin continued in a clipped voice. 'Hundred yards away. No sight of the launchers. Abhyan, the drones need to widen their arc.'

'Move the negotiators,' Yakov shouted just as another rocket smashed into the building.

'Stay in your positions,' Carmel ordered.

'The hotel will come down!' Magal yelled from the rooftop. 'We have to move them.'

'Negative,' Carmel was firm.

Shiri ran toward the parapet and peered over it cautiously. He could see the bus. Tiny. To its left and a street away, he saw a trail of smoke. Something streaked as he watched and the building shuddered again.

'Carmel,' Magal screamed, 'You'll kill all of us. Navon and I are going down. We need to evac!'

He ignored the commands that came through his earbud. Smiled briefly when the other kidon echoed his words. He fired another message to Karim.

More. Now!

An instant later, he and Shiri were racing down the stairs. 'It's us,' he told the guards on the nineteenth. 'We're going to the fifth.'

'They said—'

'I know what they said,' he cut off the soldier angrily. The Galaxy rocked on its foundation before he could finish. Metal tore and glass shattered.

'You, stay in your position,' he snapped and carried on running down.

'One rocket launcher in sight,' said Beth. Cool. Collected. 'A street behind the bus. Hostiles firing from the back of a truck.' She gave coordinates, to which Abhyan reacted instantly. He deployed one team of outside soldiers to tackle the truck.

'There should be more,' Zeb replied. 'Check for ground entry as well. Attackers on foot.'

'Checking. No sign of it at the moment.'

Zeb looked up as a beam crashed to the floor, tearing down several wall hangings. The guests in the lobby had taken cover. No screaming. No panic.

Why would they? They're experienced soldiers and cops. He grinned in spite of himself, acknowledging Abhyan's genius in that deployment.

'I'm joining Eliel and Navon,' Yakov shrieked over the comms. Several kidon joined in. 'To the fifth floor. To escort the negotiators down.'

Carmel looked at Zeb from behind her cover.

Let them go, he mouthed. She nodded.

He hadn't factored in the possibility that the kidon would break away from their positions. *I should have. They weren't clued in to the plan. Their reaction is understandable.*

He stopped thinking when more missiles landed and rifle fire increased.

'Yakov, don't come up,' Magal grunted as he took the steps two at a time. 'You'll get in our way.'

'I am coming,' the kidon shouted angrily. 'Nachman, too.'

We'll have to kill the idiots.

'Carmel, are the evac vehicles ready?'

Her reply was drowned out in another burst of sound.

He winced even as he ran. Karim was throwing everything

that he had at the hotel. *I hope it stays standing.* The building was rocking and shuddering, but so far, no cracks had appeared in the walls.

They reached the sixth floor, warned the guards to stay put and rushed down.

Fifth floor. Magal halted for a second, sweat streaming down his face. He gulped air, Shiri beside him. The three soldiers on the landing looked at them impassively. From below, footsteps pounded.

'Eliel!' Nachman and Yakov called out.

Magal didn't reply. 'Where are the negotiators?' he grated. The soldiers didn't answer. They didn't stop him when he flung the door open and raced inside the floor.

'Stop!' the IDF guards at the elevator commanded.

'Stop for what?' Magal growled. 'The hotel to come down on us?'

He ran toward the conference room with Shiri. A door slammed behind them. He snatched a glance behind. Nachman, Yakov, Uzziah and two other kidon were joining them.

'We'll have to deal with them,' Shiri whispered.

'We will,' Magal said grimly as he moved, 'but why aren't the negotiators moving out?'

The sounds of battle were muted by the thickly carpeted floor. No windows had shattered on this floor.

I asked Karim to stay away from the fifth. A rocket could take out all the negotiators. That isn't what the handler wants. Only Palestinians should die.

He approached the conference room, the guards straightening, looking at them. 'Stand back!' they ordered.

'Use your brains, you fool,' Magal swore. 'We need to move those people to safety.'

'We have our orders—'

'Screw your orders!' Yakov shouted, his face red with rage. 'Their safety comes first. This hotel is going down. We need to evac. Right now!'

The soldiers looked at each other uncertainly. Magal took that opportunity to barge through them and push the door open.

What he saw shocked him.

Thirteen people on the floor, prone. His brains caught up with what his eyes saw.

Twelve of them in IDF uniform, surrounding the American ambassador. Each soldier in the room had a weapon trained on Magal and the other kidon.

A missile hit the hotel, but no one flinched.

'You've come to kill us?' a female soldier asked sardonically.

Chapter 56

———⟨⟩———

Jerusalem Galaxy
Seven days after Assassinations
Four days to Announcement

Abhyan's soldiers were responding efficiently, even as Magal and Shiri entered the conference room.

Three IDF platoons deployed to take out the missile launchers. The sisters had located two more rocket-wielding hostiles at the two sides of the hotel.

A fourth team of soldiers approached the bus.

The attackers managed to fire one more missile, which sailed high over the hotel and vanished in the sky.

The firefight was intense but brief on the four fronts. In half an hour, all the attackers were either killed or captured. A bunch of soldiers and police went on a combing operation in the surrounding streets and the wider neighborhood. They didn't find any more hostiles.

Back at the hotel, Zeb and the sisters were surrounded by the kidon.

'You didn't think of telling us?' Yakov spat. 'All along, we thought the negotiators were in the hotel!'

'Why did you bring us here if you didn't trust us?' Nachman asked, more calmly. 'There's not a single civilian in this hotel, is there?'

'There are a few,' Zeb admitted. 'The hotel staff. The manager. They volunteered. We swore them to silence.'

He crossed his arms and let the kidon vent. Carmel and Dalia were at the rear. He shook his head imperceptibly when the two made a move to join him.

My plan. I'll take the heat.

Uzziah picked up his signal, however.

'And you!' He swung on the team leader. 'You are one of us. You should have told us.'

Carmel was up for the challenge. 'There's no us or them. We are one team. We are here to protect the negotiators—'

'There are no negotiators here,' Yakov shouted.

'Yes, but flushing out the killers is protecting them, too.'

'Why didn't you tell us? What difference would it have made?'

'They don't trust us,' Nachman snarled. 'That's why.'

'If none of us were trusted, why would Zeb bring us here? *Need to know.* We have that in our missions. Do any of you question the ramsad when he keeps details from us?'

No one replied.

'Why is this different? You see all these people?' she gestured at the *civilians* who were milling in the lobby. 'None of them knew that the negotiators weren't here. Only the hotel manager knew. Not even his staff. We aren't entitled to know just because we are kidon. This plan was primarily the commander's, Moshe Abhyan. He decided who would know the full details. Not Zeb or I.'

'You are sheltering behind him,' Yakov said roughly.

Carmel lost it. She sprang forward and grabbed him by his shirt. 'Yakov,' she said contemptuously, 'You are the only kidon I haven't worked with. Everyone here knows me. I don't hide behind anyone. I don't make excuses. I don't need Abhyan to cover for me.'

'Yakov, back down,' Uzziah warned the kidon when he made to speak. 'I know Carmel. You are in the wrong.'

Yakov walked away angrily when the team leader released him.

'Any more questions?' Carmel regarded the remaining operatives coolly.

'One,' Eliel raised his hand. 'How come the hotel didn't come down? It took so many missiles and yet is still standing.'

'It is designed for such attacks. Reinforced steel, highly toughened glass, many other features. Besides, we got lucky. The attackers were using missiles that are outdated. Modern ones would have inflicted severe damage on the building.'

'This attack … it proves no kidon was involved, doesn't it? None of those captured or killed are Mossad operatives. We are clear, aren't we?'

All the operatives turned to Zeb, who nodded. 'Yes. Mossad is clear.'

'You don't sound very confident,' Levin commented. He was with Zeb and the sisters, on the third-floor balcony.

It was five pm. Alice Monash had left for the embassy after congratulating Zeb on a plan that had worked. She had been scared, she said, not terrified, because there was this female soldier who kept wisecracking and helped her relax.

Zeb thought he knew who the soldier was. *The same*

woman who joked with me and greeted Eliel. He had sought her out later and had thanked her.

Mopping-up operations were continuing at the Galaxy. Of the fifteen attackers, six remained alive. Only two were in a position to talk. They said they were guns for hire, Lebanese mercenaries. They claimed that a man named Karim had hired them and didn't know who the ultimate paymaster was.

Karim was, unfortunately, dead. The clearing teams were searching for his cell phone. Simultaneously, the backgrounds of all the attackers were being checked. The police investigative apparatus had kicked in.

Even as they watched, EMS personnel wheeled a gurney across the lobby and loaded it into a waiting ambulance.

'How many injured?' Zeb deflected Levin's query.

'Ten. One soldier is serious but should recover. Those hostiles were poorly equipped. That kept the casualties down,' the ramsad replied, grim-faced.

That there were no deaths on the Israeli side wasn't that much of a surprise. The soldiers and police officers who had volunteered to pose as civilians were highly experienced. They had sought shelter the moment firing had commenced. They had thrown themselves to the floor and were away from windows. The hotel staff had rushed to the basement, where they had remained until the attackers were overcome.

Those tourists, they died, Zeb reminded himself. The bodies that had fallen out of the car were Japanese visitors. *The gunmen kidnapped them, killed them, and used their bodies as shields.*

His hands clenched the rail as a gust of anger surged through him. *Innocents. They had nothing to do with what went down. It's on me.*

'It's not on you,' Levin took one look at his face. 'Everyone in this hotel was a volunteer. Those tourists … all of us bear responsibility.'

'I want to know who they were. Where they were from. Their families. Everything.'

'You'll get it.'

'You didn't answer my question,' Levin asked after a pause. 'You said my people are clear. I know you, however. You sounded uncertain.'

Zeb was aware of the sisters regarding him sharply. He hadn't confided his reservations to them.

Heck, let me tell them.

'I don't know, Avichai,' he confessed and shifted to ease his throbbing leg. 'It doesn't make sense.'

'Explain,' the ramsad rapped out.

'Not a single gunman entered the hotel. How were they planning to kill the negotiators?'

'By bringing the hotel down.' Beth didn't conceal her surprise. Why didn't Zeb see what was so obvious?

'It didn't, however. So, what was their backup plan?'

'They didn't have one. They threw everything they had at the hotel.'

'What about escape? They sure weren't thinking of getting away.'

'Suicide attackers,' Beth snapped her fingers at his face. 'Heard of them? They exist!'

He nodded half-heartedly.

'What else is bothering you?' Levin asked him.

'This attack. It did what we wanted. It drew out the hostiles. But were these shooters the ones behind the first attack? That first killing was so different.' Zeb threw his hands up in frustration. 'It was meticulously planned. We still don't know who those assassins were. Masih's attack was like this one: Brute force. No refinements.'

'It's possible that today's hostiles were behind the first one. They decided to go with two assassins, then. This second time, they had no choice but to throw numbers and heavy weapons, because the negotiators were securely protected.'

'What about the EQB?'

'I don't know if they are linked to the first and last attacks. However, the police will confirm that with their investigation.'

'Uh-huh.'

'You still aren't sure.'

'I am sure none of the kidon in this hotel are involved. None of the remaining operatives showed up. You know that. You can read that two ways.'

'Either all the kidon are innocent—' Meghan watched Carmel talking with her team in the lobby. They were smiling, slapping backs. It looked like the previous rancor had disappeared. '—or the rogue operatives decided to stay away.'

'Yeah, and these Lebanese shooters saw an opportunity and took it.'

Levin looked at the activity in the lobby and made a snap decision.

'Come to the IDF camp. The three of you. We'll get Carmel, Dalia and the rest, too. I'll get Carmel to brief the agents.'

'You want the same setup?'

'Yes. That's an IDF show; however, more Mossad eyes on possible traitors will be good.'

Moscow

Andropov jerked awake when his cell rang. He glanced at his watch. Eleven pm. Of course, he wasn't sleeping. Spymasters like him never did. He was merely resting his eyes. He yawned lustily and glanced at the TV. It was replaying the events in Jerusalem.

His phone buzzed again. He checked the number on his phone and frowned. It didn't register on him.

'Da?' he growled.

'It's Mikhail.'

'Mikhail, who?' Andropov grunted. What was the world coming to? Why couldn't people introduce themselves properly?

'I am the police officer at Raskov's apartment. You gave me your card.'

'I remember. You have something for me?'

'Nothing on the killer. I was searching his apartment, however, and came across a concealed hollow behind the bookshelf in his bedroom.'

'And?' Why did this Mikhail have to draw things out?

'It had a thumb drive in it.'

Andropov sat straighter, his mind clearing up in an instant.

'What's in it?'

'I don't know. I found it ten minutes back. I haven't checked it out.'

'Who else knows about it?'

'No one. I am alone. I told my boss I wanted to follow up on some leads.'

'Why were you searching the place?'

'I wasn't, really. The forensic team had already gone

through it. But it looks like no one thought of looking behind that shelf.'

'Don't tell anyone. Don't give it to anyone. Don't leave that place.'

'I have to record the evidence,' Mikhail protested.

'What evidence?'

Ein Kerem, Somewhere in the Middle East

'Does Carter suspect you?' the handler asked Magal.

The two kidon had returned to their apartment in Ein Kerem after another briefing with the American, Levin and Carmel.

'No. We would either be dead or in a Mossad interrogation center, if he knew.'

'He duped us.'

'Yes. It was a smart play.'

'You admire him?'

'I admire good tradecraft.'

'I still want those Palestinians killed.'

'It's almost impossible now. They are in the military camp.'

'You're going there, aren't you?'

'But we will be surrounded by soldiers.'

'I thought you two were the best kidon the Mossad had. No mission was beyond you,' the handler goaded.

Magal looked at his phone and then at Shiri, who was listening.

'We'll try.' He took a deep breath. 'But you have to realize—'

'Trying isn't enough. I want the Palestinians dead,' the handler retorted, losing his temper. 'I cultivated you. I let you carry out missions in my own country. I could have captured you during any of those. It's time to repay now.'

'We will do it.'

'Good. This is the only opportunity you will have. It will be too late after the announcement.'

The handler replaced his cell in its cradle and rocked in his chair. He had put on an act for Magal, that he was angry. He was genuinely disturbed, however. He had been confident the kidons' plan would come off. So confident that he had almost boasted to the Supreme Leader to watch the news.

He was thankful he hadn't.

However, he had committed to victory to the leader, and that was still some distance away.

A chill raced through his spine.

Does Levin know I have access to his emails? Is that why the hotel had only soldiers and police?

His fingers twitched, but he didn't reach for his keyboard. Instead, he analyzed scenarios in his mind. The hotel's details had been in the Mossad director's emails. As had been the deployment of the kidon to the Galaxy.

No. The Israelis are in diplomatic trouble with the Japanese. They wouldn't have allowed the attack to happen if they knew about my virus.

He had to consider his future, though. Magal's concerns were valid.

If the two men can't kill some or all the Palestinians, I won't be able to blame Mossad.

And if Cantor and Baruti made their announcement before blood was shed, the Supreme Leader would go on a tearing rage.

The handler had no intention of being in the country if that happened. He would flee.

He would also expose Magal and Shiri.

'Are you out of your mind?' Shiri exploded when Magal hung up. 'There's no way we can kill any Palestinians and get away alive. Not in an IDF base.'

His partner smiled mysteriously.

'You think we can?' Shiri asked, dumbfounded.

'Did you see how those soldiers reacted when the attack happened?'

'They reacted like any soldier would.'

'No. Did you see what they were wearing?'

'Combat gear. What's special about that?'

'Full face helmets.'

Shiri's face cleared. 'The guards at the conference room. They, too, had their faces covered.'

'Yes. There's no way to know who's behind those.'

'We still will need to get away.'

'We can work on that. We're going to the camp tomorrow. We still have a few days in hand.'

'And if we don't get an opportunity?'

'Then, we have failed.'

'The handler will not let it rest. He is a vengeful man.'

'I have thought about that. We will have to disappear after the announcement. Our first assignment as killers will be for ourselves.'

'What's that?'

'We take out the handler.'

Chapter 57

Beit Aghion
Eight days after Assassinations
Three days to Announcement

'You have seen the news?' Prime Minister Yago Cantor addressed his visitors: Jessy Levitsky, Nadav Shoshon, Jore Spiro, Avichai Levin, Alice Monash and Zeb. They were seated around a conference table, newspapers strewn on its polished surface.

Seven am. They had finished breakfast and were sipping their beverages.

'Don't need to.' Levitsky pushed one publication away with his forefinger. 'I have been in meetings and press conferences all night. I know what the headlines are.'

'*EQB CELL STRIKES AGAIN*,' Cantor read out. 'That's just one of them.'

'That's our spin on it,' Shoshon grunted. 'We told the media that the killers were from that organization.'

'No one's talking of Mossad anymore,' Spiro grinned slyly at Levin.

351

'And no one should,' the ramsad said resolutely.

'What about the investigation? In the first killing?' the prime minister asked his team.

'That's progressing slowly, Yago,' Levitsky admitted. 'We have had to move resources to the EQB and the Lebanese attacks. Frankly, I don't think we'll find those killers before the big day.'

'What about you?' Cantor asked Levin.

'The investigator and the trusted kidon were at the Galaxy. They helped foil the attack. They have moved to the IDF base and will remain there until the press conference is over.'

'What about the remaining operatives?' Shoshon questioned.

'I think they, too, are good, but I want to be absolutely sure. That investigation will go a little slower. For the same reason Jessy mentioned.'

'Once Baruti and I make the declara—' The prime minister shot a swift glance toward Zeb and checked himself. 'I guess all the media will be focused on that day. If those killers are Mossad, we can manage it. After the event.'

'Yes, sir.'

For the first time in several days, Cantor was feeling hopeful. Yes, there had been another shootout in the streets. One in which rocket launchers had been deployed. Sure, there was clamor from the opposition that terrorists were ruling Jerusalem. And he had to deal with Japan. However, that attack had served an unexpected political purpose. It had helped bring most of his parties together. The American ambassador was dealing with the recalcitrant ones.

'Alice, how are you doing? Recovered from yesterday?'

'Everything happened too fast for me to panic,' the

ambassador said, laughing. 'Besides, I was surrounded by your soldiers. They were relaxed. They told me to stay down on the floor. They were joking. The hotel was getting hit, windows were breaking, the building was shaking, but all these soldiers could talk about was how bad the attackers' aim was.'

'They are Israeli soldiers, Alice,' Cantor said proudly.

'Yeah.' She looked speculatively at Levin. 'The Galaxy. Choosing it was your idea. Why didn't it come down? Any other hotel anywhere in the world would have collapsed.'

There was silence in the room.

'Am I missing something?'

'That hotel just might be,' Levin made a show of coughing, 'a Mossad front. Built specially to withstand such attacks.'

'You fox.'

'He's that and more,' Cantor agreed. He brought the meeting back to business. 'Alice, you met Omet Zeev?'

'I will be meeting him, later today.' She smiled mischievously. 'Did you know he has a mistress? In Tel Aviv?'

Cantor's jaw dropped. 'Omet Zeev? Are you sure?'

'Brown,' she looked at Zeb, 'found a money trail. That led to her identity. It was easy after that.'

'Isn't he the one who talks about family values?' Shoshon chuckled.

'Yeah, and that's why we hold an ace. His party will disown him if they come to know.'

'You're heading to the base?' the ambassador asked Zeb as they walked out.

'Yes, ma'am. Beth and Meghan are outside. We're going straight away.'

'I'll be joining you in the afternoon.'

'You, ma'am?' he looked at her in surprise.

'Yes. I need to be there. The U.S. has to be visible. I will stay there until the press conference.'

'Where will it be held?'

'Didn't Levin tell you?'

'I think he has a lot on his plate.'

'It will be in Teddy Stadium. It's a good venue; I have seen it.' She threw a sidelong glance at him. 'You know what's going to be announced?'

'I worked it out, ma'am. Many people in this country will be ready to die to stop it.'

'Millions more on both sides and across the world will be ready to die for it.'

IDF Base, Negev Desert

The Negev Desert covered over half of Israel's land area, in the south of the country, with the Gulf of Aqaba at its base and Beersheba, its capital and the largest city in the region, to its north.

Despite the region's size, it was home to just over half a million people, a quarter of which were Bedouins. The government had invested heavily in the desert to make it more habitable and to entice people away from the larger cities. A major IDF base was being constructed in the desert to house ten thousand soldiers and over two thousand civilian staff. A host of high-tech companies had sprung up around the military center.

It wasn't just the IDF that had camps in the desert. The U.S. had an air defense base inside the Israeli Air Force's Masha-bim Air Base. There was the Negev Nuclear Research Center, plus civilian establishments, Bedouin towns and villages, and vast arrays of solar panels in the region.

Magal had eyes for no town or historic ruin. He sat alongside Shiri in the air-conditioned bus that was transporting the twelve kidon to the IDF base, paying no attention to the stark landscape rolling past. *Negev* means *dry* in Hebrew, and the view outside the window, once they had left the urban areas, gave truth to the name.

Flat lands, valleys, dried-out streams, hills and misshapen, rocky outcrops flew past. Magal slept. Or so the other operatives thought.

The kidon was actually wide awake. He was making plans. *Today to check out the camp. Tomorrow, to attack.*

Time was at a premium. As was access.

The bus had cell-jamming technology, and no operative could make or receive calls. All Carmel had told them was that they weren't going to one of the larger military bases. Their destination was not on any map. Yes, it was an IDF camp, she said when Magal pressed for more details. 'Sayeret Matkal is based there,' is all she would say. 'Your cell phones won't work there, either. Eliel, Navon, you're from that unit. You must be familiar with the base.'

'No,' Navon shook his head. 'They move bases often. This is a new one to us.'

Some kidon had protested about the cell phones.

'Mine will work,' she told them. 'Abhyan has enabled mine. You have an urgent comms request, come to me. Carter's and the sisters' will work as well.'

A few voices grumbled, but they were half-hearted. All the kidon were mission-experienced. They knew good security protocol when they heard it. They didn't question why the

Americans had special privileges. They had seen how close their director was to them. With access came benefits.

Magal had anticipated comms challenges. He had made arrangements in Haifa and before boarding the bus, had spoken quietly to Carmel.

'You might get a call from my foster mother's house.'

'Yes, of course,' she responded, concern on her face. 'I will let you know immediately.'

'I might have to go for a few hours.'

'I am sure we can make arrangements.'

'I will come back, however.'

'You don't need to, Eliel. I understand the circumstances. Stay with her.'

'This helps take my mind off it. I will return.'

'As you wish. It will be a long ride, however.'

Haifa was a good three hours away from the base. Six hours of travel both ways. A sufficient window for Magal to travel to Beersheba, which was just forty minutes away, and pick up supplies. He had a network in that city, as he did in each major Israeli one.

Shiri and I against Sayeret Matkal. A thrill ran through Magal.

We will win.

Moscow

'Yuri,' Andropov roared when he entered his office.

The hacker scampered into his office.

'See what's in this,' he said, tossing him the thumb drive.

'What's this?'

'It's a thumb drive, *durak*.' Fool.

'I know that.' Yuri looked affronted. 'What's inside?'

'If I knew, would I ask you?' Andropov thumped his desk. A glass of water spilled, and he leaped up to mop it. 'See what you have done.'

'I didn't do anything.'

'Get out of my office.'

Yuri departed.

'Wait!'

Yuri turned around, with a long-suffering expression on his face.

'Send me the files inside that,' he pointed to Yuri's fist, 'before you do anything.'

Chapter 58

———— ◦⊗◦ ————

Jerusalem, IDF Base
Eight days after Assassinations
Three days to Announcement

'There was a thumb drive in Raskov's apartment,' Andropov told Zeb as he and Beth and Meghan traveled to the IDF base in a vehicle driven by Levin's aide.

'What's in it?' Zeb looked out at the rolling land sliding past his window.

'No idea, yet. My people are checking. I have sent a copy to you. How's Levin?'

'He's feeling more confident.'

'Da, I can imagine.' Andropov bitterly hated traitors. 'Give him my regards.'

Zeb turned on his screen and kicked the back of the seat ahead of him. Meghan turned around, flicking back a strand of hair. Her green eyes were sunshine.

'You're working? This scenery ...' she clicked her tongue in exasperation. 'It's breathtaking. The world isn't going to implode if you take some time to admire your surroundings.'

'Andropov has sent a file. I am forwarding to both of you. Check out what's inside.'

'Why has he sent it to us?'

'It was in Raskov's apartment. Did I tell you he was found dead? Knifed?'

Beth turned back as well. 'You didn't. When did it happen?'

'Yesterday. Nope,' he hurried to answer before the sisters could question him. 'No clues who killed him. Or why.'

'We'll set Werner on it.'

Which took a minute, and then the sisters were back to peering outside the window.

There was no other traffic on the road. It was a black ribbon that wound through the desert, disappearing into valleys and reappearing in the distance, shimmering in the heat.

It turned to concrete the closer they got to the base. Check posts appeared at regular intervals as they neared.

The base sprung out of nowhere, or that's how it seemed.

One moment, their vehicle was going down a steep hill, then climbing up again—and there it was.

A large, walled-off compound that contained squat, ugly buildings, a military trademark the world over. *Those will be the accommodation and admin units. There will be training grounds, clubs, fields for war games.* Zeb hadn't been to this particular base, but he had trained in a similar one in another part of the country. Military camps such as this one weren't that different around the world.

He suppressed a smile when he saw Beth and Meghan were looking around wide-eyed. It was their first time in an Israeli military camp—and one that was home to some of the best soldiers in the world.

A stern-faced officer gave them their access cards at an

admin building.

'Someone has pulled a lot of strings,' he said. 'You and those other visitors have got a free pass to go anywhere. Not many people on this base have that.' Zeb looked at him sharply. Nope, there didn't seem any rancor behind his words. *He's stating a fact. Nothing more.*

He thanked the officer and was looking around for directions when a voice hailed them. Carmel hurried across.

'Settled in?' Zeb asked.

She made a face. 'We arrived a few hours back. This place is huge; it will take some getting used to. But yeah, we know our way around the main areas.'

She led them to another building, a residential one, and showed them their rooms. All on the ground floor. The sisters stowed their gear in theirs and joined the kidon and Zeb in his.

The room had basic furniture. A table, a couple of chairs, a night lamp, a bed, an air-conditioning unit that hummed quietly, and a wall-mounted TV.

Carmel spread a map on the table and used a pen to highlight various buildings.

'The negotiators are here.' She drew a circle around an admin building in the center of the compound. 'This is where the top brass has their offices. The Israeli and Palestinian teams are secluded in a large conference room. It has steel-reinforced doors and blast-proof walls. Next to it is a canteen that provides them with food, drinks, anything they need.'

'Who cooks for them?'

'One military cook and his assistant. They are assigned exclusively to the negotiators. The servers are two guards.'

Zeb looked up skeptically. 'The guards leave their post to serve food?'

'No. Two guards at the door; these servers are extra. They are stationed at the kitchen.'

A hallway extended from the conference room for a hundred yards and opened into a central area. More hallways branched out from the anchoring space like spokes in a wheel. 'More offices.' Carmel shaded several rooms. 'Two guards every thirty feet in each hallway.'

Zeb liked the layout. One could stand in that middle space and keep an eye on the conference room as well as the entrance.

I'm sure that's why Abhyan chose that room.

'What about access?'

'That entry gate is the main control. Everyone coming or going is scrutinized, and badges with the right clearances are issued for those entering. Those cards,' she pointed to the ones around their necks, 'will gain you entry to your apartment building, to that conference room, to the commander's office, everywhere.'

'No thumbprint, iris scan?'

'Yes. At the conference room. Thumbprint, though it is usually disabled because of the servers' frequent coming and going. There's both thumbprint and iris scan at the armory.' She pointed to another building, which was set well back. 'There's no need to go there, however. We have our weapons, our gear. The IDF soldiers have theirs.'

There were more buildings on the map. 'Clubhouse, gym, lecture hall, cinema.' Carmel identified them. There were large open spaces around the buildings, which Zeb guessed were for the soldiers to train in.

'What about these?' Beth pointed to rectangular shapes well away from the admin and residential areas.

'Hangars. For choppers. Maintenance areas for tanks, vehicles. We were given a brief tour in a vehicle but didn't step out. While our passes grant us entry everywhere—'

'You won't be leaving that main office building,' Meghan guessed.

'Yes. We are here for just three nights. The grand press conference is the third day from today. We go back to Jerusalem once that is done.'

'Who is the security chief?'

'The base has its own security and military police. However, Moshe Abhyan is the commander here, too, for the security of the conference. You knew he was a Sayeret Matkal officer?' she said, aiming her question at Zeb.

'Yeah. Avichai and I knew.'

'More secrets, Zeb,' she smiled disarmingly to negate the sting in her words.

'What's your brief?'

'What the ramsad gave us. Stay close to the conference room. Eye everyone who comes and goes. Raise the alarm if we recognize anyone.'

'Twelve of you near that room will crowd that hallway. That's a security risk in itself.'

'Yes. We will be dispersed. We will be in shifts too. There's a refreshment area here,' she pointed to the central area, 'where they serve drinks and food. Many of us will be ranged from that conference room to that area.'

'Windows and exits in that conference room?'

'None. The attached kitchen has an exit. It has a supply room as well, with a window.'

'What?' Meghan read his expression.

'There should be more exits in the base. Such a large base

can't have just the one.'

'There are,' Carmel corrected him. 'They aren't marked on this map. Our guide pointed them out from a distance. There are check posts everywhere. Someone on foot or a vehicle will be stopped and questioned. And then there are the drones. They mount continuous air surveillance.'

Beth bounced on the bed, her green eyes narrowed in thought. 'I can't see how any killer can get into this place.'

'Or get out alive.'

Chapter 59

———— ✺ ————

IDF Base
Nine days after Assassinations
Two days to Announcement

Magal and Shiri broke away from the rest of the kidon, who were lingering around the central area.

The previous day, Carmel and Abhyan, accompanied by the two watchful security guards, had taken them inside the conference room.

That occurred because Magal had whispered in Yakov's ear. 'Who knows whether there really are negotiators behind that door? That's what they told us in the Galaxy.'

Back at the hotel, he had noticed that Yakov was excitable. His verbal nudge did the trick. The kidon had approached Carmel and had demanded to see the negotiators.

She had eyed him calmly and had then called Abhyan. The security commander was in uniform and cut an imposing figure, but that didn't cow Yakov. Mossad's kidon were just as well-trained and experienced as Sayeret Matkal soldiers.

'Carter and you duped us in the Galaxy. We need to see that's not happening again,' he said firmly.

The security chief had taken them without a word to the conference room and had stood back as they entered.

Twelve heads had risen up in surprise at their entrance. Magal recognized the Palestinians from the handler's files. He swiftly noted where they sat in relation to the door. They were close to it.

People tend to choose the same chairs every day, at a conference. Something about familiarity in new surroundings.

'Satisfied?' Abhyan had asked.

Yakov had nodded.

'Take out your cell,' Magal spoke softly, bringing out his device as they approached the kitchen next to the conference room.

'It doesn't work here,' Shiri hissed, but obeyed.

'Just checking,' Magal said to the two guards outside the room. The conference room's doors were twenty feet away, the security detail watching them impassively.

He and his partner entered the kitchen. The chef was busy in front of a stove. His assistant was chopping something on a sideboard.

The two servers lounged, chatting with each other. They were in uniform and, as Magal passed, he snapped their pictures swiftly.

He entered the supply room and saw that it was dark, lit by a single bulb. Rows of tall, stacked shelves extended to the rear of the room. Big freezers hummed at the back. A window at the back. No rear door.

He and Shiri returned to the kitchen and went to its back

door. Magal opened it and stepped outside. There was a parking lot next to the door. A military truck parked in it.

He went to the vehicle and checked inside. The key was in its slot.

'You got an idea?' his friend asked.

'Several. That,' he pointed to the truck, 'will be our escape route.'

Shiri looked at it and then at him. 'How will we get inside the conference room?'

'You've seen all the soldiers? All of them were armed. Even the servers.'

'Yes. M16s, Glocks; I saw grenades, too.'

'Their build?'

'Similar to ours.' Which wasn't surprising since many IDF personnel and Mossad operatives were similarly sized.

'Hair?'

'That, too.'

'Helmets?'

'On the kitchen counter.'

'You know how we will enter the conference room?'

'I know, now. But getting out of the base—'

'Working on it.'

Carmel approached him at three pm, her face worried. 'Eliel, there's a call for you.'

He took her cell, turned away and cupped it to his ear.

He adopted a grave expression and nodded silently several times.

'I will be there,' he said and hung up.

'I need to go.'

'I assumed. I arranged a military vehicle for you.'

'I need it only till Beersheba. My foster family has arranged a ride for me from there. I will return on my own.'

'I thought—'

'She's hanging on,' he smiled grimly. 'She wants to see me.'

'Go.'

Magal went.

Beersheba

He waited at Beersheba until the military vehicle departed and then climbed into the Toyota that his associate had driven.

Jud Lipman was in his fifties, and with his straggly, white hair, he looked like a university professor.

He was a master forger, a counterfeiter, a con man, a maker of disguises, and had successfully stayed clear of the law for decades.

'That thing with your mother. It's not easy, you know,' he grumbled. 'I had to record her voice and perfect it so that it could pass most audio tests. I jump whenever I get a call from your organization, checking if she is really ill.'

'You've been pulling that stunt off for a while now, pretending to be my foster mother or someone close to her, attending to her.'

'It's difficult, rerouting the calls so that it looks like I am replying from Haifa.'

'You don't complain when I pay you.'

That shut the old man up. He drove them inside the city, past office buildings and warehouses. He entered a gated, dilapidated building and called out a name at the squawk box. The iron gates opened silently.

'No one's inside,' he grunted. 'Voice recognition and iris scan at the box.'

Lipman took him up a rickety elevator and opened a door at his floor. The office was in stark contrast to the outside of the building. It was sleek, hi-tech, and had several pieces of equipment Magal couldn't identify.

He recognized the 3-D printer in the corner and a kiln the forger still used for his fakes.

'You need something?' Lipman drew his attention. 'I figure you haven't come here to greet me.'

'I need face masks.' Magal brought out his phone and showed the pictures he'd taken of the servers. 'Exact replicas.'

'That will take time. Days.'

'You have five hours.'

Zeb split from the sisters and investigated the main admin building for himself. The twins walked with Carmel and Dalia, who showed them around.

The three of them hadn't checked out the base the previous day. They had spent most of it, after their arrival, with the base's commander, and Moshe Abhyan.

He joined them an hour later and gestured to a vehicle that was waiting outside.

'Want a tour of the base? To the areas that no one sees?'

A resounding 'yeah' was his answer.

Driven by a tight-lipped captain, the four of them went to the exercise grounds and watched a drill in progress: IDF teams attacking what looked like a Syrian terrorist training camp. A chopper flew overhead and a drone made passes, as the soldiers went from stealth mode to aggressive attack, from house to house, as enemy fire tracked them

'How did you wrangle this?' Beth asked in awe, as they halted at a distance. A hundred yards away there was a team of uniformed observers, watching through binos. They didn't make any attempt to stop their vehicle. Nor did they approach it.

They are tolerating us.

That didn't surprise Zeb. No military commander liked the presence of externals in his camp.

'You have met the prime minister,' he reminded the younger sister.

Carmel and Dalia looked at them sharply. 'You have, what?'

'It was accidental,' Zeb assured them. 'We met in passing.'

Carmel gave him a long, disbelieving look. 'Really?'

'Even we, and I know Dalia and I have security clearances at par with them,' she jerked a shoulder at the soldiers, 'aren't allowed entry. Just who are the three of you?'

'Friends of Avichai,' Zeb shrugged, and the kidon had to settle for that.

Alice Monash and the ramsad were at the base when they returned.

'We arrived yesterday, but didn't see you anywhere. Checked out the place? It doesn't look like even a fly can enter this base unauthorized, at least not to my untrained eyes.'

'Seems like that, ma'am, but we can't take anything for granted.'

'You are satisfied?' Levin queried.

'Yes, but it is Abhyan you should ask. We are careful watchers, nothing more.'

At seven pm, Zeb joined Carmel, who was briefing her team in front of a drinks' stand in the open space. There was still foot traffic in the building, despite the hour. It looked like the base didn't sleep. Time merely slowed in the night.

Meghan looked back at him. 'Nothing yet on Raskov's file. He'd encrypted it. Werner's trying out various algorithms that the Russians normally use.'

Zeb nodded absently. He was counting heads and came up one short. He started again.

Eliel!

'Where is Eliel?' he asked Carmel, once the operatives broke up.

'Gone to Haifa. His mother's condition is deteriorating. Someone from his home called, said she wanted to speak to him.'

'Someone?'

'Cross-checked, Zeb. The caller *is* genuine. He does have a mother. She *is* ill. Critically.'

Navon was with Yakov, the two men talking softly, cradling drinks in their hands. Nachman was with a soldier. Other operatives sprawled in lounge chairs. Some were heading to their rooms.

Carmel had arranged shifts. Six kidon in twelve-hour rotations. She and a few others would be on watch till the early hours, till other operatives replaced them.

Zeb found no fault with her system. He had nothing to complain about in terms of security arrangements.

Still, something niggled at the back of his mind.

He reviewed the investigation he had carried out on the twelve kidon in the compound. Nope. He was sure they weren't involved. It wasn't just his gut feeling; the twins had gone through their data and given them a clean chit.

I trust their judgment better than mine.

He listed the various events that had occurred since he had arrived in the country. Found nothing that worried him. *That time outside Beit Aghion, when I thought we were being watched. Should I have dug deeper? How?*

He shook his head impatiently. It was behind him now, and in any case Masih had been killed. He continued thinking, staring unseeingly at no one in particular, unaware that Levin had joined the sisters and the three were watching him.

No. Something else was worrying him, just at the edge of his consciousness.

He gave up. It would come to him. He hoped it would be well in time and would turn out to be a harmless thought.

'Let's walk and talk,' Levin said, tapping his shoulder. 'You need some fresh air.'

The four of them went out into the night and moved away from the admin building until they came to a check post. A guard stopped them, while another trained his weapon on them.

They handed him their credentials. He made calls and waved them past the barrier.

'It's dark out there, sir,' Zeb told Levin.

'We aren't going far. Just to stretch our legs.'

Levin stopped and glanced at the sky. A pale moon was partly hidden by clouds. A few stars looked down at them.

'I hope what we are doing is right,' he exhaled loudly.

'What's that?' Meghan sat on the ground and rested her back against Beth's legs.

'You will know in less than forty-eight hours. If Zeb hasn't told you ...' he gestured apologetically.

'He never tells us anything,' she said snidely. Then smiled, and all was good.

'No one told me anything, either,' Zeb protested. 'I worked it out for myself. What's worrying you?' he asked the Mossad director.

'It will divide my country in half. Maybe forever.'

'Nothing's forever. Twenty, fifty years from now, people will have forgotten.'

'This is the Middle East, Zeb,' Levin snorted. 'Centuries of history are remembered as if events happened yesterday.'

'What do you believe in?'

'I would have resigned if I thought the prime minister was wrong. On something as significant as this.'

'Many people call me a killer, Avichai.'

Meghan got to her feet abruptly. This statement, that voice, was unlike Zeb. Beth grabbed her forearm and urged her to silence.

'There are probably kids out there who will not know their father; women and men whose lives broke down because I killed their partners. I shed blood because I believed it would further peace. I would do so again, without a second thought, if I believed in its rightness. If what Cantor and Baruti announce will help millions of people get certainty in their lives … that they will definitely see another sunrise and sunset, it is a worthy cause.'

He stopped suddenly when he became aware of three pairs of eyes on him.

'Let's head back,' he said, laughing in embarrassment. 'This fresh air is making me light- headed.'

Unknown to any of them, Shiri wasn't far from them.

He had a flashlight in his mouth and was reading a letter.

Chapter 60

—∞∞∞—

IDF Base
Nine days after Assassinations
Two days to Announcement

Shiri had found the letter in his pocket when he was in his room, as he was changing.

He took one look at it, recognized the handwriting, and hurried out.

He found a secluded spot far away from his residential building, propped himself against a boulder and opened it.

'My brother,' Magal began.

Shiri blinked. The two men were close friends, but his partner had never addressed him in that manner.

'I have lied to you.'

His grip on the letter tightened.

'You once asked who I was. Whether I was Israeli. I replied I was Eliel Magal. I lied about that.

I am eople..'

Shiri peered at the word that his partner had blacked out. He couldn't read it.

He drew a sharp breath when he read the next line.

'I am from the same country as the handler. You know that. You are, too. I belong to that country, however. It is a feeling I have never had about Israel. It is something that has grown on me as we worked with the handler and spent time with him.

Yes, I have lied about that, too. I met him on three other occasions. I didn't tell you about them. I gave the excuse that I needed to visit my foster family in Haifa.

I reached out to him all three times. I wanted to know more of that country. Not from the Mossad dossiers or from our missions to it, but to experience it for myself like an ordinary civilian.

The handler took me to a mosque; he accompanied me as we visited historical sites. He was with me while I watched their Supreme Leader give a speech to thousands of cheering people.

I felt at home, Navon. It isn't something I ever experienced in Israel.

You must be wondering, now, if I have become a Muslim.

I haven't. I still remain unreligious, like you. But I think one doesn't need to follow some religion to belong to some country.

Obviously, I now feel differently about Israel. I don't hate it. I don't dislike it. I feel nothing about it. It is why I have no problems in acting against the ramsad, even though he is a man I respect.

And it is because all these newfound feelings in me that I have accepted what happens next.

This is something you should know, Navon.

There is no escape from that base.

We are up against too much. Too many soldiers. Too many

eyes on the ground and in the sky. Too much remoteness.

We cannot kill those Palestinians and get away alive.

Levin, Abhyan, Carter, though I am not sure how much input the American had in this decision, have beaten us by moving the negotiators to this base.

But they don't know I will have the last laugh.

Because I am prepared to die.

That might sound strange to you, because we are kidon. We might die in a mission and are mentally conditioned to accept it, but we don't blindly go into an operation where the only surety is that we will die.

I intend to carry out the mission of killing the Palestinians. It is my way of getting back at the country that took us in but never made us regard it as home.

Given what I have written so far, you might wonder why I still want to kill Palestinians. The answer is simple.

I distrust the handler. You are right. He will come after us if we fail. However, he is right in this mission's objectives and its impact on Israel.

It will do maximum damage to the country and to its relationships with Middle Eastern countries and the world.

I will return, Navon, in the morning, with what we need.

You have two choices with you.

In your left pocket is another letter.'

Shiri patted his pocket. Something crinkled. There *was* a letter.

'In that one, I have confessed to the first killing as well as what we are planning on the base. I have taken sole responsibility.

You can hand that letter to Carmel. She will arrest me when I return. I will never be seen again, but you will be free.

No attack will happen in that eventuality, but you must get the handler. Otherwise he will ruin you.

The other choice for you is to join me. If you make that decision, keep an eye on the shift patterns.

Don't forget that we will die.

But I think we will be the most lethal suicide bombers ever.'

Magal signed off with, '*Your brother.*'

Shiri looked at the sky, something deep welling inside him. He cleared his throat and blinked rapidly.

He folded the letter carefully and put it back in his pocket.

At two am, he had finished thinking.

He burned both letters, buried the ashes in the ground and went to his room.

He had made his decision.

He had made peace with himself and Magal.

Chapter 61

———⊶⊷———

IDF Base
Ten days after Assassinations
One day to Announcement

Magal arrived at six am. His eyes were red and his face drooped. He looked the picture of exhaustion.

He wasn't.

He had slept in Lipman's office while the forger worked on the masks, and he was well-rested.

The base was a hive of activity even that early, and the admin office was jumping with people. The first person he saw was Shiri, who rushed over to him and hugged him.

There were tears in his friend's eyes when they separated. He thumped Shiri's back and was about to speak when Carmel joined them.

She thrust a coffee mug at him. 'What happened? Why's Navon crying? Your mother—'

'She's still alive. Tomorrow. That's what doctors say.'

'You shouldn't be here, Eliel.'

'There's no other place I would rather be. I thought your

shift was over?'

'It is, but I stayed back. Don't change the subject.'

She tried to persuade him to go to his mother, but he didn't budge. She gave up and told him to join the morning shift. 'That way, you can go to Haifa in the evening if you need to, your conscience clear.'

The morning shift was precisely what he wanted.

'Can I shower, first?' he asked her.

'Sure. Navon, go with him.'

'You shouldn't—' he began in the privacy of his room.

'Stop. Say nothing more. We have grown up together. We have gone on operations together. There isn't much I would do without you. Even dying.'

The two men embraced again and got to work, their professional selves taking over.

'You got them?' Shiri asked.

Magal held up the masks in reply.

They were made of a special rubber that allowed the skin underneath to breathe. They covered the entire face, with nose holes and openings for eyes.

'Try yours.'

Shiri fitted it over his face and looked in the mirror.

'Face me.'

He turned to Magal, who snapped his picture.

The two men looked at his image and then at the particular server's it replicated.

The faces looked identical.

'Who did this for you?'

'Someone I know in Beersheba. These look good in the pictures. In reality, up close, they will be detected as fake.'

'They will pass a quick check?'

'Yes.'

'Put on yours.'

Magal tried his. The results were the same. He looked similar to the second server.

'Didn't the security at the check post ask you about these?'

'I told them it was for a surprise, fancy dress party. I asked them to keep it to themselves. They laughed.'

'They didn't recognize the faces?'

'No.'

'Did you bring any weapons?'

'No,' Magal shook his head, removed the rubber and wiped his face. 'Those would be harder to explain. We will use what we have and take the grenades from the two men.'

'I know you said you feel nothing ... I don't, either,' Shiri said hesitantly. 'But I don't want to kill the other kidon. Not without good reason.'

'We won't,' Magal assured him. 'Unless they cross our paths.'

Seven am

Magal and Shiri returned to the admin office. They went to the coffee stand and bought themselves drinks. Dalia, Nachman, Yakov, Uzziah, Danell and Shiri were on the morning shift. Carmel and Magal were additional members.

Magal drifted to where Carmel and her partner were chatting with Danell. *I like these women. I hope I don't have to kill them.*

He felt free, knowing what was coming. He no longer had the burden of working out their escape. It was as if a weight had been lifted off him.

'Eliel,' Dalia plucked at his sleeve, 'what do you think? Danell says the ramsad wanted to give us a vacation. That's why he brought us here. There's nothing to be done here.'

'I doubt the director knows what a vacation is,' he replied, drily. 'Isn't he here?'

'Yes. He, the ambassador and the Americans are staying in a different building. He will show up.'

Eight am

Zeb came to the admin building. He had set off for an early-morning run, and before he had gone far, two pairs of footsteps had echoed behind him.

He looked back. The twins.

The three of them had proceeded silently and, after a light workout, headed back to their rooms.

Carmel brought him a coffee; Dalia brought two for the sisters.

'You don't need to serve us,' he chided her.

'Enjoy,' she mocked him. 'You can boast how Mossad was at your service. You won't get any other opportunity.'

'Anything?'

'Nothing. A few visitors in the night. IDF civilians who are security-cleared. They are in the tech department, working in shifts. They never left their office.' She waved toward a hallway.

Alice Monash came in, along with Levin. The ambassador spent a few minutes with them and introduced herself to the kidon she didn't know.

At eight-thirty am, the negotiators arrived. They were

escorted by six soldiers, who led them to the conference room. Alice Monash followed them, and the door closed behind the two teams and the U.S. ambassador.

Nine am

Magal went to the kitchen and helped himself to a glass of water. He made idle talk with the cook while he observed the servers from the corners of his eyes.

The men were at the call of the negotiators. They served beverages and soft drinks when needed. The lunch service began at twelve and ended at one pm.

'It's busiest then,' the chef said, wiping sweat from his forehead and washing his hands. 'I have cooked for larger groups, but I have also had more help. Here,' he turned around in a half-circle, 'it's just me and him.' The assistant waved lazily at Magal.

'What about the servers?'

'They don't help in the kitchen. Security protocol. They will back up the guards if needed.'

'They are soldiers?'

'Yes. I, too, have to go through rigorous training.'

Our masks will pass. Magal took the liberty of staring openly at the servers, who ignored him. *Lipman did a good job.*

The kidon checked out the various weapons on their bodies and noted how they moved. *Both are right-handed. Rifles across their backs, secured firmly, but available for quick action. Handgun across the chest. Grenades in pouches around their belly. Knife down the thigh.*

He went out of the kitchen and inspected the guards at the

conference room as well as the kitchen. They had their rifles in their hands and more gear on their bodies. The soldiers down the hallway were similarly equipped.

Ten am

'Werner cracked it.' Beth approached Zeb and led him to where Meghan was, on a couch, headphones wrapped around her ears, head bobbing to some beat. 'Cracked it during the night, but we had connectivity issues.'

'Such as?'

'Heavy cloud cover, late in the night. The satellite signal dropped.'

'You haven't hooked into the base's network?'

'And give the IDF an opportunity to hack into us?' She rolled her eyes and tapped her sister on the shoulder.

'Files. Lots of them,' Meghan told them. 'In Russian. I am getting them translated. But heck, this dude, it looks like he dumped FSB's operations on that thumb drive. This might take some time.'

'Try keyword searches,' Zeb suggested.

'Way ahead of you. Am doing that. Trouble is, which keywords to search for?'

'I don't know.' Zeb shrugged. 'You two are smarter than me, aren't you?' He walked away quickly before they could retort.

Eleven am

Andropov called. 'Raskov. You remember him?'

'Yeah,' Zeb answered. 'Meghan's going through his files.'

'She is?'

Zeb heard him bellowing at some Yuri.

'You're ahead of the curve,' the Russian came back to him. 'My cyber guy encountered some basic problems. We lost the Internet for a while. This is Russia, my friend.'

'Grigor,' Zeb stopped his friend before he launched into a tirade. 'We'll share what we have. You called for a reason?'

'Yes. Raskov's killing. It matches another killing in Saint Petersburg a year back.'

'Same cuts—'

'Same everything. I've got the photos with me. The police suspect it was even the same weapon.'

'The killer wasn't found?'

'No. Ask me about the victim.

'Who was he?'

'An arms dealer. Suspected of supplying EQB.'

Chapter 62

IDF Base
Ten days after Assassinations
One day to Announcement

Zeb's world shrank. He bowed his head to focus on Andropov's words.

'EQB arms supplier?'

'Yes. He was on our radar, too. We would have taken him out, but someone acted faster. He had enemies. Many. In Russia as well as outside.'

Zeb thanked him and headed blindly to the drink stand. He looked at no one. Was dimly conscious of Meghan's eyes on him. He didn't speak to her.

He took his coffee mug, thinking rapidly. *EQB. Israel could have killed him. Don't jump to conclusions. He had other enemies too, according to Grigor. What's his link to Raskov?*

'EQB!' He hurried to the sisters. Coffee spilled on his wrist and burned. He didn't register it. Beth sprang up and mopped his hand with paper towels. 'And Hamas. Search for those.'

'On it,' Meghan typed.

'Avichai,' Zeb called out softly on his collar mic.

Levin didn't respond.

Must be with the commander.

That feeling returned. The one he'd had the previous day. Like he was missing something obvious.

Twelve pm

Magal and Shiri drifted casually toward the kitchen. The cook was arranging plates on a counter. His assistant was working a blender. Its sound merged with that of a noisy exhaust fan, drowning out conversation.

Neither man looked up at the visitors.

Magal picked up two carrots, tossed one to Shiri, munched on his and went inside the supply room.

The servers were at the back. They were straightening their uniforms and putting on white gloves.

'You both checked these racks?' Magal asked them. 'Carmel said we have to inspect them.'

'Nothing here,' a soldier replied as he tugged at his clothing.

'Let's do it again. It shouldn't take long. NOW!'

He used his command voice. The soldiers looked at each other and shrugged. It really wouldn't take long. They still had time.

'Let's start at the back.'

Magal and Shiri spread apart. They followed the soldiers and, when it was deepest and darkest in the supply room, they struck.

'Nothing about EQB,' Meghan announced over his earbud.

'Zeb?'

'Yeah, I heard.' He went to the central space and looked down the hallway. Nothing jumped out at him. His radar was pinging, however, soft and low. He looked at the entrance.

Soldiers on guard. No vehicles arriving. Clear passage.

'Search for Hamas.'

'Copy.'

He took a step forward. Brought his mug to his mouth and sipped. Assured himself that it was nothing. He was overreacting. *We are possibly in the most secure location in Israel.*

Even as he thought that, a memory stirred. Something about knife work. Someone preferred a blade.

He tried to grab it. It remained elusive.

He took another step. Slower this time, because he wanted to focus on *knife.*

Meghan's voice came on. Strained. 'Zeb. Raskov was on someone else's payroll. Zarab Tousi. He was a double agent.'

Tousi! Shock raced through him. Major General Zarab Tousi, head of the Islamic Revolutionary Guard Corps. It was the most powerful military outfit in Iran. Its influence was far-reaching. It brutally suppressed protests in Iran and used violence and fear to keep liberal-minded citizens in check.

Tousi had openly stated that destruction of Israel was his aim.

Zeb knew of Tousi. Every intelligence agency in the world knew him. He was dubbed the Handler in some circles for running successful double-agent operations in several countries.

Iran!

Eliel and Navon are of Iranian origin. Their grandparents migrated from that country. Eliel has a Persian soldier's tattoo.

'Meg,' he knew his voice sounded coarse. 'Search for

Eliel and Navon. Their second names. Magal, Shiri.'

He moved quickly toward the hallway.

Looked around him. Didn't see the two kidon.

'Beth?'

'Yeah.'

'Get Levin. The prime minister. I don't care who. Send the police to Magal's house. Check if his foster mother is really ill.'

Another thought struck him. 'Is she really his foster parent? Just who are those folks in Haifa?'

'Got it.'

'Carmel?'

The kidon didn't reply.

'Zeb,' Meghan said, taking a deep breath. 'It's them.'

His mug crashed to the floor as he burst into a sprint. Adrenaline surged through him, drowning out the protests his body made. Her voice faded in and out as other thoughts scrambled for attention.

'Raskov was blackmailing Tousi ... photographs of Eliel and Navon.'

They showed me those pictures.

'Raskov found their identities.'

Knife work. Eliel prefers that weapon. It's in his file.

'He went to Tousi, who said he'd keep it to himself. Then he started blackmailing.'

Eliel and Navon left their post at the Galaxy. They rushed to the fifth.

'This thumb drive was his protection.'

'Find Carmel,' he panted.

'We've got to announce—'

'No! We need eyes-on. They might start killing indiscriminately.'

How did I miss all this?

He stopped thinking. There would be time later to blame himself. He was thirty yards down. Running at full speed. The first pair of guards turned toward him.

He held his credentials up. 'You saw Eliel and Navon?'

'Kitchen.'

'They're in the kitchen,' he relayed.

'Carmel's here. They're all coming,' Meghan panted, as if she was running. 'Beth's gone to find Levin.'

He looked back. Meghan running down the hallway, the Israeli behind her.

The ambassador! She's in the conference room.

Seventy feet out. Another set of guards. Same question. Same reply.

He skidded as he neared the kitchen. A server stepped out, plates balanced in his hands. He flashed a curious glance at Zeb and went to the conference room.

Zeb crashed into the kitchen door. Cook and assistant, heads down, arranging food on more plates. Blender and exhaust fan making conversation impossible.

A server came out of the supply room. Took several porcelain dishes, stacked them neatly on one forearm and headed out.

'Eliel and Navon?' Zeb yelled. 'Have you seen them?'

The server shook his head, his eyes down.

Zeb darted inside the storage room. Racks. Dim light. He moved swiftly down the rows, checking left and right, Glock appearing magically in his hand.

There, at the back. On the floor. What's that?

He took one look and lunged out of the room.

'*SERVERS*!' he bellowed.

Chapter 63

IDF Base
Ten days after Assassinations
One day to Announcement

Zeb sprang out of the kitchen. The conference room's door was opening. The second server was stepping inside. To his right, Meghan and Carmel were nearing.

'STOP!'

The server didn't stop.

Don't want to shoot him like this.

Zeb holstered his Glock in a flash, dived at him, grabbed him by his collar and yanked him back savagely.

The plates went clattering to the floor. The door started closing. The server swung round smoothly and punched Zeb in the belly. His eyes were cold, his jaws set. Zeb staggered back. The momentary respite was what the server needed. His hand flashed to his chest. Dived into a pouch and came out with a grenade.

'STAND BACK!' Zeb warned the guards, 'DON'T SHOOT.'

I should have shot him, he cursed himself, *when I had the opportunity.*

The nearest four soldiers dropped to the floor and crawled rapidly to the kitchen. Meghan grabbed Carmel and joined them. 'Go,' she yelled. 'We'll deal with him.'

There was something in the server's eyes. He seemed nervous as he backed away, holding the grenade in his hand. A muscle twitched on his face.

'Don't do this. You can't escape. Give yourself up.' He tried to recognize the server, but all he could see was his dark eyes.

All the kidon have dark eyes.

The server's hand arced. The grenade sailed in the air down the hallway. His hand flashed to the M16 behind his back.

Zeb didn't linger. He charged toward the conference room and hurled himself inside. The M16 spat behind him, followed by two flat cracks, sounding almost like one.

And then the door shut behind him.

He crashed into a chair, fell over a negotiator. His eyes sweeping around the room swiftly, taking stock.

The negotiators and the ambassador were looking at him in shock.

The room's soundproofed. But they saw some of that and must have heard the shooting.

The other server was to his front and left, jumping back from laying down his plates. His eyes were on Zeb.

The grenade exploded in the hallway. The room shuddered, its windows shook.

'DOWN! ON THE FLOOR,' Zeb ordered the negotiators, who were shrieking and cowering in fear. He repeated the command in Arabic.

The server stood immobile. He looked stunned.

Or he's working out his next move.

The Israelis and Palestinians threw themselves to the floor. Alice Monash joined them.

Zeb climbed onto the table and drew out his Glock. Then the server acted.

He grabbed a chair and threw it in Zeb's direction. It was heavy: leather-backed, with rollers. Despite that, he picked it up as if it weighed nothing. The next moment, his hands flashed to his M16.

Zeb ducked. He stepped on a paper towel, which slipped on the smooth surface. He stumbled. The heavy missile caught him on his shoulder, and his Glock went flying.

He went with the momentum, rolling on the table as rounds ripped the air above him. Moving faster than his assailant thought he could. Screams burst from the civilians.

'STAY … DOWN,' he panted, and then his feet were smashing against the server, and the two men crashed on a chair and fell to the floor.

Zeb on top, gripping the M16 firmly, directing it toward a rear wall. The server trying to gain control of the weapon, punching at Zeb with his free hand, bucking his hips in an attempt to dislodge him.

Zeb let go of the weapon. The server brought the barrel up and started turning it down. Zeb grabbed the fallen chair and pulled it hard. Its roller smashed into the hostile's neck, choking him. His grip loosened.

It was the opening Zeb needed. He slammed an elbow into the man's shoulder, grabbed the M16 from a weakened palm and flung it away. It was too cumbersome for close-quarters combat. He reached for his Glock when the server reared up and headbutted him.

The blow felt like a block of concrete. Zeb's forehead split. Blood poured down his face. He reared back from the impact, struggling to bring up his handgun after a vice-like grip clamped around his wrist. The server, who was forcing the Glock to the American's body, twisted his wrist painfully until it reached close to the breaking point.

Zeb gritted his teeth, panting harshly, and willed his body to counter the move. Sweat dripped down his nose, mingled with blood. The server's eyes were dark, fathomless, his face scrunched in concentration.

Zeb weakened his grip suddenly. His gun arm swung wide under the attacker's pressure. The weapon triggered and shot into the ceiling. He let go of the weapon, and this time, it was his turn to headbutt.

Except that the server wasn't there. He had kicked away, catching the American on the chest, and now sprang to his feet.

He ripped away his mask. His hand flashed to his thigh and came up with a knife.

'Eliel, why are you doing this?' Zeb asked hoarsely. He grabbed the edge of the table and got to his feet unsteadily.

The kidon attacked in reply.

Zeb saw the knife coming, weaving and dancing in the air, heading toward his chest. He swayed inside the arc of the slice and put out his left hand to guide the blade away.

It was misdirection.

The operative's left fist slammed into his side like a shovel. He thought he felt a rib crack. Fire lanced through him. He took a step back to make space and felt wetness down his left side.

He looked down in surprise and saw a thin, reddening slash in his clothing.

Eliel had cut him on the upstroke, even as he had punched him in the side.

'I should have killed you the moment I knew who you were.' The kidon's lips parted in a feral grin.

Zeb shook his head to clear his mind.

Eliel was possibly the best operative Mossad had. He would need his wits about him.

'I did think about killing your friends. I would have enjoyed cutting their pale skin.'

That was a mistake.

A red mist descended on Zeb. It surged through him, woke the beast in him, gave him power and speed.

He roared inarticulately. Grabbed the nearest furniture, a chair. Swung it around one-handedly and let fly at Eliel, who was charging again, saw the incoming missile and ducked. But another chair flew straight at him and crashed into his chest, and he staggered back and fell.

Eliel reacted almost instantly. He looked at Zeb. Then at the M16, which lay close by. He threw his body at it, got hold of it, and started triggering as he brought the barrel down.

Zeb moved faster than he ever had.

He left the ground, aiming for the Glock that was underneath an upturned chair. Its leg slammed into his side. A groan burst out of him, but his hand kept scrabbling desperately until it touched the weapon.

He grabbed it. Its butt fit comfortably in his palm like it was home. He turned around awkwardly, the furniture digging into his back.

The M16 had stitched a straight-line pattern on the roof,

rounds coming down the wall toward him, Eliel working the weapon with lethal efficiency, his eyes hot as if they could burn Zeb with their gaze.

Concrete chips smacked Zeb's face. He heard shouting as if from a distance. Screaming. He thought he heard Meghan's voice. Beth's as well.

He would take his time, even if Eliel shot him. He gripped the Glock, straightened his arm. Something singed his cheek and then Eliel filled his sight and his finger moved automatically and the gun bucked in his hand.

The kidon's body jerked. The M16 fell away from his hands, one last round burying itself in the wall.

Bodies moved.

Zeb looked up, tiredly.

Beth and Meghan. Behind them Carmel. Dalia. All the remaining kidon. Levin, near the door.

Voices started speaking at once. Maybe they already had been, but the sounds registered on him only then.

Beth helped him up and held a hand around his shoulder as he swayed.

'Is anyone—'

'Not a single one. But for you.'

Levin came across to them, his face like thunder. He looked down at Eliel with distaste. 'I—'

Someone yelled incoherently at the door.

Navon stood there, alive somehow, his body shredded, his face torn away, just one eye blinking at them.

He brought his M16 up slowly.

Zeb shoved Beth out of the way. He drew his Glock up but he knew he was slow.

A sharp report sounded and the kidon collapsed.

He looked around dumbly. Avichai Levin was holstering his weapon calmly.

He caught Zeb's eye.

'I am Mossad's ramsad. I haven't forgotten how to shoot.'

Chapter 64

———⊶∞⊷———

Jerusalem
Eleven days after Assassinations
The day of the Announcement

Beit Aghion, Morning

Prime Minister Yago Cantor's official residence was buzzing with activity. A small army of television vans and journalists from all over the world had gathered outside, pointing their long-range lenses at the house. They badgered the prime minister's spokesman every now and then. They wanted more details on the announcement. They wished to know who was attending.

The woman in question, an old hand at the game, tapped her watch. 'Five pm. It's not long now. Surely, you can wait till then.'

They didn't want to, but neither was she budging from her position.

Inside the residence, a high-powered meeting was taking place. The prime minister was with several of his cabinet ministers and a few other select attendees. To his right was Alice Monash; Spiro, Levitsky, Shoshon and Levin were to his left.

Their positioning wasn't lost on anyone, especially those representing the dissident coalition parties.

Cantor ran through several items of business rapidly. The announcement, which he and Baruti would be making jointly. 'I have the speech ready. You have copies in the folders in front of you.'

Papers shuffled. Heads bowed and read the speech. Zeev looked up, as did Haber.

'Nothing will be changed,' the prime minister told them grimly.

'This won't go down well with our parties,' Haber huffed. 'I know.'

'There will be riots—'

'Are you threatening me, Jaedon?'

'No, Yago. I am reminding you of what the country thinks. It is not too late to change your mind. You and Baruti can still go up there and make bland announcements. You won't lose face. In fact, the majority of the people, the world, expects to hear just that.'

'Thank you for your advice.' Cantor didn't bother to hide his sarcasm. 'I know what some parts of the country think. I know what the other parts think as well, and also what everyone else in the world feels. I didn't come to this initiative just like that. I spoke to people up and down the country. Even in Palestine. I listened to world leaders—'

'You and Baruti. You are just after personal glory. Like the Nobel Peace Prize.'

He startled when Cantor did his palm-slamming trick.

'Enough,' the prime minister thundered. 'Say no more. I have listened to your concerns, to Zeev's and the other parties who share your belief. This is the course Israel will take. Nothing will stop it, even though enough people have tried, already.'

He cast a meaningful glance at the people sitting at the back, in a line of chairs against the wall. Zeb, Beth, Meghan, Shoshon, Spiro and Levitsky's aides.

'Now, about the foreign leaders.' Cantor bent back to his papers. 'President Baruti is already in the city. Security arrangements?'

'All in place, Yago. A fly can't enter Jerusalem without us knowing about it,' Levitsky said confidently.

And this time, Cantor knew, it was the truth.

He went through his agenda rapidly. He had a full day ahead and wished to get the small details out of the way.

'Stay back, please,' he told Levin an hour later, after wrapping up. 'You too, Alice, your aides and Brown.'

'How are you, Zeb?' he eyed the American keenly, noting the cuts on his face. Levin had briefed him fully the previous day, as had Moshe Abhyan. Cantor knew what had gone down and how.

He had made an executive decision, using some of his powers. The showdown in the IDF base would never be made public. Only Levitsky, Spiro and Shoshon were to know. They had agreed with his decision. As far as the Israeli populace and the wider world was concerned, the EQB was behind the first two attacks, and that's how the story would continue to be reported.

Even the Iranian involvement was known to just a handful of people and wouldn't be disclosed to the rest of the cabinet.

'I am fine, sir.'

'You don't look it.'

'Shortage of sleep, sir. Nothing more.'

'Any other findings?' he asked Levin.

'We have filled many of the gaps, Prime Minister. Eliel and Navon were acting alone. They had an apartment in Ein Kerem. We are still going through it, but I am confident we found our traitors.'

'Tousi?'

'There's conclusive proof that he was the mastermind. We don't know how long the kidon were working with him. We are still investigating, sir—'

'Yes, I know. Time. Besides, almost every government resource is mobilized for today.'

'Yes, sir.'

'We will deal with the Iranians later.' He went to his file and brought out three ribbons, something shiny dangling at the end of each.

'Zeb—'

'Sir, I can't accept that.'

Prime Minister Yago Cantor stiffened. 'Zeb Carter, I am the elected leader of Israel. This is an honor that I am privileged to bestow on you and Beth and Meghan Petersen.'

'There is no honor, sir.' Zeb's face was wooden, his hands straight at his sides as if he was on a parade ground. 'I failed. I was taken in by Eliel and Navon. There were many opportunities for me to identify them. I was blind to all. A simple matter, like checking in Haifa—.'

'I checked that,' Levin interrupted him. 'The police checked that. Eliel was smart. His foster mother is ill, but not as critical as he made out to be. We all failed to follow up on

404

her prognosis. You can't blame yourself.'

'I still can't accept that,' Zeb replied stubbornly.

Cantor was lost for words. A flat-out refusal to accept an award wasn't something he had experienced.

'Sir, there are three people I know who deserve those,' Zeb made a face-saving offer. 'Two of them are Avichai's kidon. Carmel and Dalia. They pointed me in the right direction in the first place. They helped me when they didn't need to. The third is Colonel Moshe Abhyan. But for his planning, the body count would have been much higher at the Galaxy and the base.'

'Avichai—' the prime minister accepted Zeb's suggestion.

'I will make arrangements, sir. I will bring them to you once we are done with today.'

Cantor put the medals back in his file and returned to his visitors.

'You won't accept that, but you will take this,' and with that, he grabbed Zeb, embraced him and thumped him on his back.

He did the same for the sisters, who looked dazed and couldn't stop smiling.

'You are friends of Israel. Anytime you need anything, any help the country can provide, give me a call. Even when I am no longer prime minister.'

He glanced at his watch. 'You are coming to the announcement?'

'They are, sir,' Levin answered. 'Front row. There's something, sir …' He reached into his jacket pocket and handed over a letter to the prime minister.

He stood stiffly while Cantor read it. The leader broke off, glanced at his impassive face and went back reading.

'You have a way with words, Avichai,' he folded it and tapped it against his thigh. 'It's his resignation,' he explained to the others.

The sisters gasped and looked at the ramsad in shock.

'Zeb didn't fail, sir. I did,' Levin said woodenly. 'I had traitors in Mossad. I don't know how much damage they have done to my organization. Every mission, every kidon, might be compromised.'

'I know.' The prime minister tore the letter to shreds and dropped them in a trash bin. 'You have a lot of work to do. Go, do it.'

'Sir—'

'Avichai, there's not a single intelligence agency in the world that hasn't had traitors at some point. I know how you feel. But you aren't going anywhere. You are the best director the Mossad has had in a long while. I am not letting you go.'

'But—'

'Enough, Avichai. There will be no more discussion on this.'

'Sir, you said I was the best director.'

'In some time, yes.'

'About my salary, sir—'

'Go, Avichai. I want to spend a few minutes with the ambassador.'

Avichai went, taking Zeb and the sisters with him.

The prime minister and Alice Monash shared a laugh when they were alone, and then the leader took her by the elbow. 'Come. There's someone you should meet.'

He led her to the next room, where a single person was waiting.

President Ziyan Baruti.

Chapter 65

Jerusalem
Eleven days after Assassinations
The day of the Announcement

Beit Aghion, Morning

'President Baruti, what a surprise!' Alice Monash hugged him. 'Yago is playing his cards very close to his chest. He didn't say you were here.'

'Ziyan,' Cantor looked the Palestinian up and down. 'You are looking good.'

'If I can't look good today, when will I?'

The prime minister took out their speeches and handed one to Baruti. 'Here's yours. All changes incorporated, as we agreed.'

He waited for the Palestinian to finish reading, then handed over another sheet. 'And that's mine.'

'This won't be easy, Yago. I can see a lot of troubles for both of us ahead.'

'I know, my friend. But this is the right step. It is the seed.'

'You two,' Alice Monash beamed at them. 'You should be

proud of yourselves. I never thought I would see this happen, not in my lifetime.'

'Which is our cue,' Cantor winked at Baruti. 'Madam Ambassador,' he addressed her formally and drew out a medal. 'It gives me the greatest pleasure to make you an honorary citizen of the State of Israel. And, unlike Zeb, you can't say no,' he chortled as he placed it around her neck.

'Madam Ambassador,' Baruti quickly followed, and draped another medal around her neck. 'You are now an honorary citizen of the State of Palestine.'

Alice Monash was dumbstruck. 'I ...' she wiped tears from her eyes. 'I can't thank you enough.'

'No, it's we who should thank you,' Cantor rumbled. 'It was your tireless effort. You bullied us into pursuing this idea when we both almost gave up. But for your efforts, today wouldn't have happened.'

He looked up when there was a knock on the door and an aide poked his head in.

'Sir—'

'Go,' Alice Monash pushed him. 'I will be here with President Baruti.'

Teddy Stadium, Jerusalem
Evening

Avichai Levin picked up Zeb, Beth and Meghan from the American embassy. He was insistent on it.

'You'll come with me,' he said. 'No one else. Not even your embassy vehicle.'

Zeb knew where the stadium, the venue for the announcement, was located. It was near Malha train station and was home to four soccer teams in the city. It had a capacity of just over thirty thousand and, judging by the traffic on the roads, was going to be packed.

There was a strong military presence on every street. Choppers and drones flew overhead. Bomb squads and sniffer dogs routinely stopped cars and inspected bags and personal belongings.

'Wow,' Beth breathed, 'I have never seen security like this.'

'The prime minister of Britain, the president of France, the chancellor of Germany, they are all here,' Levin said proudly. 'Leaders of most of the G20 are here.'

'President Morgan as well?' Meghan asked in surprise.

'No,' Levin met Zeb's eyes in the mirror. 'Not him.'

'Avichai,' Zeb leaned forward. 'This isn't the way to the stadium.'

'We are going to my office first.'

'Your office is in—'

'That isn't the only office I have,' the ramsad frowned. 'You Americans think you know everything about Mossad. You don't!'

'What are we doing there, anyway? Won't we be late?' Meghan glanced at her watch.

'We won't,' Levin said comfortably, and refused to answer any more questions.

'Eyes down,' he joked when they strode down a corridor, past work stations and cubicles. A few women and men greeted him, and he responded.

'It wouldn't surprise me if you two,' he mock-glared at the sisters, 'recorded everything as you entered my office.'

He led them inside a glass-walled office, kept them standing while he went around his desk.

He pulled open a drawer and pulled out something that shined.

He came back toward them, three ribboned medals in his hand.

'You are honorary kidon, now,' he told them simply, as Beth gasped.

He draped the awards around the sisters' necks and, when he came to Zeb, he drew out his Glock.

'It's that,' he pointed at the medal, 'or a bullet. That's the Mossad way.'

The stadium was bursting at its seams when they arrived. They were stopped several times, their vehicle inspected—and the twins' bags—despite Levin's security clearances.

The ramsad had promised front-row seats, and he delivered.

On each side of them were rows of foreign dignitaries. Zeb scanned the crowd behind them. As many foreign attendees as Israelis.

He counted four choppers in the sky and spotted several more drones.

'The city is closed to private air traffic,' Levin murmured. 'There's a shoot-first policy in the air, and on the ground as well. Snipers everywhere. Stadium's been inspected maybe hundreds of times. Nothing untoward will happen tonight.'

Nothing did.

A joint Israeli and Palestinian cultural performance began at five pm.

Meghan nudged Zeb. 'Is this going where I think it is?'

'I have no idea what you mean,' he lied smoothly.

She looked at him suspiciously and then turned to the stage, caught up in the excitement.

At six pm, the lights dimmed. A solitary spotlight illuminated the stage.

Prime Minister Yago Cantor stepped out from behind a curtain, to wild applause. He greeted the crowd and waited for the audience to quiet down.

'Ten days back, President Ziyan Baruti,' the curtain parted and the Palestinian leader joined him, 'promised you something special. An announcement.'

'You will be aware,' Baruti took over, 'that teams from both our countries have been working on something. A peace treaty.'

The crowd cheered wildly.

'Such treaties take a long time. Months. What we have today is a very basic outline. The basis for further talks.'

'I promise you,' Ambassador Alice Monash appeared on the stage and took the mic, to thunderous clapping, 'that what the two countries have agreed will ...'

Motion down the line of seated attendees caught Zeb's attention. He tuned out from the proceedings on stage and looked to his left.

Major General Zarab Tousi, in dress uniform, was taking his seat. He sensed Zeb's stare and looked their way.

Zeb didn't know what came over him. He didn't know if the Iranian knew him; it didn't matter, in any case. He winked slowly, deliberately, and smiled unpleasantly when Tousi stiffened.

Levin caught the byplay. 'He's mine,' he growled softly. 'Stay away from him.'

'Only if you promise to act soon.'

'I will.'

'What have I missed?' Zeb turned to the stage.

'Nothing much. The ambassador set the scene for someone else.'

There was an expectant hush from the crowd as Alice Monash rearranged herself to stand to Cantor's right. The curtain rippled. It parted to reveal a figure.

Thirty-one thousand people roared when President William Morgan strode toward the dais.

'You said—' Meghan looked accusingly at Levin.

'He's Mossad,' Zeb deadpanned. 'They are the world's best liars.'

The president greeted the crowd in Hebrew and then in Arabic and held a hand up to quiet the rapturous ovation.

He took Cantor's left hand and raised it to the sky. 'The United States has always stood by Israel. It always will.'

The audience couldn't contain itself. Thousands got to their feet and cheered.

The president then took Baruti's right hand and raised it, too.

'From this day onwards, the United States will always stand by Palestine.'

The sound that erupted was deafening. Zeb looked about him. Several people had tears in their eyes. The leaders of the G20 had risen and were clapping continually.

Prime Minister Yago Cantor took the mic. He waited for the crowd to quiet. 'On this day and from now on, the State of Israel recognizes the State of Palestine and the rights of the Palestinian people to have their country.'

Zeb had been expecting it. He had guessed what would be declared. Still, he found himself on his feet along with the entire audience, clapping and cheering. Beth and Meghan were hollering and punching the air in delight.

President Baruti leaned forward. 'The State of Palestine thanks the Israeli nation and promises to co-exist peacefully with our dearest neighbor. We will have our differences, but what we have in common is so much more.'

The crowd roared thunderously.

President Morgan allowed the cheering and applause to continue for a good few minutes. At last, he raised his hand. The roar from the audience became quieter, but not by much.

And the applause that followed his next words could be heard around the world.

'On this day, from Jerusalem, the holiest city in the world, peace will spread and embrace the world.'

Chapter 66

Epilogue

New York
One Month from the Announcement

The world changed, but in some ways it didn't.

Riots broke out in Jerusalem following the historic declaration. Hundreds of people marched in Israel, demanding Cantor's resignation.

Demonstrations in support of him were organized, too.

The Arab states were taken aback by the announcement. Israel was the enemy. That was what thousands of their children grew up believing. Now it wasn't as stark as that. They were wary. They welcomed the historic decision, but also said words had to be backed up by deeds.

'Israel is playing games,' Iran's Supreme Leader thundered in several broadcasts. 'It will not allow Palestine to exist.'

His speeches won cheers in his country but not in many others.

Major General Zarab Tousi wasn't seen in public. He was

still in office, still heading the Islamic Revolutionary Guard Corps, but keeping a very low profile.

Prime Minister Yago Cantor had wanted to lodge a strong diplomatic protest against Iran and bring its involvement up in the United Nations.

Levin, Levitsky, Shoshon and Spiro reminded him that the Islamic country's role had been hushed up.

'Let the Supreme Leader and Tousi twist,' Shoshon said. 'Let them wonder what game we are playing.'

'You think the leader knew of this?'

'He would know some details. He and Tousi are very close.'

'We can't allow such acts to go unpunished.'

'We won't, sir,' Levin replied, flinty-eyed.

The Israeli and Palestinian governments progressed with the negotiations. Borders, capitals, governance, settlements—legal and otherwise—were always going to be the thorniest issues. Expectedly, those would take time. Both countries said a full agreement would take at least a year to work out.

Zeb switched off from the headlines after a while. He was still bitterly unhappy with himself. Especially when he discovered how Eliel and Navon had duped him in the first place.

The two had been in Jerusalem, killing Maryam Razak and Farhan Ba. Yet their personal cell phones showed they were in Amman.

He initially thought the kidon had managed to hack into their devices' location data. Beth and Meghan looked into that. Their finding was indisputable. The phones and even their laptops hadn't been tampered with. Levin confirmed the same.

And then, when Beth was buying a postcard just before they left Jerusalem, it came to him.

'Their devices never left Amman,' he spoke aloud.

'What?' Beth paid for her purchase and followed him and Meghan outside the store.

He pointed at a post office. 'That's how they did it.'

Meghan caught on. 'They posted the devices to themselves. So that they would reach them after the killing.'

Levin's people took apart their residence in Ein Kerem, as did the police. The place was clean. The burner phones on the men, however, had enough data on them. Call logs, the majority of which were to a disconnected number. They didn't have much success with that one.

'That must be Tousi's,' Zeb said thoughtfully when the ramsad broke the news to him. 'He would have set up a temporary number and bounced the calls through several exchanges.'

'We got another number, though, and that led to an arrest. One Jud Lipman, a forger in Beersheba. He made those masks. He was also the one who mimicked Eliel's foster mother's voice. It wasn't just her voice ... other family members as well. He was the one who answered all our calls.'

Other pieces fell into place. Gait analysis matched a person at Moscow's Domodedovo Airport to that of Magal. The timeline fit. It was before Raskov's killing. His absences to visit his mother now made sense.

Levin's cybersecurity team performed extensive security checks. It didn't find any virus but said it was possible the dead operatives had installed one. The team implemented several measures and also came up with its own virus that could be deployed against Iran.

The ramsad worked on reshaping his organization. He

formed a small team, with Carmel, Dalia, Riva and Adir. The five of them looked at every mission and kidon and determined whether any were compromised. They rewrote ops procedures, and how kidon were vetted.

'We are rebuilding Mossad from scratch,' he told Zeb, who nodded.

I would have done the same.

'You didn't have to kill Eliel,' Levin told Zeb one evening when the team was back in New York.

Meghan looked sharply at the phone and then at him. Beth frowned. She didn't understand what the Mossad director meant.

Zeb knew, and he attempted to stave off his friend's probing. 'I had no choice, Avichai. He had an M16. He was bringing it down on me.'

'I have seen you shoot in the most desperate situations. You have always picked your shots.'

'You are forgetting I was injured, bleeding. There wasn't much time to conduct a detailed threat vector analysis.'

'You killed him because he was better off dead. If he was alive, he could have become a thorn in Mossad's side. He could have exposed operations, he could have revealed how he hoodwinked all of us. Tousi could have played his dirty tricks. He could have started rumors on social media. No, you killed him because you thought it would be best for my career.'

'You give me too much credit.'

'Perhaps I don't give you enough.'

'About Tousi.'

'Yes?'

'Let's begin.'

And Zeb Carter and his Warriors began planning a joint mission with Mossad.

Coming Decmber 2018

Burn Rate

Zeb Carter Series, Book 3

By

Ty Patterson

Bonus Chapter from Burn Rate

'Drive, Mister.' A gun pressed tight against the back of Zeb Carter's head.

He didn't move for a moment, stunned at the turn of events.

'Move,' the speaker gritted his teeth. He jammed the weapon harder. 'Didn't you hear what I said?'

It was just after noon. A New York afternoon in the summer. Bright sunlight on the sidewalks. Hordes of chattering tourists, cameras around their necks, following their tour guides dutifully. Office workers returning to their workplaces after hastily snatched meals. Skateboarders speeding through crowds in the daredevil way only they could manage.

Zeb had been out for lunch as well, along with Meghan and Beth. A Vietnamese joint near their Columbus Avenue office had opened up and the younger sister had talked them into trying it out.

And so they had gone.

They had returned from Jerusalem a few months back, high from the events of their previous mission. Israel had recognized Palestine as an independent country and the two nations were working on the finer details of a historic accord.

That single development had dramatically reduced terrorist incidents around the world. Zeb's Warriors were benefiting
from that lull. Nothing much was happening at the Agency.

'You want to join?' he asked the others as he followed the
sisters.

'Nah,' Broker replied distractedly and focused on better-
ing his golf shot. Bear and Chloe, engrossed in something on
their cell phones didn't look up. Bwana and Roger were playing, aiming shots at the hoop on a wall. The two men waved
them away.

Zeb went with the Petersen twins. Him and sunshine and
laughter. He had taken their SUV to the joint and parked it in
an empty space.

It had happened on their return.

He had slid into the driver's seat, Meghan, next to him at
the front, Beth in the rear. Standard seating when the three of
them were in a vehicle.

He saw the blur of motion from the corner of his eyes. Felt
the rear door open and bodies slid in.

By the time it registered on him and the sisters, it was too
late. A barrel was digging into the back of his head.

His eyes flicked to the rear-view mirror. He was still
stunned. Anger growing in him at his carelessness.

*I'm losing my edge. I wasn't paying attention to my
surroundings, at possible threats.*

He blinked when he took in the assailants. Two of them.
Male and female. The former's weapon was on Zeb, the
woman's on Beth.

They're kids! In their teens.

The boy looked to be sixteen, the girl a year or two younger.

Not that I am an expert on ages.

The gun at his head jabbed again. 'How many times do I have to tell you? You want to die?' the boy shouted. 'You,' he yelled at Meghan, 'don't turn back or your friend dies.'

Zeb looked swiftly at the elder sister who nodded imperceptibly. She too had caught the undertone of fear in the kid's voice.

He's scared. He isn't a seasoned carjacker. Could be his first such gig.

'Where to?' he asked.

'Columbus Avenue. Near the Lincoln Center.'

He turned the key, flashed his indicator and joined the stream of traffic.

Do they know who we are? They're aware of our office location?

It didn't seem likely. Zeb and his crew worked in a covert outfit that only a handful of people knew of. It was called the Agency, its director reported only to the president. It went after terrorists and international criminals.

The two kids didn't fit that bill. They were smartly dressed, the boy in a Tee over jeans, neat haircut. The girl, her eyes wide, in a mid-calf dress. Both blonde-haired, green eyes, well-shaped features. They looked like high-school students.

Not scruffy, though. Preppy. Private school?

'Where exactly on Columbus Avenue?'

'I'll tell you when we get there,' the boy snarled.

There were ways Zeb could overpower his assailant. The gun was too close to his head. A swift move to the left or right and the barrel would be exposed. An elbow to the rear, break the kid's jaw and the tables would be turned. Beth could easily overcome the girl.

He didn't do any of that, though. Neither did Beth. Meghan didn't react.

The three of them could read one another without having to speak. They wanted to see how this would play out. It didn't feel like a mugging or car theft.

Ahead, a light turned red. Traffic slowed. Zeb eased on the gas.

'Go!' the boy showered spittle on the back of his neck. 'I'll tell you when to stop.'

'You don't want me crashing in those vehicles,' Zeb explained reasonably. 'We'll draw attention. Cops might show up. I'm guessing you don't want that.'

'Please, mister,' the girl broke her silence. 'Drive as fast as you can.'

Her voice was breaking. *The two of them are close to breaking down. They're just about holding it together.*

He looked in the mirror, at the girl, whose jaw was set tight. She stared straight ahead, didn't meet his eyes. Her gun was jammed in Beth's side.

The light changed. The snake of vehicles moved. Zeb accelerated. Overtook a cab. Honked to get a lumbering van to make way, got an upraised finger as they swept past.

New York. Attitude first, manners second.

Lincoln Center loomed in the distance. Their office building to their left. The kids didn't look at it as it slid behind them.

Nope, this isn't about us.

'Left, at West 62nd Street.'

Zeb turned on his blinker and navigated. He felt the boy's breath on his neck. Could hear him breathe harshly. Gulping as he swallowed. He spread out the fingers of his left palm.

A message to the twins.

Be ready.

A car nosed out of its parking space. He floored his SUV and squeezed in its place before another vehicle could.

'What are you doing?' the boy screamed. 'I asked you to drive.'

Zeb turned off the ignition and swung around in his seat.

'Shoot me.'

'What? Can't you see I have a gun?'

'Yes. Use it. Go ahead.'

The boy swallowed. His face turned red. The gun, a Glock, shook in his hand, its barrel pointing at Zeb's face.

'Mister,' the girl's voice trembled.

He and Meghan looked at her. Beth was watching as well.

'Please do as he says,' a tear rolled down the young woman's face. 'We need to go fast.'

'Why?'

'There's a gunman in our apartment,' she sobbed, her gunhand falling limply to her lap.

'If we don't take this vehicle to our building,' she shuddered, 'he'll kill mom.'

Author's Message

───⬦⬦⬦───

Thank you for taking the time to read *The Peace Killers*. If you enjoyed it, please consider telling your friends and posting a short review.

Sign up to Ty Patterson's mailing list (www.typatterson.com/subscribe) and get *The Watcher*, a Zeb Carter novella, exclusive to newsletter subscribers. Join Ty Patterson's Facebook Readers Group, at www.facebook.com/groups/324440917903074.

Check out Ty on Amazon, iTunes, Kobo, Nook, and on his website www.typatterson.com.

Books by Ty Patterson

Warriors Series Shorts

This is a series of novellas that link to the Warriors Series thrillers

Zulu Hour, Book 1
The Shadow, Book 2
The Man From Congo, Book 3
The Texan, Book 4
The Heavies, Book 5
The Cab Driver, Book 6
Warriors Series Shorts, Boxset I, Books 1-3
Warriors Series Shorts, Boxset II, Books 4-6

Gemini Series

Dividing Zero, Book 1
Defending Cain, Book 2
I Am Missing, Book 3
Wrecking Team, Book 4

Zeb Carter Series

Zeb Carter, Book 1
The Peace Killers, Book 2

Warriors Series

The Warrior, Book 1
The Reluctant Warrior, Book 2
The Warrior Code, Book 3
The Warrior's Debt, Book 4
Flay, Book 5
Behind You, Book 6
Hunting You, Book 7
Zero, Book 8
Death Club, Book 9
Trigger Break, Book 10
Scorched Earth, Book 11
RUN!, Book 12
Warriors series Boxset, Books 1-4
Warriors series Boxset II, Books 5-8
Warriors series Boxset III, Books 1-8

Cade Stryker Series

The Last Gunfighter of Space, Book 1
The Thief Who Stole A Planet, Book 2

Sign up to Ty Patterson's mailing list and get *The Watcher*, a Zeb Carter novella, exclusive to newsletter subscribers. Join Ty Patterson's Facebook group of readers, at www.facebook.com/groups/324440917903074.

Check out Ty on Amazon, iTunes, Kobo, Nook and on his website www.typatterson.com.

About the Author

Ty has been a trench digger, loose tea vendor, leather goods salesman, marine lubricants salesman, diesel engine mechanic, and is now an action thriller author.

Ty is privileged that thriller readers love his books. 'Unputdownable,' 'Turbocharged,' 'Ty sets the standard in thriller writing,' are some of the reviews for his books.

Ty lives with his wife and son, who humor his ridiculous belief that he's in charge.

Connect with Ty:
Twitter: @pattersonty67
Facebook: www.facebook.com/AuthorTyPatterson
Website: www.typatterson.com
Mailing list: www.typatterson.com/subscribe

Made in the USA
Columbia, SC
04 January 2021